The Lights of Pembroke Road

a novel

Stacey Roberts

julu press

To Mary,

Thank you so much! I
hope you enjoy this story~

Stacey Roberts
2/28/19

The Lights of Pembroke Road
Copyright 2018 Stacey Roberts

ISBN: 978-0-990-69663-6

First published in 2019 by Julu Press, an imprint of Huqua Press
An operating division of Morling Manor Corporation
Los Angeles, California

Cover Illustration by Yoko Matsuoko
Graphic Design: designSimple

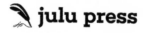

huquapress.com

For the family and friends that encircle me.

Acknowledgements

Sincere thanks to Ellen Knight, Winchester's dedicated town archivist. Ellen provided numerous resources for reference, took hours out of her busy schedule to sit for an interview, and ensured my site research was as easy as possible; and to my Aunt Donna, who spent the better part of a day driving me to all the locations I wanted to see, and shared her own favorite memories of growing up in this wonderful town.

Thanks also to those who provided comments as this book was being written: Linda Sansom, a delightful member of my local book club; my daughters, Michelle and Vicki, who took time out of their very busy lives to assist me with research and review; and especially my mother, Blanche Roberts, who read each draft with care, and patiently provided her comments and concerns in the most tactful way.

I must also express my heartfelt gratitude to my dear husband, Vince, for his patience and support through the long haul; and to Judy Proffer, for believing this story was worth sharing, and her encouragement to move forward with publication.

Finally, I would be remiss if I didn't mention my deepest gratitude to my grandparents. Winchester was your town, and this book would not have been possible without your influence, your stories, and your love; and to the Town of Winchester, Massachusetts, where my parents passed a reasonably idyllic childhood, and where my paternal grandparents reside forever in Wildwood Cemetery.

Chapter I

Walter Hannigan leaned back in a worn leather chair. He liked his old office, liked the way the late afternoon light beamed in from the bay window, the way it illuminated an array of awards arranged neatly on a nearby shelf.

Walter had done well for himself. He'd worked in the newspaper business his entire career, the last two decades as editor-in-chief for his own local paper, *The Weekly Boston Reporter*. When he finally retired, he'd handed the business over to his sons, who expanded the paper's customer base into much of New England, as far north as Bangor, Maine; west into New York, with accounts in Syracuse, Ithaca, and Rochester; and south, too, into Baltimore and Annapolis.

Now, at 68, Walter spent most of his time on the golf course, or at the park with his grandchildren, or puttering in the garden with his wife, Susan. Aside from a touch of arthritis, he felt good physically, felt he had most of his marbles still in play. Once or twice a month he came downtown to visit the paper, watch his sons and their staff at work, maybe grab a bite at the corner deli, or offer advice on the occasional instance he was asked. And he'd kept his private office, just so he could step away sometimes and think, maybe tap out a letter or two on his old IBM Selectric.

Today he'd gone into the office with a singular purpose, to write the invitation for the 50th Class Reunion of the Winchester High School Class of 1942. He would post the invitation to those for whom he had an address, and place it as a notice in some of the larger local papers, the *Globe*, the *Herald*, and of course, his own *Reporter*.

There were three people, in particular, that Walter wanted to be sure would attend, and he had spoken to each of them the previous week. There was Louise Duncan, who lived in California. She'd answered Walter's call on the second ring, with an efficient "Duncan and Associates, this is Louise, how may I help you?"

Her tone softened when she heard Walter's voice, genuinely happy to hear from her old friend. Of course she would be at the reunion, she kidded, had she ever missed one?

And then Walter explained, and he heard her sigh, a soft 'oh' on the other end of the line. "Of course, Walter, I'll be there. Thanks for letting me know."

A similar conversation followed with Dorothy Humphrey, recently widowed, and in the process of moving from New Hampshire to Florida with her daughter. She also assured Walter that she would be in attendance.

It had taken a little longer to reach Henry Smith. An acclaimed psychiatrist, Henry had spent his career devoted to repairing the battered psyches of men and women who had seen too much in war, for whom peace of mind had become an elusive, if not irrecoverable, state.

Walter first tried to call Henry at home, a little cottage on Martha's Vineyard, and Henry's own refuge when he needed one. Henry's wife, Jennifer, a well-respected psychologist in her own right, answered.

"Henry's gone this entire month," Jennifer said. "He's got two conferences, and in between he's making a few appearances for his new book. He started off in New York, then spent a week in Oslo, and I think this week he's in Paris. Let me check, Walter, I have his itinerary here somewhere." She paused, and Walter heard a shuffle of papers in the background. "Oh, yes, here we go. Hotel Gérard, on the Rue d'Armand. He'll be there the rest of this week. I only have the number for the hotel. How's your French?"

"Rusty," Walter laughed.

"No matter," she said, a smile in her voice, "between your French and their English, you'll get a hold of him. In any case, he calls home every few days. If you don't catch him, I'll be sure to let him know you need to speak to him."

She gave him the number of the hotel, and he dialed it as soon as they hung up. The sleepy receptionist who answered told Walter that it was two o'clock in the morning, was he sure he wanted to disturb Monsieur Smith at such an hour? Walter had forgotten about the time difference, apologized for the late call, and said no, would she leave a message for Mr. Smith to call Walter Hannigan at his earliest convenience?

"Mais oui, but of course, I will put the message in the box of Monsieur Smith right away," she replied, now more fully awake.

Walter was in his kitchen the following afternoon, making a ham and cheese sandwich, when the phone rang.

"Hello?" Walter answered, crooking the phone between his neck and ear as he tried to spread mustard on the bread.

"Walter Hannigan? You old codger, this is Henry. I hear you've been scouring the Earth for me."

"Henry? Where the hell are you, you sound far away."

"Paris. The room phone isn't very good. Here, is this better?" The voice seemed closer.

"Yes, yes, that's better. Geez, it's good to hear from you. You seem to be on quite a whirlwind tour these days." Walter sat at the kitchen table, the telephone cord stretched from the wall behind him, the sandwich forgotten.

Henry chuckled. "I suppose I am, but I promise, it's not my idea. Between the university and my editor, I'm booked through to the end of the year. I've had to rearrange all my private consultations, and my hospital schedule. But I plan to retire next year, so things should slow down soon. I may teach a class or two at BU, you know, just to keep my hand in."

"That'll be great, Henry. I like retirement, although I don't know about the slowing down part. Grandkids keep you on your toes, you know!"

"I'm looking forward to that, Walter," Henry said, a wistful edge to his voice. "Anyway," he started, "I wanted to call you back. Is everything okay?"

"Ah, well, I did want to talk to you about something. Our 50th reunion is coming up in November, and I was hoping you could make it. For Mike." There was quiet on the end of the line, and for a moment Walter thought he'd lost the call.

Henry's voice came back, serious. "It's like that, is it?"

"Yes, it is."

"When and where?" Henry asked.

Walter told him.

"I'll be there. Thanks, Walter. It'll be good to see everyone again, it's been too long."

Now, in his office, Walter reviewed the brief invitation he would send out to the rest of the class. His days at the *Winchester Star* had taught him the value of factual, pointed, and invariably short copy. It would be enough.

Chapter 2

Elizabeth Crowley looked out her living room window, a dust rag caked with beeswax clasped in one hand, the other hand fumbling for the back tie of her apron. It was hard for her to see much over the snowdrift in front of her house, but she caught a glimpse of Walter Hannigan as he stepped out onto his front porch, bundled up against the cold. She watched as he tromped toward the hill, Flyer in tow.

During the summer, the hill that jutted up at the end of Pembroke Road was covered with morning glories, a Monet of purple and dark green that flourished up and over the ground, untamed. But it was mid-December now, and the morning glories, long shriveled away, were replaced by more than a foot of packed snow, perfect for sledding.

Beth balled up her apron and dust cloth and dropped them together into a large cut-glass bowl on the sideboard. The bowl was a prize her mother won the previous August at the Feast of the Assumption Day Festival. It was the fourth year in a row that Amelia Crowley had taken home a blue ribbon for her peach pie, and the prize this year included the bowl, a relic dug out of someone's basement and polished up. It now sat in the center of the walnut sideboard, a cherished possession, and for the moment, keeper of Beth's work apron and dirty rag.

Beth slipped as quietly as she could toward the mudroom. She had to pass the kitchen, where her mother was vigorously scrubbing a breakfast pan at the sink; and where her grandmother, Hazel Crowley, sat repairing the hem of a skirt, one of several items piled on a nearby table waiting to be mended. Amelia and Hazel were discussing the upcoming Christmas Eve luncheon, an event that Rose Hannigan, their friend and neighbor across the street, hosted every year. Beth stood by the door, listening, waiting for the right moment to cross the opening.

"Rose said she'd make a ham, and pumpkin pie this year. She always does such a fine job with the Christmas holiday. We're supposed to bring your gingerbread. I'll help you with that if you like." Hazel paused as she finished off the hem. She picked up another article of clothing, a shirt missing a button, and squinted through her spectacles as she threaded her needle. She continued with a new line of thought.

"Do you think Irene will make it to the luncheon? She looked quite poorly the last time I saw her."

Amelia stopped scrubbing and began to rinse the pan as she replied, "I know she hasn't been feeling well. Father Glenn has been bringing her communion for months. I think the last time I saw her was at Thanksgiving. When did you last see her?"

"Last week, after church. I brought a jar of that broth you made, convinced Louise to let me upstairs to say hello to her mother. Irene was just a limp washrag under her bedclothes. I asked her if I could do anything, she just said no, and thanked me for the broth, and for stopping by. That was it. The house seemed clean, Louise seemed well, but Irene looked like death warmed over, poor old girl." Hazel sighed and shook her head. "And so soon after her husband passed."

Beth peeked quickly into the kitchen. Her mother's back was turned now as she dried the pan, and her grandmother, eyes focused on her needlework, continued talking, something about the decorations on Rose's Christmas tree. Now was the time; but as Beth crossed the doorway, she glanced into the kitchen. She froze as she locked eyes with her grandmother. Without skipping a beat with her sewing or her conversation, Hazel smiled and gave a half nod of acknowledgement to her granddaughter.

Beth returned the smile, and continued on her stealthy path into the mudroom. There, she took her green wool coat and matching cap from a wall peg. Quickly, she pulled them on, careful to hold her shirt sleeves by the cuff so they wouldn't bunch up in the coat. She sat on the mudroom bench and shoved her feet into her rubber snow boots. She stood up, balancing awkwardly as she worked her heels down into the bottoms of the boots. The right foot went in smoothly enough, but the left heel of her shoe got caught up. She tried to again to work her foot into the boot, until finally, impatient with the struggle, Beth jumped up and landed hard on her left side. Success! The boot was on, but at the cost of a noise her mother could hear. Without a moment's hesitation, Beth grabbed her scarf and mittens, and headed toward the door.

"Elizabeth?" called her mother from the kitchen.

"I'm going to the hill, Mom!"

Beth was out of the mudroom and down the steps before her mother could voice an objection.

"Oh, that child!" exclaimed Amelia, irritated, as she put the pan away in the oven. "Wait until she gets home!"

Hazel stopped to examine her handiwork. "Amelia, dear, why do you let her perturb you so? She's a good child, and on holiday from school. Let her go have some fun."

The air was brisk, but not biting, and Beth saw more blue sky than clouds as she made her way to the little storage shed at the side of the house. She walked as quickly as she dared on the icy path, buttoning her coat and tugging on her mittens as she went. She opened the shed door and peered into the darkness. Her Flyer sat just inside, leaning up against the wall, waiting for her.

Chapter 3

As she approached the hill, Beth saw that Walter was already at the top, and Mike was with him. Ray and Henry were dragging their sleds up the side, billows of steamy breath visible with the effort. Walter was easy to pick out, for although all the boys were bundled up in their winter gear, Walter was by far the leanest of the four, pale except for the apples at his cheeks, his black hair in stark contrast to his fair skin.

The four boys had known each other all their young lives. In second grade, a coincidence of timing and uncommon freedom brought them together at the base of the hill to sled on the first Monday of Christmas break, a singular event that developed over the years into a day-long holiday for the boys. They always met at the hill, sledding for an hour or so to start the day. After that, they trooped over to Winter Pond to skate, and race each other across the inviting expanse of frozen water.

By midday, hungry and tired, the boys stopped in at Ray's house, a cozy Tudor-style home nestled snugly between Winter Pond and Pembroke Road. There, Ray's mother, Mrs. Simard, fed them lunch, always cheese and bread, and a thick hot stew full of potatoes and carrots and bits of beef. They would eat quietly, ravenous from the morning's exertions, unwilling or unable to divert energy from the task of consuming the bounty before them for the sake of a joke or a question.

It was after lunch, as they sat warming themselves in front of the fireplace, that their banter resumed; and by the time they were off to Walter's house, they were warm and dry and fed, ready to spend the afternoon sprawled out on a big blanket in Walter's den, eating Mrs. Hannigan's special holiday cookies and drinking hot cocoa as they played checkers or read through the latest Dick Tracy comics. Rose Hannigan, Walter's mother, had affectionately dubbed the young foursome 'the Hill Boys,' and the name had stuck throughout their grade school years.

Walter stood still for a moment, looking out over the street below, and the snow-ridged houses lining either side. From this vantage point, he could see the intersection a quarter-mile away, where Woodside Avenue cut across Pembroke Road. He could see Mike's house, which sat proudly at the corner, an expansive Colonial Revival home built in the late 1800s. It was painted a stately white with black trim, and boasted a huge covered porch that ran all the way around to the back of the house. The Andrews' had a formal garden in their large yard. Even in the winter, they kept the walkways cleared, and Walter thought it looked like a miniature of the gardens at Versailles, especially from the hill.

Walter could also see Ray's house, which sat on the opposite corner, and Henry's house as well, just beyond. Walter liked having his best friends so close, all together on the same street. Their proximity gave him a sense of stability and cohesiveness, of friendship and belonging.

"This is great," Walter said to Mike, inhaling the freedom that seemed to accompany the light, cold air. "This is my favorite day of the year." Walter's father traveled during the week for work, and it was understood that Walter shouldered the responsibility, as the eldest son, to care for his mother, his brothers and sister, and for a list of never-ending chores. This day was a golden opportunity for him to be the fourteen year-old boy that he was.

Walter looked down at Ray, who was huffing and puffing up the slope, a step behind Henry. Ray was, for the most part, an average-looking kid, although he had been graced with an especially wide, bright smile that invariably reached up to crease his large, dark brown eyes, so that he had the look about him of a very sweet puppy. He was a somewhat chubby teenager, not inordinately so, but just enough to slow him down a bit. His weight didn't seem to matter, at least as far as Walter could tell. Ray was very popular at school, quick-witted, and charming. The coaches may not have given him a second look, but his teachers found him agreeable and trustworthy, and he made friends, or at least good acquaintances, easily. Walter knew Ray a little better than most, and, behind the wit and charm, found a caring, warm, empathetic young man, easy-going in nature, and devoted to his family. Walter felt honored, in a way, to be one of Ray's closest friends.

"It's a perfect day," responded Mike, turning to view the cemetery behind them. His eyes followed the slope that dipped away from them down into Wildwood Cemetery, where a knee-high stone wall ran the natural curve of the landscape, dividing the living from the dead. Beyond the wall, the earth rose up into a high broad hill, dotted with barren trees and snow-topped burial markers, and bearing the black cutout of the roadway that circled through the graveyard.

Mike Andrews was happy to be out of his house, with something to do besides attend school, or church, or one of the endless social functions his parents hosted so frequently. He was tall for his age, with dark hair and dark flashing eyes. As a young child, Mike had been somewhat clumsy, unable to adjust easily as the growth spurts pushed him out of clothes and shoes as soon as they were bought, and sometimes sent him, literally, tripping over his own feet. His parents, in a responsible effort to help their son through these 'awkward years,' dragged him to every major social event on their calendar where it was remotely permissible to bring a well-behaved child, and included him in every event they held at their own home. They hoped that a refined, formal adult atmosphere would help Mike slow down and become more conscious of his physical movements, while giving him a sense of social wherewithal. Mike knew his parents meant well, but he found the constant effort of being polite to patronizing adults exhausting. Today was special, and Mike was happy to be with his friends, and especially with Walter, who had been his best friend for as long as he could remember.

Walter noticed that Henry seemed unusually quiet this morning. Walter wasn't really concerned, though. Henry could be introspective at times, and

Walter chalked Henry's subdued demeanor up to one of these pensive moods. He had no doubt that as they started sledding, Henry's focus would shift to the activity at hand, and he would revert to his usual, genial disposition.

Henry Smith was nearly as tall as Mike, and transitioning quickly from an adorable child to a handsome young man, handsome in the classical sense, as though Michelangelo's David had come to life in the little town of Winchester. His sandy blond hair grew in gentle waves when he wasn't fresh from the barber. He'd lost the roundness of face that some of the boys in his class still carried, replaced with high cheekbones, a strong, angular jaw, and a cleft at the chin. Large, sea-green eyes and an infectious grin completed the picture of this burgeoning Adonis.

His physical person was no less attractive. Henry spent his summers digging graves and mowing lawns at Wildwood Cemetery. During the winters, he shoveled snow from neighborhood walkways and split cords of wood for his family. These activities left Henry well-muscled, the kind of muscle that coaches look for when choosing the next round of potential halfbacks and quarterbacks for the high school team. Coach Franklin had approached him already, asked him if he'd like to join the football team, or maybe the baseball team, when he started at Winchester High next year. Henry balked at the suggestion, but Coach had taken no note, only told him enthusiastically that he'd be looking for Henry at the fall tryouts.

Henry did like baseball. He liked the weight of the bat in his hands, and when the pitch was right, the power he felt when he made contact with the leather ball, sending it hurtling over the heads of his friends. But playing in the vacant field with his friends was the extent of Henry's inclination to participate in sports. To join a school team, to play offense or defense, went against his reserved, careful nature, a notable deficiency in a small town that revered sports almost as much as it did formal education.

Henry's true strength resided in his innate ability to absorb and analyze information, to pull details from the hundreds of books he consumed every year, and to weave the volumes of knowledge he acquired into tangible works of academic distinction. His scholastic aptitude won high praise from his teachers, and more than offset any disappointment over Henry's reluctance to participate in organized athletics.

In the presence of strangers or passing acquaintances, Henry tended to be quiet, content to listen and observe the interactions of others. A few people were put off by this, finding his seeming detachment rude; others simply thought he was shy. With his friends he was much more comfortable, affable and warm, but disinclined to discuss some of the more substantial thoughts that swam around in his brain. It was with those few adults he trusted, his parents, his Uncle Eric, and two or three particular teachers, that he discussed those deeper subjects, matters of philosophy and science, spirituality, the effects of physics on human activities, the way mathematics infiltrated nature at every turn.

Walter was right; Henry was deep in thought, though for reasons Walter would never imagine. A week earlier, Henry's family had gathered by the fireplace after an early supper. Henry and his younger brother were playing a card game, while his twin sisters, just out of diapers, sat on the floor nearby, stacking wooden blocks. On the radio, *Hansel and Gretel* played low in the background as his parents, Carl and Emma Smith, talked lightly about the upcoming holiday plans. There would be the tree lighting and caroling on Christmas Eve at the Common, an annual event put on by the Fortnightly Club, a local women's charitable and civic organization. There would be a reception at the Unitarian Church afterwards. Henry's mother planned to make her special Christmas cake for the reception table, a once-a-year event that involved cracking open and mincing pecans, chopping dried apricots, and a flurry of mixing eggs and cake flour and spices. Henry relished the sweet, heady scent of nutmeg, cloves and cinnamon that filled the house as the cake baked, and lingered for days afterward.

An announcement on the radio broke the happy tenor of the evening. Caroling and cake and smiles fell away as they heard the news: the Reich Minister for Foreign Affairs, Joachim von Ribbentrop, had brokered a 'No More War Treaty' with France, signed in Paris that day by von Ribbentrop and his French counterpart, Georges Bonnet. Henry's parents, who had discussed the movements of Hitler and his Nazi party over the last two years, at first in whispers, then more openly, stopped mid-sentence to listen, suddenly serious and quiet. They did not say much afterward, but Henry absorbed the new tension, and the news still weighed heavily on his mind.

"Here comes Beth," said Walter.

"What?" Mike turned from his view of the cemetery to scan the street below. Mike scowled when he saw her. "Bad enough that baby trails after me on the way to school every day. Now she's following me when I'm on holiday." Mike was unsure of the chain of events that led to his assignment to walk Beth Crowley to St. Mary's parochial school every day. He only knew that his mother, Margaret Andrews, and Beth's mother, Mrs. Crowley, both belonged to the Home and Garden Club. Somehow, that meant he had to walk Beth to her school every day, a chore which put him a block out of his way before he could turn toward the Wadleigh Middle School, which he attended.

"Aw, come on, Mike, she's just a kid." Walter raised his arms and shouted a hearty "Hiya, Beth! Come on up, the snow's perfect!"

She waved back at him. "Hiya, Walt!"

Beth was the only person who called him Walt, and he liked it.

Mike watched her as she made her way to the bottom of the hill, shaking his head. Elizabeth Crowley was not like any of the other girls he knew in the neighborhood, or even in school, for that matter. She was a skinny eleven-year-old, with muddy-brown hair that was always in disheveled pigtails. She was too tall, and at least a hundred freckles dotted her nose. Even the dimples that appeared on her cheeks when she smiled were too pointy, so that she looked like a marionette. She ran races with the boys in her class, and rode her bicycle too fast.

"What an ugly girl," he muttered under his breath as he jumped onto his sled, belly down, the momentum carrying him to the base of the hill for the first run of the day.

While Mike did his utmost to ignore Beth, the other boys did not. As Walter predicted, Henry managed to join in the fun as he, Ray, and Beth jumped aboard their sleds and whooshed down the hill, snow flying. They raced each other, sometimes sitting up, feet on the steer bar, hands clenched around the rope as they flew down, laughing all the way to the bottom.

Walter liked Beth, even if she was just a kid. Last summer, he'd watched from the living room window of his house as Beth and her father threw a ball back and forth in their front yard. At first, watching them produced a twinge of jealousy to rise up somewhere in his core. But she could pitch and catch, and before summer's end, Walter invited her over nearly every day to play catch off the back side of his house, where Rose had set up a large plank of wood for the purpose. Beth Crowley would be a good addition to Walter's team next summer if he needed an extra player. He was mindful of how he treated her, if for no other reason than that.

Chapter 4

Louise Duncan pushed aside a lacy curtain and looked out of her second-story bedroom window. The clouds that had delivered three inches of snow the night before were giving way to blue sky. Dabs of sunlight shimmered off the bright white powder, reflections that made Louise's eyes smart.

She took in the signs of holiday cheer that graced the little cul-de-sac below. Most of the houses on Pembroke Road were decorated much like the Crowley house across the street, with holly and red ribbon around the porch railings, a wreath carefully centered on the front door, and a few strings of colored electric light bulbs threaded along the eaves. Each front-room window framed a hand-picked pine or spruce, decorated with cherished ornaments and tinsel, popcorn strings, and more colored lights. An angel doll or foil star topped each family tree, a reminder of the holy event that occurred so long ago. It was at night that passersby saw how pretty the houses were, with the trees lit up, glowing out into the street. It was at night that nearly all the houses in the little town of Winchester cast a similar warmth of light and cheer into the dark chill of the December evenings.

Even Gus Osprey, the widower who lived in the corner house up the street, had placed a pretty wreath at his door; and a small tree, rather overladen with tinsel, could be seen through his front window. Louise had been inside the Osprey house once, when Gus and his wife Helen first moved to Pembroke Road, tagging along as part of an informal welcoming committee formed by some of the neighborhood women. Louise didn't remember much about the house itself, but she remembered the two pug puppies that were safely confined to the kitchen; and then sitting on the back porch step, drinking a glass of cool, sweet lemonade while the grown-ups talked. After that day, Louise sometimes looked out her mother's bedroom window, where she could see over the neighbor's fence into the Osprey's back yard. She watched as Gus and Helen worked in their garden during the long summer evenings. Louise imagined they must be very happy together, the two of them smiling and laughing as they pulled weeds or harvested tomatoes or green beans or peppers.

When Helen passed away, Louise noticed the Osprey house was suddenly very quiet. Aside from her weekly visit to the butcher shop, where Gus would hand her order to her with a strained smile, Louise rarely saw him or the little dogs. His garden lay fallow the first full summer after Helen's death, and his house was invariably dark and bleak during the holiday seasons that followed.

This year, though, as Louise walked home from the grocer one early December evening, she was startled by the light emanating from the Osprey house. She stopped short, thinking at first that somehow she had turned onto the wrong street. Then she noticed Mr. Osprey in his front window next to a half-decorated pine, waving to her and smiling. Relieved and comforted, she smiled and waved back.

Of course, Mr. Osprey's decorations were simple compared to those of Louise's neighbor, Rose Hannigan. Louise thought that this year, the Hannigan house, bedecked with ribbons and lights, evergreen and holly, was by far the most festive house in the neighborhood, maybe even in all of Winchester. Louise had stepped outside one night, just so she could stand in front of her neighbor's house and take it all in.

Mrs. Hannigan's usual array of pine boughs and ornaments adorned her porch rail. A flourish of red and gold ribbon, tied in an ornate bow, sat proudly affixed to the large wreath on her door. More ribbon, fashioned in barber-pole stripes of gold and red, wound around each column of the front porch. Strips of holly, woven through strand after strand of colored lights, graced the front eaves. In addition, Mrs. Hannigan had lined each of the front-facing windows with more holly and lights, a decidedly bold decorating move. But Louise could see, as she stood in the street in front of the Hannigan home, that it was the tree that was truly amazing. It seemed to sparkle, with a hundred jewel-like ornaments placed just so on the branches, and another hundred colored light bulbs strung around the tree, in an artfully random way; and between all these ornaments and lights sat carefully arranged red and gold satin bows, their tails gently woven downward through the branches, reflecting the lights and giving off their own flashes of bright color as they peeked out from the rich green of the spruce.

Louise had smiled, sighed, and gone back up the steps to her quiet, dimly lit house. No decorations placed by loving hands cheered a neighbor's glance; no tree stood in the window to warm the hearts of those who passed, no, nor the hearts of the home's solitary inhabitants. Only a small, simple sprig of holly, a token of acknowledgement of the season, adorned the front door.

It was nearly a year ago, on a cold, clear winter's day, much like this one, that Louise's father, Frank Duncan, died of some mystery illness. It had robbed him, over more than a decade's time, first of his energy, then his breath, and finally his life. For the fourteen years Louise lived in the same house with her father, she knew surprisingly little about him. She rarely saw him, and he took scant note of her on those occasions when he garnered strength enough to hobble downstairs for an hour or two. Toward the end he remained confined to his bed; and with the exception of the occasional wracking cough that seemed to shake the whole house, she often forgot he was there. Louise's mother, Irene Duncan, tended to her husband's essential needs, and relied on her married son, George, to support the majority of the household, although she took in ironing and mending on occasion when pressed for extra funds.

Louise caught sight of Walter Hannigan as he stepped off his porch and headed toward the hill. She saw Beth from across the street follow a few minutes later. She knew they would meet up with Mike, Henry and Ray, who had crossed her line of sight ten minutes before. Louise had watched as they passed her house, Mike and Ray laughing and talking excitedly, Henry a step behind, as they stomped through the snow, unmindful of the cold.

Louise used to go to the hill to sled with her friends when the boys weren't there; but she was a young woman now, discomfited with young women's concerns over unmentionable breasts and menstrual cycles, no longer inclined to the type of physical exertion that sledding engendered. She still went skating over at Winter Pond, usually with her best friend Dot, occasionally with some of the other girls in her class. Today, however, she stayed home to make soup for her mother, who was not feeling well; and to read *Jane Eyre*, which she picked up from the library just before school let out for the Christmas holiday.

Louise moved away from the window, and stood for a moment before the mirror at her dresser. Her figure was well-proportioned and slender. Her hair, gathered in a loose tie at the nape of her neck, fell in shiny, gentle waves of rich mahogany between her shoulders. Her complexion was fair and clear, her large emerald-green eyes framed by long dark lashes and a gently arching brow. A delicate nose and slightly full lips completed the picture. Louise knew she was pretty, and could not help but be pleased with the reflection she saw. She felt that one day, it would matter. One day, perhaps being pretty might help invite the right young man to her side, one with money, or at least, one with prospects.

Louise retrieved her book from a shelf in her closet. She stopped to look at the coat hanging there, and ran her hand along the wool scarves and hats that sat on the shelf above. She loved the feel of the soft wool. These were her favorite pieces of clothing. Last August, her mother had taken her to Franklin E. Barnes & Co. for a special birthday shopping trip. The new fall season was out, and the selection was ample. Mrs. Duncan, sweltering in her black mourning dress, insisted that Louise try on countless garments and accessories, until Louise was exhausted and nearly in tears. They walked out with a beautiful black wool pea coat, with silver buttons down the front and a satin inner lining; two hats of fine black wool; and soft wool scarves, one dyed a dark cherry-red, one light gray, and one periwinkle. Mrs. Duncan also purchased a pair of black leather gloves and two pair of knitted mittens. As they walked out of the store with their boxes, she said, "I want to get you boots, too. Mrs. McGurty said the shipment will arrive next Wednesday, and they will have everything out on the floor by Friday. We will be there."

Louise and her mother never made it back to the store. Mrs. Duncan didn't feel well the next day, or the next, and was still too weak to leave the house when the new shipment of footwear was placed carefully on the shelves at Franklin E. Barnes & Co. Since then, she had gone out infrequently, spending more and more of her time in bed, or reclining on the couch in front of the living room fireplace. Louise went to the butcher, or the grocer, or the drugstore when they needed something. She took over the housework; and as the summer waned, she worked diligently in their back garden, which consisted of a half-dozen large raised beds, and a patch of raspberry vines trained up along the fence. She cleared away the dead and dying, watered and harvested the last of the bramble berries, turned the pole beans and peas and peppers when they shriveled in the late summer heat, and tended the new trails of winter squash. She put up fruit preserves and canned the last of the summer tomatoes, tasks she and her mother usually shared, sweating together in the hot September kitchen as they filled the jars, talking about the new school year, the latest radio program, God, life. Louise took on the work, without being asked, knowing only that it needed doing, and she was the only one to do it. At the end, Louise was proud of her effort, proud to show her mother the jars of purple, red and orange lined up neatly on the pantry shelves.

George came by to visit nearly every week since the middle of September, still providing money for living expenses and paying the bills; and sometimes meeting with Dr. Murray behind closed doors, to carry on calm discussions in low, unintelligible voices. Dr. Murray prescribed a steady supply of laudanum, which Irene Duncan used sparingly at first, more frequently as time went on.

At Thanksgiving, Mrs. Duncan rallied, venturing out onto the back porch for a few minutes in spite of the cold weather, and eating her fair share of roast chicken and potatoes, and a hearty slice of cherry pie that George's wife, Claire, brought for the feast. That was three weeks ago.

This morning, Louise's mother simply stated that she was tired and needed to rest. Louise helped her back into bed, noting her mother's ash-gray skin and blue lips.

"Shall I call Dr. Murray?" Louise asked.

"No," the simple reply.

"Do you want your medicine?"

"Already had it."

"I'll make some soup for lunch," offered Louise. Her mother nodded.

"That sounds fine. I'm just going to rest now." And Irene Duncan settled back into her bed and fell asleep almost immediately.

Louise picked up her book and shut the closet door. Heading downstairs and into the kitchen, she gave the stockpot a stir, watching the thin slivers of chicken and chunks of carrot, potato, and parsnip swirl up and dance with the white barley pearls. She stood over the pot, stirring gently, the steam carrying the heavenly aroma into her lungs, spreading through her body until she felt almost giddy. She looked at the clock. It was still early; the soup would need to simmer a while longer. Her mouth was watering. She would wait, of course. It would be nice to share lunch with her mother, so she would wait.

Louise settled onto the couch to read. An hour later, when a young Jane Eyre had only just arrived at Lowood School, Louise glanced up. From her seat, she saw Beth heading back to her house, dragging her sled; and the Hill Boys tromping up the street, rosy-cheeked and smiling, a dusting of snow on their jackets and caps.

She returned to her book. A few seconds later, Louise heard her mother moan.

At the bedroom door, Louise peered in.

"Murray," her mother gasped.

Louise ran downstairs to the telephone, and rang Dr. Murray's office on the exchange.

The doctor's wife, Annabelle Murray, answered crisply, "Dr. Murray's office, this is Mrs. Murray speaking, how may I help you?"

"Mrs. Murray, this is Louise Duncan. Mother is sick, and asking for the doctor. Can he come?"

There was silence on the other end of the line.

"Mrs. Murray, are you there?" Louise heard the unnatural pitch in her own voice.

"Oh yes, dear, I'm sorry, I was just looking at doctor's schedule. Please hold a moment."

Louise waited. She heard a muffled discussion in the background. Then Mrs. Murray was back, her voice softened. "Doctor will be there in a few minutes, dear."

"Yes, thank you," was all Louise could answer. She was suddenly afraid. A few tears pushed up, and she pushed them back. She went to the front window, looking out expectantly, wanting the doctor to come, so she wouldn't be alone. Ten minutes passed. Would he never arrive?

Her mother moaned again, and Louise knew, by the lightheaded wash that tingled down from the crown of her head, that this was very bad. She wanted so desperately to stay downstairs, because if she stayed downstairs, then maybe everything would be all right. Still, she could not ignore the sounds from her mother's room. She pushed herself to go back up the stairs, feeling dizzy and a little sick as she returned to the bottom of her mother's bed.

"He's coming right away."

Another groan from the depths of the sheets. Her mother's hand fell away from the sickbed, more bone than flesh.

"Glenn," she whispered.

There was a knock at the front door, and Louise heard Dr. Murray step in.

"Louise?" he called out.

"Upstairs," she called back. She nodded to her mother, "I'll call Father Glenn. And George."

Then, almost as an afterthought, she whispered, "I love you. I'll miss you." Her eyes stung as she looked into her mother's thin, gray face, seeking some acknowledgement. Her mother looked up at her with difficulty, and nodded. Louise went out to the landing as the doctor made his way up the stairs.

"Thank you for coming so quickly."

"Well, let's take a look."

She followed as he pushed aside the door to Irene Duncan's bedroom. All was still.

Chapter 5

George Duncan was only eight years old when his brother and two sisters each succumbed, one after the other, to scarlet fever during the winter of 1919. Watching his siblings fall ill and die, watching their coffins as they lowered into the cold deep earth, left George with an acute awareness of mortality well beyond his years.

George was twelve when his sister, Louise Elizabeth, was born. It was a difficult event for him to bear, not because of jealousy or resentment, but rather due to an unpronounceable fear, a fear of future loss, a gnawing at his core that he should not become attached to this child, for she could be swept away like the others. He avoided being at home, which was easily managed. There was a building boom in Winchester, and George spent much of his spare time working at construction sites. At first, he picked up nails, swept debris, stacked lumber or bricks, anything the job foreman would let him do. As he got older, he learned how to lay shingles, run pipes and pull wire. For the first time in his young life, George received payment for his work; the wages were nominal, but George liked receiving compensation for his efforts, liked the feeling of worthiness that being paid for his honest labor afforded him.

When George was sixteen, his father fell ill and lost his job at the Beggs and Cobb Tannery. George wanted to quit school to work full-time, but his father, rasping from his sickbed, insisted George finish his education. Frank Duncan's word could not be snubbed. But then George's mother asked him to give up working altogether that year, to come home right away after school. She needed his help, she said, to cope with their new circumstances. George considered ignoring his mother's request. With neither his father's income from the tannery nor his after-school earnings from construction, the Duncan family would be hard-pressed to manage through the winter on their scant savings. In the end, George did as his mother asked, in large part because his father promised that he would be permitted to work full-time at the end of the school year.

"Just do as your mother asks for now," Frank Duncan wheezed, a heavy brogue lacing his words. "When you're done with school, ye kin work day and night if you've a mind to, and neither your mother nor I will hold you back. But your mother needs you now, here, at home, while Louise is still small and I'm a...a burden." He closed his eyes, trying to collect his breath.

George looked at his father, heard the labored breathing. He could already feel the sick angst of his youth rising up, a dread of long afternoons cooped up in a house where someone lay sick, and possibly dying. And there was another layer to his anxiety, a resentment at the loss of productive activity in the outside world, where he could earn a few hours' pay with the sweat of his brow.

"I'll do as you like," George replied, resigned to the inevitable, unhappy about it.

That year proved as difficult as George imagined. Sustenance during the harsh winter months consisted of bread, broth, eggs, and the canned vegetables and fruits his mother put up the summer before. Irene Duncan took in sewing and ironing while her husband languished in the upstairs bedroom. George did his best to help wherever he was needed, chopping wood, performing minor house repairs, or entertaining Louise. In the spring, Mrs. Duncan was able to convince her husband to apply for assistance through Winchester's Public Relief Committee, which bit at their pride, but improved the family's circumstances significantly.

For all the privations of that winter, the only clear memory George had was of the daily ritual his mother insisted he share with his little sister. After the first frost set in, Mrs. Duncan sent her two children out onto the back porch every morning, each with a chunk of stale bread in hand. They stood out there, George towering over his little sister, breaking off small pieces of bread and throwing them onto the bare ground below the railing. Sparrows and finches and white-breasted nuthatches gathered expectantly, fluttering out from their hiding places in the underbrush, eager to snatch a precious share of the crumbs. It was here on the porch, helping his sister, talking with her, laughing at her childish view of life and the world, that George laid aside his fear and found a better purpose. It was on the porch that he became her protector and guardian, her teacher, her big brother.

In June, George graduated from high school, and found work at a small machine shop in Medford. Mr. Van Meter, the shop owner, saw potential in young George, and taught him how to run the accounts, order supplies, and manage customers. George liked his work, liked Mr. Van Meter. More importantly, George was bringing home a steady income, just enough to support his family and take them off public assistance. His father told him how proud he was of him; his mother shed a few tears of happiness herself, an extraordinary display of emotion on her part. And as George beamed outwardly at the relief of his family, the leaden weight of implied responsibility for their welfare clasped onto his shoulders, digging in with talon-like grips. From then on, George worked tirelessly to provide for and protect his parents, and to ensure a happy childhood for Louise.

The last quarter of 1929 nearly crushed all of his hard work. He saw some of his best friends move away, their parents ruined, their beautiful homes sold for a fraction of their original worth, the sum of unpaid property taxes or interest on the mortgage. In nearby Lowell, more than half the men lost their jobs, and the number of applications for public assistance in Winchester piled up. It was obvious that Mr. Duncan would certainly never work again, even if work were plentiful. He was frail now, never leaving the house, rarely coming downstairs. Women who previously sent ironing or sewing to Mrs. Duncan now did the work themselves, saving their precious pennies; but leaving Mrs. Duncan without the meager income she depended upon, along with George's earnings, to make everything work.

Mr. Van Meter sat with George one blustery afternoon the following March, hovering over stale coffee and cigarettes, to discuss the prospects for the machine shop. Business was languishing. Formerly steady customers had either reduced their orders significantly, or gone out of business altogether. As far as Mr. Van Meter could see, the prospects sat somewhere between bleak and hopeless.

But George was a determined young man, hard-driven to keep himself and his family afloat. The difference between George and a thousand other men was that George had a gift. He was the young man who remembered your name, remembered your wife and children's names, spent time with you talking about you, building you up, making you feel like you were the most important person in the world while he was in your presence. Whether you chose to do business with him or not, you were a great man and personal friend. With a winning smile and a warm handshake that carried a golden touch, George obtained a handful of new minor accounts, and rebuilt the ones that were lagging if there was anything to salvage.

Mother Nature helped. She dried up some machining companies in the Dust Bowl, and others she drowned out in Louisiana floods, leaving a space that George pounced to fill. In the fall of 1930, George landed three healthy regional accounts, and by Christmas of that year, Mr. Van Meter's shop was literally buzzing and humming with new business. They expanded the shop, and hired four machinists from Boston. Mr. Van Meter made George his partner, and George brought home enough income to ensure his family remained comfortably independent.

George built on his success. In 1931 he opened a small shop of his own in Winchester, Back Bay Machining. The shop consisted of a large main floor which held a dozen machines, a variety of mills and lathes, saws and drills. His business grew steadily, with several new contracts from small manufacturers throughout New England. He hired two men to help him at the Winchester shop: a black man from the north end of town, Joseph, who had worked at one of the machine shops decimated by the Louisiana floods; and an Italian immigrant, Antony, who spoke a variegated form of English, but knew how to interpret specs and run the machines, turning out everything from nuts and bolts to replacement parts for soda fountains, all while singing and talking to himself in Italian.

Back Bay Machining expanded twice in two years, the second expansion a direct result of Roosevelt's New Deal. George bought Mr. Van Meter's business in Medford, and moved everything to his shop in Winchester. Mr. Van Meter stayed on as a consultant of sorts, and while George was happy to have his mentor's expertise at hand, he was happier still to have full control of his own company. At twenty-two years of age, George was fast becoming an important businessman, not just in Winchester, but in Middlesex County, and beyond into much of New England.

Chapter 6

Up until the moment Claire Radcliffe entered his life, George had not thought seriously about women. He'd dated some nice girls from school, who all smiled the same nice girl smile, gave the same nice girl peck on the cheek goodnight, and left the same dull feeling of wasted time clinging to the back of his neck. But Claire was not like the girls from school, or church, or the neighborhood. He first saw her at a Saturday afternoon art exhibit at the Winchester Library. He was staring at a watercolor still life, sorting out how he was going to fit a new drill press into his shop, when she stepped in front of him. His thoughts shifted, his focus sharpened as he took in the changed view, now the backside of a blonde, well-dressed, curvy young woman.

She must have felt him staring, because she turned around and looked directly at him, her slate-blue eyes seeming to pierce into his brain, putting thoughts into his head that hadn't been there a moment ago, maybe had never been there. She moved toward him, passing close enough to brush his jacket with her arm; and as she did, she flashed a wicked smile at him, a smile that said she could make him very, very happy, oh, if he only knew. Her perfume, something earthy and rich, lingered on his jacket, so that he couldn't forget her, couldn't shake off the arrow that had hit somewhere closer to his groin than his heart.

He asked about her casually, after the event. He found an old high school buddy who knew of her, knew something of her family. She lived in Boston, her family was very posh. She came to Winchester to visit friends, and an old aunt who lived on High Street. George had heard of some of her friends, and understood immediately that they ran in different social circles, that any pursuit might be more effort than it was worth.

But then he saw her again, two weeks later, at a fundraiser for the Winchester Hospital. Her effect on him this time was nearly paralyzing as he watched her flit from table to table, chatting with the patrons, and then adjusting some of the bows that adorned the silent auction offerings.

"Pretty girl," said Amelia Crowley, who had come up beside him, breaking his reverie.

"Oh, hello Mrs. Crowley," George stumbled over his words a bit. "Well, yes, all the ladies here are pretty."

Amelia smiled at George. She had watched him grow up into a handsome young man, watched him take responsibility for the Duncan household when his father fell ill, and build a successful business in spite of the economic depression. Certainly he deserved an opportunity at happiness, she thought.

"Some are prettier than others. Would you like to be introduced?"

"Umm, oh, well, I don't know," George flustered. "She's very busy, I don't want to disturb her."

"Well, let's see. Don't run away. Speeches are next." With that, Mrs. Crowley returned to her seat at a nearby table.

George, his train of thought disrupted, returned to his table as well, and made a sincere effort to listen to the speeches. He heard about linens and new steam heaters for the wards, new equipment for the operating theater, advances in medicine, and the constant need for qualified nurses.

The speeches ended, and the last call was given for the silent auction bids. George sauntered over to the tables laden with decorated baskets and boxes, each arranged to entice the highest offer possible. He felt a touch on his arm, and turned. There she was, in front of him, less than three feet away; along with Mrs. Hammond, the Chairlady of the Fortnightly Club, the local women's charity that hosted the Annual Winchester Hospital Fundraiser.

"Are you enjoying the event, George?" Mrs. Hammond asked sweetly.

"Oh yes, very much, Mrs. Hammond, thank you," he replied graciously, glancing from Mrs. Hammond to Claire.

"We have some interesting items for auction, don't you think? Have you seen anything in particular upon which you would like to place a bid?"

"Oh, well, yes," he turned to look at the basket next to him, laden with piccalilli relish, jams and lemon cake. "This one looks very nice," he said, looking back at Claire. He could feel a flush of heat rising up his neck.

"Well, dear," Mrs. Hammond continued, "don't wait too long to place your bid. Have you met Claire Radcliffe? Claire, this is George Duncan, one of our wonderful up-and-coming young businessmen; and George, this is Claire Radcliffe, of Boston. She is always so helpful during these little functions. She's in charge of the silent auction, so if you have any questions, be sure to ask. Now I must see about the next announcements, it's almost time!" Mrs. Hammond flurried off, leaving George looking wide-eyed at the young lady in front of him.

"It's nice to meet you, Mr. Duncan," Claire said, and the smile appeared. "If there's anything I can do to help you, please don't hesitate to ask."

"Thank you," he replied, hoarsely. "I'll just bid on this, I think."

He turned and wrote a number on the ticket. "I've seen you—," he started as he straightened up, only to find she was engaged in conversation with another patron some distance away. He caught her eye, and she winked at him.

George was done for.

After that, they saw each other from time to time at a party, or at a Winchester Country Club function. They spoke to each other in groups at first, then more intimately for a minute or two while standing in line for a picnic buffet, or next to each other during a raffle drawing at a charity event. George found her self-assured, bright, and charming; and always the smile, just for him, which left him unhinged, and unable to think about work with any serious depth for hours at a time.

He asked her if she would like to see a moving picture, and she agreed. They ate lunch together, sometimes at Randall's Diner in Winchester, more often at a small, chic café in Cambridge. They talked about art, politics, and local news; sometimes they walked along Upper Mystic Lake, bringing along a picnic hamper and blanket so they could sit for a while and watch the sailboats and swans meander through the water. One afternoon, she asked about his business, and he showed her his shop, showed her the machines, his little office off the work area, the lists of his customers. He asked about her family, and was invited to dinner to meet her parents, a civil enough event, if not entirely warm. Somewhere in all the formality, apart from his business and her family, they began to share more intimate thoughts and feelings. These skimmed the surface at first, tentative in the newborn trust they shared; and as the trust grew, the depth and surety of their exchanges grew as well.

For Claire, it was never so much a falling head over heels in love, her ideals regarding romance squashed at an early age through close observation of her own parents' example. But she found in George a man who was smart, and driven, and who shared himself openly and honestly. He had a sense of humor, but more importantly, a sense for business. She knew he liked her from the very beginning, at the art show; and she found she liked him, too, maybe even loved him, in her own reserved way. Above all, she felt comfortable with him, a feeling she had not experienced with the boys she had dated before, clumsy, inarticulate children who drank too much and tried, too obviously, to grasp onto the bloom of glowing sexuality which radiated from Claire; nor with the old men her mother kept inviting over to dinner, men who leered at her as they ate their salmon or lobster; and who attempted to corner her sometimes after dessert, smelling of cigars and brandy and something else, something revolting, a naphtha-laden mustiness laced with old age and death.

As for George, whose experience with the opposite sex was limited to a few simple dates squeezed in between caring for his family and building a business, Claire had become the tangible, flesh-and-blood reality of an elusive, hazy dream. With her, he could envision a defined, contented future he'd never imagined for himself, a home and family of his own, an expanse of comfort and companionship; for in Claire, George found his best friend, a woman with whom he could share his fears and hopes, the woman with whom he wanted to spend the rest his life.

George proposed to Claire one afternoon in early July, during one of their picnics at Mystic Lake. He'd picked out a square-cut diamond, set in a delicately filigreed white gold band. Claire accepted, laughing through tears as he placed the ring on her finger.

"I'll need to speak to your father, of course," George said.

Claire was suddenly quieter. "Yes, we'll talk to my father."

For it was Mother who stood aghast as Claire's father clapped George on the back and granted his enthusiastic blessing of the union; and it was Mother who made an unannounced visit to George's shop one morning shortly after the engagement.

George, surprised and nervous, invited Mrs. Radcliffe through to his office and offered her a chair.

"I'll come right to the point," began Mrs. Radcliffe. "Claire is obviously smitten with you; however, she is very young, and as her mother, I see things more clearly. I see you have a nice little shop here, and you appear to be busy."

She looked doubtfully at the small office, the simple furniture.

"Still," she continued, "I'm not convinced that you can care for her properly. I'd like to see your accounts, if you don't mind. Just the last eighteen months or so should suffice."

George was flabbergasted. The woman was rude, invasive, and horrible. Nevertheless, she would be his mother-in-law, and he wanted her to tolerate him, at least, for Claire's sake. He pulled two ledgers from a shelf and set them before her.

Mrs. Radcliffe stood up after perusing the documents silently for the better part of a quarter-hour. "Not as impressive as I would have hoped. At any rate, I'm sure I've made myself understood. Is there another door by which to exit other than going through that shop again? That racket has given me quite a headache." George, fuming, showed her out through a side door. She left without saying another word.

George mentioned the visit to Claire that afternoon as they ate lunch at Randall's.

"Don't worry about my mother," she reassured him. "Daddy approves of you, and that's all that matters. And I love you. Mother will soften up. She just needs time."

They were married the following May, an ostentatious affair, orchestrated under Mrs. Radcliffe's close supervision. As a wedding gift, Claire's parents gave the couple a Queen Anne-style home on Dix Street, just a few blocks from downtown, but worlds away in luxury. A wide marble floor entry extended through the center of the house, leading to large, spacious rooms off the corridor to the right; and to the left, a gently curving staircase floated up to the second story. The house boasted three large fireplaces with handsomely finished maple wood mantels and surrounds. An inviting porch, augmented with several ornately turned colonnades, extended across the full front of the house.

Claire decorated with plush couches and chairs, furniture of gleaming oak, maple and walnut, and luxurious curtains and carpets. Wedding gifts of silver, china and crystal provided the finishing touches to an absurdly lush standard of living in the midst of the Depression. The initial expenses blindsided George, who spent most of his considerable savings to avoid debt. Still, Claire glowed with satisfaction, and once the house was furnished, the extravagance seemed to diminish. George decided his life was very good, with that smile sending him off to work every morning, and greeting him as he walked through the door of his beautiful home every night.

Within a few months of their marriage, Claire was pregnant. George was elated with the news. If he ever noticed that Claire became a bit cooler toward him, or that her sense of humor seemed faded, he never mentioned it. He was going to be a father. His world was complete.

Chapter 7

Claire delivered a son, Oliver James, in the spring of 1935. He was a large, healthy baby, with wisps of sandy brown hair and a well-developed set of lungs. The delivery had been very difficult, and by the time Claire was transferred to Winchester Hospital, the surgeon was already waiting in the operating theater. The Caesarian section was performed with haste, leaving Claire with a nasty scar, and an inability to bear more children.

George hired a wet nurse, and a nanny. He asked his mother and sister to come as often as they could, and Irene and Louise happily took turns fussing over Oliver, changing his diapers, bathing him, and cradling him in their arms as they walked back and forth along the expanse of the Dix Street house. At first, Claire was too ill to protest, but after a few weeks, she reminded George that he had hired a nanny; and, after all, Irene should be tending her husband, and Louise should be helping out at her own house. Something about Claire's comments disappointed George. He enjoyed having his mother and sister visit his home, knew they cared more for his son than a hired stranger. Claire was still so sick, though, and George dared not upset her. He asked his mother and Louise to come rather less often, and let the nanny do her job.

Claire was slow to recover, and it wasn't until two months after the birth that she formally invited her parents to meet their grandson. Mr. Radcliffe was as proud as if it were his own. He shook hands with George vigorously as they walked through the door, and handed him a box of cigars.

"Good job, son! Where is the little fellow, I can't wait to meet my new grandson!"

"Good heavens, Lyle, we've only just walked in the door!" chided Mrs. Radcliffe. "Here, George, take these from me, will you?" She handed him two bottles of champagne. "So, his name is Oliver James, I understand?"

George did his best to balance the cigars and champagne as he made his way to the dining room table.

"Yes, Oliver James. He really is a lively little fellow, we're enjoying him immensely." George gingerly placed the box and bottles on the table. "Thank you so much for these, we'll have to pop open a bottle to celebrate."

"Have you set a date for the christening?" asked Mrs. Radcliffe.

"Oh, yes," George replied, "August 17th. It's been delayed a bit, of course, but we'll be ready by then. The notice will go out next week."

Mrs. Radcliffe continued, "And how is Claire? Fully recovered, I hope?"

George looked at her, incredulous. Her daughter had been through a grueling surgery, and a long, painful recovery. She had been told that she could not have more children. Yet in all that time, through all the agony Claire experienced, Mrs. Radcliffe had not once stopped by, had not telephoned, had not written so much as a note of encouragement or congratulations.

"Yes," George replied with a hint of condescension, "she's much improved."

Then, to Mr. Radcliffe, "She should be downstairs shortly, she's just getting dressed. The nanny will bring Oliver down in a few minutes. Won't you please sit down? Ruth is here as well, and I believe she made coffee."

"Well, I'm glad to hear you have help in." Mrs. Radcliffe seated herself at the dining room table and removed her gloves. She sat ramrod-straight, purse in her lap, her face expressionless.

At that moment Ruth, a middle-aged black woman bearing a large silver coffee service, entered from the kitchen. She placed the tray on the dining room table. "Would you like me to pour?" she asked Mrs. Radcliffe.

Mrs. Radcliffe ignored the woman. George answered, "Thank you, Ruth, I'll take care of it."

Ruth nodded and returned to the kitchen. Mr. Radcliffe made his way to the large window seat near the table, and looked out over the garden. "Well, I see the hydrangeas are coming along. And the lilacs, they should bloom nicely next year. Thought of putting in some vegetables back there, George? It's a little late for tomatoes, but I bet you could get some pumpkins this fall if you started soon."

"We'll put some in, Daddy." Everyone turned. Claire had appeared at the bottom of the stairs, and was walking slowly into the dining room. She was pale, but well-dressed, and her hair was neatly tied with a bow. She held Oliver in her arms.

"Daddy, would you like to meet your grandson?"

Mr. Radcliffe hurried over to his daughter, hugged her carefully, and peered at the baby. "Well, he certainly is a good-looking young man! Sleeping, is he? Well, that's fine. And how is my kitten? Feeling better? I know you've had a rough go of it, but you're on your feet, and I'm heartened to see it."

"Now, Lyle, don't make a fuss over her," said Mrs. Radcliffe to her husband. Then to George, "I thought you said there was a nanny." George opened his mouth to reply, but Mrs. Radcliffe turned away. She stood up and made her way over to Claire, glanced into the blankets to see the new baby for herself.

"Well, it's a boy. I suppose I'm glad to have a grandson." She returned to her seat at the table, where she motioned to George to pour her a cup of coffee.

A week after the christening, Claire and George sat at the dining room table, eating dinner. George was, as his usual custom, reviewing a stack of business papers as he ate. Claire reached over and touched his hand. He looked up at her.

"George," she began, "I know things have been very difficult, for both of us, the last few months. I want you to know how much I appreciate all you've done for me, for us, Oliver too."

George smiled at her. "Of course, Claire. I was glad to be of help." He turned again to his paperwork. "The thing is, George," she continued, "I want you to know that I'm better now." This was a delicate subject, and she wanted to broach it carefully. "The doctor says we could...be together, again, if we wanted."

George put down his fork and wiped his mouth with his napkin. Looking up at Claire again, he said gently, "I know what the doctor said. I also know that you have been through a horrible ordeal. I want to be sure you have plenty of time to heal completely, so let's wait a bit longer."

Claire looked down at her plate.

"All right," she said. George returned to his papers, and they finished the meal in silence.

Months passed before Claire prompted George again. This time, he finally agreed, but their lovemaking was tentative and awkward; after that, they made love infrequently, George decidedly hesitant, Claire quietly resentful, and increasingly bitter.

Claire thought, at first, that it was the scar that made George so reluctant to touch her. It was, in truth, a horrible-looking slash that extended downward from her bellybutton, still red, and uneven with bulbous scar tissue, the large stitch marks pointedly visible. Claire knew it would take years to heal to a less noticeable white, bumpy line.

But it wasn't the scar that set George on a course of near celibacy with his wife, nor the seriousness of her operation, nor the length of her recovery.

While Claire had been in the operating theater, George had been ushered into a waiting room and left alone. He sat for a while, his head in his hands; then he rose, and paced for several minutes, the length of time it took to smoke a cigarette. He sat again. A nurse brought him coffee, told him the doctors were doing their best, and returned to her station down the hall. George pondered what had gone wrong, if there was something he could have done differently to prevent the chain of events that led to this point. Claire could die; for that matter, he suddenly understood, so could the baby.

After the first hour, he got up, and started to pace again, this time breaching the borders of the waiting room, and wandering through the white halls, peering surreptitiously into rooms here and there, wherever a door happened to be open.

He stopped short at one open door, recognizing the boy in the bed, a young fellow that had come looking for work at his shop a few months before. George remembered the thick mop of dark brown hair that sat atop the boy's head, remembered how he'd asked if there were any menial tasks he could do. George's shop was fully staffed, and so he'd sent the boy away, telling him there were a few other businesses up the road that might have an opening.

Now the boy was in a hospital bed, his dark hair in stark contrast to the pale skin and white sheets surrounding him. A woman wearing a bulky brown sweater, her hair pulled back into a tight, neat bun, sat next to his bed. His mother, George thought. He knocked lightly at the door. The woman looked up, anxiety seared across her face.

"Yes?"

"Sorry to intrude," George said softly, "but I know that boy."

"Oh, are you a friend of Sam's?" the woman inquired.

"Acquaintance might be better."

"Well, friend or acquaintance, what's your name?"

"George," he smiled at the woman.

"Hello, George, I'm Iris," she replied.

"Pretty name," he said. The woman herself was not pretty, although she may have been, once, George thought. As she sat by her son, she looked plain, puffy, and haggard.

"Thank you."

"What happened to him?"

"Accident at work. He got a cut, it got infected. They'll be taking off his left hand today, hoping it will save his life," she trailed off with a deep sigh.

"I'm very sorry, Iris. I'll say a prayer for him, for you both." George withdrew quietly, leaving the mother and son to their own agony.

George made his way back to the waiting room. He hated this, hated hospitals, hated sickness and death, and the cutting open of people, the cutting off a hand, the cutting out a baby. He couldn't be here any longer, he'd have to tell the nurse he had to go out for a while, that he would come back later, after he'd gotten some fresh air, or even gone into the office, where work— safe, steady, healthy work—awaited him.

As he approached the nurse's station, he saw his mother was there, waiting for him.

"Where have you been?" she chided. "The nurse has gone looking for you. You have a son!"

"What about Claire?" he asked, his desperation overwhelming any joy.

"Claire is out of surgery, George. I heard the nurses talking. I guess it was very rough for her, but she's out of surgery, and alive, although it seems she'll need to stay in the hospital for some time."

Irene Duncan reached out for her son's arm before she continued, her brow furrowed with deep concern.

"And George, you might as well hear it from me. Claire, well, Claire won't be able to have any more children. I'm so sorry."

George rubbed his temples, shook his head.

"Come on," said his mother, trying to encourage him, "let's go see the baby, and then we'll ask about Claire."

They stood at the maternity ward window, a wavy glass partition through which George and his mother could see the new baby, wrapped in a white blanket, held in the arms of the charge nurse. Looking at his son, George asked his mother the most difficult question he'd ever asked her, ever asked any woman.

"Do you think…do you think Claire and I are…mismatched? That's why the baby was so big, why she had such a difficult time?" He hadn't expressed exactly what he was thinking, but Irene Duncan knew her son, knew what he was asking.

"George, God gives us our burdens as well as our gifts and pleasures. Marriage is a sacred commitment, you know this. You're not mismatched as long as you keep your vows. Love comes and goes, believe me; but the commitment remains. Now, Claire has given you a healthy son. It's cost both of you something, but the truth is, Claire has borne the brunt of it. This may be the time to think about what your commitment means, and how best to keep it."

She was silent for a moment, then added, "You may have to suppress some of your own needs in consideration of Claire's delicate nature."

Chapter 8

Back Bay Machining continued to do well for the next year. By the end of 1936, however, business started to flatten out, and then slowly decline, in bumps and starts, like a motor running out of gas. George wasn't concerned at first. A minor slowdown from time to time was a normal part of his business. By the spring of 1937, he realized that the loss of business was not a temporary setback; the economy in general, which had recovered somewhat from the horrible crash of 1929, was diving again, and Back Bay Machining was sinking with it.

One evening in early June, George tried to express his concerns to Claire as they were dressing for dinner. The wet nurse was long gone, but George suggested they could do without the nanny; certainly Oliver was old enough.

Claire shook her head. "That is absolutely out of the question. I'm swamped with work for the Fortnightly Board, and you know I've been elected to serve as Chair for the Home and Garden Club. Oliver still requires constant care, and I won't consider letting the nanny go until he's at least through first grade."

George was irritated by Claire's stubbornness, but he didn't want to argue with her. He tried another tack.

"Maybe your parents would be willing to give us a loan, just until we get over this rough patch. What do you think?"

Claire looked at him doubtfully.

"You know Mother and Daddy have been more than generous to us. They have their own business to attend, and I will not ask them for…charity." She hissed the word as if it were something vile-tasting. "I don't need to remind you that it's your job to provide a certain standard of living for our family. You were fortunate enough to marry into one of the best families in Boston. Your success in business proved you worthy of our marriage. I have every expectation that you will maintain that worth."

Claire turned to face the mirror at her dresser, leaning in to check her make-up.

"You know I love you, George. I'm saying these things only because I know you are a capable, strong man, and you don't want anything less than the best for our family. The best has always meant our beautiful home, nice clothing, and a few extras. I do my part, and I know you will do yours."

She stood back from the mirror, adjusted the collar of her blouse, and checked the seam on her hose. Finally, she looked up at him, smiling her wicked smile. "Now finish getting dressed for dinner. We're expected at the Andrews' at 6:30, and I don't want to be late."

George's savings were depleting steadily. If things didn't improve, they could last another year, maybe a little longer, with their current expenses. For the first time in George's life, hard work and a winning personality were not enough. His golden touch was melting away, leaving drossy mortal flesh in its place.

Chapter 9

It was in the middle of George's financial struggles that Frank Duncan passed, mercifully, in his sleep. Irene Duncan had found her husband deceased one afternoon when she brought up his lunch. Without shedding a tear, she performed the duties for which she felt responsible under such circumstances, actions she had rehearsed in her mind hundreds of times over the years, knowing it was not a matter of if, only when.

It took her an hour and a half to wash his body and dress him in his one black, slightly moth-eaten, woolen suit, the one he had worn at their wedding, and to every church service until he fell ill. Once he was dressed, she pulled his body from the bed and, finally getting him into position on the floor, grabbed him by the ankles and pulled him through the bedroom door. She stopped twice as she maneuvered him down the stairs: first, when his right arm got hooked up in the bedroom doorjamb; and again, to place a blanket under his head when the 'thunk, thunk, thunk' of his head hitting each step started to make her feel queasy.

From the base of the stairs, she dragged him to the couch in the front room. She was warm, now, and beginning to tire, so she sat for a few minutes on the couch, her feet placed gingerly between her husband's legs. Once she'd caught her breath, she gathered herself for the remaining tasks, and set back to work.

She placed a thick layer of newspaper and several blankets down on the cushions, and hoisted the body onto the couch. She had considerable difficulty with this, for although she was a strong woman, and her deceased husband didn't weigh more than 140 pounds, he was, of course, a dead weight, and it was clumsy work. Once she succeeded, though, she stepped back from her handiwork. His hair needed combing. He needed a blanket to cover everything below the chest, and a string of rosary beads placed in his hands. These tasks accomplished, Irene Duncan surveyed her husband again, and decided this was by far the best he had looked in a long time. She called Father Glenn, and requested he come to the house to administer whatever last rites remained for her husband; and as an afterthought, she called Dr. Murray and told him to stop by on his way home from work, her husband was dead.

Louise had come home from school that afternoon to a scene she could never quite forget: her father, blue and skeletal, neat and formal, stretched out on the couch as though he were taking a very rigid nap; and her mother and Father Glenn sitting in chairs across from the body, engaged in quiet conversation, coffee cups and a plate of sugar cookies on the table between them.

Dr. Murray arrived, and made a cursory assessment as Louise, her mother, and Father Glenn looked on. It was probably a heart attack, the doctor said. It didn't matter. Frank Duncan was a man his family hardly knew during the last ten years, who had occupied an upstairs guest room for the better part of the last five. In the end, he was a thin shadow of the hearty Irishman who blustered his way from Cork County to Canada, fished and trapped his way into America, and finally settled in Winchester to work at the tannery and marry a good Irish-Catholic girl from Stoneham. After the burial, Irene Duncan gave George his father's Winchester rifle; and Frank Duncan's only other worldly good of any value, a Waltham pocket watch with a coin silver case, etched on the outside with fine whorls.

George knew his mother was terminally ill the following September, just after her weakness left her unable to return to the store for Louise's winter boots. Dr. Murray made it plain to George that his mother had a cancer, and it was growing quickly. George discussed the situation calmly with his mother one afternoon in late October. He assured her that he would look after Louise, make her finish high school, support her through college if she wanted to go, make sure the man she married was decent. Mrs. Duncan nodded her head.

"Mother, I would like to see the will, if possible, so that I can make sure everything is in order."

"Oh, ayah, to be sure. I have it in the closet." A combination of Irish brogue and Boston accent clipped her speech. George watched his mother as she rooted around in her bedroom closet for the better part of ten minutes, sitting down twice to catch her breath. "I have it here somewhere," she panted. George offered to help, but a firm "No, no, I can still do this," was the sharp reply. Finally, she found it, folded up and wedged between two old wool blankets. She handed it to him without looking at it.

"Would you mind if I took this with me? I promise to return it in a day or two."

"Keep it," his mother said. "After all, you're the executor, and I have no intention of trying to find it again when our heavenly Father is calling me home. But for heaven's sake, don't lose it!"

George sat in his den that night after dinner and carefully unfolded the document. It was simple, only a few lines written in his father's shaky hand, followed by his father's shaky signature. George read it twice, more slowly the second time, to be sure. The property, the house, its furnishings, every-thing—was left to Louise, without encumbrance, after Irene Duncan's death. There was nothing mentioned about what would happen if the Duncan ma-triarch should die before Louise reached the age of 21. There certainly were no savings or other financial backing to offset the cost of living in and main-taining the house, nothing Louise could live on while she finished school. There was nothing for George, the will executed at a time when he was flush with successful business, a beautiful new wife, a beautiful new home.

George sat back in his chair. It was obvious to him that his father hadn't thought this through, that he had assumed Irene would live a long time, and that Louise would most certainly be an adult with a family of her own when Irene did pass. George had hoped, actually expected, that the property would pass to him, at least in part. He could borrow against it, giving him something to prop up his business until the economy improved.

Claire was washing dishes when George sauntered into the kitchen an hour later.

"Well?" she asked, aware from the look on his face that all was perhaps not well. George poured a cup of coffee, sat heavily at the kitchen table, and lit a cigarette.

"Tell me, dear," Claire said. "Perhaps I can help."

"The house goes to Louise, lock, stock and barrel." Claire stopped mid-rinse of a plate, just for a second, and then placed the plate in the drainer carefully before responding.

"Well, Louise will need some sort of security, won't she? Your parents are providing that for her, aren't they?"

"Yes, I suppose that was the intent. But they didn't leave any funds for management of the property, or for Louise to live on. I think my father expected that I would continue to support the house. He obviously thought my mother would live a long time, and Louise would inherit as a grown woman."

Claire started to dry the dishes and put them away. George went on, more cheerfully.

"But I think I have a plan, which will be good for everyone involved. First of all, Louise will have to move in with us. After all, she's only fifteen, she can't rattle around in that old house by herself. And then, I'm going to rent it out. There's a steady income, which would be useful—and then the house would be there for her when she's old enough." George took a drag from his cigarette, tapped the ash from the end into a little crystal ashtray.

Claire knew this was coming, at least the part about Louise living with them, when it became obvious that the cancer would kill her mother-in-law sooner rather than later. Claire turned to George, smiling sympathetically. "Of course she should come live with us," she said. "She'll need her family around her, people who will make sure she's protected, and who will care for her. That's you and me, George, we're her family."

That seemed to be the end of the conversation until the day of the burial. The service was well-attended, and Father Glenn gave a lengthy eulogy for Irene Duncan, who had taken her turns working at St. Mary's, polishing the extensive woodwork, washing and ironing the linens, and tidying the rectory. At her graveside he said the blessing for the dead, offered condolences to the family, accepted a contribution for his services. The reception was held at George's house, and Claire patiently received the Duncan's neighbors from Pembroke Road: the Hannigan family; young Beth Crowley, along with her mother, Amelia, and grandmother, Hazel; Gus Osprey, the butcher; the Smith family; and dozens of others from the Parish, some of whom Claire recognized, most of whom she did not. Claire was unusually receptive of Mr. and Mrs. Andrews, and when Margaret Andrews was filling her plate with a second helping of sandwiches, Claire looked across the coffee service at Philip Andrews, and gave him her most wicked smile. He raised an eyebrow ever so slightly, a faint grin momentarily crossing his face. And then he turned his attention to the coffee pot, and very, very carefully poured a half cup.

That evening, as they lay in bed together, Claire turned to George. He looked at her in the darkness, a sliver of moonlight casting a shadow over her face that made her eyes seem like hollow pits. He closed his eyes.

"George," she said.

"Hmmm."

"George, I've been thinking of a better way to get you out of your little difficulty." He opened his eyes, closed them again. He was so tired.

"What," he said.

"George, are you awake, this is serious. George, I think you should sell the house, and not rent it out. If you rent it, you won't get very much every month, and renters are sometimes so difficult to manage. On top of that, you would be responsible for all the upkeep." Claire moved closer. "I think that's more of a burden than you should have to bear. George, are you listening?"

"Hmm."

She waited a moment to let the idea sink in.

"You could use the money from the sale to help rebuild your business, with plenty of time to replace any funds you use, maybe even giving Louise a little bit of interest."

Claire pressed on. "Wouldn't that be best? You would have the funds you need right now, and she would have her inheritance, plus a little bonus, when she's old enough. Don't you see, this is an opportunity that will help all of us."

"I hardly think my mother's death is an opportunity," he snorted, turning away from her, from the empty eye pits. "I'm very tired, Claire, it's been a long day."

She put her hand on his shoulder. "It's just an idea, I just want to help both you and Louise. Good night, sweetheart," she whispered.

George lay awake for the next hour thinking about it. He considered this new option. It was true, he could use the money. The way the will was written, the soonest Louise could truly inherit was still six years away. Surely that was plenty of time to bring his business back up, and replace any funds he'd borrowed. He dozed off, the new plan jelling in his mind.

The next morning, George agreed at breakfast that selling the house was a better option. The next step was to find a buyer.

For Claire, the decision to sell was a foregone conclusion. Now she had to manage the circumstances of Louise's room and board.

"When Louise moves in, she'll need her own room, you know—it's very important to a girl her age. I don't want to move Oliver, and of course, we have our room…"

"What about the back bedroom? Or one of the other rooms on the second floor? Maybe she could stay in the room next to Oliver," George suggested.

"Oh dear, no, none of those will do," replied Claire. "I need that back bedroom for Mother when she comes. You know she can't climb stairs. Besides, what if we have guests? As for the other rooms upstairs, I don't think Louise would be comfortable cramped in one of those. Certainly not next to Oliver, he might keep her awake. No, the only thing to do is fix up the attic. It will be perfect for her. We'll get it all cleaned up, move her furniture in there—I'll even get some new curtains. She'll have plenty of privacy, and lots of room. It will be just perfect, and I think she'll love it."

There was no further conversation on the subject. In the end, George cleaned out the attic himself. Claire begged off from the tiresome project, saying Oliver had a terrible cold and needed tending. Oliver's 'terrible cold' consisted of two sneezes, a single cough, and a refusal to eat lima beans at dinner.

It was just as well, thought George. He went up the wooden stairs leading from the second floor to the landing at the attic door, carrying a bucket full of cleaning supplies in one hand, a broom and a mop in the other. The door squeaked as he opened it, and frigid, musty air filled his nostrils as he groped for the pull chain to turn on the single bulb, an unshaded sconce light near the door. The room was large, finished with wooden planks from ceiling to floor. Small, four-paned, double-glazed windows were situated on either end of the room.

George warmed as he worked, trying to figure out how he would get Louise's furniture up the stairs, how it might be arranged so that she would be most comfortable. He moved boxes and trunks to the basement, dusted and swept, and damp-mopped the floor. He washed the windows with vinegar and water, polishing them with newspaper until they fairly sparkled. As he worked, he imagined how Louise could be happy here, how she would be cared for, and how he would help her with her schoolwork. Maybe she would babysit Oliver sometimes so that he and Claire could go out more often.

In the end, the attic seemed, if not overly inviting, at least tolerable. With Louise's furniture in place and new curtains at the windows, George thought the room would be quite pleasant, and certainly a safe haven for his sister in the midst of so much loss.

Chapter 10

"Louise," George said, "I've found a buyer for the house."

Louise drew in a sharp breath. This was all wrong, it was happening too fast. George had mentioned something about selling the house after the funeral, but Louise thought it would take months, not three short weeks. The shock made her dizzy. Her mother was gone forever; and now George, the one she could always count on to make things better, was selling the only home she had ever known.

George saw the look on her face. "No, no, Louise," he said, "it will be fine. Don't you see, you'll come live with us. You'll have your own room, and you'll have your family right there for you, to help you and take care of you."

Louise was stunned. Not only was George wrenching her from her home, he was thrusting her into the icy abyss of the Dix Street house. She protested as best she could.

"Please, George, I don't want to leave home." Her voice was raised, on the edge of panic. "There must be some other way." Hot tears began to drop. George handed her his handkerchief. He glanced around casually as he lit a cigarette. He had hoped to avoid a scene, bringing her down to Randall's

Diner to break the news, but apparently it could not be avoided. Maybe it could be contained.

"I know you love the house, Louise. But you're too young to live on your own—you know this. And Dot's mother has her own family to take care of. She's been very kind to let you stay there the past few weeks, but you can't live there forever."

George sat back and smoked his cigarette. He let her cry for another minute or two, waiting until, he hoped, the worst of it passed. When she quieted, he continued, trying his best to soothe her.

"Now, then, everything will be fine. And when you're old enough, you'll have an inheritance waiting for you. You can go to college if you like. You could even buy your own house. But right now, I need you to be brave, and do the right thing." He bent across the table to peer at her downcast face. "Can you do that, for me?"

Louise was angry, and hurt, and exhausted. She knew she had no choice. With only a few dollars saved of her own, she was at the mercy of her brother and his wretched wife; and while George might truly have her best interests at heart, Louise could not believe the same about Claire.

When Louise first met Claire, their relationship had been friendly enough. Louise was still very young, just eleven years old, and Claire was disposed to think of her as the child that she was. But everything changed one afternoon shortly after George and Claire moved into the Dix Street house. Louise was sitting at the dining table, carefully unwrapping a crystal decanter, one of what seemed like a hundred wedding presents stacked in front of her, all to be opened and sorted and put away or displayed. Claire and her mother were in the kitchen, their discussion quickly turning from conversational to argumentative. As their voices rose, Louise couldn't help but hear the vicious words Claire's mother was directing most emphatically toward her daughter.

"I would never have allowed this marriage. You deliberately went against my wishes." There was a pause. "I still don't know what possessed your father to purchase this house and just give it to you. It took everything he had, it was so foolish; but he has always allowed sentiment to cloud his reason. Such an extravagance." Louise heard Mrs. Radcliffe heave a great sigh of disgust.

"I think Daddy just wanted us to have a good start, Mother. I didn't realize it was a financial concern."

"Well, now you know. And all the training I lavished on you, the best schools, the nicest clothes, the most appropriate friendships—even when you got into trouble with that boy from Medford, I took care of that, too—all so you would have the best life possible. All my work, wasted on this, this Irish laborer. If I'd thought for one second you were thinking anything more of this heathen than a passing fling, I would have..."

"We're all Catholic, Mother," Claire inserted.

"Yes, but we're French," Mrs. Radcliffe retorted.

"George is very good to me. I'm happy with him." Claire's voice was shaky.

"Happiness is *not* the point, here, young lady. Wealth and position are the point. You had better hope your little man can pull his weight, and if he starts to lag, you'll need to push him along. The whole family is depending on you, Claire. I had a nice rich gentleman all ready for you, for us. But you refused him! And your father is an absolute idiot for supporting you in this preposterous farce."

"Please leave Daddy out of this. George is a good businessman, you know that, you saw his shop. You made him show you his books."

Mrs. Radcliffe continued, unrelenting. "What's more, you also have his family with which to contend. That little girl out there, along with her mother, will be nothing but an albatross around your neck. They will siphon money out of your hand every month, you'll see. You could be married to old money, Claire, instead of this, this, mechanic..."

"Machinist," Claire corrected, her voice now taking on an acerbic edge. "And he owns the business, and it's very profitable."

At this, Louise heard a loud clap, and an "Oh!" from the kitchen. She debated if she should leave the room, or simply duck under the table and hide.

"Don't take that tone of voice with me, young lady." Mrs. Radcliffe's voice was venomous. "You could have married the old man and had George on the side—that's how women in our position find their happiness, Claire. But what's done is done. You are responsible now—*not* me, *not* your father—*you*. Do you understand?"

"Y-Yes, I understand." Claire's voice was hoarse, strained with tears.

The Lights of Pembroke Road

A moment later Claire came out of the kitchen, her eyes red, her left cheek a deep pink. She saw Louise standing at the dining room table, staring at her.

"I suppose you heard all that. Didn't even have the good grace to leave when you knew it was personal."

"I'm sorry, Claire," said Louise, now wishing desperately that she'd hidden under the table when she'd had the chance.

"Yes, I'm sure you are. Just go home, Louise. I have to lie down."

Claire headed up the stairs without another word.

Mrs. Radcliffe came out of the kitchen, handbag over her arm, pulling on her gloves. She took no notice of Louise until she stood in front of the mirror by the front door, adjusting her hat, checking her make-up and hair.

"Be sure you leave all those gifts where they belong. I'll know if something's missing."

With that, Mrs. Radcliffe walked out the front door, closing it quietly behind her.

In the ensuing weeks, Louise sensed Claire's increasing antipathy, and gave her a wide berth. At family functions, Claire and Louise simply made the concerted effort to stay as far apart from each other as possible, a dance which had worked well enough for both of them. Now, after three years of careful avoidance, they would be living under the same roof.

"Claire doesn't like me," Louise sniffled, wiping her eyes.

"Yes, she does."

George sighed. This was more complex than he had anticipated. Still, Louise was his little sister, and he was sure she would be happy once she was settled into his house. "She just doesn't know you very well, and she wants to get to know you better. We can become closer as a family, Louise." He paused, and beamed an understanding smile at her. "No more tears now. It's all settled, and you'll see...I promise, it will be fine."

They left the diner, and he dropped her off at the house on Pembroke Road, saying he would return on Saturday to help her pack and move. He smiled and waved as he pulled away. Louise raised her hand to wave good-bye, George's handkerchief still crumpled in her fist. She watched until his car turned onto Woodside Avenue, and then trudged up the walk to the porch.

At the steps, she glanced up at the house, quiet and dark and still. She would miss the flowers, she thought, that would overtake the front of the house in the coming spring, the roses and morning glories, and the irises and daffodils that she and her mother carefully nestled into the ground near the porch two years ago. Louise decided that was the best summer of her young life. She and her mother spent most of it working in the back garden, growing plump tomatoes and tender pole beans, crisp sweet peppers, peas and squash. Nearly every Saturday from July to the end of September was spent canning or drying the abundant harvest. When the blueberries were in, they went with Beth and Amelia Crowley to a little farm in Tewksbury, where they filled as many buckets with the sweet fruit as they could carry, returning home to make cobbler, and then jar after jar of sweet, thick preserves.

They had twice gone to Wingaersheek Beach, taking Dot with them. They hired a young nursing student to tend to Frank Duncan while they took the precious time away. Louise reveled in the excitement of a day at the beach with her best friend, picnicking, digging for clams and splashing in the surf. As for Irene Duncan, it was enough to stroll back and forth along the quiet span of Ipswich Bay, with the Annisquam Lighthouse sitting as a beacon in the distance, and little white cottages nestled serenely along the shore.

Now the iris and daffodil bulbs were sleeping. The rose plants, which bloomed red and pink in effusive waves of show during the summer, had been cut back hard, so that only the nubs of the stems poked out from their white winter blanket. The morning glories, which would grow fast and furious over and through the porch slats at the first hint of late spring warmth, also lay confined under a thick layer of mulch and snow. It would be months before all the bright colors of life would hold dominion again. Louise reflected that she was like the house as it stood now—cold, dormant, waiting. She walked up the steps and went inside, hoping that a warm fire would ease the gray chill that permeated through to her very soul.

She turned on the radio, and built a fire in the fireplace. Unable to eat much at the diner, she warmed soup for herself, and sat at the hearth as she ate. She thought of how her family would gather in this room on Saturday evenings to listen to an episode of *The Shadow Knows*. She and her mother would fold laundry, or knit, or mend clothes as the radio mystery unfolded. In earlier days, her father would sit with them, settled in his chair, perusing the *Winchester Star* newspaper, an unlit billiard pipe draped at the corner of his mouth. George was there too, until he married Claire. Louise wondered if they listened to the radio at the Dix Street house. Somehow, she doubted it.

Louise knew there was no miracle to save her from the inevitable. But maybe she could take something tangible with her, something to help her hold on to her memories.

Louise went from room to room, looking for any bits or pieces she could salvage. There wasn't much. The exterior of the house was always neat and fresh, but a necessary frugality, imposed by circumstances both external and internal, prevented the acquisition, or even the holding, of much in the way of material goods. Louise ended her search in her mother's room. She went through her mother's drawers, her closet, her jewelry box. She found a small silver brooch, which her mother wore every Sunday to church; and a faded picture of her parents on their wedding day. These would have to suffice. Louise put the items into a little box. She bundled up, and taking a last look behind her, stepped onto the front porch, shut the door, and made her way to Dot's house for the night.

George reflected on his conversation with Louise as he drove home. He was concerned that Louise was right, at least to some extent, about Claire. He never really thought about it. He'd never had to, or at least, hadn't wanted to. It was true, after he and Claire were married, he'd never seen his wife and sister interact with friendliness. In fact, he couldn't think of a recent time when they'd spoken more than a passing word to each other. Even at his mother's funeral, Claire sat by George; but Louise, pale and still in her black mourning dress, sat at the far end of the pew at the church; and stood on the other side of the grave at the cemetery.

George pulled into his driveway, and looked at the beautiful house in front of him. He considered the deep sighs that emanated from Claire whenever he mentioned Louise, the irritation in her voice when she talked about the move, and the convenient excuses she made to avoid the preparations to receive his sister. George dismissed the thoughts one by one, excusing them as one would a dog passing wind. Confident in his ability to make everything work, and ultimately, seeing no other reasonable course of action, he set his mind to the immediate task at hand—that of getting his sister safely moved into his home.

A month after Irene Duncan was laid to rest next to her husband in Wildwood Cemetery, George moved Louise and her few belongings into the attic at his house on Dix Street. Claire was already complaining that they were using more coal to heat the attic space. "The heat will rise, you know—she'll be sweltering and we'll be catching our death down here."

George simply said, "We'll be fine."

On the evening of Louise's arrival, over a dinner of roast chicken, carrots and potatoes, Claire made it clear, in a calm, straightforward manner, what she expected from Louise while she remained under their roof.

"Louise, dear, I know you'll want to help out here at your new home. Your duties are really quite simple. We have a housekeeper, Ruth, who comes in two days a week. She does most of the heavy cleaning, but I expect you to help with the housework on the days that she isn't here. You are responsible for washing the dishes, and keeping the house tidy. I'd like you to prepare dinner a few nights each week, I'll let you know when. I'd also like you to keep up our back garden, you seem to know your way around the raised beds."

Claire continued as she spooned potatoes onto Oliver's plate. "We also have a nanny, although now that you're here, we'll end her employment next week. I expect you to look after Oliver on the days you don't have school. And of course, you'll look after him when George and I go out."

At this, George, who had been engrossed in paperwork as he ate his dinner, looked up.

"Oh, yes, Louise, if you can look after Oliver from time to time, that would be wonderful." He returned to his paperwork, lost again in his own train of thought.

The unspoken requirements were that Louise should stay out of the way, up in her attic room if she was not actively engaged in housework or child care; that she should not complain; and if she wanted anything beyond the most basic of necessities, she would have to acquire it without Claire's assistance.

Louise did her best to adjust to her new circumstances. In the summer she found work at Dr. Ferguson's office three afternoons a week as a receptionist and file clerk. She continued to work there as she began her sophomore year at Winchester High School. Her earnings allowed her some small niceties, as Claire was loath to provide anything more than the essentials. The job also gave Louise time away from the house, for if she and Claire had been unable to tolerate each other while living in separate households, the situation was not improved by closer proximity.

When she wasn't at school, or working at Dr. Ferguson's, Louise spent her precious free time with her dearest friend, Dot. Dot was perpetually cheerful, which Louise might have found grating, except that she knew that it was a deliberate choice that Dot made every day of her young life. Dot's family had once been very wealthy, but the Depression had taken its toll on the Humphrey family. Dot's mother sold her jewelry, including her exquisite marquise-cut diamond engagement ring, to pay off the mortgage on their home, so that at least they would have a roof. Over time, furnishings also went to market—the camphor Chinese chest and silver service for taxes, a collection of Dresden figurines for clothing, pieces of Waterford crystal for food and coal. Now, when Louise went over to Dot's home, the living room was empty of furniture, save an expansive, down-stuffed sofa sitting in front of the fireplace, and precious family pictures carefully arranged on the mantel. The guest bedroom, once plush with teakwood furniture and satin comforters, now held only Mrs. Humphrey's sewing table and a single chair.

Ever the pragmatist, Mrs. Humphrey explained once that she really didn't mind doing without all the furniture and bric-a-brac, as it made cleaning the house so much easier. It also gave her more time to make her special line of children's clothing, smart little dress clothes and matching caps, which she sold in Winchester and Boston at a few small shops. Mr. Humphrey, once a financial analyst in Boston, found work delivering milk in nearby Medford and Lexington, which kept his family afloat, if only with the humblest of life rafts. Dot, following her parents' example of practical acceptance, chose to be grateful for the simplicity of her life, for the good things she did have—her loving parents, a warm home, and her dear friend, Louise.

Dot's room was unpretentious, composed of a bed, desk and chair, and dresser. Its minimalism protected it from being emptied in pieces for cash, and Dot and Louise found refuge there, gossiping about teachers and boys, and doing homework, until the inevitable hour arrived when Louise would make her way home to begin her work for the evening, whether it was cleaning, or cooking, or looking after little Oliver, who proved to be the one bright spot in her dismal life at the Dix Street house.

Chapter 11

Rose Hannigan stepped onto her front porch, bell in hand, ready to call her boys home for supper. She stood at the railing and surveyed her neighborhood, savoring the expanse of sharp, bright color that surrounded her. It was the third week in May, and the town of Winchester was fully alive under the late spring sun. Front yards shimmered with lush green lawns, and abundant cascades of leaves floated on the tops of the alder and birch and maple trees that lined the streets. Vibrant flowers of every hue popped in artfully arranged groupings from sidewalk plots and window boxes.

Rose's sons, Walter, Daniel, and Patrick, were playing baseball at the vacant field two streets over, a pick-up game that would be repeated nearly every day of the summer once school let out. Rose could hear them in the distance, the voices of young boys raised in a chorus as someone caught a ball that signaled the end of an inning, echoes carried by a gentle wind. The day was far along, the late afternoon warm and fine. The fragrance of fresh-cut grass floated in the air, fading away quickly as a heightened breeze pushed along the heavy, heady scent of lilacs, Rose's favorite flower.

Supper was ready. Still, Rose waited a minute, then another, her senses reveling in the singular pleasure of the moment. She closed her eyes and breathed deeply, slowly, angling her head to catch the sun's warmth across her cheeks. At a glance, anyone passing by on the street would see a pleasant-looking woman in her mid-thirties, with an unremarkable figure, her face a bit thin, perhaps, but not gaunt. Her dark blonde hair, which reached her waist when loose, was caught up in a neat bun on the top of her head. Her dress was simple, her shoes sturdy and sensible.

Rose thought back to when they first moved to Winchester, nearly six years ago, to this new home on Pembroke Road. She was early in her pregnancy with her fourth child, and on the first night, when she and her husband Joe finally fell into bed after a long day of emptying boxes and positioning and re-positioning furniture, Rose lay awake for some time, silently thanking God for her family, for her husband, and for the beautiful new home. It was a big step for them, moving from Stoneham. Joe had been promoted at work, taking a well-deserved position of regional manager for Lever Brothers. His advancement meant they could afford a home in Winchester, one that would accommodate their growing family. Their children would attend good schools, and they could enjoy some comforts, in spite of the recent Depression that gripped the country.

Rose took God's generosity to heart. She wanted her husband to be successful, her children to be popular and well-educated, and her home to be the center of everything for her family. She spared no effort ensuring her vision became a reality. Family pictures in pretty frames sat in a well-arranged line on the fireplace mantel, starched doilies were centered perfectly on highly polished furniture, and flowers grew from spring through fall in lovingly tended pots lining the front steps.

Rose made friends easily, and enjoyed the company of her neighbors, especially Amelia across the street, and Amelia's mother-in-law, Hazel. Friendships aside, Rose had, with purpose and diligence, cultivated useful relationships with many people in the community, in particular the staff at Lincoln Elementary School, where all of her children would pass their early education; and with carefully selected members of St. Mary's Parish. Rose baked cookies for the neighborhood children and church bake sales. She supported the food bank with blackberry preserves made from the overflowing bramble canes that lined the fence of the Hannigan's back yard. Now that Christine, her youngest, was in kindergarten, Rose volunteered two mornings each week at the Lincoln School, helping the younger children with art projects and managing some of the school files. She planned to join the Winchester Home and Garden Association, and perhaps even support one of the local theater groups.

Rose's efforts had borne the fruits she sought. Her boys did well in school, scholastic awards attesting to their success displayed proudly on a bookshelf near the fireplace. Walter, now fifteen, joined the newly formed local chapter of the Boy Scouts. Daniel and Patrick served as altar boys at St. Mary's. Rose's house gleamed, decorated every Fourth of July with red, white and blue bunting along the porch rails, every Christmas with a well-ornamented spruce prominently displayed in the front window. She felt that she was well-liked in the community, and well-received, and that she and her children wanted for nothing.

Sometimes, though, she missed her husband.

Rose and Joe had discussed, in some depth, the practical benefits and sacrifices that would result from his promotion and their subsequent move to Winchester. Joe listed the new house, the increase in salary, the opportunities for the boys, and Rose, as well. He also mentioned the sacrifices it would mean—time on the road, time away from his family, time away from Rose.

"Will you be all right?" he asked.

"Oh, yes," she replied, her strength of resolution pushing aside any doubt. "We always do what we need to do to make it all work. I don't want you to worry about a thing. Walter is old enough to help out, so are Patrick and Daniel, for that matter. I just want you to know how proud we are of you, Joe. You've always worked so hard, and you deserve this promotion." She smiled at him, and he was, for the most part, reassured.

Joe Hannigan started his career with Lever Brothers when he was just sixteen, packing boxes with Welcome Soap. Over a five-year period, he worked every job on the factory floor, from receiving raw materials to troubleshooting broken equipment. Affable, intelligent, and respectful, he was promoted to floor manager at twenty-one, and transferred into sales a few years later. Lever Brothers was growing, and profits were up. By 1929, the American arm of Unilever was the third largest soap manufacturer in the country, employing a thousand workers in their Cambridge facility alone. Lux, Lifebuoy, Rinso, and Welcome were household brands, and Joe, who had proven himself talented at local sales, was the obvious choice for the regional manager position when it opened up. The promotion was a good one, financially; but it meant Joe spent four nights of every work week on the road, managing accounts and visiting prospective clients throughout New England. It had been a strain on the family at first, but after a while, Joe's schedule became routine, and Rose and her children learned to thrive during his week-long absences.

Weekends developed a regular, if onerous, pattern that provided the boys with structured interaction with their father. Saturday mornings, Joe handed out work assignments to his sons. Joe's Hudson had to be washed and waxed, and his shoes shined. Depending on the season, grass had to be mowed, or leaves raked, or snow shoveled. Joe happily volunteered his sons to provide similar services for the neighbors. Mrs. Livingston, a widow who lived next to the Crowley's, invariably needed her lawn mowed, or leaves raked, or snow shoveled; and old Mr. Davis, who lived near the end of the cul-de-sac, needed his back garden weeded every weekend from the last frost of winter until mulch was laid on the beds in late fall. Payments the boys received for these services were handed over to Joe, who gave each of his sons an allowance in return. The remainder he gave to Rose to cover any little emergency that might arise.

On Saturday afternoons, once chores were completed, Joe took the boys into town. They stopped at Gus Osprey's butcher shop to pick up chicken livers and gizzards for Sunday morning breakfast. If the boys were due for a haircut, they went to the barber shop, where Bert, the lone barber, trimmed and clipped until the boys were restored to respectable neatness. Finally, Joe took his sons into Ford's drugstore for ice cream cones, always chocolate, always one scoop for each of the brothers.

On Sunday mornings, Joe stayed home to cook breakfast while Rose took the children to St. Mary's eight o'clock Mass. Sunday afternoon was Joe's quiet time—sometimes he would play catch with the boys, but mostly he liked to lie on the couch and read, often falling asleep with the book on his chest. By seven on Monday morning, he was back in his polished Hudson, off to the first appointment of the week.

Rose had heard some gossip that Joe spent an evening or two while on the road in the company of other women. Rose didn't really know for sure, and more pointedly, she didn't want to know. Her world was full of purpose, and she enjoyed the life she had built for herself. Her husband did his part to maintain that world for her, and that was, in a practical sense, what she needed from him.

The moment passed, and Rose was back again, on the porch. From the upstairs bedroom, she heard Christine cough. Rose turned her head, listening. Another cough. It sounded coarse and deep. Rose's brow furrowed. The spring cold Christine developed a week ago had seemed to be getting better, but today the cough came, and with it, a fever. Rose had given her an aspirin, and confined her daughter to bed for the day. At first, Christine complained bitterly at the restriction, as it was her nature to play with her schoolmates at kindergarten, and with her big brothers when they came home. Finally, after much cajoling and a reminder that Santa was taking notes, she resigned herself to coloring and looking at picture books, finally sleeping a bit in the afternoon. Rose had seen no need to call the doctor. But now Rose heard the guttural rattle of the cough, suddenly so much worse than this morning.

"Mommy," called Christine. The sun and lilacs and fresh-cut grass were forgotten.

"Coming," Rose called. She rang the bell quickly, loudly, to call the boys home, went inside, and headed upstairs.

Chapter 12

Walter heard the bell. Daniel and Patrick heard it too, and looked to Walter for the right response. Sometimes they lingered a few minutes to finish up an inning, but Walter was hungry, and the ring of the bell seemed insistent. He nodded to his brothers, and called to the other boys.

"Hey guys, we have to go."

The brothers trotted across the imaginary infield, picked up the notebooks they had dropped near the sandbag that served as a makeshift home base, and started home.

When the boys piled through the front door, Rose called to Walter from Christine's room. He headed up the stairs, directing his brothers to go wash up at the kitchen sink. Walter saw his mother standing at Christine's bedside, peering at a glass thermometer.

"Walter, honey, run over to Dr. Murray's house, ask him to come over as soon as he can. Christine is really not well. Tell him her temperature is," Rose looked at the glass thermometer, squinting, "a hundred and two."

Walter looked at his little sister lying still on her bed, her eyes closed and sunken in. Her breathing sounded funny. He glanced at his mother, just long enough to see the crease of worry on her face.

"Sure, Mom, I'll go get him." He was down the stairs and out the door, running. Dr. Murray lived on High Street, not more than a half-mile away, but Walter felt like it took forever to get there.

Walter fumbled with the latch on the fence gate at the front of the doctor's house. He swore under his breath. No one else's house had a fence, or a gate of any kind in their front yard. All the others were just fields of grass, dotted with trees and lined with flowerbeds, and he could run right up to anyone's front door—except Dr. Murray's.

Walter stepped back, forced himself to be patient, and tried again. This time the fence swung open gracefully, admitting him. He bolted forward, and, landing at the top of the porch steps, rapped with purpose on the large oak door. He looked around. He took no notice of the well-manicured lawn on either side of the walkway, intended to guide guests gently to the entry of the elegant home. Walter did notice the roses that lined much of the fence surrounding the property, and he thought the doctor must have a hundred of the damned things. Walter didn't like roses. Their thorny stems leaped out at him when he mowed his neighbors' lawns during the summer. Then, when the first frost bit, the spikes would stab him again with defensive anger as he cut the plants back for the winter.

Walter liked Dr. Murray, though. When Walter was ten, he contracted a mild case of polio, which left him unable to lift his left arm above the shoulder. The doctor sat with Walter through much of the illness, giving encouragement, reading short stories, telling bad jokes. When the illness passed and the damage was assessed, Dr. Murray told him how lucky he was. Not only could he breathe and walk, but since Walter was right-handed, the residual effects would not hamper him. These words were reassuring to a boy who wanted to play baseball in the summer and skate in the winter; and to his mother, who had hovered in vain during his illness, unable to make anything better for her son of her own volition.

Walter knocked again. Almost immediately, the door opened wide, and Dr. Murray stood there, a napkin tucked in at his shirtfront, with some kind of gravy sitting in spots against the white linen. Walter wondered what the doctor was eating for dinner. It smelled good, whatever it was, the rich scent of roasting meat pouring from the house. The doctor looked down at his uninvited guest, expectantly. They locked eyes. The doctor prodded.

"Hello, Walter, is there something I can do for you?"

"Dr. Murray, Mother sent me. Christine has a temperature of a hundred and two, and is very sick. Can you come to the house?"

The doctor sighed, exhaling his resignation with a whoosh.

"It's dinner time, Walter. I'm just in the middle of dinner, and I'm having a very important discussion with Mrs. Murray at the moment."

Walter thought maybe they were having an argument, because important discussions always seemed more like arguments to him, but he would not be deterred. In his father's absence, he was the man of the house, a responsibility he took very seriously. Christine was sick, and needed the doctor. He pressed.

"Could you come after dinner? Please?"

Dr. Murray nodded. "All right, tell your mother after dinner. I won't be long."

"Thank you, Dr. Murray!" Before the doctor could say another word, Walter bounded off the porch, and was running again, pausing only to shut the fence carefully behind him before racing the rest of the way home.

Dr. Murray arrived just before seven o'clock. Upstairs, he found Christine feverish, glassy-eyed, and listless. Her breathing was raspy. By now, Rose was frantic, but trying hard to control her voice and her anxiety.

"Is it the croup?" she asked, hopefully, knowing she could handle that— but knowing already that this was not the croup. Dr. Murray sat at the edge of Christine's bed, listening to her lungs.

"I think it's pneumonia," he stated matter-of-factly, removing his stethoscope. Dr. Murray made a few notes in a little book. "You'll have to watch her. We can perform an X-ray tomorrow if you like, but it's best to keep her comfortable tonight. Maybe tomorrow you could take her outside for a bit, go for a walk. The fresh air will help."

Dr. Murray left. Rose heard him say "Good night, boys!" as he walked out the door. Rose came to the top of the steps and looked down. Her three young men were gathered at the bottom, looking up at her. She smiled down at them, determined not to worry them unnecessarily. She kept her voice light and cheerful as she spoke.

"Well, then, boys, did you eat your dinner? Everyone have enough?" The three boys nodded their heads in unison. Rose found their silence unnerving. She made her way downstairs.

"All right, then, you know the routine. Walter, would you take the basin in Christine's room and fill it with fresh water? About halfway full should do. Daniel and Patrick, I need you to pick up your jackets and books and put them away. Let's tidy up a bit. Then we'll get you ready for school tomorrow." She scanned their faces and arms.

"You seem clean enough. Did you wash up properly for dinner?"

"Yes, Mum," the two boys chimed in unison.

"Is Christine very sick, Mum?" asked Patrick.

Rose gave her two young sons a reassuring smile.

"Yes, Patrick, she is sick, but we're going to take care of her, so I don't want you to worry. Now let's get busy and tidy up, shall we?"

Walter came down the stairs.

"The basin's all set. Anything else I can do?"

"Thank you, dear. Would you take care of your brothers while I tend to Christine? It would be a help if you could get them ready for school tomorrow and into bed."

Walter nodded, and Rose made her way back up the stairs.

Chapter 13

Rose pulled a rocking chair next to Christine's bed. She sat by her daughter, talking to her as she lay still and hot, telling her she would feel better soon, and they would have a party when she was well, and there would be cake and punch.

Rose wet a washcloth in the basin of cool water, wringing it out and folding it into careful thirds before placing it on Christine's forehead. She pulled the chair closer to Christine's side. Her daughter had finally fallen asleep. Rose prayed. Dr. Murray's words seemed to indicate that Christine would recover, but a few words in God's ear wouldn't go amiss. After all, this was her special child. Christine had come into her life when everything was new—the new house, the new job for Joe, the new schools for the boys. Rose loved Christine, loved her childish sweetness, her temper and stubbornness, her unending questions about everything in her little world. Rose made sundresses for her each summer, and knit little scarves and caps for her each winter. Christine was her constant companion, and Rose felt closer to Christine than she'd ever felt with the boys. Not that she didn't adore her sons, but Christine, well, Christine was her little girl.

Rose wanted desperately to call Joe, to let him know he was needed at home. The scare with Walter's polio had made its mark, and Rose wanted

Joe home to take charge, to give her a strong shoulder to lean on. But there was no phone number to dial, she only knew he was somewhere in Concord tonight, and tomorrow he would be in New Hampshire. Rose said another prayer, and for a time, she passed the damp cloth gently over Christine's arms, neck, and forehead, rinsing it every few minutes in the basin of water.

And then, it was broad day, and Rose was in her back yard, hanging laundry on the line to dry. The boys were darting in between the sheets, playing hide and seek. Suddenly Patrick was at her side, asking when Christine was coming home, because they couldn't have dinner without her.

Rose awoke slowly as the first rays of sunlight peered over the Atlantic and through the window of Christine's room. She was still half-dreaming of laundry on the line, comfortable in the rocking chair that had cradled her during the night, unaware that sometime in the dark, early-morning hours, Christine had shuddered for just a moment, fighting the loss of her last little breath. Years later, Rose would say that the first memory she had of that morning was the ghastly quiet of the room, and feeling the warm, damp cloth balled up in her hand.

They buried Christine in a little plot across from the hill at the end of Pembroke Road. As the family, friends and neighbors stood around the open grave while Father Glenn droned on about ashes and dust and life everlasting, Walter looked across the way to the backside of the hill, his hill; and could only think that he would never again stand at the top of it without drawing his eyes into the cemetery to seek out this particular spot.

Joe, consumed with his own sorrow, and uncertain of how to comfort his wife or sons, returned to work the day after the service. Rose tidied Christine's room, and shut the door. It was all she could manage. In spite of the flurry of community support offered, and the multitude of condolences received, Rose had never felt so very alone, so very much abandoned by Joe. The sharp pain in her heart and her gut never let up, and the guilt she felt for falling asleep in her daughter's final hours sent her to bed wracked with fits of deep sobbing. Dr. Murray prescribed a tonic, which sat unopened in the kitchen cupboard. No medicine could heal the deep cleft in Rose's heart, or the wrenching ache in her soul.

Chapter 14

If Rose Hannigan was the heart of Pembroke Road, Gus Osprey was its eyes and ears. Situated at the corner of Pembroke Road and Woodside Street, the Osprey home sat tall over the gently sloping cul-de-sac, and its many curtained windows belied a sense of privacy that extended only to the interior of the home. Not that Gus spent his days peering furtively from behind drapes to spy on his neighborhood; to the contrary, Gus went to great lengths to be fully occupied with his own business. It just happened that, as the local butcher, he had contact almost every week with his neighbors as they stopped into his shop. These interludes were more than just a matter of cutting meat and serving customers. They were a sharing of confessions and opinions, gossip and news, about his neighborhood and his town. Gus absorbed the sorrows and elations, the concerns and discernments his customers expressed. His responses were simple, whatever was customarily acceptable—a nod or a grin, or an 'I'm sorry to hear that,' as he passed the package of hamburger or chops or liver over the counter.

Gus still missed his wife terribly. He missed her bright wide smile, and her hearty, honest laughter. Helen had been the vivacious one, who visited with all the neighbors, baked cakes for fundraisers, and volunteered with the local Red Cross; and it was Helen who shared her time and energy with him in their little vegetable garden, who made him laugh at corny jokes, sometimes until his sides ached; it was Helen who knew him, who made him feel special and whole.

It was hardest for Gus right after Helen passed. Every day he went to his shop, not knowing what else to do with himself. In the months that followed Helen's death, the neighborhood ladies would all say the same things to him. 'Gus, how are you getting along?' they would ask, invariably, in a sympathetic, soothing way, that sounded vaguely patronizing. 'If there's anything I can do for you, Gus, anything at all...' trailed off as the lady picked up her little bundle of meat. And he would pass over her change, and smile pleasantly, and say, 'Thank you, that's very thoughtful.' Sometimes he would catch a glimpse of true concern, but it seemed to him that it was mostly just women saying what was expected. Mercifully, time passed, and the condolences, real or perfunctory, faded away, with the exception of those proffered by the persistent Mrs. Clemens.

The Widow Clemens was a regular Tuesday morning customer, and Gus steeled himself for her arrival every Tuesday at breakfast, when he indulged in a finger of peppermint schnapps with his tea and toast. Mrs. Clemens arrived at his butcher counter promptly at 9:30 in the morning, and the conversation always ran the same horrifying course. She would start off cheerily enough, with a bright hello, followed by a comment about the weather or a local event. But within just two minutes—Gus had actually timed it—Mrs. Clemens started to talk about how lonely she knew he must be, and would he like it if she brought over a casserole for dinner sometime, or perhaps some cookies? Maybe he would like to accompany her to one of those moving pictures she had heard about—there was always something playing at the new movie theater on Main Street, and wouldn't he like to go?

Gus knew she was desperate to marry again. He knew because Mrs. Clemens stopped in at the grocer's on Wednesday mornings, running the same conversational track with James, a long-widowed gentleman of 62, who managed the stock at the store. Even Mr. Leonard, the librarian, received Mrs. Clemens' attentions. For Gus, it wasn't so much that he didn't like Mrs. Clemens, didn't feel some sympathy for her loneliness; he just didn't have the heart to love another woman. Helen had been his bright shining star, his whole world, and he had determined long ago that no one would take her place, simply because no one could. Certainly not Mrs. Clemens, who had wiry hair that rolled around her head like Brillo pads, and whose full, fatty wattle jiggled as she spoke her words of consolation.

It was enough, now, for Gus to follow a routine that gave him purpose and kept him involved with the world around him, even if his involvement was on the outskirts. And each night, Gus closed up his butcher shop and walked back to his house, where his pugs, Lulu and Didi, greeted him enthusiastically at the door.

"Hallooo," Gus would say to them as he walked in the door, "yes, yes, meine kleinen schatzchen, let's go have dinner."

They yipped and danced at his feet as he walked into the kitchen. From his coat pocket he pulled a small paper-wrapped bundle of waste scraps from the day's work and carefully opened it, dividing the meat into little bowls. Gus would make a bowl of soup or a sandwich for himself, and the three of them ate their evening meal together.

In the warmer months, if the evening was fine and the mosquitoes weren't too thick, Gus, Didi and Lulu went out to the back porch, where Gus sat on a worn comfortable chair, smoking his pipe, sometimes sipping a beer if the weather was particularly warm. In between puffs, he threw a little rubber ball for the girls to fetch.

The pipe finished, Gus made his way out to the back of the property, where sat the plot of land he and his wife had planted and tended every year. He'd spend an hour or two in the early twilight pulling weeds, digging the earth, and harvesting what was ready. He and Helen had always enjoyed their vegetable garden, and he found solace there, as though she were still working along with him, talking to him about whether a tomato was ripe enough, or if the potatoes should have more or less water. Most nights, he would answer her, ask questions of his own. As far as he was concerned, this was where she was, at least during the summer, and this was where he found peace, communing with her in the garden.

As twilight faded, and the moon began her domination of the darkening sky, Gus finished his gardening and returned to the house. He always looked back over his little plot of land before pulling open the screen door. It was hard to walk away, thinking Helen was still out there, out in the garden, tending the plants.

As late fall rolled in and the garden lay fallow, Gus didn't go outside after supper. Instead, he built a fire in the fireplace, and sat nearby in his favorite chair to read, or listen to the radio, perhaps work a crossword puzzle. Didi and Lulu would join him on the chair or the couch, sometimes playing tug of war with an old dishcloth, sometimes just snuggling. And sometimes, when Gus couldn't keep his mind busy enough, he would just think—about Helen, about how things were supposed to be, and weren't. Helen never joined him on the couch, never called to him from the kitchen, never sat with her sewing in her chair. During the winter, Helen was nowhere to be found, and the loneliness Gus felt sat as a deep hard rock in his heart. His greatest consolation was the knowledge that she would come back with the first thaw, and he would find her again, waiting for him in the garden.

Chapter 15

After Christine's burial, life went on for the Hannigan family, albeit much changed. Walter, Patrick and Daniel went back to school. With Joe's return to the road, Rose faced the loss alone. The first few weeks she spent most of her time in bed, sleeping and crying at intervals. When she started to move through the house again, it was to wander from room to room; sometimes she managed to straighten a pillow or water a potted plant, but her heart and mind were elsewhere, her energy unfocused.

Amelia stopped by every day at lunchtime to check on her friend, to bring her a cup of coffee and a sandwich, and sit with her for a while, at first at her bedside, later at the kitchen table. They didn't say much. It was enough to sit together for an hour or so, to share something to eat, and talk vaguely of nothing. Walter, Daniel and Patrick no longer lingered at the library or joined a game at the vacant field; but rather, hurried directly home after school. Walter cooked dinner, washed laundry, or worked in the yard, whatever was most needed.

The younger boys helped out as well, sorting and folding clothes, sweeping floors, washing dishes. Daniel, neat and orderly by nature, fell into a pattern of after-school chores that kept the house dusted and organized. He helped Patrick with his homework, and ran errands for Walter; for while Daniel felt the sting of Christine's loss, he found sanctuary in keeping to a routine that carried him from morning to night, ever busy, ever useful.

Patrick performed his tasks in Walter's shadow, for of all the boys, he missed Christine the most. He would have sought comfort in his mother's arms, but she could not begin to comfort herself, and so Patrick stuck close to Walter, who understood his youngest brother's anguish, and did his best to soften the blow.

The school year came to a close, and one afternoon in early summer the three brothers sat together on the front porch, taking a break from the day's chores.

"By the way," Walter started, "Dad got me a job. At Lever Brothers."

Daniel looked up at his brother, startled. "Wait a minute, what will happen here at home? You've always been in charge. I don't want to be in charge. You have to stay here this summer."

Walter half-smiled. "I don't know what to tell you. It's all arranged. I start day after tomorrow. But I don't know what you're worried about. You'll be fine, you know what to do."

Patrick leaned his head on Walter's shoulder.

"Will you come home, sometimes?" he asked, a tremor in his voice.

Walter laughed a little. "I'll be home every night, I promise."

"Oh. Well, that's okay then," Patrick sighed with relief.

"It's just you two really need to be strong, and help each other, okay?" Walter looked at each of his brothers. They nodded.

"Okay, then. And I'll save out some of my pay to take you for a treat once in a while if you're good."

By July, Rose seemed better. If she hadn't completely recovered from the blow, she was at least able to manage the necessities of domestic life. The boys sensed their mother's improvement. It was an especial relief for Patrick, who had not only lost his little sister, but thought he might lose his mother as well, in the way that young children know when a parent is teetering on the brink.

Daniel did his best to step in and fill Walter's shoes, running errands, making minor house repairs, and keeping the yard work up. Patrick stayed by his mother's side, and learned how to cook scrambled eggs, how to wash

The Lights of Pembroke Road

the kitchen floor. He pulled weeds and gathered green beans and tomatoes, and polished the furniture with carefully poured wood oil. Patrick knew he was helping, for his mother hugged him often, sometimes through tears. It was all he needed. Everything would be okay.

Work filled the long summer days for the Hill Boys. Henry and Ray spent most of their time at Wildwood Cemetery, mowing the interminably growing grass and digging the occasional grave. Walter worked on the factory floor at Lever Brothers, doing what his father had done twenty years ago, packing box after box with soap. Walter liked the work. It paid well, and he didn't have to lift his left arm to load the boxes.

Mike went to Boston every day with his father, to 'learn the auto business from the ground up' as Philip Andrews put it. Mike spent week after week learning about vendors and sales, accounts payable and receivable, and trying desperately to stay out of the way of an army of secretaries. He wondered to himself how he was supposed to learn about auto manufacturing when the actual factory was in Michigan, but he never asked the question out loud. It was enough to know that school would start up again in September, and his torture would come to an end.

It wasn't until mid-August that the Hill Boys were able to meet again for a series of pick-up games at the empty field. They played in the late afternoons, after work, before the mosquitos made it impossible to hold the bat steady. Patrick and Daniel joined in, along with some of the other boys from the neighborhood. Walter was glad for the games. They marked a milestone for him, a return to a normal life, at least as much as could be expected.

One afternoon, Patrick stayed home instead of joining the game. Rose planned to clean out the room he shared with Daniel, an event that held potentially catastrophic repercussions if not properly managed. Daniel's neatness ensured his mother would not scrutinize his belongings too closely; but Patrick, whose belongings were stuffed into drawers and cupboards when not strewn across the floor, was in a near panic, and insisted on overseeing his mother's work in order to avoid any possible loss of a favorite toy or shirt. Walter asked Beth to come along and fill in for Patrick if she felt like it, and she did.

It was the last inning. Mike was pitcher, Walter was catcher, and Daniel covered first base. Beth covered the spread between second and third. She watched intently as each of the boys from the other team picked up the bat and stood over home plate, the dusty sandbag set into the hard dirt.

The first half of the inning was almost over, and the other team was winning by a run. Mike pitched a fastball, which passed the boy at the plate before he even saw it. It was the third out, and Walter's team headed in. Daniel went up to bat first. Beth sat on the wooden bench at the edge of the infield, waiting for her turn. Mike gave her a dismissive glance. She still had mousy brown pigtails dangling like limp washrags over her ears and down her shoulders. Scabs blundered across both her knees, visible as they peeked out from the hem of her skirt when she swung her legs under the bench. At least he wouldn't have to walk her to school anymore. Beth was now deemed old enough to walk to school by herself. Mike was glad to be relieved of that responsibility. With his sophomore year looming, he would be attending Winchester High School, and was sure to be occupied with more important matters. Still, here she was, at the field with the rest of them.

Mike had done his best to ignore her through the game, but now she was sitting in his favorite spot, and he was suddenly irritated by her presence. He took Walter aside.

"What is she doing here?" he asked, loudly, jerking a thumb in Beth's direction.

Walter was dismayed by Mike's contempt. He liked Mike, they had been best friends for as long as he could remember, but Mike's inability to accept Beth as part of their team didn't sit well with Walter.

Walter answered evenly, "She can pitch and catch. I've seen her. She's good, and we need someone to fill in for Patrick."

"Geez, Walter, why'd you invite her? Do you like her, or something? She's like a puppy dog, tagging along all the time, and now I have to play ball with her? Does she fetch?" He was smarmy now, not quite teasing in his disparagement.

Walter was not biting. He and Mike were friends, but this was business, and he liked to win.

"You don't have to play, Mike, if you don't want to." He walked over to the other side of the bench, closer to home plate, to watch the action.

"I don't like it," Mike muttered under his breath.

Henry took his turn at the plate, catching the ball low on the bat, sending it toward third base. He managed to get to first, just ahead of the ball. Mike was up next. Still fuming, he swung twice when the ball was too low.

Walter called out to him, "Come on, Mike, eyes on the ball!"

The next ball was low again, and Mike held his bat steady. Finally, the pitch came in even, and he swung hard and sure, sending the ball over the head of the second baseman toward the tall grass at the end of the field. Henry moved to second, and then third before the ball was flying back toward the infield. With Henry on third and Mike on second, Beth came up to bat. Mike shook his head in dismay, sure that she would ruin the game. He looked down at the second base sandbag, thinking that Walter should be at bat. Beth was a last resort, at best.

It wasn't until he heard Walter yelling, "Come on, Mike, move!" that he realized Beth had actually hit the ball, square and solid over the back fence and into a neighbor's yard. She was running toward him after rounding first base, her battered knees pumping like a machine under her flopping skirt, her pigtails flying behind her. He started to move toward third just as Beth nearly barreled into him crossing second. He barely outpaced her as he rounded third, and she was hard on his heels as they crossed home plate. Mike was flustered and angry. Beth was triumphant.

August melted into September, the heat and humidity of late summer seeping over into early fall as the new school year began. The Hill Boys entered their sophomore year at Winchester High School just as the German Army advanced into Poland, as England and France declared war on Germany, as the United States declared her neutrality. World War II was underway.

Henry and Walter teamed up to write for the high school newspaper, *The High School Recorder*. Walter had aspirations to join Student Council, and the newspaper was one way of getting to know students who were already taking the lead at school.

Henry was simply hungry for any news from overseas. Radio kept him informed about some things, but the reports seemed limited in depth and breadth of war news, and his parents often tried to prevent him from hearing what was broadcast. Henry knew he wouldn't write about the war, but he figured he might hear more in the school newsroom than he would at home, and maybe even more than he could read in the *Winchester Star*.

Mike had no desperate need for news, nor any lofty ambitions other than to pass his classes with respectable grades. He thought he might join the JV baseball team, and perhaps a club or two, just to have an occasional excuse to bow out of his parents' hectic social calendar.

Ray's focus on school was diverted by an incessant prodding from his parents and Father Glenn to join the choir at St. Mary's. They could hear what Ray could not—that his voice had developed as a clear, strong tenor. Ray declined vigorously at first. Singing in front of an audience was a nerve-wracking proposition, and he had no intention of embarrassing himself; however, through a persistent campaign on the part of his mother, which included much flattery, a liberal application of guilt, and a promise of a new bike at Christmas, Ray finally relented. The second Sunday of October found Ray doing his best to hide in the back line of the choir, mouthing the words to "Ave Maria," sweating profusely through stomach cramps.

By November his nerves settled, and Ray discovered he almost liked being on stage, and could manage to put some breath through his vocal cords when performing for the parishioners. Father Glenn, hearing Ray's voice gain strength and consistency, clasped on to the slim hope that he might be ready and willing to sing a solo at the Christmas Eve performance.

Chapter 16

By December, the harsh sting of Christine's death had faded for the Hannigan family, a salve of time and continuing life spread gently over the deep wounds of guilt and loss. Walter helped his mother put out the Christmas decorations, watched her trim the carefully chosen spruce. He helped her clean the windows and polish the silver and woodwork, until the Hannigan house gleamed once again; although to Walter the brilliance seemed ever so slightly muted, as if his mother's lingering tears muddled some of the ornaments, or dimmed some of the lights.

Christmas break arrived, and the Hill Boys decided to forgo their customary sledding in favor of a full morning skating at Winter Pond. They met at Ray's house, and as they passed through the mudroom door and into the kitchen, they were embraced by the heady fragrance of freshly made spice bread, muffins, as it turned out, which they could see cooling on the counter; and drummed by a tumultuous din which pervaded the room, a whirlwind of commotion that surrounded Mrs. Simard as she stood in the middle of her kitchen.

The youngest of Ray's sisters, only a year old, was happily emptying a cupboard of its pots and pans, each article clanging noisily as it hit the floor, much to the delight of the child. Two other girls were jumping up and down excitedly in front of their mother, clamoring for her attention as they showed off their costumes for the church nativity play, one dressed as a snowy sheep, the other as a robed shepherdess. Jane and Ann, the oldest of the brood, chattered with each other about a new boy at school as they washed and dried the breakfast dishes. Ray looked at his friends and shrugged his shoulders. Walter smiled to himself. It was always like this, at least every time he'd been here.

"Want a muffin?" Ray asked, almost shouting.

The boys each grabbed a muffin from the plate on the counter.

"Let's go," he suggested. Ray turned to his mother, his voice raised over those of his two costumed sisters.

"Bye, Mom, going to the pond, we'll be back for lunch!"

Mrs. Simard nodded her assent in Ray's direction, turning her attention immediately back to the sheep and shepherdess in front of her. The boys hastily made their way out the kitchen door, collected the skates they had dropped at arrival, and headed out into the blustery air.

They trudged across Ray's back yard, and through the stand of silver maple trees that divided the Simard property from Winter Pond. It was cold and overcast, but the dampening effect of the snow lent an ethereal tranquility to the air, a relief after the pandemonium of Ray's house. Mike broke the stillness.

"Geez, Ray, I don't know how you do it. I mean, every day. Do things quiet down when your father gets home?"

"Oh, yes. It's like a beehive when it's just me and Mom and the girls. But when Dad gets home, it's suddenly like," he searched for the word, "...church. Well, except for little Alice, of course, she's still a baby...but a lot of times she's already asleep when he gets home."

The boys fell quiet again as they crunched through the snow, the bare branches of the trees interlacing overhead, a web of thin dark limbs breaking the span of ashen sky. It took only a few minutes to pass through the wood and come out on the other side, at the edge of Winter Pond. Looking out over the expanse, they saw that an old black walnut tree had fallen over at the south end, blocking one of their unofficial racing lanes. Henry and Mike tried to move it, but it was an unwieldy mass, and the boys decided they would simply skate on the other side of the pond.

Soon they were racing each other back and forth across the ice. Walter was quick, and did well in the sprints, while Henry was unmatched for the longer races. No one kept track. They were having fun, out for the morning, free for the day.

It was nearing eleven. Lunch at Ray's house was next, although Mike silently wondered how Mrs. Simard could manage it with all the girls at home. He was sure Jane and Ann helped, but still. His thoughts on the subject were lost as he watched Walter and Henry, still on the ice, line up for the last race. He and Ray, already changed out of their skates and into their boots, were sitting at the pond's edge near the finish line, an old overturned boat serving as a makeshift bench.

Walter and Henry started their sprint. The competition was close, but it looked like Henry would win this one. Mike and Ray stood up, cheering. As the two racers closed in on the finish line, there was a loud crack, and a splash, and the cheers stopped as the crack echoed on the air. Walter had disappeared. At first, Henry didn't notice. But then he heard the shout from Mike, and turned to see the large, jagged hole, a thin splatter of blood glistening at the near edge. Walter was under the icy glaze.

Henry scrambled to get to the opening. He dropped to his belly as he approached it, and dug the rounded toes of his skates into the ice, hoping for any added leverage he could gain. Ray slid on the ice behind him, grabbing his ankles, careful of the blades of Henry's skates. Mike picked up a fallen tree branch and scurried out onto the ice from the side, sliding the branch toward Henry.

Henry reached into the open hole, feeling desperately for his friend in the frigid water. He reached in further, the cold biting into his arm up to the shoulder, and he prayed to grab anything, any part of Walter. And then he felt it—the collar of Walter's jacket. He grabbed it and pulled hard.

"I got him!" he yelled, and Ray tightened his grip on Henry's ankles. Henry managed to pull Walter's limp arm up and out of the water, and was grappling, searching for more. The cold water splashed against his face and neck, and he gasped for air at the shock. Henry felt the ice start to buckle under his chest, and with the threat of a further break, he renewed his efforts. He reached in with his other arm. Walter's head and shoulder bobbed up, and Henry grabbed at them.

"Pull!" Henry yelled to the air behind him. "Pull!" he yelled again, "I don't want to lose him!" Mike slid beside Ray.

"Use the branch!" Mike yelled.

Henry didn't see how. It took everything he had to keep his grasp on Walter, his hands aching from the deep cold, his arms shaking from the weight that seemed like it would pull them out of their sockets. Henry's left hand slipped, but just as quickly he grabbed, catching Walter's arm before it disappeared. The ice under Henry buckled again, and this time the frigid water hit him square in the face and soaked through the front of his sweater, a shock of cold that took his breath away.

The shift in the ice was a gift. It was just enough to allow Henry to grasp his friend under his arms, to gain enough purchase so that Walter slid out of the watery tomb at an easy angle, with Henry, Mike and Ray now grappling to pull Walter away from the hole. Once free from the pond's clutches, Walter slid easily to the edge, a dead weight in the hands of his friends.

They turned him over. He was white, almost blue. Henry started to push on Walter's stomach.

"Gotta get the water out! Come on, Walter, please!" Henry was soaked and shaking with cold now, but unable to stop the process in which he was so heavily invested. He pushed on Walter's stomach repeatedly, a technique his Uncle Eric showed him when they had gone swimming one summer at the Cape. Mike and Ray stood quietly behind him, watching, still trying to comprehend what had happened, what was happening in front of them.

Walter coughed. Quickly, Henry started to turn him on his side, and Ray knelt down to help him. Pond water spewed from Walter's mouth onto the snow. He coughed again, retching. Finally, he drew a breath in, coughed, sputtered and spit, took another breath. Within a few seconds, Walter started to shake violently.

"Get his clothes off!" yelled Ray. Mike and Henry pulled off Walter's soaked coat, and tugged urgently at sleeves to remove the wet sweater and shirt underneath. Ray removed Walter's skates and socks, and Henry helped him pull the freezing woolen pants off. Mike took off his jacket, and wrapped it around Walter. Ray pulled off his scarf and cap and transferred them to his friend, careful of the wound on the side of Walter's head, which was starting to bleed.

Henry stood up. Sopping wet himself, he took off his sweater as he made his way along the pond's edge to the overturned boat. There, he sat down in a heap, shaking, clumsy in his efforts to change out of his skates and back into his boots.

Mike and Ray, each taking a shoulder and a knee, carried Walter to where Henry was shoving his boots on.

Henry looked up. "I'll go ahead and let your mom know, Ray. Do you two have him?"

"We have him," replied Ray. Henry stood up with an effort, and set off through the trees toward Ray's house, moving as quickly as he could through the snow.

Walter was starting to come around, still shivering uncontrollably, but his eyes were open.

"Come on Walter, it was close, but you made it. Let's get you back to my house." Ray and Mike adjusted their grips, and lifting again, hauled their friend toward the Simard house.

Henry strode through the mudroom, and stuck his head into the kitchen.

"Mrs. Simard?" he called.

"Are you boys done already? Come on in, lunch is just about ready," Mrs. Simard replied from the hallway.

"Mrs. Simard, Walter had an accident, he needs help."

Mrs. Simard bustled into the kitchen. She took in Henry's wet undershirt and the look on his face.

"Good heavens, what happened? Where are they?"

"Coming now, they should be in the yard. Walter fell into the ice. He hit his head."

"You go sit in the living room by the fire, Henry, right now, and warm yourself up. Take that shirt off. There's a blanket on the couch, wrap yourself up in it."

Henry went through to the living room as Mrs. Simard stepped out onto the mudroom porch. She propped open the door, and from the top of the steps, she saw that Ray and Mike were still supporting Walter, but he had found his legs, and was trying feebly to help get himself up the stairs.

"Bring him in, boys, get him onto the couch in the living room," she ordered. She hurried inside ahead of them.

Mrs. Simard called upstairs. "Janie and Annie! Where are you?"

The girls' heads popped over the banister.

"Right here, dusting. Why?"

"Stop dusting, bring down blankets and towels, right now!"

A few seconds later the contents of the linen closet began to tumble over the banister to the floor below. Mrs. Simard picked up an armful of towels and two blankets, and hurried into the living room.

The boys were now inside the house and heading toward the fireplace. Mrs. Simard placed the blankets on the couch, along with some towels. Ann, now downstairs, brought more blankets into the living room. Mrs. Simard directed Mike and Ray over to the couch.

"Put him down here, boys, then help me get these blankets on him." They worked quickly, heaping the blankets on top of a shivering Walter. Mike handed another blanket to Henry, who was sitting quietly at the hearth warming himself.

Mrs. Simard sat next to Walter, assessing his condition. She saw the cut on his head, a small gash behind his right ear. It wasn't bleeding anymore, but it was beginning to swell. Walter would have a bit of a bump for a while. His hands felt very cold, but he was lucid, and his shivering was beginning to calm.

"Annie, love, get Dr. Ferguson's on the exchange. Tell him there's been an accident, and he's needed here at our house." Ann nodded and headed toward the kitchen. Mrs. Simard then turned to Janie.

"Janie, go get the hot water bottles and fill them up. The teapot on the stove is full, you should be able to start with that." Janie scurried to the kitchen.

Donna and Patricia, the sheep and shepherdess of the morning, now changed into play clothes, appeared at the living room entryway, quiet, knowing something was wrong. Mrs. Simard saw them, and said, "Girls, I need you to watch after your baby sister for a while. She's napping now, but if she wakes up, you'll need to take care of her. In the meantime, I want you to take the blankets and towels that are on the floor there by the stairs and bring them back up, fold them and put them away."

Mrs. Simard turned her attention back to Walter.

"Walter, I know you're very cold. We're going to warm you up. You stay here by the fire, under these blankets for a while. We'll get you some warm flannels to put on, and you'll be just fine. I'll call your mother."

"No!" Walter cried through chattering teeth. "Sh-sh-she c-can't know. Don't tell her—please. I'll b-be fine. I don't want her to worry."

"Well, we'll see what the doctor says."

She turned to Ray. "Ray, run upstairs and get your flannels...the clean ones! And a shirt and sweater for Henry."

Then to Mike, "Mike, please go out to the mudroom. You'll find a few logs out there for the fire. Would you bring them in and get them on the grate?" Mike nodded, and retrieved the wood. He set the logs gingerly onto the fire, positioning them so that they would burn long and hot.

Ann returned to the living room, and Mrs. Simard looked at her expectantly.

"Dr. Ferguson has another patient he has to see, and then he'll be here," Ann reported.

"Hmmph. We're on our own, then," Mrs. Simard muttered. Then, brightly, "Well, Walter, I'm sure Dr. Ferguson will be by soon, and we'll see what he says. But you seem to be recovering. In the meantime, here are some flannels." She reached for the pajamas proffered by the now returned Ray. "Can you get changed by yourself, or do you need help?"

"I-I can do it."

"Well, then, I'll leave you to it. Here's another towel if you need it. And Henry, here's a towel for you as well, and I think," she paused as she glanced at the shirt and sweater Ray handed her, "yes, I think these clothes will fit you."

"Thank you, Mrs. Simard," Henry said as he took the shirt and sweater.

"Henry, when you've changed, come on into the kitchen, and we'll have lunch." Mrs. Simard paused for a moment, and beamed at the three bedraggled boys that had saved Walter.

"I think you were all very brave today. You must be starved after such an adventure. Go on into the kitchen, and you'll have a nice hot stew and biscuits in just a few minutes. Walter, I'll put together a little ice pack for the bump on your head."

Somehow the promise of warm comforting food ended the event, and the tension that had sustained the boys throughout began to slip away. Ray and Mike went into the kitchen, followed by Mrs. Simard, after she assured Walter that she was just a footstep away if he needed anything, and she would return in a few minutes to tend the cut on his head.

Henry and Walter remained in front of the fire.

Henry stood up and put on the shirt and sweater. He set the blanket aside, and sat again on the hearth.

The two boys were silent for a moment.

"Are you really okay?" asked Henry, staring into the flames.

"I think so. Thanks for saving me, Henry. I know Ray and Mike helped. But I know you were the one who saved me." Henry turned to Walter.

"I was just being selfish. Who else would help me write the school newspaper?"

"I knew there was an ulterior motive," Walter replied quietly.

"Get changed. Are you hungry? Want some stew?"

"Maybe a little."

"I'll go get it." Henry got up and sauntered into the kitchen.

By the next day, the news had spread through town. The *Winchester Star* sent a reporter to interview the boys for a piece in the paper.

Henry was a hero.

Chapter 17

The rest of sophomore year followed a simple, if busy, routine for the Hill Boys. Ray willingly accepted more responsibility with the choir, and Mike finally convinced his parents that he could miss out on all but the most critical of social events.

The summer of 1940 returned each of the boys to the previous year's occupations, Henry and Ray at the cemetery, Walter at Lever Brothers. Mike had a singular reprieve, for although he joined his father each morning on the train into Boston, they now parted ways at the station. Philip Andrews headed to his office as usual, but Mike walked three blocks in the opposite direction, to the law offices of Andrews and James, where his grandfather and uncle, both executives with the firm, welcomed him with open arms. For the Hill Boys, the highlight of the summer was listening to the broadcast of the Louis-Godoy fight for the World Heavyweight Championship. Only Henry, ever searching for war news, knew that France had surrendered in mid-June, and that the Nazis now occupied Paris.

Louise continued to work for Dr. Ferguson. She kept the files, took appointments, tidied the office bathroom, and handed out aspirin. She accepted payments as they came—most patients paid with cash if they could, but just as often they handed over a couple of loaves of bread, or a package of soap, or even, once, a painting by a patient, a still life of fruit and flowers, which hangs in that office still today.

She and Claire had worked out a schedule that allowed Louise to minimize the time she spent at the Dix Street house while still fulfilling Claire's work requirements. Louise didn't see much of George, as he was continually preoccupied with his business; for that matter, she rarely saw Claire except at dinner time, for Claire was consumed with her own agenda. Oliver was Louise's constant companion when she was home. It didn't take long for them to become fast friends. Louise found Oliver to be loving and cuddly, and willing to play, or read a book, or go for a walk, whatever activity Louise chose. They shared cookies and milk, read *Peter Pan and Wendy* a hundred times, listened to *Let's Pretend* on the radio on Saturday mornings, and played with trucks and blocks in Oliver's room. If Claire was jealous of the time Louise spent with Oliver, she didn't show it. But if Louise ever thought that her nephew needed protection from Claire, she dismissed the idea out of hand. Claire was not an overtly loving mother, but she was not unkind to her son, and cared for him well enough when Louise was not at home; but when Louise was present, Claire readily passed her responsibility off, eager to apply her energies to more important social obligations.

Summer waned, and junior year at the high school began. Louise thought, as she settled into her new classes, that most everything was in balance. Her work at the doctor's office allowed a few niceties; her schedule at home was set, and Claire's animosity was limited to the occasional unkind word or criticism; and an icy aura that emanated from her, lending a chill to the atmosphere of the house, even on the hottest summer days.

School started off well enough, but somewhere in the second week, Louise became confused in her math class, and the confusion quickly snowballed into a complete loss of understanding. The agony of bewilderment was made worse by the torture of sitting through the class itself. Mr. Bennett, a corpulent, balding, officious man, droned through his lectures, his back to the classroom as he placed an unending series of chalk marks on the board. One day, nearly a month into the semester, Louise's eyes grew heavy, and closed for what seemed like only a few seconds.

Smack!

The ruler missed her nose by an inch, whacking the hardwood of the desk in front of her.

"Stay awake in my class, Miss Duncan." Titters from her classmates burned in her ears.

"Quiet!" Mr. Bennett scolded. He returned to the chalkboard. "Perhaps Miss Duncan would like to complete the problem on the board." She was mortified. She looked at the problem.

"I'm sorry, sir, I don't…" Her voice trailed off.

"Then after school you will please return to this classroom for detention." Her heart sank. She couldn't come back, she had to work at Dr. Ferguson's that afternoon.

The next day, Mr. Bennett called her up after class.

"You didn't come back," he said, stern and impassive.

"I'm sorry, Mr. Bennett, I had to work," she replied.

"What work?" he asked, incredulous.

"I work at Dr. Ferguson's. I take care of the office in the afternoons."

Mr. Bennett was silent for a moment.

"You know that you were recommended for this class last year by Mr. Jamison. He said you showed promise, perhaps you might even go to college. For you to have difficulty so early in the semester shows a lack of application, and perhaps Mr. Jamison was in error."

Louise was near tears, sick with the thought that she had failed already at a class that others thought she could manage. Mr. Bennett saw the look on her face, and softened a bit as he continued.

"Now, I understand you have had some, well, some difficult circumstances at home. And I must say, I'm sorry for that. But I've often found that the structure of the classroom and concentration on one's studies can help one retain a sense of order, which can be most helpful in dealing with upsets at home, even when, and perhaps particularly when, those upsets are of a serious and somber nature. I will excuse you this once, Miss Duncan. But, if I find you falling asleep again in my class, or if your grade slips below a C, I will report your deficiencies to the principal and to Mr. Duncan. Do you understand?"

"Yes sir, thank you Mr. Bennett," she said, her voice strained with unshed tears.

"Well, we'll see," he said. "We have a test next week, and I expect you will pass it. Go on, go to your next class." He dismissed her with a wave of his hand.

She was relieved to be out of the room, scurrying down the hallway—but pass the next test? She tried hard to focus on her geography lesson, but her mind raced in a dozen different directions, looking for a solution to her dilemma. At lunchtime, Louise searched for Dot in the cafeteria. Louise was sure Dot would have an answer, or at the very least, make her feel better.

As she scanned the room, she saw Mike at the far end, sitting with Ray Simard. She hesitated, looking again for Dot. Dot had once suggested that Louise talk to Mike about helping her with math—and hadn't he offered at the beginning of the semester? Louise didn't know that much about Mike Andrews. She knew his family had moved to Winchester from Boston, and that they lived in the beautiful white house at the corner of Pembroke Road. She'd heard his father, Philip Andrews, made a good living in the automobile industry, but wasn't sure. She did know that Claire and George mixed with Mr. and Mrs. Andrews socially, and that Claire and Margaret were both members of the Home and Garden Club, and both active on the Library Art Committee.

Louise looked over the room again. Finally, the decision made by the absence of her friend, Louise started to make her way through the busy cafeteria.

Ray Simard saw her over Mike's shoulder.

"Hey," he said to Mike, "don't turn around, but Louise Duncan is headed in our direction."

Mike, unable to resist, glanced as unobtrusively as he could over his shoulder.

"Hah! I knew it," said Ray, teasing. "You like her. She's..."

Ray stopped short, then whispered, "She's coming up behind you!"

Mike blanched, and sat very still, a rabbit hiding in plain sight from the hunter.

"Hello, Mike," Louise said. She was standing beside him now.

Mike cleared his throat, and made a concerted effort to regain his composure.

"Oh, well, hello Louise. Please, have a seat." Mike couldn't believe this beautiful young woman was speaking to him, and was even more surprised when she sat down at his invitation. He stared at her, at a loss for words. Ray kicked him under the table.

Mike started, and glaring for a moment at Ray, said, "You know Ray, of course. We were just talking about, ummm, football."

"He's lying," said Ray, who was not quite as overcome by Louise's presence. "We were talking about Mr. Villée's toupee, you know, 'Villée, toupee.' Hey, maybe Walter and Henry can do something with that in the school paper! Wouldn't that be swell?"

Mike looked at him to see if he was serious, then they both laughed.

Louise smiled politely. She was on a mission, and while she didn't want to offend these boys by mentioning that they were no longer ten years old, she didn't want to feed the flames either. She opened her sack and took out a cheese and jelly sandwich.

"I was wondering, Mike, did you mean it when you said you'd help me with math? I'm really having a bit of a problem with, well, some of the problems." She looked at him for a brief moment, then down at her sandwich.

Ray looked at Louise, then at Mike, raising an eyebrow.

"I think I hear my mother calling. You two have fun." With a nod to Louise and a wink at Mike, he was gone.

"What was that?" she asked.

"Pay no attention to him," said Mike, "You know Ray, he's always joking around. But sure, of course I'd be happy to help you. Should we meet after school?"

"No, I can't. I work after school most days. I would only be able to meet on Saturday."

She thought for a moment, then said, embarrassed, "Oh, Mike, you probably have chores on Saturdays. I'm so sorry, I shouldn't have asked." She started to collect her lunch and get up.

"No, wait," he said. He reached for her arm and pulled her gently back down. Mike was usually shy around girls, but he had fallen for Louise Duncan when he'd first seen her a year ago, when they had taken a history class together. She spoke exactly four words to him that whole year, a soft 'Nice to meet you,' when Dot introduced them. Louise had graced him with a polite smile, and he was smitten. He had been quietly overjoyed when he saw her sitting in his math class this year, and reintroduced himself on the first day, making the offer to help her with the course if she needed it. At the time she had thanked him, and said it was thoughtful of him, but had not even looked at him since then.

And now here she was, actually asking for his help. She was warm, and her skin was soft and smooth, and she smelled of Ivory soap and something else, something simple and sweet, like oatmeal cookies. He wanted to sit with her forever.

"Saturday is fine," he said quietly, looking at her squarely, with a gentle grin. "Can you come to the library at ten?"

She looked at him more closely. He was not beautifully handsome, not like Errol Flynn or George Brent, or even Henry Smith. He was rougher at the edges, like Humphrey Bogart maybe. A warm Bogart, gentleness in the crease of his eyes, the curve of his lips. He was tall, just growing into himself, and with a little time he would be quite…breathtaking.

"Yes, I can do that. I'll meet you at ten in front of the library. Thanks so much, Mike."

Before either of them could say more, the bell rang. They got up, and with a quick good-bye, headed in opposite directions. It was only when she was seated in her history class that Louise realized how hot her face was, and that she hadn't eaten a bite of her sandwich.

Chapter 18

Mike sat at the library steps. He was early, he knew. He pretended to read a chapter from American History while he waited. At ten o'clock precisely, Louise rounded the corner. He stood up and waved. She smiled, waved back.

Mike felt a little nervous as he watched her walk up to him. She wore a white blouse, tucked neatly into a light blue skirt, which swayed gently as she walked. Her hair was pulled back, up and away from her beautiful face, her sweet smile, her bright eyes. He could hardly believe it. She was so pretty, and here she was, smiling at him, needing his help.

"Hello, Mike," she said. "Thank you again for offering to help."

"No trouble at all," he said, his voice breaking slightly as he said the words. He was suddenly aware that they were standing on the steps of the library, and he was grinning at her like a goofball, as his father would say.

"Shall we go in?" he asked, breaking the moment.

They sat next to each other at a quiet table in the corner of the first floor. Mike explained the problems, demonstrated how to work them; Louise asked questions, Mike answered. They worked together through one homework assignment, then another. Mike was a good and patient teacher, and Louise found the gray cloud of confusion clearing as she practiced.

Just after noon, the pair left the library and walked to Randall's Diner. Over cherry phosphates and grilled cheese sandwiches, they talked about school, their families, their friends. The conversation was easy, and by the time they finished lunch, their new friendship had grown, reaching beyond Louise's prettiness and Mike's willingness to tutor her.

As they were leaving the diner, Helen Grimsly, one of Claire's closest cronies, entered and stood in the open doorway.

"Hello, Louise," she said. She spoke with a vulturous rumble, as though carrion was still in her throat. Mrs. Grimsly looked at Louise, looked at the boy beside her. Mrs. Grimsly took a step forward and closed the door behind her. She stood there, blocking the exit, trapping the couple.

"Oh, hello, Mrs. Grimsly." Louise was suddenly nervous, as though she'd been caught doing something terribly wrong.

"And who is this young man? Michael Andrews? My, Michael, you've quite grown up. Your mother must be very proud of you. Well, and what are the two of you up to, now? Just having a little lunch? How cozy. Louise, I thought Claire needed you at home. And here you are with young Michael Andrews."

She stood there, unmoving, her back against the door, eyeing them.

Mike didn't like Mrs. Grimsly, didn't like feeling cornered by an overstuffed woman who wore much too much make-up and too much perfume. She was insinuating something, and he liked that even less.

"Excuse us, please, Mrs. Grimsly," he responded. Then, moving past Louise, and effectively pushing Mrs. Grimsly out of the way, he opened the door.

"There you are, Louise," he said as he ushered her out. "Nice to see you, Mrs. Grimsly, enjoy your lunch." He followed Louise outside, and, clasping her elbow gently, escorted her away from the diner toward the library.

"What a horrible woman!" he exclaimed. "I thought we were all going to be gassed into unconsciousness by her perfume."

Louise laughed a little, but then turned serious.

"She'll say something to Claire, I just know it. I got permission from George to study this morning, but it won't make any difference to Claire."

The clock tower at Town Hall chimed the hour. It was two o'clock.

"Oh, good heavens, it's later than I thought!"

Louise stopped short, and looked at Mike, concern etched over her face. Mike gave her a reassuring smile.

"Louise, don't worry about anything. We were studying, we had lunch, we had a nice talk, that's all. And I had a good time. Did you have a good time?"

Louise was thoughtful for a moment, then nodded. "Yes, Mike, I did. I had a good time, even if we did study math. And thank you again, you're a good teacher."

"Well, you're very welcome. You're a good student. Next Saturday?"

Louise looked at him. "Yes, if the wicked witch of Middlesex County doesn't send out any more of her flying monkeys."

Mike laughed out loud. It was true, the way she was made up, all Mrs. Grimsly needed was a pair of wings and a tail.

As she walked home, the encounter with the vile Helen Grimsly faded from Louise's mind. Her thoughts turned to Mike, how patient he'd been, how easy it had been to talk to him, and how he'd taken control when Mrs. Grimsly entered the diner.

Louise and Mike continued to meet on Saturday mornings. Sometimes they would study at the library, but just as often they would go for a walk around the Common if the weather was fine, or share a bite to eat at the diner when winter settled in. Mike made Louise laugh, made her look a little beyond her current circumstances. After all, one day she would be out of school, she wouldn't always be a vassal in Claire's domain. Mostly, though, Mike made her feel beautiful and special, and encouraged her to have faith that things would turn out well.

One Saturday afternoon Mike and Louise were walking around the Common, and Mike reached out his hand. She took it in hers. It was a simple gesture, full of meaning for both of them, but it was comfortable, and neither one let go until it was time to go home.

Chapter 19

Dot saw the notice on the board by the cafeteria, and pulled Louise along with her to get a closer look.

'Wanted! Actors, Actresses, and Crew Members for this year's Spring Play Production of *You Can't Take It With You*.'

"Look at this!" Dot exclaimed. "I bet I could get the part of Penny, or maybe The Grand Duchess, don't you think so? Tryouts are..." Dot squinted at the handwriting at the bottom of the notice, "...this Thursday!"

"Do you want to be in the play with me? You are so pretty, Louise. I bet you could get the part of Alice."

Louise laughed out loud.

"I couldn't possibly be in the play!" she said. "First of all, I couldn't bear to be on stage. I've never acted in anything in my life, and I don't plan to start now. Second, I'm still working three afternoons a week at Doctor Ferguson's." Louise saw the disappointment on Dot's face.

"I'll tell you what," Louise offered in consolation. "*You* should try for the lead, because *you* can act, and *you* are pretty. And *I* promise to come watch rehearsals whenever I can. And of course, I'll be in the front row to give you a standing ovation at the end of every scene."

Dot smiled. "Well, it won't be the same without you in the cast, but I think I will try out. It would be so much fun!"

There were at least thirty students who showed up to try out for a part in the play. There were three rounds of trials, and Dot made each cut. Finally, Mrs. Henderson, the drama teacher, released the remaining students, saying the final role assignments would be posted outside the auditorium on Tuesday afternoon.

Tuesday came, and Dot waited anxiously for the school day to end. When the final class was dismissed, she rushed over to the auditorium. Louise was already there, waving as her friend approached.

"Go take a look," she encouraged. Others had gathered around the posting, each eager to see what role, if any, they would play. Some moved away, crestfallen; others saw what they wanted, and left the group obviously thrilled. Dot pushed through the remaining students, trying to catch a glimpse of the handwritten list.

The boy next to her looked at her and said, "Hey, you got the lead!"

Congratulations whirled around her as Dot stepped closer to see the list more clearly. There it was, in bold capital letters: 'ALICE STORM-WATER...............DOROTHY HUMPHREY' and at the bottom of the page, 'Rehearsals begin Monday afternoon at 3 p.m. sharp. Don't be late!'

Dot looked at the rest of the list. Raymond Simard got the part of Tony. Dot had known Ray most of her life. He was in the choir with her at St. Mary's, and she knew he had a wonderful voice. She was fairly sure he did well in school. Still, he was always joking about one thing or another, and she wondered whether he would carry through with something as serious as a play. Dot decided it didn't matter. She was going to be the best Alice, and that was all there was to that. She pulled away from the group, smiling at Louise.

"I'm Alice!" she exclaimed.

"Yes, you are! Let's go celebrate. I have a little pocket money, let's go over to Ford's, and I'll treat you to an ice cream or something."

Rehearsals started in earnest the following week. If Dot had any doubts about Ray's commitment to his role in the play, they were quickly swept aside. Ray appeared at each rehearsal ready with his lines, eager to learn his blocking, eager to be a good player. He even suggested that he and Dot should rehearse for a few hours on the weekends since most of Scene II was just between the two of them. They began to spend an hour or two on Saturday afternoons in Dot's living room, rehearsing their lines, and trying different ways of moving within each other's space.

One Thursday afternoon, Mrs. Henderson stopped the rehearsal of the final scene.

"Something doesn't seem right here," she mused. "Dot, where the direction says 'And she is in his arms,' it seems stingy to me. Perhaps Mr. Hart and Mr. Kaufman are leaving this open to interpretation. I think this needs a more definitive, romantic twist—after all, Tony and Alice are a couple again."

Mrs. Henderson looked up from her script.

"Dot, when you run into Tony's arms, I want you to give him a kiss on the cheek, and then settle blissfully into his embrace. All set, then? Let's see how that looks. Everyone, please take it from 'And speaking of dinner, Mr. Kirby...'"

Dot did as instructed, giving Ray a quick kiss, and nestling into his arms. As the scene ended, Mrs. Henderson applauded.

"Yes, yes! That's much better! Well done, everyone!" A few minutes later Mrs. Henderson dismissed the group, with a reminder to bring their costumes to the next rehearsal. Ray and Dot walked out of the auditorium into the crisp, late afternoon air.

"Well, that's a bit of a twist," said Dot.

"I liked it," said Ray. "We'll have to be sure to practice."

Dot turned her head away, pretending to be shocked.

"Why, Raymond Simard, I'm surprised at you. I suppose I'll just have to endure it. The sacrifices I make for my art..." Placing the back of her hand to her forehead, she pretended to swoon. She laughed, and Ray laughed with her.

The following Saturday, Dot and Ray continued their private rehearsals in Dot's living room, now including the kiss, and Dot nestling into Ray's arms. The kiss was timid at first, Dot and Ray both self-conscious as they practiced the simple act on their own, with Dot's mother in the kitchen making dinner, her father down in the basement tinkering with the furnace. By the time they had run through the scene a few times, though, the kiss was performed with more surety; then, with something almost approaching passion. At the last run-through, Ray turned his head as she approached him, and kissed her on the lips, holding her in his arms just a bit long. Dot stepped back for a moment, then turned her face up to him, and they kissed again, with heat.

"Do you think," whispered Dot as she pulled away, "that it counts as a first real kiss if you're doing it for a play?"

"Hmm, I don't know, maybe not," whispered Ray in return.

"Oh."

"Are you disappointed?"

"Well, no, of course not, I just wondered."

"Ah. Would you like it to be a first real kiss?"

"Well, I don't know. I suppose it all depends on who it was with. And the circumstances."

Ray thought a moment.

"Dot, would you like to come to the movies with me tonight? *The Philadelphia Story* is playing. I hear it's a good movie, Cary Grant and Jimmy Stewart. And Katharine Hepburn. Will your mother let you go?"

Dot looked at Ray, thinking. She liked him. There were layers to him. He was the easy-going comedian that everyone knew and loved. He had a lead in the play, and was the debate team captain, roles that gave him credence with his teachers and acceptance among his peers. Dot now saw more than these, though. She knew he was committed to the choir at St. Mary's, that he worked during the summers with Henry Smith, earning money that helped support his family. He could be serious and determined when the situation called for it. He was sweet and caring, patient with his sisters, loyal to his family and friends.

"I like Katharine Hepburn. I can ask my mother."

"Let's go ask."

And at the end of the movie, after Ray took Dot home and walked her up to her front porch, he took her in his arms, and kissed her, slowly, tenderly, shaking. It was a kiss that said, 'I love you, Dot Humphrey.' And Dot knew it, and kissed back, with a kiss that said, 'I love you too, Ray Simard.' And they pulled away from each other, looking into each other's face, into each other's eyes, holding onto each other's hands.

"Good night, Dot."

"Good night, Ray."

She went into her house, watching him from the doorway as he went down the steps and along the walkway, waving back as he waved to her when he turned the corner to head home.

Chapter 20

The Fourth of July celebration was a tremendous social success for Claire. As usual, Winchester put on a spectacular fireworks display, said to rival any found in Boston. Most of the town turned out for the day-long celebration, and Claire was at the hub of activity, overseeing the Red Cross booth, directing the food vendors, and assisting Mrs. De Mans with keeping the many speeches in order and moving along. Claire loved feeling important and in charge, giving direction and having others obey. At the end of the event, Mrs. De Mans thanked her personally for all her excellent hard work, for her diplomacy with the speech givers, for her tireless assistance with the vendors and booths. Claire was elated.

July was coming to a close now, and Claire headed downtown to Filene's. She had three events coming up, and desperately needed a new dress, new shoes, and perhaps a new hat.

Claire picked out two pieces and handed them to the salesgirl. She continued to look through the displays, choosing another two. She debated as to whether she should buy more than one dress, then decided she needed one for each occasion. She was tired of the dresses hanging in her closet. She was sure everyone had already seen them at least two or three times last season.

At the end of her excursion she walked out of Filene's with three new dresses, two new pairs of shoes, and one stunning sun hat, navy blue with a white satin band and three small peacock feathers arranged on one side, a perfect accompaniment to one of the dresses she had purchased. Once home, Claire put on each outfit again, admiring her reflection in the mirror, thinking how her figure made the best of each piece. She would be absolutely radiant at the Garden Club luncheon on Tuesday.

That night at dinner, Louise placed a bowl of mashed potatoes on the table, along with a plate of hamburger patties, and fresh green beans from the garden. As Claire portioned out the food onto Oliver's plate, Louise asked if she could go with Dot to Wingaersheek Beach the following Saturday. It would be the last opportunity for such an outing before school started in the fall, as the month of August would be consumed with a filing project at Dr. Ferguson's office; and at home, with putting up jar after jar of preserves, the product of mounds of lush raspberry vines trained along the entire back fence; tomatoes in such abundance that Louise already had two shelves in the basement lined with tomato sauce; and piccalilli relish, her mother's special recipe, made from green and red tomatoes, young bell peppers, and sweet summer corn.

"I don't think you can go," said Claire as she spooned some potatoes onto her own plate. "I have two meetings that day, and George and I may go to the movies with the Andrews'. I'll need you here for Oliver."

Claire continued to speak as she started to cut up a hamburger patty for Oliver. "We all need to pull our weight around here Louise, and that most certainly includes you. I expect you to fulfill your responsibilities. Besides, I've seen your little friend Dot, and I'm not sure she's the best company to keep. She's quite...flirty."

Louise looked at Claire in disbelief. She turned to George, who was chewing a mouthful of hamburger, thoroughly engrossed in a stack of papers next to his plate. She looked back at Claire.

"But," Louise started, only to be cut short.

"No, dear," Claire looked at Louise now, keeping her voice calm, even friendly. "Not this time."

July passed, and August sweltered. George was on an even keel with his business, but he saw new opportunities popping up all around him. Roosevelt's Lend-Lease Act with England practically guaranteed a boom in all sorts of manufacturing concerns, whether the United States joined in the fight overseas or not—but only for those who could manufacture the required goods while the ink was still wet. He could bid on military contracts, especially if he could overhaul his facility quickly to meet the specs the government would demand. He'd heard of manufacturers in the South obtaining lucrative government contracts already, contracts for fabrics, rubber products, even paper.

The money from the sale of his mother's house would once again come in handy, and this time, with the potential for a real return. It was true he'd used some of the funds right away to pay off debts and keep his business afloat last year. George left the remainder in the bank, hoping for a real upturn in business that would allow him to replace what he had borrowed. Now a new opportunity was knocking, and George was ready to answer.

He knew which machines needed a retrofit, and which should be replaced entirely. He planned to hire four new machinists, and another secretary. It was only a matter of months, maybe even weeks, before bid requests would be issued for any number of metal parts, parts for guns and tanks, ships and fighter planes. He knew he could supply almost any of the smaller metal parts, he just had to get the right machines and the right people in place.

He drove over to the Winchester Savings Bank on a Wednesday afternoon. The moist heat of the mid-August sun beat down oppressively, and George felt as if his clothes would smother him as he walked in the door. Inside the bank it was only marginally cooler, and while relieved to remove his hat, George wished fervently that he could take off his jacket and tie, and unbutton the collar of his shirt. Still, his business wouldn't take long. All he needed was an exact balance on the remainder of Louise's inheritance account. He would run the figures tonight after dinner, and order the parts and machines as early as Friday. By the end of the month, mid-September at the latest, he would be ready to bid. For the first time in a long while, he was excited about something. It felt good.

"Hello Mr. Duncan, how are you today?" Joey Liston greeted George enthusiastically as he walked into the bank.

"Doing well, Joey, how are you?" George liked this young man, thinking sometimes that he was very much a younger version of himself. "And how is your mother? Still winning prizes for her cakes, I hear."

"We're both well, thank you, sir. And yes, her Black Forest cake took first place at the Middlesex County Fair last month, kind of you to notice." Joey smiled. "How can I help you today, Mr. Duncan? Perhaps a new account?"

George followed Joey over to a little office, simply furnished with a plain wooden desk, and plain hard-backed chairs. Papers were piled neatly on the desk, with more neat little piles of papers stacked on the bookcase along the side wall.

"There are new military contracts coming out that would be perfect for my business," George started, "but, if I want to get some of those contracts, I'll need a few new pieces of machinery, and a retrofit for some of the pieces I already have. I'd like to get a balance on my savings account so I know what I have to invest."

"Well, Mr. Duncan, I have to agree. Putting some money into your shop right now would be an excellent investment for those funds. Please wait here a moment, and I'll go pull your account records. We'll see what you have to work with."

It took Joey nearly ten minutes to step back into the office. He held three large folders, which he placed carefully on his desk. Sitting down, Joey looked at George with some concern.

"Mr. Duncan, it appears that you have three accounts with us—two separate savings accounts, and your business account. Is that correct?"

"Yes, that's correct. What's wrong? Is there something wrong?"

"Well, let's take them one at a time," Joey said. He showed George the bank records for his business account. "Please take a look at all your deposits and withdrawals over the last several months. Do these seem correct to you?"

George looked. There were several entries, and they were all familiar to him. He nodded.

"Now, let's take a look at your personal savings account. You normally deposit between ten and twenty-five dollars into this account every month. There have only been two withdrawals in the last year, one for twelve dollars, and another for six. Do these seem correct to you?"

George glanced at the ledger sheet. "Yes, all of these entries make sense. But I'm talking about the third account, the savings account I opened almost two years ago. The funds were from the sale of my mother's house…" George stopped. He could already read what was in Joey's now carefully neutral face.

"Let me see the ledger for the third account," George said evenly.

Joey slid the ledger in front of him.

George looked at the entries. Someone had been siphoning the money out of the account at frequent intervals. Most of the funds had disappeared in little chunks, ten or twenty dollars. But there were several larger withdrawals as well, some of them in the hundreds.

George leaned forward on the desk, his hands clasped together in front of him. Sweat trickled down his back, but his hands and stomach were like ice. He felt sick, and a little dizzy. He took his handkerchief from his breast pocket and wiped the sheen of sweat that he could feel on his face. He looked down at it in his hand. Fine cotton, with his initials monogrammed in blue silk in the corner…KGD—a gift from Claire for his last birthday.

"Who has been making these withdrawals?" George already knew the answer.

Joey looked at the withdrawal slips in the file. "All of these withdrawals were requested by you, Mr. Duncan, and delivered to Mrs. Duncan, per your written request." Joey handed a typewritten note to George, along with several of the withdrawal slips. George's signature appeared at the bottom of the note, which simply said that Mrs. Duncan was to receive funds upon the bank's receipt of an appropriately signed withdrawal slip. The withdrawal slips also bore his signature. But not quite. From the ledger records, George could see that Claire popped into the bank several times a month, and in less than two years had effectively wiped out nearly $4,000… Louise's inheritance, and funds that would have set him up for the coming boom.

George drove home. He'd left the bank with a new loan in hand, for as loath as he was to borrow money, he saw no other recourse, not if he intended to push through with his plans. As he walked in the door and hung up his hat, he scanned the living room. He noted the two new wingback chairs, the new rug, the new crystal vase, all supposedly purchased at the thrift store in Woburn, all now carefully placed in the living room. Claire had made a big deal when the items appeared a few months ago, excitedly telling him about the wonderful bargain she'd landed. He went upstairs to the bedroom to change his shirt, but stopped first to look in Claire's closet. Opening the doors, he saw more than a dozen hatboxes, and countless silk scarves on the top shelf. On the closet floor were nearly two dozen shoeboxes, neatly stacked; and, hanging on padded hangers, were dozens of dresses, skirts, and blouses, many of them with the price tags still attached.

The dinner parties. The fundraisers. The membership to the Country Club. The brand new silver coffee service that Claire said was an anniversary gift from her parents. Parents that had slowly declined to the verge of bankruptcy over the last ten years, like so many others.

"George?" Claire called from the bottom of the steps. "Dinner's almost ready."

George felt nauseous.

"George?" she called again. He closed the closet doors.

"Coming," he whispered, then loudly, "Coming!"

At dinner he looked at the table. New china. New flatware. He'd never noticed.

Claire looked at him, and said, "You're awfully quiet," adding playfully, "Cat got your tongue?" He looked up at her. Yes, he thought, the cat has my tongue, and apparently everything else.

After dinner, George suggested they go out for ice cream. Oliver gave his enthusiastic approval of the idea. The heat of the day had waned, and so they walked the six blocks to Ford's. George gave Louise a quarter, and told her to go ahead with Oliver, that he and Claire would meet them there. He waited until Louise and Oliver were a block in front of them, out of earshot.

"Where's the money, Claire?" He didn't have to ask, but it was the start to the conversation he was going to have with this woman, a woman he thought he knew and understood, a woman he loved, and who he thought loved him in return, in her own way. Now he realized he really didn't know her at all, except that she was capable of forgery, and stealing, and lying to his face.

"What money?" she answered distractedly, watching Louise and Oliver ahead of them, Oliver skipping, a new trick he learned just a week ago.

"The money in Louise's savings account. It's gone, Claire. You forged my signature on that ridiculous note, and on all those withdrawal slips, and bled the account dry over the last two years."

She was silent as they continued a slow walk.

"Now I need the money, Claire, to invest in the business, an investment that will pay big returns, and it seems to me you've frittered it away. But I'd like you to prove me wrong. Where is the money, Claire?"

They were passing by the Beauchamp house, tall and stately, one of the older homes in Winchester. Ivy Beauchamp was pruning her roses, cutting away the blown hips, gathering a few new buds.

Claire turned her attention to her neighbor. "Hello, Ivy, how are you? Your roses are certainly holding up well in this heat."

Ivy Beauchamp looked up at Claire and George, and waved a gloved hand.

"Thank you, Claire! Wish I could say the same for my tomatoes out back! Can't keep enough water on them, it seems." And she turned her attention back to the task before her, wiping a trickle of sweat from the side of her face, leaving a thin smear of dirt on her cheek.

Once out of earshot of Mrs. Beauchamp, Claire spoke. "Now George, I will admit I did use just a little bit of that money to fix up the house, just to make sure we kept up decent appearances. But really, it wasn't that much."

George stopped and faced Claire. "Three thousand, eight hundred, and sixty-two dollars, Claire. That's what was left after I refurbished the garage and shop two years ago. You knew things were difficult, that this goddamned Depression was eating away at my business. Now I need that money, and it's gone. You took it. Where is it?"

"I'm not going to have this discussion in the street, George."

"I am. Where is the money, Claire?" his voice louder now, booming.

George smiled and waved at Mr. Jenkins, who was pushing a mower across a stretch of lawn in front of his house. Mr. Jenkins had slowed a bit, hearing the tone of George's voice, but smiled and waved back. Claire beamed at Mr. Jenkins, waving as well. Under her breath, she said, "Would you please keep your voice civil? I'll not have the neighbors think anything less than the best of us."

They continued on. Claire spoke quietly, through smiling lips, but with a decided note of determination in her voice.

"George, if business isn't what you would like it to be, that isn't my fault. We've had this discussion before, do I need to remind you? You promised to keep me happy, and that means providing a certain standard of living for me and Oliver. God knows, I've kept up my end of the bargain, making a wonderful home life for you and Oliver, and even your sister. I've made sure we're involved in all the right committees, know all the right people, and attend all the right functions. Everything I've done, I've done for our family. I think you need to consider your son, George. Don't you want him to have a better life? I know you do. We both do. For that, it's important to have the right connections, and George, that takes money—money to look right, and to support the right causes."

"Besides," she continued, "I don't see why I shouldn't have been at liberty to use that money. I've lived with your sister for more than two years now, clothing and feeding her, putting up with her antics."

George was aghast. It was almost too much for him to take in, what she was saying. But it wasn't over yet.

Claire continued, her attention divided as they passed a newly painted house.

"Look at that awful color combination. Ugh. I'd never allow that color of green trim with the white paint. I would have chosen something much deeper, a hunter green, perhaps." She prattled on, still looking at the house. "Now you take a look at someone like Philip Andrews. He's done well, and continues to do well, in spite of this little downturn in the economy. He's a very smart man, and I think you should be more like him. In fact, Philip gave me some very good advice, and you should be proud of me for listening to him. He suggested I start saving some of the basics—sugar, coffee, cigarettes. He thinks that we might end up in the war, and if we do, some things might be in short supply. Helen, Mildred, Evelyn too—we've all been storing away extra supplies, you know, just in case."

George and Claire were friends with Philip and Margaret Andrews. He was a Vice President at Buick, and served as a Town Selectman. He was on the Building Commission, and on the Winchester Hospital Committee. Margaret chaired the Winchester Art Association, and served as Secretary at the First Congregational Church. Their son, Michael, tutored Louise in math.

"When was this?" asked George. The last time they had seen Philip and Margaret was at a dinner in late July. They'd gone to a movie afterward.

George didn't recall a discussion about storing up supplies.

"Oh, a little while ago." Claire was looking straight ahead as they walked, but George could see she was smiling, the same wicked smile that had first captured him.

For the second time that day, George felt as if he'd been sucker-punched.

They arrived at Ford's. Louise and Oliver were sitting at the counter, Oliver kneeling on a stool, intent on consuming a giant scoop of chocolate ice cream; Louise sat next to him, sipping a root beer float, watching to make sure he didn't get too messy. Claire ordered a scoop of vanilla ice cream.

"Soda water for me," said George, his voice tight.

They sat across from each other at a booth. George was silent as Claire babbled on about an upcoming Red Cross fundraiser. He couldn't hear her, he couldn't speak. It was all he could do to grasp the breadth and depth of his own ignorance.

Chapter 21

George was not without words for long. He stayed home the next morning, and insisted Claire join him on the back porch after sending Louise and Oliver to the library.

They settled into the porch chairs, sipping iced tea, for the day was warming quickly, and the air was already heavy, almost oppressive.

"This is nice," George said as he surveyed the back garden. This was Louise's domain, and the vegetables in the raised beds were doing well enough, in spite of the heat.

"Yes," agreed Claire.

Another minute passed. Claire watched a butterfly, something with iridescent blue wings, flutter haphazardly across the yard, finally settling on a bell pepper plant.

"Are you seeing Philip Andrews?" George asked calmly, already knowing the answer.

Claire looked down into the glass in her hands. She didn't answer.

"Claire?"

"You're never home. You don't touch me. Ever since Oliver was born, it's been…civil. All you do is work. Even at the dinner table, you sit with stacks of paper."

"That's true," George admitted.

Claire hesitated, then blundered forward, her defenses aroused.

"So, what difference does it make? If I'm seeing him or not, it doesn't affect you, or anyone for that matter."

George found himself choking up. He took another sip of his drink, put the glass on the little table near his seat, and regained his composure.

"It makes a difference to me, Claire. I may not have…"—here he stopped short, shook his head—"but this is a betrayal, a betrayal of me, and of us, of our marriage. First, I find out that you've been siphoning away Louise's inheritance, and then," an incredulous note creeping in, "I find out you've been having an affair with Philip Andrews? Honestly, Claire, it beggars belief."

"You can't begin to understand betrayal," she countered, her voice low, but arrogant. "Everything I've done, since the day we were married, has been to benefit our family, including any little flirtation with Philip. You have no idea what I've sacrificed. You've spent the last five years buried in your work, assuming all was perfectly fine at home without ever questioning how it stayed fine, never touching me beyond a kiss on the cheek, never considering that I might have…needs. And now you have the nerve to accuse *me* of betrayal."

George understood the role he may have played in Claire's affair with Philip Andrews, and as hurt as he was, he blamed himself in part for her unfaithfulness. Still, between the affair and the money, George's trust was shattered.

"Stop seeing him, Claire. Today, now, break it off."

Claire sighed. "Will you take his place?"

"Don't push, Claire. Break it off." He was all business now, and insistent.

She looked away, sighing. "Oh, all right. It wasn't much fun anyway."

Claire stood up. "Do you want more iced tea?"

"No. I'm going in to the shop, but I'll be home early tonight. I expect to find everything settled, understand?"

Claire nodded, picked up George's glass, and headed into the kitchen.

Over the next six weeks, George completed the planned retrofit of his shop. He bid for, and won, two lucrative federal contracts. Back Bay Machining would provide tens of thousands of nuts, bolts, rivets, and washers to the

United States government; and this was only the beginning, as other likely bid requests crossed George's desk with increasing frequency.

Winchester itself was gearing up for what looked like the unavoidable entry into the conflict in Europe. The community was already heavily involved in supporting those in bombed-out London, the ladies of the Fortnightly and Winton Clubs, along with those from various church groups, making scarves, afghans, wool socks and sweaters, and shipping them to unknown English recipients. They were even able to purchase and send a mobile kitchen to help feed those suffering in London. The local chapter of the Red Cross, which took over the third floor of Town Hall, raised funds to purchase and send an ambulance.

The Winchester branch of the Civil Defense Organization, calling itself the Committee of Public Safety, was established, and volunteers were plentiful. Winchester equipped itself to care for refugees if needed, and the Boy Scouts were mobilized to serve as couriers. The first war bond drives were frequent and successful, so that by the end of November, local businesses, organizations, and residents had purchased nearly $260,000 worth of war bonds.

Each person in Winchester found a role to play. The Hill Boys volunteered to assist with air raid drills, preparations for Victory Garden allotments along the Aberjona River, and bond drives. Walter and Henry, who now edited the high school newspaper, ensured articles and advertisements supporting Winchester's efforts were placed throughout each edition of the *High School Recorder*; and Walter, who had been elected Winchester High School Class President, served as diligent liaison between the school and community organizations, so that any student wanting to volunteer was assured of useful occupation.

Louise and Dot spent one afternoon each week at the Red Cross, sometimes rolling bandages or assembling safety kits, other times filing papers or filling out forms, whatever work was needed at the moment. Rose Hannigan and Amelia Crowley volunteered with the Fortnightly Club, and soon became experts at collecting, sorting, and shipping piles of donated clothing to England.

Claire was one of the few people in town who found herself restricted as to what she could do. She ended her affair with Philip, and when George was sure it was finished, he told Claire that she was to stay home and care for Oliver. There was no arguing. Louise was busy with school and work, and was now volunteering at the Red Cross. Claire was needed at home. In exchange, George provided Claire with a more generous allowance, and a promise that, eventually, he would allow more leeway in her activities.

Claire did her best to bide her time. She could be patient when it served her purpose. That patience came to an end on December 7, 1941.

Chapter 22

Joe Hannigan was napping on the couch in the living room, an open book resting on his chest, when a frantic knock at the front door pulled him from his slumber. His first thought was that he must have slept through part of the radio broadcast of the game: the New York Giants were playing against the Brooklyn Dodgers, and he wondered what the score was.

Rose hurried to open the door. Amelia, flustered and breathless, pushed in. Rose could tell she'd left her house in a hurry, she didn't have on a coat, or even her boots.

"Did you hear? Oh my God, did you hear?" Amelia was pale, her voice shaking.

Joe got up and made his way into the dining room, where Rose was pleading with Amelia to sit down.

"Oh, Joe, have you heard the radio?" Amelia asked when she caught sight of him.

"What? What's happened?" he asked, still not fully awake.

"The Japanese. They bombed us. Someplace out in the Pacific called Pearl Harbor. You know what this means…" Amelia worked furiously to combat the emotion that was threatening to close down her voice.

Joe went back into the living room, Amelia and Rose following close behind. He turned up the radio, adjusted the station. There it was, a newscast. The announcer was in between stories, all seeming to revolve around the attack.

Rose heard Walter come in the kitchen door.

"Mom!?" he called out, making his way into the living room. "We've been hit..." he started excitedly as he saw his mother.

"Shhh," Rose looked at her son, a dart of fear striking her as she realized he was a full-grown man now, and would undoubtedly be called to fight. "Come in, warm up by the fire, your father has the news on," she said in a whisper.

The four of them sat huddled around the radio, listening intently to the report from Albert Warner, out of Washington D.C., just as hundreds of other families in Winchester were listening, as hundreds of thousands of families across the country heard the news.

"...The attack was made on all naval and military activities on the principal island of Oahu. The President's brief statement was read to reporters by Steve Early, the White House Press Secretary. A Japanese attack on Pearl Harbor naturally would mean war. Naturally the President would ask Congress for a declaration of war. There is no doubt that such a declaration would be granted." Warner cut out, and another reporter, John Daly, took his place.

"Well," said Joe in a whisper, "that's that. Finally."

They listened as John Daly repeated the White House statement about Japanese attacks on Hawaii, and on Manila in the Philippines. Other reporters came on the air, some debating the Japanese intent, some focusing on the end of diplomatic relations with Japan, or the response from England.

Toward the end of the report, John Daly returned to the air: "They report that the attacking planes numbered between fifty and one hundred, the attack is still on, and antiaircraft fire can be heard as the attacking planes are coming in. This latest report now, from KGMB, is all that we have to the moment."

Joe turned the radio down.

"I better call in to work, see what they want to do." Joe headed toward the kitchen.

"My God, Rose, they're still under attack!" Amelia exclaimed. Suddenly she was up on her feet. "I need to get home, I need to check on Beth and

Hazel. Come over later if you want."

Rose nodded. "Thanks, Amelia, for letting us know."

As Amelia shut the front door behind her, Rose turned to Walter. He stood up, and looked at his mother.

"Where are Daniel and Patrick?" she asked, an edge to her voice.

"Down the street, on the hill. I'll get them."

Joe came back into the room.

"I'm to go out on the road tomorrow, but call in to the office every day until they make a decision."

Rose nodded. "I better get dinner started."

As she headed into the kitchen, she turned to Joe, who had returned to the radio. "I still can't believe it."

The next day, radios were set up in the schools, at the Winchester Library, and even over the public address system at the town center, so that everyone could hear President Roosevelt's speech.

Louise sat in her classroom, listening intently to the broadcast with her classmates. It made her hair stand on end to hear the President's words, to hear his voice, deep and resolute, as he spoke of the attacks, as he spoke of the American determination to defend herself, of the state of war with the Japanese Empire.

At Back Bay Machining, George stopped the machines, and collected his workers around the radio. At the end of the speech, George looked at his men.

"You know what this means. Some of you will go to fight; I'll do my best to retain those of you with more experience, or who are older, or have families with children, if I can, and if it's what you want. Either way, we have our work cut out for us. Let's get back to it."

Claire sat at her dining room table, with Oliver playing with his trucks on the floor nearby. At the end of the speech, she turned off the radio, and, stepping over the convoy of trucks Oliver had lined up on the plush carpet, she headed toward the phone.

"Well," she said to herself, "time to get busy."

Her first calls were to Helen, Mildred and Evelyn. They would meet for lunch at Randall's the next day, when Ruth would be at the house and could watch Oliver. Claire knew she would have to ease into her work. A few hours a week at the hospital or the Red Cross, maybe some time devoted to helping organize a fundraiser of some sort. She would have to wait until Louise finished school before she could really make an impact. But Claire would start now, and build up her connections, so that when the time came, she would be in perfect position to take a leading role in Winchester. A working lunch with her friends would set the stage for it all.

Chapter 23

On Monday morning, Joe drove to Springfield, the first stop for the week. He made a few calls on clients, but some were closed, others unwilling to do business, everyone still reeling from the news of the Japanese attack, everyone waiting for the President's address to the nation.

At lunchtime, Joe stopped in at Charlie's Diner, a small restaurant nestled in among the storefronts that lined Main Street. He sat with a half-dozen other men at the counter, riveted to the radio. Each one of them had stopped eating when the speech started, and as Roosevelt finished his address and a reporter took up the air, most of the men paid their bill and left, including Joe. He would call the company from his hotel in another hour or so. He hoped that would be enough time for them to make a decision.

Privately, Joe was elated that the United States was finally in the fight. He'd paid attention to the fleeting news stories as they were broadcast—the Axis agreements, the fall of Warsaw, the first air attacks on Britain—and then dug deeper. Traveling gave him consistent access to the larger newspapers, and even some of the smaller, more vocal rags that surfaced as events unfolded overseas. Joe knew that most of America didn't grasp the full story, the massive shifts of power and the incredible losses at the hands of the Nazis. But Joe did. On the evenings he wasn't otherwise engaged, he scoured the newspapers, reading the headlines, searching carefully for the buried articles that fed his interest. He pieced together a sort of storyline that started in May of 1939, just before Christine died, when he heard that Italy and Germany had formed the Rome-Berlin Axis. Less than two weeks later, Churchill signed a British-Russian Anti-Nazi Pact. In September of that year, the Germans invaded Poland, and the Second World War was officially underway.

When the 1940 Olympics were canceled, Joe was not surprised at all, although some of his neighbors and co-workers wondered aloud if the cancellation wasn't an overreaction to the skirmish in Europe. Joe was heartened when Winston Churchill became Prime Minister, heartened to read his speeches in the newspaper when they weren't broadcast on the radio; chilled when he heard the Germans had occupied Paris. He wept each evening in his hotel room as the Blitz of London raged, and quietly donated a hundred dollars to the Red Cross one Saturday afternoon, between haircuts for the boys and ice cream at Ford's. He'd read a line or two in some of the underground papers about the atrocities the Nazis imposed on their conquered nations, and even on some targeted groups, Jewish people, gypsies, the disabled, but it was hard to tell if these accusations were true.

The last year saw the Axis powers occupy Athens, and constant air raids over England. Germany, Italy, and Romania declared war on the Soviet Union. Joe fully anticipated the United States would join the war, rally to England's side with guns and tanks, ships and bombers, all tangible war machines, and all a far cry from the limp-wristed Lend-Lease Act.

But Joe had not expected the attack from Japan. That had caught him by surprise.

Joe called in at work. The decision was made. He was to return to Winchester to stay, at least for the foreseeable future. He would have an office at the factory, and work from there.

Joe paid his bill and left the hotel. He drove west, across the Memorial Bridge, toward the outskirts of Springfield. He turned down an unfinished driveway, slowing to avoid the jarring of the rough road underneath, grateful that the little road was dry and clear of snow. A small farmhouse came up on his right, white with dark blue trim, a light visible in the kitchen window. Joe continued past the house, and pulled around to the back, parking in front of a dilapidated shed.

Ellen Chandler, a round, fortyish woman with large lips and over-plucked eyebrows, stood at the kitchen door, waiting for him. She welcomed him with an affectionate kiss, handed him a scotch and soda as he entered her house.

Joe sat at the kitchen table as she finished making dinner, watched her move easily from cabinet to counter to stove. He finished his drink, and she gave him another. Conversation was usually scant and light between the two of them, but this time Ellen was asking questions, questions about what happened with the Japanese, was the United States really at war, would he have to go fight? Joe found himself drained by the conversation, by the too-much sound of her voice. He ate quickly when she put the plate in front of him, hoping to move away from the kitchen table, away from the talk, and into the bedroom. Upstairs, the questions subsided, and they fumbled a little in the dark, until there was no talk at all, only slow, rudimentary sex. They slept, and in the morning, she made breakfast while he sat in the tub, washing the night away.

He dressed. Downstairs, she gave him coffee and eggs, and burnt toast with jam. She sat down across from him, dragged her toes up the shin of his pants.

"When will you be back? Next week?" she asked, kittenish.

"No, sorry. Everything's changed. I won't be on the road anymore, at least for a while. I'll let you know when things go back to normal."

"I see," she said, her demeanor changed, a little anger pushing through. She stood up stiffly and went to the kitchen sink, and began washing the breakfast pans. He slid a ten-dollar bill under his coffee cup, picked up his jacket and keys, and headed out the kitchen door.

He loathed going home. After Christine's funeral, Joe found the distance between himself and home a relief, each mile a gauzy layer dropped between aching sorrow and dull nothingness, between his conscience and guilt, the guilt of not being there to help, of not knowing how to comfort his wife or his children; of not knowing anything had happened until he rolled into his driveway on Friday afternoon to see the black crepe on his door, Rose standing on the porch in a black dress, Walter beside her. She'd looked at him as he hurried up the steps, unable to speak, only able to give him the most sorrowful look he'd ever seen in his life.

It was Walter who finally spoke.

"Christine."

A single word, and Joe bolted into the house, caught by the sick smell of too many flowers heavy in the air.

Now he would be home every night. As he pulled into his driveway late Tuesday afternoon, he felt out of place, a stranger sitting in front of this pretty house on Pembroke Road. He hardly knew the boys, hardly knew Rose, for that matter. Joe considered the circumstances. There was nothing to do but make the best of it, see the glass half full, as it were. Maybe this would be an opportunity to make things better, to gather together the ties he'd once held so neatly, to put back into place the fragments of his life that had shifted from too much time on the road. After all, he had a good job to go to every day, and a good woman to come home to every night. He reassured himself that everything would work out.

It dawned on him suddenly that Walter was old enough to serve. The thought left him washy, not wanting to get out of the car until the nausea passed, even though the car was cooling fast, the snow-laden air seeping in. It wouldn't be good for Rose to lose Walter. Joe would have to find a way to fix that.

Joe settled readily into his new office and new routine. The commute was easy, by train if he wanted, and he enjoyed working with the factory team again. Sometimes, when things were slow or he needed a break, he went down to the floor to pack a few boxes, or troubleshoot a faulty machine.

One afternoon in February he stopped in at the Winchester Town Hall to drop off some paperwork. His business finished, he made his way downstairs, curious to see what offices still remained buried underground. As he came to the bottom of the steps, he stopped short.

Everything was different. The offices had been enlarged, partitions removed, tables and desks and chairs arranged for the new services that now occupied the Town Hall basement. There was a large room across from the stairs, obviously an induction center of some kind. Another area was reserved for various volunteer services, and a few private offices sat at the far end of the hall.

He was about to head up the stairs when someone called to him. "Can I be of assistance?"

Joe turned back, and peered down the hallway. Mr. Jeremiah Lowell was walking toward him, smiling.

"Jerry? What are you doing here?" Joe strode forward to clasp his friend's hand.

"Joe Hannigan. I haven't seen you in a long time. Never mind what am I doing here, what are you doing here? I thought you were bound to the road."

"Well, things have changed, haven't they...I'm at the factory now, home every night, regular hours, the works." He looked around. "Things have changed here, too."

Jerry Lowell nodded. "Ayah, lots of our young men signing up, lots of volunteers. We needed more space to accommodate the military folks and the volunteer groups, so we made a few changes, and, well, here we are. I got to oversee it all, and now I hang around and coordinate, making sure people end up in the right place."

"A bit of a step down for you, isn't it, Jerry? I mean, you had your own business, the bookstore on Vernon; and you were on the Building Commission, weren't you? A lot to give up to direct people."

"Oh, I didn't give anything up." A sly smile crossed Jerry's face. "How do you think this all happened? I ordered it. I'm the official head of the Office of Civil Defense for the Town of Winchester, although we call ourselves the Public Safety Committee. I get to coordinate the whole works, serve as liaison with the Boston OCD, and keep my post on the Building Commission. And I still own my business, the wife runs it beautifully, better than I ever did. Come see my office."

They sat for a while in Jerry's office, a small box of a room a few steps from the stairs. They discussed the war, the critical events that led to Pearl Harbor, the current state of the U.S. military. Joe expressed his concern about Walter.

"Didn't he have polio?" Jerry asked, reaching for a cigarette, offering one to Joe.

"Yes, he was nine or ten, somewhere in there. But he recovered from that, except he can't lift his left arm very high." Joe accepted a light from Jerry, inhaling deeply. Cigarettes would be in short supply soon, he thought.

The Lights of Pembroke Road

"Get Doc Murray to write a note. If your son had polio and his mobility is impaired, the letter will keep him home." Jerry paused as he took another puff from his cigarette. "Actually, I'd like Walter to work for me, if that's okay with you. We had plenty of volunteers at first, but with so many young men signing up, we're starting to see a shortage, so I can use him. When he's out of school, send him over. I'll have plenty for him to do."

By March, Joe was as busy as he'd ever been. Phone orders were coming in by the hundreds. Lever Brothers landed a hefty federal contract, and the company was running at full speed. Joe managed the incoming orders, and even lent a hand with accounts receivable whenever he could.

One morning the CFO knocked on his door. Joe saw who it was and stood up.

"Good morning, Mr. Kendall," he said, almost automatically.

Mr. Kendall stood aside, and ushered in two men dressed in dark gray suits.

"Joe, I know you're busy, but, ah, these two gentlemen would like to speak with you." There was an awkward pause, and Mr. Kendall backed out of the office. "I'll leave you to it, then. I'll just close the door, give you some privacy." And with that, the door to Joe's office shut, and he was faced with the men in suits.

As Joe walked out of his office later that afternoon, he could barely remember the rather one-sided conversation he'd had with the two men. He could only roll around the old adage 'there's no such thing as a free lunch.' It was true, Joe had followed Jerry Lowell's advice, and obtained the necessary note from Dr. Murray. When the time came, Walter would remain stateside. In turn, Jerry Lowell had evidently recommended Joe to the Boston OCD as a discreet, loyal, intelligent man. Boston OCD needed volunteers in Middlesex County, a few trustworthy men who could tackle the delicate work of sorting through dossiers and files, materials related to the loyalty of the local population.

The men in suits strongly suggested that Joe would be one of those men. Joe felt it was in his best interest to agree with them.

Chapter 24

"Michael invited me to the prom."

Louise tried to sound nonchalant as she said the words at dinner. In her chest, though, she could feel her heart beating hard and fast, and she felt a little light-headed. George smiled broadly at her.

"That's nice, Louise! You'll have a wonderful time. Would you pass the potatoes?"

Claire hovered for an almost imperceptible second as she cut Oliver's chicken into manageable bites, and resumed her task without comment. George glanced at her, noted the silence, and continued.

"I had a great time at my prom. I took Mary Margaret Winters. We danced, drank punch, ate the most awful cookies that one of the teachers made, Miss Olsen, I think. Nice teacher, terrible baker. I don't think I ever danced so much in my life, before or since. Anyway, now it's your turn, and I like Michael. We've had dinner with his parents a few times, haven't we, Claire? I know his father is a Selectman, and I think he's on the Building Commission, isn't he? And he does something in the auto industry, in Boston, I think. An executive with Ford or Hudson," George snapped his fingers, summoning the correct name. "Or maybe Buick—yes, Buick, that's it. And his mother, I believe, does something with the Art Association, and I think she serves on the School Committee. Isn't that right, Claire?"

As if pulled from a dream, Claire answered quietly, "Yes, Mrs. Andrews is active in the community."

Turning her attention to Louise, Claire asked sweetly, "When is the dance, dear? Do you know the date?"

"April 29th. So, I can go?"

Claire started with, "Well," only to be cut off by George's hearty, "Of course!"

Claire started again. "I believe we have a dinner engagement that evening at the Country Club, a fundraiser for the Red Cross. It's an important occasion, and I need Louise at home to babysit Oliver."

"Nonsense! I just checked my calendar this morning, and that dinner is in early May, the weekend after Louise's prom date. So there's no conflict at all."

Claire glared at him. He looked back at her, a smile still at his mouth, but his eyebrows raised to return the challenge. Claire turned her attention to Oliver. "Oliver, dear, eat your peas, they're good for you."

An emphatic "NO! I don't like them!" followed by a spray of peas launched from Oliver's spoon left Claire wiping her face and clothes, and picking up peas that had landed on the table. Oliver laughed, and attempted to follow his first strike with an equally well-aimed spoonful of potatoes. Claire stood up, near violence. Louise reached over and prevented Oliver from hurling the mashed potato missile.

"No, Oliver, that's not nice," said Louise.

"We don't do that, Oliver. Stop it right now," George reprimanded.

Claire regained her composure, and sat again, turning away from her son as he stuffed the spoonful of potatoes into his mouth, still laughing.

George continued with the conversation. "Hey, you'll need a new dress, won't you?"

Until this moment, Louise had only been concerned with getting permission, and was still working through the relief at gaining her brother's approval. Her heart had slowed, and felt she had pulled back from the brink of a precipice. She knew that Claire was seething under her calm surface, and George was playing some sort of game. Louise could feel the warm anger emanating from Claire's body, in spite of her silence. But with George there, so supportive, it didn't seem to matter what game was being played. Still, she decided to be careful. Louise was sure that Claire would find some way to even the score later, when George was not there.

"Umm. Well, yes, I would need a new dress. I have some money saved from working at Dr. Ferguson's, I was going to use that."

"Not at all," George said as he pulled his billfold from his pocket. He took out five crisp five-dollar bills, and handed them to his sister. "You buy yourself something really special, Louise. Get your hair done, and make sure Mike gets you a nice corsage. Don't forget to get him a boutonnière."

Louise was speechless, but only for a moment as she looked at the bills in her hand. She had never seen so much money at one time.

"Oh, George, thank you!" She rose up and came around the table, giving her brother a tight hug and a kiss on the cheek. Without looking at Claire, she carefully folded the bills up and buried them in her shirt pocket.

Later, as Louise finished drying the dinner dishes, Claire walked in and stood next to her at the kitchen counter. She was so close, Louise could smell her stale perfume, mixed with fresh cigarette smoke and Scotch. The hairs on her arms prickled, but she continued her work, slowing so that she could maintain control, glad to have something to do with her hands while Claire was so close.

"That's a lot of money George gave you. Be careful you don't lose it."

Louise glanced at her before picking up a stack of plates to return to the cupboard. There were still two peas clinging to her hair.

"I won't," she said.

Claire moved a little closer. "Would you like me to hold it for you until you find a dress you like? Perhaps we could shop together?"

Louise replied with her back to Claire as she put the glassware away. "Claire, that's very kind of you, but I've already picked out a dress, and I promised Dot we would go together to buy it." She closed the cabinet and turned around, her kitchen work finished. "Thank you, though, it was very nice of you to offer. I'm going up to bed now. Good night, Claire." And with that, Louise escaped up to her attic bedroom.

She sat on her bed, the bills laid out in front of her. With this money, she could buy not only the dress, but shoes, and a little purse to match. She could have her hair done at Mrs. Singer's salon. She would have to make an appointment right away. Prom would be a very busy day for every salon in town. Louise got up from her bed and went to her desk, fishing in the drawer for her red pencil. Having found it, she sat back on the bed, and placed a single red dot over the pyramid's eye on each bill. Not noticeable unless you were looking for it, she thought, but just enough of a mark. She hid the money between the pages of her old history book, knowing Claire's resentment of her, knowing she was not to be trusted.

At school the next day, Louise told Dot about her brother's generosity. Dot's eyes grew wide.

"Why, Louise, you'll be the belle of the ball! Now you really can get that dress at Filene's, that beautiful green one in the window. When do you want to go?"

"Let's go Saturday morning—can you come with me?"

"Of course, silly! Then we can take it to my house, and I'll help you with the hem if you need it, and you can help me with mine. Decided to wear my mother's dress, you know, the blue one I showed you last week? It needs to come up an inch." Dot sighed, a faraway look in her eyes as she envisioned the dance. "Mike is going to be the luckiest guy at the prom. Except Ray, of course," she winked.

On Friday evening, George and Claire went to Mildred's for dinner. Oliver was finally asleep in his room after a fussy evening. Louise had her work cut out for her, soothing him first through the distraction of playing with trucks, then coloring pictures with him, and finally offering warm milk and cookies, and a chapter of *Peter Pan and Wendy*. He nodded off on the couch, a half-eaten cookie in his hand, just as Wendy arrived at the Island of Neverland. Louise picked him up ever so carefully, and carried him up to bed, waiting a few minutes to be sure he was asleep. Finally, breathing a sigh of relief, she headed up to her room. Tonight she would retrieve the money George had given her, and tomorrow she and Dot would go shopping at Filene's.

She opened her history book and flipped through the pages.

The bills were gone.

She flipped through the pages again. She held the book upside down, shaking the book over her bed.

Claire.

Louise flipped through the book one last time, looked at the cover again to be sure she had picked up the right book. She was angry now, angry with Claire, but just as angry with herself for not choosing a better hiding spot.

Louise went back downstairs to Claire and George's bedroom and pushed open the door. Only the light from Claire's closet illuminated the room, a bright beam of light crossing the bottom of the bed, casting the rest of the room in shadow. It took a moment for Louise's eyes to adjust. She never went in here, really, except to place folded laundry on the bed, or to run a dust rag over the furniture. Ruth always took care of this room.

Louise heard the downstairs hall clock chime ten. Claire and George would be home soon, she knew. She started to search methodically, carefully, working her way through Claire's bureau and her bedside table. Nothing.

She opened Claire's closet door, and searched through the pockets of the clothes hanging on the rung, the purses and clutches sitting on the shelves. She went through again. Nothing. Louise sat for a moment on the closet floor. The shoes. Claire loved her shoes, and kept them in perfect order, in their original boxes, stacked three high on the closet floor. Claire had twenty-one pairs of shoes. The clock chimed the half-hour.

Louise looked at the boxes. She noticed the cover of the bottom box in the middle stack was slightly lifted. Carefully, she removed the two boxes on top of it. As she put them aside, Louise heard George's car in the driveway, the heavy motor of the Packard growling up to the garage.

Louise lifted the bottom box top carefully. Inside were the blue satin pumps Claire wore with her blue and white summer dress, the shoes dyed to match perfectly with the blue satin belt that came with the dress. Louise heard the garage door open, and the car move inside. She pulled the shoes out. The box was empty. She heard the car doors close, then the garage door lowering.

Crestfallen, and beginning to panic, Louise fumbled with the shoes as she tried to put them away. And then, from the toe box of the left shoe, a neatly folded packet of five-dollar bills fell into Louise's lap. One red dot on the back of the top bill left no doubt. No time to waste, Louise replaced the shoes carefully and quickly in the box, replacing the other two boxes on top. She pulled the light switch off, and opened the closet door slowly. She could hear the key in the front door downstairs. Louise crept to the bedroom door, hoping desperately to avoid stepping on any creaking floorboards. Reaching the door, she opened it a sliver and peered out. She saw the light over the stairs, and heard snippets of conversation from below. It seemed George and Claire were in the kitchen. Was everything in place? She couldn't remember. She had been careful, even with the last scramble with the shoeboxes. But she couldn't remember if the closet door had been open or closed when she had first entered the room—open, she thought, yes, and open when she left it. Right? The light! She had turned it off! Too late. Maybe Claire wouldn't notice.

No time to spare, Louise slipped out of George and Claire's room, holding her breath as she gently turned the knob into place. Now to get to her room. She had to cross in front of the top of the staircase from the first floor to get to the stairs leading to the attic. Claire and George were already at the bottom of the steps, talking quietly, something about Mildred's husband being tipsy at the table before dinner even started. Louise made a quick turnaround and headed back down the hall, away from the stairs, past George and Claire's room, to the alcove next to the bathroom.

"I just want to check on Oliver," said Claire. Louise was caught. She could just see them from her hiding place as she pressed into the shadows of the alcove. Louise wanted desperately to move, but she dared not even look in their direction.

They both entered Oliver's room. The moment they were inside, Louise thought about moving. Maybe she could make it to the attic steps. No. She waited, keeping her breath shallow and light and quiet. They came out of Oliver's room, and went into their own bedroom without another word, closing the door part way behind them.

Louise took her chance now. She stepped lightly and quickly past their door, past Oliver's room, and to the base of the stairs leading to the attic. She breathed a sigh of relief as she placed her feet on the steps leading up to her room, the money clutched in her hand.

At the landing, something made her look down. Claire was at the bottom, looking up at her with a cold, unflinching stare. Louise waited.

George called to Claire from their bedroom door, a half-whisper, "Claire, what are you doing? Come to bed." Claire narrowed her eyes. She turned, her face calm and cool as she faced George and headed back to the bedroom.

Louise shoved her chair under the door handle that night.

Chapter 25

The emerald-green dress, a fuss of satin over tulle at the skirt, and topped with a fitted waist that extended upward to a sweetheart neckline, fit Louise perfectly. It was one of the few pre-war dresses that Filene's had on hand, so different from the 'new' style of dress, where hemlines remained the same, but the skirt sweep was gone, and along with it any attractive swish of material that followed a woman as she moved. Louise had even been able to get satin pumps dyed to match, and real silk stockings, her first pair, and, she thought ruefully, probably her last. Dot's mother loaned Louise a pair of ivory kid gloves that extended up past her elbows, and Mrs. Singer herself had put Louise's hair in a soft, elegant chignon that afternoon. As the hour drew close for Mike to arrive, Louise made her way downstairs. George, sitting in the front room reading a newspaper, took one look and whistled. Claire glanced at Louise as she came down the steps, turned away, and went into the kitchen.

Mike simply said 'wow' when he picked Louise up at the door, kissing her gently on the cheek as he greeted her. Mike looked quite handsome in a well-tailored dark gray suit, with his hair trimmed perfectly, his black shoes polished to a high shine. Louise pinned a single white rose boutonnière at his lapel, and Mike's cheeks flushed pink as he carefully pinned a corsage of white roses at her left shoulder.

George stood at the front door as they made their way to the car. "Take good care of her, Mike! Have a wonderful time!" he called.

Mike opened the passenger side door of his father's Buick, borrowed for the occasion, and helped Louise in.

"Louise, you look great!" he said. Mike had always thought Louise was very pretty, but tonight, with her hair up, and her beautiful dress, Mike was in awe.

She smiled at him, a little blush rising to her cheeks. She knew she looked nice, but it felt good to hear him say it.

"Thanks, Mike. You look nice too. I don't think I've ever seen you in this suit. This one is gray, it's very sharp."

"Ah," he said as he got into the driver's seat, "This is my dad's suit. He said I should wear it tonight, make sure I made a good impression on you."

"Really?" Louise laughed, "Well, you be sure to tell your dad that I was very impressed."

Walking into the gymnasium on Mike's arm, it all seemed so perfect. As Mike handed the tickets to the young lady at the reception desk, Louise took in the decorations, the music, the brocade of colors that shimmered as the young couples danced, and the scent of Old Spice and a dozen perfumes, blended together in a heady aroma. Above, the ceiling was draped with red, white, and blue streamers, and silver-star cut-outs seemed to float in the air amidst the multi-colored crepe. Long tables set up near the home end of the court, draped in red, white, and blue bunting, were laden with punch and cookies and little cakes.

At the other end of the court was a platform, where the Jibers Band was playing Glenn Miller's "Blueberry Hill." Small round tables with chairs were arranged in the corners of the gym. Mr. Dougherty, the principal, and Mr. James, the vice principal, stood near one of the tables, while their wives and two of the school secretaries poured punch and plated cookies. Most of the court space was filled with dancing couples. Chaperones danced along with them, enjoying the music, enjoying the party as much as they could. All knew that after tonight, most of the young men in attendance would make final preparations to join the armed forces. By midsummer they would be gone, leaving dance partners behind.

Louise turned her attention to the couples on the floor. Each of the young women wore the nicest dress she could afford to buy, or make. Many were reworked from a hand-me-down, some made by hand from a pattern, a few newly store-bought, but all an array of taffeta and tulle, all the colors of the rainbow gathered in this center of the high school gymnasium, shifting and swirling before her. And clasped to each spot of swirling color was a young man, someone Louise had known most of her life, with whom she had gone to school, attended church, passed a hundred times at the library or the grocer's. Each of them was grown up now, each wearing his best suit and tie, each showing his best gentlemanly demeanor.

Within moments, she and Mike were in the middle of the room, his arm around her waist, drawing her closer by gentle increments as they moved among the other dancers. Louise let him pull her closer, exultant, in her own way, as she felt the pressure of his hands, the strength of his arms, knowing she fit perfectly, knowing he only saw her in this roomful of pretty girls. She looked up at him, and he looked at her, the way she knew he would, an expression of tender excitement across his face. Louise felt at once connected with it all, alive and beautiful too. And as happy as she felt at just that moment, there was a scratching, a gnawing at the periphery, a something she wanted desperately to push back, to push away, at least for tonight. Just now she wanted to dance, and feel Mike's warmth, and receive everything she could from him, give everything she could in return.

The song ended, and Ray sauntered up to claim the next dance. Louise smiled as she looked at her dance card. It was full, and Ray was next on the list. Mike made his way over to Emma Simms, who sat next to him in French class. And so the evening went. Couples danced, changed partners, stopped to sit for a few minutes to chat over punch and cookies, got up to dance again. Dot and Ray danced nearly every dance together, stopping now and then to sit at a table and watch the other couples on the floor.

As the evening came to a close, Louise began to look for Mike among the crowd. The last dance was just starting, a slow, sultry rendition of Glenn Miller's "Moonlight Serenade." Louise and Mike had promised to save the last dance of the evening for each other. Dot and Ray were already on the floor, holding each other as closely as they dared in the darkened gym, her head on his shoulder, both his arms clasped around her. Walter was dancing with Hannah Miller, a pretty girl in the junior class, Dr. Murray's niece. They were in the center of everything, dancing slowly, carefully, self-conscious. Louise stood at a table, waiting for Mike—where was he? This was their special dance, the last one before everything changed.

She saw him, finally, at the other end of the gym. He was talking to a young woman, Josephine, a junior. She had arrived with Mark Hines, a senior who had enlisted with the Army just two days before. She was crying, no, sobbing really, her back turned to the dancers, as Mike offered her his handkerchief and a consoling arm. He looked up, caught Louise's eyes, shrugged his shoulders.

Louise sat down, near tears with frustration. As she resigned herself to disappointment, Henry, who had come stag that evening, came up to her and asked if she would like to dance. She started to say no, but looked over again at Mike. He was engrossed with comforting Josephine, talking earnestly with her. Henry would be signing up at the end of the school year, just like all the others. So Louise said yes, took his hand, and danced the last half of "Moonlight Serenade" with Henry Smith, trying not to look at Mike, trying to be a good dance partner for the young man in front of her. If it couldn't be helped, then she could give someone a decent last dance. Henry was as deserving as any of them.

The party ended. Revelers walked dreamily out of the gym in pairs or small groups, leaving behind the few responsible souls for whom the evening wouldn't end until the last tablecloth was bagged up for laundering, the last bit of crepe swept away into the dustbin. Mike and Louise made their way slowly to the car.

"I'm so sorry, Louise," Mike said. "I saw her crying and started to talk to her before I realized it was the last dance, our dance. I'm so sorry…" he trailed off, miserable.

"Oh, for heaven's sake, don't be morose," replied Louise, laughing a little at his gloomy mood. "I knew what was happening, you couldn't help it—and if you had walked away from Josephine at that moment, I'd think you were an ogre, and wouldn't have danced with you anyway." She smiled. "Now, you're not mad that I danced with Henry?"

"Oh, no, of course not," Mike replied. "You couldn't just sit there when all the other girls were dancing, that wouldn't have been right. But," he stopped, turned to her, serious. "You owe me a dance, now. I expect full reimbursement when I return from wherever they send me. Is it a deal?"

"It's a deal!" Louise offered her hand, and Mike took it, and they shook hands on it, a real gentleman's agreement.

Mike drove Louise back to the Dix Street house. They sat in the car at the curb, the dim light at the front porch casting a pale yellow glow onto the steps below, a footlight for the deepening evening's own band, a boisterous harmony of singing crickets and croaking frogs. Mike took Louise's hand, leaned toward her, and kissed her. He was gentle at first, then more open, exploring, his arms wrapped around her, his hand cradling the back of her head. Louise returned the kisses, warmth growing inside her. She imagined what it would be like to be in bed with him, like this, arms around each other, his strength surrounding her, taking her.

And then Mike sat back, and glanced up and down the street. Louise waited a moment, wondering what would happen next, if he would want to go further. If he did, she didn't think she would say no, but was unsure about the logistics. Mike's next words spared her further concern.

"Wait for me, will you?" His voice was hoarse and thick. "I mean, it's a lot to ask, but I plan to wait for you if you'll wait for me."

At first Louise didn't know what he was saying. Wait for him to do what? Then it dawned on her, in a flash, that he wasn't going to go any further, that he was asking her to wait for him to come home from the war. She began to recover her composure.

"I didn't think there was any question about that, Mike." A moment passed. "After all, I owe you a dance."

Chapter 26

High school had all but come to a close. There were no more tests, no more assignments, just half-days of practice for the graduation ceremony a few days away. The prom, two weeks past, nestled in Louise's memory as a warm, pleasant dream. Her future, apart from graduation and saying good-bye to Mike, stretched in front of her, murky and untouchable; and in between the known and the unknown was an unusually warm, sunny Saturday afternoon in mid-May, where Louise sat curled up in the big, cushioned wicker chair on the front porch of the Dix Street house. She was attempting to read a chapter of *Jane Eyre*, the book she had picked up more than three years ago and never finished. She wasn't having much success. Her thoughts drifted vaguely to the young men in her class already signed up, with only graduation day standing between home and an uncertain future, both for those going, and for those left behind.

She reflected particularly on her relationship with Mike, what it would be like to wait for him; and more persistently, what she would do while waiting. She assumed she would continue to work at Dr. Ferguson's, and that she and Dot would probably spend more time volunteering at the Red Cross. Perhaps they could assist with a bond drive, or a metal drive, or demonstrate gardening techniques at community meetings. She would have to think about it.

As Louise sat on the front porch, with *Jane Eyre* and musings about the future competing for her attention, Claire sat inside at the dining room table with Helen, Mildred and Evelyn, shuffling cards in preparation for their monthly bridge game. Claire had opened the downstairs windows to allow the luscious warm air to move through the house, and Louise could smell the heady combination of hot coffee and cigarettes as the aromas wafted by her.

Louise's attention sharpened as she heard her name mentioned in snippets of conversation between Claire and her cronies. Claire was either oblivious to Louise's proximity, or to the way her voice carried. Now diverted from both her book and her private thoughts, Louise sat up quietly in her chair, her eyes still on the page in front of her, her ears intent on the discussion inside.

The conversation among the four women started with general dismay over the new sugar ration. Mothers and daughters and wives waited in long lines at the elementary schools, where ration coupons were doled out carefully and methodically to registered recipients. These same mothers and daughters and wives then waited in long lines at the S.K. Ames store in Town Center, where they could exchange one coupon per month for a newly precious pound of sugar. Rumors were flying about which sundries would be rationed next, and shoppers found many items in scant supply, coffee, flour, even cornstarch and baking soda, hoarded by those lucky enough to be on hand when the shelves were being stocked. Claire and her cohorts had been gathering supplies for months, and each of the women was pleased to have a full larder while others scrambled for the basics.

The discussion shifted from rationing to that of volunteer opportunities in town, and which ladies were chairing which groups.

"Now that Louise is graduating, I'll have the chance I've been waiting for to volunteer full-time," said Claire. "Winchester has so many openings at the Red Cross and the hospital. The Public Safety Committee is desperate for volunteers, although I hear they need people to serve as lookouts in the middle of the night, which I simply won't do. And it seems there are so many different drives—scrap metal, paper, even rubber bands!" She took a sip of her coffee, and offered cigarettes from a silver case to the other ladies before taking one for herself. She lit it, and inhaled deeply before she continued.

"Mrs. De Mans is chairing the Fortnightly Club, and is on the Board of the local Red Cross, and I intend to work with her. I spoke with her at last Wednesday's War Bond Committee meeting, and she mentioned she was looking for an assistant, and I said I would do it. And she accepted on the spot!"

Claire smiled at the thought. It was what she'd been working for ever since the war started. It was the perfect opportunity to get out of this wretched house, away from the sniveling shadow of Louise, and Oliver's unceasing demands for attention. She saw herself counted among those few who would take the lead in the local war effort. She would now come into the regular company of women like Mrs. Hammond and Mrs. De Mans, rich, older women whose opinions carried as much weight in Winchester as those of their well-respected husbands, and who gave sumptuous parties, rather less often in light of the war, but unsurpassed nonetheless when they did occur. She would finally take her proper place, a place to which her family's history and previous wealth entitled her. Claire smiled dreamily, imagining herself at one of these parties, being introduced by Mrs. De Mans to others as her 'indispensable right hand.' She would wear the finest dresses she could, respectful of any wartime limitations, of course, but the nicest to be had.

Evelyn broke into her reverie. "But, Claire," she started cautiously. Mildred raised her eyebrow in warning. Evelyn continued, "You're talking about a full-time commitment, and, well, you have Oliver still at home. Every organization calling for volunteers, and all the job openings for women, now... well, they're really calling for single women."

Mildred chimed in, following Evelyn's lead. "I've heard that, too. I read in the *Star* just last week that they want women with young children to stay at home, and take extra care of them while making do with less..." Mildred surreptitiously scanned the opulence around her.

Claire dismissed Mildred's words, and the obtuse glance at her furnishings, with a wave of her hand.

"Oh, you are absolutely right," Claire responded. She sighed, and leaned back in her plush, cushioned chair, looking at her cards. "That's where dear Louise comes into my plans. Remember, we discussed this at the very beginning, how we would each play an important role in the war effort." She took a deep drag off her cigarette, following the smoke with sparkling eyes as she blew out and up. "Louise has been here for three years now. She knows how to run the house, and Oliver adores her. School is over in another few days, and she can take care of everything here."

Helen glanced up from her cards. "My, what a good idea," she said, a knowing smirk crossing her face as she repositioned the cards in her hand. Helen saw Claire as her opportunity to advance socially, and was happy to ride on the coattails of Claire's plans. Mildred and Evelyn looked at each other, knowing that they'd missed something, then back at their cards.

Claire went on as she refilled her coffee. "Actually, this is a perfect opportunity for Louise, bless her heart. She isn't all that bright, you know, and she couldn't possibly do any serious charity work, or even get one of those factory jobs. Of course, she'll have to give up her little filing job with Dr. Ferguson to stay at home, but it will be her valuable contribution to the war effort, while I make the contribution that I can. It's really the best way."

Claire took another long drag off her cigarette, and lifted her eyes heavenward as she blew the smoke upward, as if she were receiving divine commendation for her sacrifices through the fumes. She then sighed and looked at her friends.

"Which means," she said, "this may be our last regular bridge game for a while. Your lead, Helen."

As the women began playing, Louise got up quietly from her seat, and made her way down the front steps. She walked quickly down the street, hot anger growing with each step. For three years she had lived under Claire's roof, lived by Claire's rules, put up with Claire's derision, her selfishness, and her overbearing narcissism. Indentured servitude had seemed an unavoidable consequence of her situation while she was in school, but school was fast coming to an end, and Louise was not required to stay at the Dix Street house if she could find another way of managing.

After a good half-hour of walking through the neighborhoods, Louise found herself in front of Dot's house. She knocked on the door, and Dot opened it, her hair in pin curls, her face slathered with an egg-white mask.

"Don't make me crack my face." Dot muttered through tight lips as she stood aside to admit her friend.

"What are you doing?"

"I have a date with Ray tonight, I want to look fabulous."

They made their way to the kitchen.

"I have sun tea and sour lemonade," said Dot through unmoving lips. "Which do you want?"

"Ugh. Why make lemonade if you don't have sugar? I'll take the tea."

Dot poured out two glasses. "Let me take this awful stuff off." She bent over the kitchen sink and rinsed off the mask, dabbing it dry with a towel. Her face clean and rosy, Dot sat with Louise at the table.

"You look like you're a little upset. Is it the wicked witch of Middlesex County again?" Dot took a sip of her tea.

"She wants me to quit my job when school ends and stay at the house full-time, cleaning and cooking and looking after Oliver. All so she can take on more volunteer duties with her ghastly friends."

Dot looked at her friend coolly. "And you don't think that's a good idea? Do you think you could do something more productive to support the war effort? What if she's right, and you staying at the house and taking care of things there really is the best way to help?"

Louise looked at her friend in disbelief.

Dot saw the expression, and placed a gentle hand on Louise's arm. "Of course you have more to offer than what Claire sees. But whatever you do, you need to look beyond this moment, beyond being angry with Claire. What do *you* want to do?"

"I don't know, really. Up until an hour ago, I hadn't thought about it—I planned to continue to work at Dr. Ferguson's, join you with more volunteer work at the Red Cross. Now, I only know that I'm irritated, and feel desperate to get away, to get out of that house and get on my own somewhere."

"Maybe this isn't the time to make big changes. After all, Mike and Ray, and almost all the other boys in our class are gone or going. Families are being pulled apart, and I suppose some of them for good." Dot paused for a moment, sipped her tea. "Those changes are big enough."

Louise buried her face in her hands. "So you think," she said, her words muffled by her hands, "that I should stay with George and Claire? I simply can't."

Dot laughed, and Louise turned her head, near tears.

"Oh, Louise, come on," Dot said through her laughter. "Nothing's that bad. If you want to get out, there are scads of jobs open for young women. As it is, I will be teaching grade school over at Ambrose Elementary. Mr. Hawkins and Mr. Post have signed up, and there are no other young men to fill in, so voilà! Mr. Jamison asked me if I would teach first and second grade at the fall term, and of course I snatched it up."

"Well, that's all well and good for you, Dot," Louise replied, an edge of bitterness flitting through. "I can see you now, elbow deep in finger paint and clay, and reading stories to all those horrid little creatures."

"So, if you really want to get out," Dot continued, ignoring Louise's disparaging comments, "you need to get a job, and something more than filing for Dr. Ferguson. Have you checked the board at the school office? Or at Town Hall? Lots of jobs posted, you just have to pick one and get to it."

"I suppose Dr. Ferguson could find a replacement," Louise said, her brows furrowed as she considered the idea of finding new work.

"And as for moving out, well, I have an idea. You get a job, and I think I can help out with a place to live. It won't be the Taj Mahal, mind you, but it would be nice enough. The place I'm thinking of is here in Winchester, though, so don't get a job in Maine or South Carolina, or you'll be on your own. What do you think?"

Louise felt a little lightheaded. This was all of a sudden serious, finding new work, moving out of George and Claire's house. As angry and desperate as she felt, the reality of it all momentarily overwhelmed her.

Dot saw her wavering.

"We have to grow up sometime, Louise, and I think we're all going to grow up a lot faster now. But we're very lucky, you know. We have each other, so we don't have to do it alone."

The following Monday afternoon, with Claire's plans and Dot's encouragement still fresh in her mind, Louise made her way over to Town Hall. She stood in front of the advertising board that now hung in the downstairs hallway across from the makeshift induction center. She perused the multitude of flyers, leaflets, and hand-printed ads that crowded the board space. It seemed that there were jobs everywhere, jobs for any young woman who wanted one, most of them at good pay. There was an ad for a salesgirl at Filene's, and several ads for office assistants. Public Safety was looking for volunteers, as was the Red Cross; further afield, in Woburn and Lexington and Boston, there were openings for machinists and mechanics, no experience necessary. There were ads for farm labor as far away as California.

Mr. Lowell came up behind her, and asked if he could help her find something.

"Oh, hello, Mr. Lowell. I don't know, maybe you can help. I'm looking for work. Seems like there are an awful lot of ads, and I'm not sure exactly where to start."

"You're Miss Duncan, aren't you? Here's an advertisement your brother posted just two days ago. Wouldn't you want to work for him?" Louise looked at the handbill. George never mentioned that he was advertising for help. She knew he had expanded his shop, and was very busy, but no more than that.

She reflected on the opportunity, then shook her head. "No, I'm casting my net further afield."

"Ah, well then, how about this one?" Mr. Lowell asked. He pulled down a square of printed paper and handed it to her. "This is close, and I know the man who owns the company, Mr. John Davenport. The hours seem fair, and the pay is the best outside of Boston."

Louise looked at the ad. 'Workers needed, ladies welcome! Assembly line work, building engines/other parts for military vehicles. Fair pay! Inquire at 26 Newcomb Street, Woburn.' Louise smiled. She knew the street, a five-minute walk from the train station in Woburn.

"Yes, I'll give this a try. Thank you, Mr. Lowell!"

Louise wasted no time. Suddenly her future shifted into motion, all she had to do was reach out and grab it.

Chapter 27

Courage in hand, Louise took the next train into Woburn. She was nervous that she might not be able to find the shop easily, but when she turned onto Newcomb Street, all doubts disappeared. A large sign reading 'DAVEN-PORT MACHINING' in large black letters stood plainly over the entrance to the building, a long, tan structure which encompassed the better part of the block.

Louise pushed through the entrance. It took her eyes a moment to adjust to the dim light of the office. Across from the entrance was a desk, where sat a plump, middle-aged woman with graying hair and soft gray eyes. A small placard placed at the front of the desk intimated that it was Mrs. Davenport seated there. Louise watched from the entryway as Mrs. Davenport handed a piece of paper to a young black woman.

"You'll start tomorrow morning, Miss Dayton. Be here at seven sharp, and we'll get you started."

Miss Dayton looked at the paper. "I'll be here, seven o'clock. Thank you, ma'am." The woman fairly flew past Louise and out the door, a huge smile on her face.

"Yes, young lady, may I help you?" asked Mrs. Davenport.

Louise approached the desk. "My name is Louise Duncan. Mr. Lowell from the Winchester Public Safety Committee suggested I call on you to see about the advertisement for help."

Mrs. Davenport looked at Louise more closely. "Yes, we need help. But you seem awfully young. How old are you, dear? Are you through with high school?"

"Yes, ma'am, I graduate this week."

Just then a man blustered in from a door along the rear wall. He was middle-aged, thick in the waist, but not quite portly, with a bit of gray at the temples of his closely cropped hair. He wore no jacket, and his tie was loosened. Rings of sweat pooled on his light blue shirt at his armpits.

"Honestly, Marge, they've moved up the due date for the Georgia order!" He dropped a stack of papers on the desk.

Mrs. Davenport turned to the man and said, sweetly, "Mr. Davenport, this is Louise Duncan from Winchester. Mr. Lowell kindly suggested she come by to see if we might have a job for her."

Mr. Davenport looked at Louise. "Oh, ayah, I just got off the phone with Jerry. That was fast, you're obviously a go-getter. Jerry says you're George Duncan's little sister. I know George, we met when he was first setting up his shop. Why don't you want to work for him? Don't tell me he's got all the help he needs." Mr. Davenport shot her an expectant look.

Louise, startled by Mr. Davenport's blunt manner, hesitated for a moment, one that seemed to hang in the air a bit too long, until Louise, feeling pressed to fill the awkward silence, offered a clumsy stab at the truth.

"Well," she finally sputtered, "no, George does need more workers. But, umm, it's just that I don't want to work for George, or rather, it's too close to home." Louise felt a tinge of guilt as she stumbled over her explanation.

"Ah," said Mr. Davenport, seeming to understand. "You want to meet some new people, learn something new about the business. Well, that's fine then, you're more than welcome aboard. Margie here, or rather, Mrs. Davenport, will take care of you. Hope you can start soon."

Turning back to his wife, he said, "Anyway, wanted you to know the new due date is the fifteenth." Without another word, he returned through the door from which he had entered, closing it behind him.

Mrs. Davenport sighed as she fingered the newly delivered paperwork. Most were change orders, some were new orders, others receipts for expenses, and on top, the most pressing, the change order for the delivery of a thousand riveted molds, now due in six weeks instead of eight. She knew they could do it, it was just a matter of getting bodies in and trained and working. They had hired four new women in the last week. They needed at least four more.

Turning her attention back to Louise, she said brightly, "Well, it seems you'll be useful! Do you think you can start next Monday? Shift starts at seven each morning, and ends at five p.m., Monday through Friday. You get a break for lunch, and sixty-five cents an hour to start. The work isn't too bad, and you'll be busy!"

Louise nodded. A nervous 'yes' came from her mouth, although a voice in her head was yelling at her, 'Wait a minute, wait, think about it first!' Too late, Louise found herself seated at a little table near Mrs. Davenport, filling out a form that asked for her name, birthdate, and address. She hesitated only a moment before putting Dot's address down instead of her own. No sense in letting Claire get her clutches on any correspondence. It was none of her business, anyway. Mrs. Davenport took a quick look at the form.

"Do you have one of those Social Security numbers, dear? You'll need one to work here."

Louise furrowed her brow in confusion. "I—I don't know what that is."

"Not to worry, a lot of people starting off at work don't have one. Here, fill out this form," Mrs. Davenport pulled a sheet of paper from her desk drawer and handed it to Louise. "You didn't always need one, you know, but now that we're working with the government, well, they're awfully fussy about it. Something about putting a bit of your wages aside so you'll have something for yourself when you're older. Usually you'd have to do this at the post office, but desperate times, you know. Just fill it out, and I can take care of everything for you."

Louise took the form and provided the few pieces of information requested.

"Everything looks fine," said Mrs. Davenport, perusing the paper when Louise returned it. "See you next Monday, Louise. We'll give you a uniform to wear, but be sure to wear a sturdy pair of shoes, and put your hair up nicely so that it doesn't fall in your face. Understand?"

"Yes, Mrs. Davenport. Thank you so much!"

Louise left the building and fairly floated back to the station. She felt jubilant—and nervous. How would she break the news to George? Looking back on the events of the last few hours, she considered that she may have acted rashly. She hadn't consulted her brother, after all, and he would be within his rights to be upset. Doubt began cloud over her triumph, but the certain knowledge that she had to get away from Claire pushed the doubt back. She had to follow through with her plans to leave the Dix Street house. Still, Louise decided she wouldn't say anything right away, at least not until school ended.

Louise caught the train back to Winchester. During the ride, she pulled a napkin and a pencil from her little purse, and tried to figure out how much she would earn. Sixty-five cents an hour, nine hours a day, five days a week—probably enough to get a place of her own, and considerably more than she was making at Dr. Ferguson's.

When she stepped off the train in downtown Winchester, she headed to Randall's. It was midafternoon, and, still heady with the boldness of what she had just done, Louise wanted to collect herself before going home. She took a booth and ordered a root beer float, and began to mull over the figures again. She wanted desperately to talk to Dot now. Perhaps she would stop at her house on the way home. Dot had intimated some prospect for living arrangements, but given no details. Louise was suddenly anxious again. What if Dot's idea didn't work out? Where would she find a place to live? People were coming from all over the place to work in Boston, and housing was in short supply.

"Louise?" Dot was suddenly sitting across from her.

"Ooh, that looks good, I'll have the same, please," Dot said to the waitress at the counter. Then to Louise, "What are you doing?"

Louise smiled at her. "I'm glad you're here, I was just thinking about you. I'm figuring out if my new job will pay enough so that I can move into a place of my own."

"Really? Did you really get a new job? Tell me about it!"

"I'll be working at Davenport's in Woburn—you know, that big machine shop where they make metal parts. I don't know what I'll be doing, I only know that I'll be making sixty-five cents an hour."

"Good heavens, Louise, you'll be rich as Croesus!"

The float arrived at the table, and Dot took a long sip, and ate a spoonful of the luxurious vanilla ice cream. She watched as Louise scribbled a few numbers on a napkin.

"Oh, Louise, don't do that! I told you I had a place for you, for both of us. Mother and Daddy have decided to rent out the upstairs bedrooms. They're going to convert the downstairs den into a bedroom for themselves, so there will be three rooms available on the second floor. Jennifer Haynes, you know her, she graduated last year—well, she took one of the rooms; but there's another room up there, the sewing room, and it's for you if you want it. Mother's moved all her sewing down to the basement, so that bedroom is empty, just waiting for you. Your furniture would fit in there nicely, and you'll have a wonderful view of the garden. She's charging thirty dollars a month, which is cheap these days. If you're serious about moving out of your brother's house, you simply must move in with us. I've already mentioned it to her, and she would love to have you take that room. Oh Louise, it would be such fun! Please say yes, and don't give anything else a second thought."

"Oh, Dot, that would be perfect! You can't possibly know how relieved I am. Yes, yes, of course I'll take it!" It seemed Providence had supplied all the components Louise needed to make her leap to independence, and as the pieces fell into place, Louise became more assured in her heart and mind that she was doing the right thing.

After the graduation ceremony on Thursday, there was a congratulatory luncheon at the Winchester Country Club, put on by the School Board, the Winchester Art Association, and the En-Ka Society, a local charitable organization. Claire made good use of the occasion, chatting with Mrs. De Mans and Mrs. Hammond when she wasn't sitting with Helen, Mildred and Evelyn, although she went out of her way to avoid Philip and Margaret Andrews. George made his way from table to table, congratulating the students, wishing them all the best of luck. He noticed that at no time did Claire look in Louise's direction, much less say a note of congratulations. In the three years that Louise had lived with them, they still took pains to keep their distance from each other. George had long ago decided it was just as well.

At dinner that night, Claire asked Louise, "So, now that you're graduated, do you have any plans for the summer?"

Louise had not planned to have this conversation quite yet, but with the question posed so directly, she answered back directly as well.

"Yes, I do."

Claire smiled, and cut off any further explanation. "I'm sure you do, dear. I have some plans too, and I'm sure we can work out a schedule that will leave you some time to yourself."

Louise smiled at Claire, and went on as if she hadn't heard her sister-in-law. "It's time I started taking care of myself. I've taken a full-time job in Woburn. I start Monday, and my shift is from seven in the morning until five at night. But you won't have to worry about my disturbing Oliver so early in the morning. I'm moving out this weekend. I spoke to Mike, and he and Ray will be over this Saturday to help me move my furniture out." Louise took a bite of her potatoes, and waited for the reaction.

She looked at George, who sat chewing his carrots quietly, an amused look on his face. He thought Claire very much resembled a codfish, her mouth dropped open in a most unladylike gape.

The stunned silence didn't last long. Claire caught the look on George's face, and her fury blew like a steam engine. For the first time since Louise had known her, Claire completely lost her icy composure. She yelled at George, "Did you know about this? You knew about this! You can't do this, you have to make her do what I tell her!"

Oliver started to cry. George opened his mouth to reply, but Claire cut him off, her voice venomous and hoarse.

"You both owe me something for what I have endured with this, this, creature in my house for the last three years!"

George stood up, and over Oliver's crying, boomed, "That's enough, Claire. No one owes you anything! Not one more word from you!"

Louise picked Oliver up from his chair and took him out of the dining room into the kitchen.

"We'll just step in here for a minute, sweetie, and dry your eyes."

Louise sat the child on the kitchen counter. She washed his face, and spoke soothingly to him. It was as much an effort to soothe herself, as she found she was shaking, and feeling a little dizzy. After a few minutes, the irate conversation that had ensued in the dining room died down. Oliver hiccupped, and yawned.

"Oh, now, there's a good boy. Let's go finish dinner, and I'll read you a story and tuck you into bed." She paused for a moment, looking at her little nephew.

"I suppose you'll be all right without me," and here she hugged him, "but I'm sorry for it, and I'll miss you. I promise to come see you as often as I can." Louise felt tears well up, but kept them in check. There was no sense in upsetting him all over again.

Back in the dining room, Louise found that only George remained at the table, calmly eating his dinner.

"So, tell me about your new job," he said, "and where you will live, and what your plans are." He smiled. "And don't worry about Claire. She's got enough problems of her own without making any for you. She can bluster away if she wants to, but she'll be fine—if there's one thing I've learned, Claire knows how to take care of herself."

That weekend, George worked alongside Mike and Ray to move Louise to the upstairs bedroom at Dot's house, six blocks down the road, and light years away from Claire's clutches. George put down the first month's rent so that Louise wouldn't have to dig it out of her savings. As they placed the last box of clothes in her room, George took Louise aside.

"Louise, now that you're out on your own, I want to talk to you about something. It won't take long, but," he hesitated, "let's step out onto the back porch for a moment." Louise nodded.

The group headed downstairs, and at the landing, George said to Mike and Ray, "Excuse us, gentlemen, I just need a moment with Louise, she'll be right back."

George leaned over the porch rail, while Louise sat in an old rocker that Mrs. Humphrey put outside on fine days.

"Louise, first of all, I want to apologize. I think I didn't realize how difficult the last three years have been for you, living with Claire. I want you to know that there was no other way, you couldn't stay in the old house by yourself...but perhaps I could have been more aware, maybe helped manage your situation a little better."

Louise shrugged. "Claire was always a certain way with you. I just thought you couldn't see the full picture. It doesn't matter, I'm here now, I have a new job."

"Yes, and that brings me to my second apology. I sold our house, the one on Pembroke Road, as you know. And I think you know that you were due to inherit that house, or at least proceeds from the sale. What you don't know is that I used some of that money to cover business expenses when times were tough, and then, last August, well, I found that there was no money left." Louise was silent, her lips pressed together. George continued.

"However, with the war, business has been very, very good, and I have the money now to repay you, to give you your inheritance, plus some interest. It amounts to just over four thousand dollars. I've set it aside for you. So, I wanted to tell you, and ask you what you want to do with it."

Louise looked up at her brother, the shock evident on her face.

"Louise, are you okay? Should I get you a glass of water?"

"No, no...I'm not sure...did you say *four thousand dollars*?"

George nodded.

"What am I going to do with that much money? I can barely fathom sixty-five cents an hour."

George laughed. "Well, I'll tell you—you can do everything, or you can do nothing. You can invest it, or buy property, although I think I'd have to help you with either of those. You can put it in a savings account and let it earn interest."

"I don't know, George, it's too much to think about all at once. Will you hold it for me until I have a chance to decide?"

"Absolutely—but I want you to know, it's set aside in a separate account, and the only two people on the account are you and me. It's over at Winchester National. Think about it. We can talk about it some more after you've had some time."

George looked out over Mrs. Humphrey's garden. "This really is beautiful. What a fine day. And I'm happy for you, Louise. I think you're very brave to strike out on your own, I'm very proud of you. Now, I think Mike is waiting to take you to lunch, so I'm going to head back to the house. We'll keep in touch."

Louise stood up and gave her brother a hug. "Of course! I'll miss you, George, and I'll miss Oliver, but I'm still close by, and we'll visit."

"Wouldn't have it any other way."

Chapter 28

Mike felt a little shaky. He was more excited than anxious, really, but he wanted this part to be over, so he could prepare for the business that lay ahead, the business of training and fighting. He and Ray stood in line outside Town Hall, waiting their turn to sign up, to take on American enemies, to save the world. They joked a little back and forth, keeping the tension at bay.

"Where are Henry and Walter?" Ray asked. "I thought we were all going to do this together?"

"Walter came in with his dad earlier this morning, and I think Henry came in with them. That's okay, we're all still going to meet at Walter's house tonight. I guess Mrs. Hannigan is going to put on quite a spread for us."

"She's a good cook," Ray agreed. Then he asked, "So, what are you and Louise going to do? Does she know you're signing up today?"

Mike nodded. "She knows. We're going to wait until I get back, you know, do everything right. We'll write to each other, of course, and I'll visit whenever I'm on leave. But we talked about it, and she'll wait for me."

Ray looked at his friend, trying to read the expression on his face. Deciding everything was okay, he slapped Mike on the back. "That's swell, Mike!

Anyone can see you two are meant to be together. She's a looker, and really nice. You lucky dog." Mike cracked a smile back. He knew he was lucky.

"You and Dot are doing well, too, aren't you? Everyone can tell the two of you are really close, a great couple already. She'll wait for you, right?"

"Uh-huh, we worked it all out. Hey, Mike, you should be my best man—will you do that for me?" Ray elbowed his friend in the ribs.

"Wait a second, what do you mean? You're not getting married now, are you?" Mike's voice broke over into a near panic.

"No, not now, later, when we get back. Geez, Mike, you should see the look on your face. You'd think I'd said I was going to eat a bowl of bugs or something."

"Hey, I just don't want anyone I know setting an example that I'm not ready to follow right now. But, sure, Ray, when we get back, I'd be honored to be your best man."

The line moved forward, and it was their turn. Entering Town Hall, they made their way downstairs to the basement, where the converted offices housed the Winchester Recruitment and Induction Center. Middle-aged men, representing the Army, Navy, and Air Force, dressed in sharp, crisp uniforms, sat or stood at tables squeezed into the space. There were a lot of young men in the room, most of them freshly graduated from high school, and the chatter was high as neighbors and friends talked to each other when they weren't filling out forms or talking to the military representatives. Finally, the paperwork was completed, and with a signature and a handshake, Mike and Ray officially joined the United States Army.

They stepped out of Town Hall, passing others just going in. Mike thought the air seemed crisper, the sun brighter, sounds sharper. The shakiness had passed, relief replacing any anxiety he'd felt. He and Ray made their way to Randall's to grab a bite to eat, but it was hard to sit still. The two young men threw questions at each other, trying to anticipate the future.

"How long do you think before we're called up?" asked Mike.

"Soon, I think. A week or two, maybe. Where do you think they'll send us for training?"

"Don't know—could be anywhere. Do you think they'll keep us together?"

"That would be great, but I doubt it. We'll see. I hope we can go through basic training together, at least."

"I hope so, too," said Mike.

From the diner window, Ray saw Walter walking by on the other side of the street.

"Hey, there's Walter!" he exclaimed as he scrambled to the diner door, calling out to his friend to come join them. Walter jogged across the street, and sat with them at the booth. The waitress came by, took his order for a sandwich and soda.

"So, how'd it go?" asked Ray. "Which service are you in?"

Walter looked at his friends, and then down at the table, shaking his head.

"Actually, I didn't make it. My dad brought me in this morning, showed the Army reps a letter from Dr. Murray. The polio disqualifies me, or rather, not being able to lift my left arm up disqualifies me. So they sent me upstairs to Public Safety. I'll be working with them. They'll train me to conduct air raid drills, check blackout curtains, kill spies—you know, that sort of thing." Walter tried to make a joke out of it, but his disappointment was obvious. "Although I'm awful jealous of the two of you."

Mike turned to him. "Geez, Walter, I'm truly sorry. You'd be an ace up the sleeve for us. But if there's anyone I'd want protecting my family and my neighborhood it's you. You've always been a straight arrow."

Ray changed the subject. "How is it to have your dad home, now?"

"Great, great, you know he's the best. Mom's happy he's home, and Patrick and Daniel are always bugging him to play catch or go to a movie."

Walter kept to himself the doubts and frustrations that seemed to be closing in on him. At first, he'd been happy when the company called his father home for the duration of the war, but it didn't take long before the friction between the two of them began to surface. Walter had a routine, a list of duties he fulfilled when his dad was on the road. In truth, as Walter got older, he began to despair a bit when his dad rolled in on Friday afternoons, feeling relief when he pulled away in his shiny Hudson on Monday mornings. But now—well, now his father was there every day, asserting his dominance, not overtly, but quietly and consistently...

'Walter, take the trash out.'

'Walter, did you pick up the groceries for your mother? Better hop to it, son.'

'Walter, Mrs. Livingston needs her lawn edged.'

These were all tasks that Walter knew had to be done, and which he scheduled into his week, but his dad insisted things be done instantly. Walter didn't want to fight with his dad, and didn't want to upset his mother. He couldn't help but believe that the military would have been a graceful way of escaping the increasing oppression that he felt. But at his medical exam that morning, the doctor had told him, in no uncertain terms, that he could not serve with his left arm mobility so limited. The examining doctor must have seen the frustration on his face.

"Look, son," the doctor said in a consoling tone, "I know you're disappointed. So am I, we need young men like you. But you have to believe that you are perfectly fit to serve right here at home. Why don't you check in with Public Safety? They've moved upstairs, they're on the second floor now. Go on up, ask for Mr. Lowell. Tell him I sent you. He'll find a good spot for you." And with that, Walter climbed up from the basement to the second floor of Town Hall.

An hour later, he walked out of Town Hall with a training schedule and assignment forms in his hand. He felt better, but he knew it wouldn't be enough. This was a volunteer position, and he felt a sharp desire to get out of the house, to be on his own. He would need a paying job.

"Did Henry come with you this morning? What happened with him?" Mike asked through a mouthful of grilled cheese sandwich.

"He came in with us. It was really strange. Dad talked to the officer about me first, gave him the note from Dr. Murray. Then he disappeared with Henry. They went into a separate office. I saw a couple of men in uniform in there, but then the door closed, and I didn't see them again. But I know he's coming to dinner tonight, I'm sure we'll find out then."

Chapter 29

As Walter, Ray and Mike sat discussing that evening's dinner, Henry Smith stepped out of Town Hall onto the sidewalk, and into the bright, brisk light of day. He stood there for a moment, then turned right, and made his way around to the back of Town Hall. From there he crossed the cool expanse of lawn that led to the stone steps of the library. He went up, and then inside, where he picked out a book about farming, and sat in an isolated chair on the second floor, the book in his lap, his eyes unfocused.

Henry's entry into the armed forces had been an entirely different experience from that of his friends. When Walter's father ushered him into the office that morning, apart from all the other young men signing up, he became nervous. Something was wrong, and he washed over with fear that this was it, this was where his ancestry would become a falling sword of Damocles, where he would be shut into a prison for the duration of the war, maybe forever.

Mr. Hannigan had introduced Henry to the officers, and invited Henry to have a seat. The younger officer was introduced as Lieutenant Williams, a rigid young man, who spoke very little, and moved out of his firmly placed stance behind his superior officer even less. The older officer, Major Branson, was a well-muscled graying man in his fifties. Sitting behind the small desk, Branson did his best to put Henry at ease.

"Son, you look like you've seen a ghost. Don't worry, you're not in any trouble. But Mr. Hannigan here has told us a little bit about you, and we'd like to talk to you for a few minutes, ask you a few questions. Would that be all right with you?" Henry looked back at Mr. Hannigan, who had taken a seat behind him against the rear wall of the room. Joe Hannigan nodded at him.

Turning back to the officer, Henry said, "Yes, sir, that's okay."

And so it began. The first interview took just over an hour. Major Branson asked simple questions at first: where was Henry born, what was his favorite subject in school, what were his hobbies. The questions soon moved to more in-depth topics, and with these, Henry had a better feel for what was going on.

"Henry, do you speak German?"

"Yes, I can speak German, but at home we speak English, so I don't get much practice."

"Tell me how your parents came to America, Henry. Do you know how they came here?"

"My father and mother were both raised in Meissen after the war. My father lived with his parents, my mother lived with her aunt and uncle. My father's parents and my mother's aunt and uncle each owned bakeries, and they were rivals. My parents fell in love, and got married, but none of the relatives in Meissen accepted the marriage. So, my parents came to America. Now my father works at Winchester National Bank."

"Have you ever been to Germany, Henry? Maybe to visit your grandparents or see the country?"

"No. I've never met my grandparents, although I've seen pictures of them. Never been further from Winchester than Boston."

The train of questions continued. Henry was on guard, but in fact, there was nothing to hide. Finally, Major Branson closed the folder in front of him.

"Well, everything seems to be in order. Why don't we take a little break, and then Henry, if you don't mind, we'd like to give you a little test—nothing too strenuous, just a brief exam, which Lieutenant Williams here will administer. What do you say?"

"I don't understand. Why am I not out in the other room with everyone else?"

Joe Hannigan chimed in. Henry had forgotten he was there, and jumped when his voice came from behind.

"Henry, I want to assure you that the interview and test are simply a way of making sure your placement in the military serves the best interests of everyone, including you. I know you want that, I know that's why you showed up today. Take the test, Henry. It'll be all right."

Two hours later, Henry was back in the chair in the office, sitting across from Major Branson. This time they were alone in the room.

"Henry, I want to thank you for your cooperation today. I know it was an unusual experience, but you handled everything very well. Lieutenant Williams has given me the results of your test. What did you think of it?"

Henry shrugged. "It was challenging, but not too bad."

"No, not too bad for someone with an IQ of..." The major looked at the papers in front of him. "...an IQ of 168." Major Branson set the papers aside.

"Henry, we have a special place for you, if you'd like to consider serving your country in a unique position. Now, consider yourself signed up, either way. But I'm offering you stateside work, nice accommodations, top-end privileges once you've gotten some time and experience under your belt. What do you think?"

"What kind of work?" Henry asked. He was getting tired, his nerves frayed by the long interview, the long exam, the little cat-and-mouse game that seemed to be going on.

"Unfortunately, Henry, I can't give you details. I can tell you that it's good work at good pay, a situation that would require your apparently suitable brain-power. I'll tell you what. You think about it tonight. Go home, have a good night's rest, come back here tomorrow at, say, nine o'clock, and let me know your answer."

Henry nodded. He wanted to get out of this little office, out of the Town Hall basement, out into the fresh air.

"But, uh, one little thing before you go, Henry. It's better if you don't say anything about your experience today—not to your folks, not to your friends, not to anyone. If anyone asks, just say that you signed up, which is the truth. Understand?"

Henry looked at Major Branson, looked straight into his eyes, and weighed out the activities he'd experienced that day. The separate interview, the test, the offer of a different kind of service from that of his friends, all rolled around for a moment in his head, and then they fell into place. Henry understood, perhaps more than Major Branson intended. Henry would be useful in the intelligence sector. That was the obvious conclusion. But Henry saw a bigger picture, one where he might be in a position to protect his parents, his uncle Eric, perhaps even help his friends.

Henry nodded. "I understand. I just signed up today."

The major stood up and extended his hand across the desk. "Nine tomorrow morning, then."

Henry took his hand, returning the firm handshake. "Yes, sir."

Chapter 30

Walter, Mike and Ray stepped out of Randall's Diner. It was just before noon, and the bright, cool morning had given way to a bright, temperate day. With a confirmation that they would all meet together again at his house that evening, Walter left his friends, claiming an errand for his mother. In truth, he just needed to think a bit. His friends were going away, and he would be left behind. There had to be something else he could do besides make sure blackout curtains were drawn and everyone obeyed curfew.

Walter walked downtown, looking into the shop windows as he passed by. Each storefront displayed advertisements for various fundraisers, posters encouraging passersby to support the war effort, to participate in an upcoming metal drive, to buy war bonds.

On Church Street, he stopped in front of the *Winchester Star*. While the newspaper was housed on the second floor, the first floor was a general store, which carried a wide selection of useful sundries. Notepaper, toys, tennis balls and garden supplies, and a hundred other diverse items lined the shelves or filled bins and baskets.

Walter walked in to see if they had anything on hand that would help him fulfill his new assignments, perhaps a pocket calendar so he could track his training and work schedule. He perused the shelves, and found them oddly barren, or rather, filled with a different stock. Pamphlets on growing and canning vegetables replaced kites, and flags of all sizes filled the bin where rakes used to stand. A shelf previously devoted to children's toys now held hurricane lamps. Walter noticed that the toys now sat jumbled together in a large basket on the floor.

Mrs. Wallace, sitting on a stool at the register counter, looked up from her newspaper, peering over the top to observe the young Walter Hannigan.

"Did you sign up yet?" she asked.

Walter looked between the shelves, over the blackout curtains and pamphlets. Finding Mrs. Wallace's sharp blue eyes, he replied simply, "I tried. They said I couldn't because of my arm."

Mrs. Wallace prodded. "So what will you do with yourself?"

Walter thumbed through a pamphlet entitled *Victory Meal Planner*. 'Victory Dinner I' included a recipe for a tuna fish loaf with horseradish sauce. Walter thought about what that really was, and decided he hated the war already.

"I picked up an assignment with Public Safety," Walter replied, pushing the pamphlet aside and picking up a small calendar. "I'll be working with them, whatever they tell me to do. But I think it's only a few hours a day, or really, probably mostly at night. I'll need to do something else the rest of the time."

Mrs. Wallace looked back at her paper. "Why don't you run up the back stairs and see if Mr. Wallace could use you."

At the top of the stairs Walter found a short hallway. At one end he saw the printing room, the old typesetting machine gleaming from behind reams of unprinted newspaper. At the other end was the open wooden door leading into the office of the *Winchester Star*. Walter felt a little nervous, and attempted to creep stealthily toward the office door, an attempt he abandoned almost immediately as the old wooden floor protested at the slightest pressure with alarming creaks and groans.

Walter stopped at the doorway and looked into the office. Sanded wood flooring, whitewashed walls, and sturdy metal desks with chairs on rollers served as the cog room for the *Winchester Star*. Two walls held articles, highlights of just over sixty years of local news, captured in frames, most of the papers yellowed under the glass. At one end of the room a large grandfather clock stood at attention, and chimed the half-hour. At the opposite end, a solitary, unreadable document hung on the wall, askew; and beneath this, sitting at the largest desk, was Mr. Hamish J. Wallace himself, a large, brawny man, with dark ginger hair and thick fingers, and a cigar stub clenched between his teeth, unlit. He was intent on the work in front of him, scribbling wildly at a piece of paper. Walter knocked on the doorjamb.

"What?" Mr. Wallace asked, his voice gruff. He looked up at the lanky young man darkening his office door, and then returned his attention to the paper on his desk.

"Mrs. Wallace said come up," said Walter.

"Oh, she did, did she?" He peered up for another second, taking in the face and stature of the young man in a single glance, and returned again, with diligence, to his task. "You're little Walter Hannigan, aren't you? Well, not so little now, huh? Want a job, do you? You wrote for the High School paper, *The Recorder*, didn't you? Can you still write? Can you type?"

Walter nodded. "Yes, sir."

"Well, let's give you a try. God knows, I need the help and beggars can't be too choosy. See those desks with those papers piled on 'em? Those papers are the unusable notes of the men who used to work here. Sort 'em out, and stack up anything you think might go into next week's paper. Then write up a few stories from the notes. You know what the paper looks like, bright young man like you can figure it out. There's a typewriter on that desk you can use. Get as much decent copy as you can to me by three p.m." Walter glanced at the clock. It was just past twelve-thirty.

"Yes sir," he said, and set to work.

Each desk was covered with papers in various states of disarray. He collected the papers, piled them up onto one desk, and started to sort through them. Four items meant nothing to him, and he discarded these, along with two drafts for old news from the previous week. But there were several items that Walter thought would work—fourteen meeting notices, two notices of accidents from the previous day, one obituary, and one engagement announcement. There were two full story items, one about Roosevelt, another about rationing.

The notices were easy. He'd read them hundreds of times growing up, and they were always the same. Walter put together the few lines needed to inform readers about a meeting at the Winchester Country Club, at the Rotary Club, a change in choir practice at the Unitarian Church. The obituary was harder. Walter knew the man, Mr. Breen, who owned the grocery store on Skillings Road. He had been nice to the Hannigan boys, handing out suckers to each of them whenever they went in for a loaf of bread or bag of sugar. Walter didn't know he'd passed until he read it in the draft: 'Mr. Frederick Breen, heart attack, age seventy-two.'

"Aw, hell," he muttered under his breath, and rewrote the copy, adding a few lines about Mr. Breen's kindness to his customers and his generosity to those in need.

He didn't know the girl who got engaged. She was two years older than he, so they may have crossed paths at school, but he doubted it. The head-shot that accompanied the announcement showed a round-faced, dewy-eyed young woman, her dark hair swept up softly away from her face. He knew the man she was marrying, though. He was a rough-and-tumble kind of guy, had been a fullback for the Winchester High School Varsity team. Walter had watched him play a few times, had watched him shoot the pigskin into the air to a teammate, a great throw, only to have it intercepted. Walter could only wonder at how they were getting married, as the rough-and-tumble football player was surely already enlisted.

He arrived at the drafted article on Roosevelt, 'that man in the White House,' as Mr. Wallace would say in his most disparaging tones. Walter scanned the piece, compared the draft with the accompanying notes to be sure everything matched up, made several edits, and finally, in desperation, rewrote the entire article. He set it aside. It was one-thirty, and he was hungry. His stomach growled. One last article remained, the one on rationing. The previous newsman had scribbled a dozen incoherent notes on his pad of paper. Walter would have to do more than rewrite a draft here, he would have to do the write-up properly, from scratch.

A ham sandwich and a ginger ale appeared in front of him.

"Eat, I can hear your stomach from across the room." Mr. Wallace walked back to his desk, and Walter inhaled the sandwich and swallowed half the soda before he looked again at the cryptic scrawls.

"No way around it," he muttered. He got up. "Mr. Wallace, to do this story I need to head over to the Public Safety office."

Mr. Wallace grunted, his head buried in a stack of papers.

Walter made his way to Town Hall, and for the second time that day took the stairs to the second floor. He asked for Jerry Lowell again, and explained what he needed.

"Working for the *Star,* are you? That could be very helpful, we always have announcements." Mr. Lowell smiled. Walter was young and enthusiastic, and his 4F status meant he had something to prove. Jerry would make good use of those attributes. He handed Walter several flyers, each of which gave pointed information about one war-related topic or another—sugar rationing, war bonds, vegetable gardening, which scrap metals should be saved. He then handed Walter a series of booklets containing recipes and helpful hints for wartime, products of the War Food Administration.

"You can print sections of these in the *Star,*" he said. "It will help our ladies at home with cooking ideas, provide information about the best fruits and vegetables to grow in their allotments, and help them make do with less in general."

Walter hurried back to the *Star* office. He had an hour left to pound out this last story, and clear away the vestiges of a man who left this work behind to answer another call. At ten minutes of three, Walter laid the stack of articles on Mr. Wallace's desk, and waited. Mr. Wallace picked up the pile, and thumbed through the papers. He pursed his lips at Mr. Breen's obituary.

"I get the feeling you liked Mr. Breen," he said, out of the corner of his cigar-laden mouth. "It's long, though, for what it is. Don't forget, everything that goes into the *Star* has to be typeset by hand—by me, by myself now, although I'll train you if you work out. Anyway, we have a policy here—don't get fussy. Keep things simple, I don't print any of those sensationalist headliners you'll see in papers from Boston or New York."

He glanced through the article on Roosevelt, and set it aside. He turned last to the article on rationing, and read it through from start to finish. He put the copy down and looked at Walter, the cigar still between his teeth as he spoke. "I can tell what's yours. It looks good. You'll do." Mr. Wallace stood up and shook Walter's hand. "Be back at nine tomorrow. You get eighteen a week, plus a bonus for specials. You'll see. Now get out, you're done for the day."

Chapter 31

A light step carried Walter as he headed home. So much had happened in one day—refused by the military, but welcomed to serve with the Winchester Public Safety Committee, doing necessary work. Then, as a stroke of chance, hired at the *Winchester Star*, making money doing something he liked, something he knew. He felt good about the steps he'd taken to volunteer, and the good fortune that would move him toward independence.

"Walter, is that you?" Rose called from the kitchen as he walked in the door.

Joe, sitting at the dining room table poring over papers, followed up, "Better check in with your mother, son, she wants your help."

Walter responded, "Yes, sir," and then, in the direction of the kitchen, "Coming, Mom!" He hesitated a moment. He wanted to ask his father about that morning, about what happened to Henry, and tell him about his assignment with Public Safety, and about the *Star*. A quick glance from his father prompted him to make his way to the kitchen without any further conversation. It would have to wait, perhaps indefinitely.

Rose was drying her hands on her apron as Walter walked into the kitchen. "Oh, good, I'm so glad you're finally home. I was beginning to worry!"

She looked at her son. She knew Joe had made arrangements for him to work for Public Safety, and was deeply comforted that he would stay home.

"Everything all right?" she asked.

He nodded, "Yes, a lot happened, but it was a great day."

She smiled at him. "Well, I hope you have a little energy left. I need some help in Christine's room. Daniel's going to move in there tomorrow, and I need help cleaning some things up and moving furniture around."

Walter raised his eyebrows. Rose saw the look, and answered it.

"Yes, it's time. Daniel should have his own room, and, well, three years is long enough. And you can tell me all about your day while we work." As an afterthought, she added, "And then I need you to help me get ready for dinner tonight—we'll have quite a full house, I think!"

Walter and Rose emptied drawers, shifted furniture, put new sheets and covers on the bed. He told her about his volunteer work with the Safety Committee, and about his new job at the *Star*.

"Well, Walter, you really have had a busy day!" she exclaimed. Then, more quietly, "Does your father know about the newspaper?"

"No, I haven't had a chance."

"Well, I think it'll be a perfect announcement at dinner. I'm very proud of you, Walter."

She stood up from filling a box. She reached out to give Walter's shoulder a reassuring pat, and suddenly realized he was taller than she was, by several inches.

"You're really all grown up, and soon you'll be on your own. I hope you'll stay close to home, I don't want to miss you too much." Rose sighed, and went on. "Now let's finish this up, I've done most of the work for dinner already, but the table needs setting, and I need to get a few things warmed up in the oven."

They finished boxing up Christine's clothes and toys, donations for the Red Cross. The exceptions to these were Christine's christening gown and her little gold cross necklace, which Rose wrapped together in tissue paper and placed carefully in a small wooden box, which she tucked away on the closet shelf; and the picture little Christine Hannigan drew on her last full day of life, a childish rendering of a horse in a grassy field below a bright yellow sun and rainbow, which Rose framed and hung in the upstairs hallway for remembrance.

Walter and his father pulled the dining table apart, placing two leaves in the center. Extra chairs from the kitchen and den filled in the new space. Mismatched chairs aside, when all the services were set out, the table was quite impressive. Rose had insisted on using the good china and silver plate, and set a low arrangement of hydrangeas, lilacs and roses, freshly cut from her garden, in the center of the table.

A half-hour before the guests were due to arrive, Rose called her three boys into the kitchen.

"Now, boys, this is a very special dinner, and I want you all on your best behavior! No shaking knees under the table, and for heaven's sake, don't shovel your food in. Chew with your mouths closed, say 'please' and 'thank you,' and use your napkins properly. And Patrick, for heaven's sake, don't eat with your knife. Use your fork, you're a big boy now. Everyone understand?"

Heads bobbed in vigorous assent.

"That's fine, then. Daniel, put the salt cellars at either end of the table, and Patrick, I want you to run upstairs and change your shirt, and then both of you wash your hands and faces. Go on, now, get going. I want you to look nice!"

Rose had made one of her specialties, Shepherd's Pie, two large pans filled to the brim with ground round of beef, tender carrots, and young sweet peas, all swimming in a rich beef broth, and topped with mounds of freshly mashed potatoes. Rose and Amelia had combined their allotment of sugar, and Rose made a special dessert for the group, a three-layer chocolate cake with a whipped buttercream frosting.

Beth and Amelia arrived first, each bearing a large pitcher of cold punch, a concoction of ginger ale, corn syrup, and orange extract, a recipe Amelia had found in an issue of *Good Housekeeping*. Walter and Beth grabbed a baseball and mitts and headed out to the back yard, pitching the ball against the house, trying to catch it before it landed in the garden beds. Mike, Ray and Henry arrived together. Henry stopped to talk for a moment to Mr. Hannigan, while Mike and Ray headed out to the back porch.

"Hey Walter, hey Beth!" called Ray.

"Hi back!" Beth pitched a hard ball, and it flew back neatly into her mitt.

Mike called out, "Hey, Walter, Henry's inside talking to your dad. He wouldn't tell us what happened to him this morning. Did you find out anything?"

"No, I've been busy, haven't talked to anyone since we left the diner. Actually—" Walter stopped mid-sentence to run to the back of the yard to catch a pop-up fly. "Actually," he continued as he walked toward the porch, "I'll be working days at the *Star* for Mr. Wallace. I get paid and everything."

Ray nodded in approbation. Walter was a serious young man, and Ray was glad to hear that his friend would be at home, and with prospects.

"Should we go in?" Walter asked. "Mom's been working all day on the dinner."

"I think so," replied Ray. "It smells wonderful in there, and I saw the cake sitting on the sideboard. Your mom is such a good cook, Walter. It was swell of her to invite us over."

Beth followed Walter, Mike and Ray into the house. The two great pans of Shepherd's Pie sat on trivets on the table, along with two large bowls of extra mashed potatoes, and plates of sliced tomatoes, the first of the season. Glasses, already filled with Amelia's punch, sat at each place setting. The chocolate cake and a plate loaded with oatmeal cookies were placed invitingly on the sideboard. The Hannigan dining room was filled with laughter and excited conversation as everyone eyed the mounds of food, figured out where they were supposed to sit, caught up with each other about the day's events. Joe tapped his glass with his fork, and everyone quieted.

Joe bowed his head. Not normally given to prayer, he recited an old invocation he remembered his father said at Christmas Eve dinner and on Easter Sunday:

"We thank you, Lord, for the many blessings of this day, known or unknown, great or small, temporal or spiritual. Amen."

"Amen," resounded through the room. Rose and Amelia dished out the Shepherd's Pie, and the boys fell to eating as though it were the first meal they'd had all day.

"Walter," asked Rose, "did you tell your father your exciting news?"

"Not yet," he replied, mouth full.

"What happened at the Town Hall when everyone signed up this morning?" asked Amelia. "Ray, which service did you join?"

Ray made the polite attempt to swallow at least some of the food in his mouth before answering.

The Lights of Pembroke Road

"Army. Mike too. We joined together."

"Well, I think that's just wonderful. Mike, did they tell you where you would do your basic training?"

Mike didn't answer right away. He'd been looking around the table as he ate, and his eyes had lingered just a bit on Beth. Baseball or not, Beth had changed somehow. Her hair was different, pulled back in a new style; her freckles had disappeared, and her figure, well, her figure had somehow softened.

"Mike?" Amelia asked again.

"Oh, sorry Mrs. Crowley. No, they didn't really tell us very much, other than it would be about two weeks before we shipped out."

Amelia continued with her questions, her way of keeping the conversation going.

"And Henry, what service did you join?"

Henry looked up from his plate, wide-eyed. "Oh, the Army, of course. Mrs. Hannigan, this is the best casserole like this I've ever tasted." Then, as an afterthought, "Don't tell my mother."

Rose laughed. Her house was full, at least one last time, with the young people that had been a part of her children's lives since they moved to Winchester.

Joe Hannigan chimed in now. "Beth, I heard you've taken on some serious volunteer work."

Amelia nodded to her daughter.

"Yes, I'm very lucky. I'll be working with Mrs. De Mans and Mrs. Jamison, helping them at the Red Cross. I think it's going to be exciting work, and I hope I get to make a difference."

"I have no doubt you will make a very important difference. Winchester is very lucky to have such dedicated volunteers."

Joe Hannigan continued, "Now, what's this news you have to share, Walter?"

Walter was caught between mouthfuls of food, his fork in mid-air, ready to shovel in the next mound. He finished chewing and swallowed. Everyone was quiet, waiting for his response.

"Ah, well, you know I'm assigned with Public Safety—I'll be helping with whatever is needed here in town. I also stopped by the *Star*. Mr. Wallace hired me to help with the paper. I already started today." Walter looked around the table, finally meeting his father's gaze.

Amelia Crowley chimed in, breaking the silence. "Why, Walter, that's wonderful news! You can keep us informed about all the goings-on, everything we need to know."

In a cacophony of approval, Walter's friends offered their congratulations. Rose looked at Joe, waiting to see his response. Joe nodded his head approvingly.

As the boys quieted down, Joe said, "Well, son, I'm very proud of you. You're going to be a busy young man in town. We'll have to get Patrick and Danny here to take over your chores. See me, boys, after dinner, and we'll sort this out. In the meantime, I'd like to propose a toast."

The assembly raised their glasses.

Joe continued, "To our young men, may God bless you and keep you during this difficult time."

"Yes, God bless you all," Amelia echoed.

After the dinner was finished, and the chocolate cake consumed down to the last crumb, the young guests took their leave. Rose sent each of the boys home with a packet of oatmeal cookies to snack on later. Amelia stayed for a while to help clean up, and then she and Beth left also, crossing the street with a plate of food for Hazel, who had stayed home with a summer cold.

Joe sat at the kitchen table while Rose finished drying the last of the dishes. The boys were upstairs, getting ready for bed.

"What happened with Henry, today?" she asked. "He seemed so quiet at dinner, and a little evasive. Did something happen to him? I saw him talking to you."

Joe didn't like to keep too many secrets from his wife. The affairs didn't matter, she didn't need to know about them. But Henry's situation was different. Joe didn't know the details, but he knew Henry's work would be classified. Joe decided it was time to draw the line he would have to draw sooner or later. His work with the Boston arm of the Office of Civil Defense was becoming increasingly sensitive, and he was privy to more information about his neighbors and friends than he ever wanted to know.

"Rose," he started. She looked at him. "Things are different now. Working with OCD limits what I can share with you. Suffice to say, Henry will be fine. But I want you to know I won't be able to answer the questions you have, and it might be easier for both of us if you didn't ask."

Rose put the last plates away in the cupboard.

"I understand," was her only response. They had grown apart in the last several years, and it seemed to her that even though he was home now, the war would maintain the barrier between them. Maybe it was just as well. Rose had already determined to continue her life as she had built it without him. No need to muck things up.

Chapter 32

Claire watched from the front porch as Mike lifted the last box onto the back of the truck. Louise really didn't have that much. Mike and Ray helped George muscle down her few bits of furniture: a single bed, a small dresser, a desk and chair. Books, clothes, and a few bits of junk from the old house filled three boxes and a small trunk. Within an hour's time everything was loaded up, and then Louise was gone, as though she'd never been there.

Claire went back into the house, and sat with Oliver in the living room as he played with his trucks. There just had to be a way she could move forward with her plans. She certainly wasn't going to let Louise's actions interfere. It was true, her move would make things more challenging, and for that, Claire would make sure Louise paid dearly. But not now. She could bide her time where Louise was concerned. Claire had other things to arrange first.

It wouldn't be easy. George had tightened the reins at the bank, and put her on an allowance—enough for groceries and a few sundry items, but not much more. No new dresses, no new shoes, no new anything. Claire could just about work with that, at least for the time being. Wearing the same clothes, remaking last season's dresses, made one patriotic rather than out of fashion. But with Louise's departure, George had also cut Claire off from the Country Club, the Fortnightly Club, and the Home and Garden Association. He made it clear she could volunteer three hours a week at the Red Cross when Ruth was there to clean and help with Oliver. Aside from that, George expected she would stay home and take care of their son.

Initially, she pleaded to hire help in several days a week, making the case that the local war effort needed her, that she could be useful, that she could make a difference. But George, still smarting from the revelations of the previous August, stood firm.

Claire's frustration was magnified by the knowledge that George's business was now flourishing. He had contracts to supply several manufacturing concerns in the region; and more lucrative contracts to provide supplies directly to the federal government. He bought the parcel of land next to his shop, and twice expanded the building to accommodate the increase in business. He hired and trained fourteen women, and they were producing rivets and washers, nuts and bolts, and dozens of other small metal parts at a furious pace, shipping them out as fast as they could be made.

Claire knew the money was rolling in. Of course, some of it rolled out again to keep the business running. But the bulk of the income was filling George's bank account. In addition to the untouchable wealth, George was becoming more important in the community, more important than Claire ever envisioned. He had been approached to serve on the Board of Selectmen, a powerful position, not just in the Town of Winchester, but in Middlesex County, as Winchester was taking the lead in supporting the war effort, making decisions that other towns in the County, and beyond, emulated.

Most pressing upon Claire's mind was her promise to assist Mrs. De Mans. If she reneged, she would be displaced from the great lady's society, no matter what the reason. Claire sat for a few more minutes, fuming about George's spitefulness. After all, she'd given up her little affair with Philip Andrews. Philip had completed his term as Selectman, and it was really his place that George would fill on the Board. George would need Claire's support if he accepted the position, but he seemed oblivious to this fact, digging his heels in on the limitations, both financial and social, he had imposed. George's support of Louise's move, and of her working for a competitor, no less, was the last straw. It was all so frustrating. There just had to be a way to make things right.

She thought briefly about asking her parents to help with Oliver, but Claire knew they could barely afford to help themselves. They still had their house in Boston, which they owned outright, but struggled to pay the taxes. Claire's father had finally taken a job overseeing accounts at a mill in Lowell. Claire's mother volunteered at a branch of the Boston Public Library, but professed she would rather starve than put her hand to manual labor, or paid labor of any kind, for that matter.

Claire's last viable resource was Ruth, who still came faithfully each week to do the laundry and heavy housework. Claire had always kept Ruth at a distance, but thought she'd treated her fairly enough, always providing lunch and a snack when she came, and never yelling at her that she could remember. Claire knew there were other jobs now that paid more, so she would have to work something out to make her offer more attractive. Ruth would come to work the following Tuesday—and Claire would be ready. Her first step was to call Philip Andrews.

Tuesday morning arrived, warm and winsome. George reviewed the *Star* as he ate his breakfast, kissed his son on the head, and left for work. His only words to Claire as he walked out the door were that he would be home on time for dinner. She felt his eyes on her as he told her, and she looked up from dusting the living room furniture and smiled at him, not her wicked smile, but something else, something decidedly innocent and supportive.

"I'll have dinner ready for you. I hope you have a good day, dear."

He nodded, and closed the door behind him. He drove to his shop slowly, distracted by her change of demeanor. In all the time they were married, she had never lifted a dust cloth. Why would she dust? Ruth was coming today to clean the house; besides, since Louise's departure, and the subsequent restrictions he'd placed on her social activity, Claire had barely spoken two words to him. Something was going on. But when he arrived at his shop and entered his office, his misgivings disappeared as his secretary handed him the first orders of the day.

Claire watched George from the front window until he rounded the corner and headed west on Church Street. Once he was out of sight, she raced to the kitchen and put on a fresh pot of coffee to percolate. She filled the sugar bowl, and piled macaroons on a plate, precious commodities just for Ruth, who liked sweets almost as much as she liked coffee.

Claire welcomed Ruth at the door when she arrived a quarter-hour later.

"Ruth, would you mind if we sat down and talked for just a few minutes? I have some fresh coffee just perked, and some macaroons I think you might like."

Ruth was stunned. Mrs. Duncan had barely said ten words to her in the last three years, preferring to give any direction through Louise.

"Well, Mrs. Duncan, that's very kind of you. I hope you aren't dissatisfied with my work."

"No, no, Ruth, nothing further from my mind," Claire reassured her. "Come in, let me take your sweater, and we'll chat for a few minutes over a treat."

At the dining room table, Claire Duncan poured the coffee. She asked after Ruth's family, her children, her other housekeeping jobs. She asked if she had thought about working at one of the factories.

"Oh, no, Mrs. Duncan. My children are grown up enough to look after themselves, but my mother needs help in the evenings and early mornings, so I wouldn't be able to work outside of Winchester, and not the hours most of the factories want. I'm doing well enough with my housekeeping, and Lloyd, you know, my husband, well, he's too old for military service, so he got to keep his job at Davenport's, so we're doing fine."

"Is that the Davenport Machining in Woburn?" Claire asked as she topped off Ruth's coffee cup.

"Why yes, have you heard of it? It's a pretty big company, and they are just swamped with work for the government. Lloyd won't tell me what they're working on, he always says 'loose lips sink ships.' But I do know that he's working hard every day, long hours." Ruth bit into a second macaroon, a wave of delight crossing her face. "These are just delicious, Mrs. Duncan, I haven't tasted something this good in, well, I don't know how long."

"I'm glad you're enjoying them, Ruth. You've worked here for so long, you certainly deserve a treat, and I'm glad to get to know you a little better. I did want to discuss something with you, as I said before."

Ruth took a sip of her coffee, and put the cup down on the saucer.

"Yes, Mrs. Duncan?"

"Ruth, you know that our country is at war. Each of us must do the best we can to help our country win, to help our young men overseas."

Ruth nodded, "Yes, ma'am."

"I know you are a smart woman, and a hard worker. You've taken care of our family for a long time, even before Lloyd got the job at Davenport's. I remember when he was out of work for a while. All that time, no matter what else was going on, you've been consistent in your service to our family. So first of all, I want to say thank you for all that you've done for us."

Ruth's eyes grew wide. "Are you sure you're not firing me, Mrs. Duncan?"

"Good heavens, no. No, in fact, I want to offer you an opportunity. I would like you to continue to work for us as you usually have, but also to take on some added responsibilities, with an increase in pay, of course." Claire refilled Ruth's coffee cup, and slid the macaroons closer to Ruth's plate. "These added duties would be of service to our war effort here in Winchester. Would you consider something like that?"

"Well, of course, Mrs. Duncan," and Ruth leaned in closer, a third macaroon in one hand, the cup of steaming coffee in the other, listening intently as Claire outlined her proposal.

The arrangements were simple enough. Ruth would come three days each week instead of one. She would watch Oliver, maintain the house, and prepare dinners. While Ruth was there, Claire would be out, working with Mrs. De Mans, attending meetings, suggesting plans and projects for fundraisers, providing direction to the younger volunteers. Philip Andrews would provide the funds to cover Ruth's additional wages.

Claire enjoyed every mouthful of her dinner that night. The hard ball sitting in her gut ever since Louise announced her move was gone, replaced by a contented warmth. Claire's plan was taking shape, a plan that not only allowed her to pursue her society work, but provided an unexpected bonus, one that would, in due course, knock Louise down a peg or two.

Chapter 33

As the day approached for Mike, Ray and Henry to depart for basic training, Louise and Mike scrambled to make the most of the last few hours they had left. On their final evening together, they ate a quiet dinner at Randall's, then walked downtown, passing shops and storefronts. They ambled along the path that lined the newly divided community garden allotments near the Aberjona River, and sat for a while on a bench that overlooked the spillway, where the Aberjona gently fell at the underpass of the Main Street Bridge. Their conversation veered toward practical matters—the logistics of writing to each other, plans for the holidays if Mike was on leave, Louise's new job and living situation.

At the end of the evening, they stood in front of Dot's house, hidden in shadow, with only the half-moon to witness the long kiss, and longer embrace, Louise resting her head on Mike's chest. She would not see him again until it was time for him to leave on Saturday morning, just two short days away, when they would be surrounded by his family and a throng of well-wishers. This was her only time, and she lingered, listening to the sound of his heartbeat, feeling the warmth of his arms around her as the evening cooled. And then they parted, and he watched as she walked up to the house, held up a hand as she turned at the door, and she offered her own hand up in return.

Dot and Ray were inseparable those last few days. They spent mornings lingering over breakfast at the diner. During the day, Ray worked alongside Dot at the Red Cross, rolling bandages, and packing first aid kits and knit scarves into boxes to be shipped overseas. They joked with each other about her questionable filing skills, and his inability to roll a bandage evenly; they spoke seriously about the future, plans for the kind of house they wanted, how many children they would have, where they would spend their vacations.

In the evenings, they ate dinner at Ray's house, Mrs. Simard offering a warm welcome to the sweet young lady who would likely one day be her daughter-in-law. Dot was quick to join in the chorus of female voices as bowls and plates were passed, and it seemed as if she had always been a happy member of their family. As it was, Mr. Simard didn't notice until the third evening that Dot was eating dinner with them, and she was not, in fact, one of his five daughters.

The evening before Ray's departure, Dot sat with him on the front porch of the Simard home. Dinner was finished, and she and Ray could hear the rattle of plates and glasses from inside as Mrs. Simard and Annie cleared away the kitchen. It was early yet, the moon low in the east, the sun hovering, trembling and shimmering just above the western horizon. Dot stood up.

"It's time for me to go."

Ray stood up next to her. "What? No, why don't you stay a while longer?"

She looked up at him, wanting to stay, but knowing that she had to leave, to give him a last few precious hours with his family.

"Ray, you need to spend time with your family tonight. As much as I'd like to stay, it's important for them, and for you, too. I'll see you in the morning," she reassured him.

Ray kissed her. His kiss was warm, and passionate, and Dot came away from it lightheaded.

"Let me walk you home," Ray said.

"Not this time, Ray. It's still light out, and I'm not far. You should go inside, sit with your mother and father and sisters. I've taken up too much time from them as it is."

Dot looked to the west, saw the sun start to slip away. She turned back to Ray, and smiled.

"I'll be there in the morning to see you off," and then, "I love you."

"You know I love you, Dot," he whispered back. One last kiss, and she stepped away, letting go of his hand only as she started down the steps. At the bottom, she turned, looked up at him, and nodded. He nodded back. This was how he would remember her, he thought, in her light blue dress, with a white sweater over her shoulders, her long hair pulled away from her sweet face, her kiss still on his lips. He would wait for her, he knew, but he didn't want to. Now that the moment was here, he only wanted to stay home, to keep her close, to share dinner every night, to hold her in his arms. In that moment, if he could have pulled her into his house and hidden away with her there, he would have. And as she disappeared, finally, from his sight, he felt a hard, burning cold lump rise in his chest, just under his ribs, making it hard to breathe, hard to hold back the tears brimming just at the edge of his eyelids. He took one last look at the sunset, and went in the house.

The next morning was bright and cool, a fresh light breeze keeping the warmth of the day at bay until the sun could gain height and strength. A crowd of friends and family gathered in front of Town Hall, Dot and Louise among them, all waving good-bye as a town Selectman and a member of the American Legion drove Mike, Ray and Henry, along with two other young men, to South Station in Boston. There, each of the young men would climb aboard a train that would carry them to Georgia, or New Jersey, or South Carolina, wherever their assignment dictated.

A new routine settled over Winchester, as each family adjusted to the absence of their sons or brothers; to new rations on butter, coffee and meat, then cigarettes, gasoline and rubber; to bond drives and metal drives, to volunteering, to scrimping and saving, to extra hours tending backyard gardens or the assigned allotments along the Aberjona River; and to doing the best they could to support high hopes for a quick end to the war.

For several months, Dot and Louise enjoyed a simple routine divided between work, the Red Cross, and home. Dot spent much of her summer preparing lessons for the upcoming school year, meeting with the other teachers and administrators often to ensure she would be ready to fulfill her teaching assignment. When school started, Dot fairly threw herself into her new role, teaching not only letters and reading and rudimentary math, but also art, basic science, and simple geography and history. She loved her little students, and spent not an insignificant amount of time looking for arts and crafts projects for them to do, staying after school to help some of the older girls refine their drawing skills. More days than not she would come home with smears of paste glue on her clothes, and finger paints under her nails and sometimes clinging to strands of her otherwise neatly coiffed hair.

Louise continued her work at Davenport's. Within a few months, she learned to repair most of the machines. She learned each job, and filled in if someone was sick, or late. She got to know the other women in the company, from Davenport's wife, who never gave up the paperwork, to the cleaning ladies who came in at four in the morning. A sense of camaraderie pervaded the shop. It was important work, and Louise was proud to be part of a team of good people devoted to a common cause. But there was something else, a stirring of self-confidence that grew within Louise with each swiftly passing day; and for the first time in her life, she saw the possibilities that opened up for a young woman, any woman, for that matter, who had an income.

She wondered, sometimes, what it must have been like when the shop was full of men. Davenport was able to acquire a special dispensation for some of his original workers, especially the older men, those with families, or those who were expert machinists. But the bulk of the current workers were women, white and black, of all ages. It had been hard for John Davenport at first. The idea of hiring women was completely foreign to him, but the pressure of contract obligations and the coaxing of his wife led him to place his first advertisement calling for ladies to apply to work at his shop. When Davenport saw his advertisement in the newspaper, he noticed it was surrounded by twenty or more similar advertisements, all seeking factory or farm workers, from all over the country. At least he wasn't alone.

Initially, Davenport thought that the women should, and would, be paid less.

"What do you think is a fair wage for these new ladies?" he'd asked his wife on the day his advertisement first appeared in the paper.

She looked up at him with a determined set to her face.

"Exactly what you paid the men, of course," she replied.

John Davenport laughed a little, then saw she was serious. "No, really, what percentage should I pay them? Maybe fifty percent of the men's wage?"

Mrs. Davenport sighed heavily. She pressed the newspaper open on her desk, and pointed to several of the notices for work in Boston, New York, Harrisburg.

"Take a look at what everyone else is paying. I think you'll see that the wages are comparable to the men's wages."

"Hmmm," Mr. Davenport looked over his wife's shoulder, scanning the other ads more closely.

"But still…" he started.

"No 'buts' here, my dear. I think you should consider two very important points. First of all, these women are stepping in for their menfolk, responsible now for the welfare of their families. They are taking the place of husband and father, and should be paid as the husband and father would be. Second, if you want to keep your workers, you'll have to pay competitive wages—and fifty percent of these wages," she pointed to the ads in the paper, "simply won't do."

Davenport saw the sense of it, and although he had some lingering doubts, agreed. As it turned out, the women proved themselves hardworking and meticulous, and as each quota was met, and each order shipped, Davenport was immensely pleased. At the end of each quarter, he happily handed out generous bonuses to each and every employee.

November rolled around, and Louise stopped by George's shop the Saturday before the Thanksgiving holiday. She missed her brother, although they both made an effort to stay in touch, often meeting for a late breakfast after church on Sundays.

George was happy to see his sister. He worried about her, especially as the weather was turning colder and the darkness of night lasted longer than the light of day. They sat in his office and talked over luxurious hot coffee, some of Claire's secret stash that he had found, and a portion of which he had taken into work.

"I've decided what I'd like to do with the money, George," Louise said as he poured her a second cup of the sacred fluid.

"Good! What would you like to do with it?"

"I'd like to take one thousand of it—and keep it as cash in the bank. That's more than enough to get me through the next several years, especially if I continue to work. But the remaining three thousand—well, I'd like to invest that."

George pulled out a sheet of paper, and, with pen poised to take notes, said, "Very good! And how would you like to invest the remaining funds?"

"I'd like to put it into Back Bay Machining."

George put the pen down.

"Are you sure? I can't promise an overwhelming return. I mean, things are going very well right now, and I plan to continue the business long after the war ends, but are you sure? It's a lot of money to put into one investment."

Louise was sure, although she spent the better part of the next hour convincing her brother that she was making a sound business decision, and not limiting her choice to something—and someone—that she knew. In the end, George relented, promising Louise he would do his best with her money.

George and Louise spent Thanksgiving apart, the first time they ever celebrated the holiday in separate houses. George and Claire went to her parents' posh, if declining, home in Boston; and Louise and Dot, along with Mr. and Mrs. Humphrey, enjoyed a sumptuous feast of chicken and dumplings and pumpkin pie, cozy and warm in the Humphrey's dining room, a hot fire burning in the grate nearby.

The days grew very short after Thanksgiving. The cold chill that permeated the next two months seemed to hold hands with a constant companion of downpour, either of snow, or rain, or sleet. Louise worked her shifts faithfully, but was, in truth, exhausted by the end of each work day. She only managed to make it home every night by breaking this final task down into increments. The first was the easiest, leaving Davenport's each evening with some of the other women, company and comfort as she passed through the darkened streets with them toward the train station in Woburn; then, enduring the short train ride itself, working hard not to fall asleep and miss her stop.

The longest part of her trek was next, the eight blocks she had to walk from Winchester Center Station to Dot's house; and finally, the climb up the outside stairs that led to the second floor rooms, and to a warm, welcoming sanctuary from the elements. It seemed, sometimes, a singularly unbearable effort. But Louise pushed through, and was often rewarded with a note from

Mike, or a hot cup of tea and a warm bath that Dot would make just for her on those bitter days.

The most disconcerting aspect of her nightly sojourn was the darkness, a necessary blackout imposed by the war, which prevented warm and cheering lights from spilling out onto the street as Louise made her way home. Louise supposed she should have been uneasy, walking alone in the dark, with every building she passed curtained against the least ray of light escaping the inner confines. Her nerves were steady, though. Her only desire was to get under cover, and sit in front of the fire with Dot and a cup of hot tea.

Her calm determination, however, was scattered one evening as she approached home.

"Who are you?" yelled a male voice from somewhere on the other side of the street. Louise stopped in her tracks, and looked into the darkness from the direction of the voice.

"Who are *you*?" she called back. She was too tired to play games, but was ready to fight if she had to.

"Louise?" Walter stepped out from the shadows, crossing the street quickly to where she was. She finally recognized him in the scant moonlight as he approached her.

"Walter," she said with a sigh of relief.

"You shouldn't be out now, it's after dark. I mean, it's not past curfew, but it's awfully dark to be out on your own." He seemed so serious, she didn't dare tease him.

"Walter, I'm walking home from work right now. I work in Woburn, the shift doesn't end until five. So these days, I'm always out after dark when I'm coming home. But don't worry, Walter, I live only a block away, I'm almost there."

He looked at her. She was cold. He softened.

"Well, of course, that's all right, Louise. I just want you to be safe. I'll walk you the rest of the way—part of the service, you know."

As they walked together, Walter asked about her work, and if she liked it; he asked if she heard from Mike at all. "Oh, yes. I write to him every week, and he writes back, although not every week. He's still stateside, training in Georgia. I keep praying the war will end before he's sent overseas."

"Well, don't forget I'm working days at the *Star*, so if you hear anything encouraging from him, please pass it along. I'll make sure we don't print any national secrets, but you know, everyone likes to hear something good."

Louise nodded. "Of course, Walter, I'll be happy to do that." They stopped at the front gate of the Humphrey home.

"Walter, would you like to come in and have something hot to drink? Dot's home, she'd love to see you."

He looked up at the shadow of the house, dark against the backlight of the moon. It seemed tall to him, looming up and almost scary, like something out of a haunted house story.

"Oh, no, I have to finish my rounds, but thanks for the offer. I'll look out for you from now on, now that I know you're coming in from Woburn at night."

They said good night, and he watched her climb the steps up the side of the house to the second story, thinking that she was probably one of the bravest young women he knew.

Chapter 34

The New Year of 1943 found Winchester heavily invested in the war effort. The military attrition rate in the senior high school class was high, and the School Committee voted to give an automatic diploma to any senior who either volunteered or was drafted before the end of the school year. Those not military-bound continued to contribute to the war effort in other ways. High school students made blankets for the Red Cross, held their own paper drives, and bought so many defense bonds and stamps they were able to fund two jeeps for the Army. Elementary school children knitted afghans and scarves, contributed their pocket money to purchase defense stamps, and collected heaps of salvage metal for the scrap drives.

Rationing was now a way of life. Most highly prized was the acquisition of real butter, for oleomargarine, the prescribed replacement for butter, came as a white lump of lard-like grease. It could not help but be considered unappealing by even the most indelicate palate, even when the packet of yellow food coloring, which accompanied the loathsome material, was well blended in to make it look like butter's distant cousin.

The rations on gasoline and rubber prevented all but the most necessary of motored excursions. Carpools were standard, and tires were patched until they were more patch than rubber, for there were no new tires to be had. Some fortunate locals were able to pull an old rig out of a barn or shed, and hitch up a horse, a bygone mode of transportation renewed in its usefulness.

Winchester Library was designated as a war information center, and became the local headquarters for civilian work. The Civil Defense Food Committee held meat-cutting preparation demonstrations in the Library Art Gallery to show people how to stretch rationed meats. Library meeting rooms housed the War Bond Committee, divisions of the Red Cross, and the Victory Book Committee, which sent literature to military personnel.

Carl and Emma Smith, initially nervous about their German heritage, found comfort in the routine of their daily lives. Both of them actively supported the war effort, and the country that had become their home. Carl purchased war bonds and organized various drives at his work; Emma repaired bed linens for the Winchester Hospital, something she could do at home while tending her younger children. Once a month they received a letter from Henry, which never stated quite where he was or what he was doing, but only that he was well, and not to worry about anything.

One Wednesday evening in late September there was a knock at the Smiths' door. Carl got up from the dinner table, saying, "I'll get it, it's probably the Jenkins boy collecting for the newspaper." He opened the front door to find, not little Billy Jenkins, but a grown man, a man he recognized, one he'd seen in town. It took him a moment to place him. It was Walter's father.

"Oh, hello—Joe Hannigan, right?" Carl smiled on the outside, but wondered why in the world this man was standing at his door. He regained his composure, remembered his manners. "Won't you come in? We're just having supper, would you care to join us?"

Joe Hannigan shook his head no. Carl watched as Joe looked down the quiet street, took a quick glance behind. Joe seemed to make a decision. Carl waited, and Joe finally looked squarely at Carl's quizzical face.

"Mr. Smith, you should know that you have been accused of being a Nazi sympathizer. It's a serious allegation; however, I know, or at least am reasonably certain, that it's not true. Your dossier fell into my hands today. I reviewed it, and am now giving it to you. I remember very well that your son,

Henry, helped my son, Walter, many years ago at Winter Pond."

Joe handed the file to Carl, who held it as if it were a live grenade.

"I think we're square now. Good night, Mr. Smith." Joe Hannigan turned and walked away. A few seconds later, Carl heard the roar of an engine. He poked his head out the door and looked up and down the street. Nothing moved except the few remaining autumn leaves trembling at the tips of branches as a cool breeze nudged them.

Carl closed the door, his heart beating hard in his chest. What did this mean? He glanced at the file, then tucked it into his briefcase and returned to the dinner table.

"Was that Billy?" Emma asked, scooping another spoonful of potatoes onto the children's plates.

Carl looked at Emma and his three young children, then down at his plate.

"Uh, no, just someone asking for directions."

Later that evening, with the children bathed and tucked safely in their beds, Carl looked out his front window, checking the street again, before closing the blackout curtains for the night. He made sure the doors and windows were locked. He took the file from his briefcase, and sat at the kitchen table.

He thumbed through the papers. There was a copy of his birth record, and Emma's. There was paperwork from the couple's arrival in America from Germany. Finally, he saw the statements from three people, each only a line or two, indicating that Carl Smith and his wife Emma were members of the Bundt Party, and Nazi sympathizers. Carl didn't recognize the names of the three accusers, but he remembered the incident in New York, only two months prior, that had left him unnerved and eager to get home.

Emma joined him at the table.

"What's all this?" she asked. He handed her the file.

"Look. Joe Hannigan dropped this off when we were at dinner. He said he remembered how Henry saved Walter's life at the pond. He said we were even now."

She looked through the papers slowly. Her color drained as she realized what they were, what they meant, how much information someone had collected on them. Her hand started to shake when she came to the paper with the statements.

"What is this? Who are these people who accused us?"

"I didn't tell you. It didn't seem important. Remember when I went to New York in July? That meeting for some of the local bank associates?"

Emma nodded her head.

"Well," Carl continued, "one morning, the last morning I was there, I was standing outside the hotel waiting for one of the other men to come down. We were going to go to breakfast. I saw a group of boys, maybe fifteen years old, maybe a little older, roughhousing, and they knocked a woman into the street. I ran over to the lady to help her, and scolded the boys for their rudeness. They started to fight with me, one of them knocked me down, took my wallet. There wasn't much in there, just a few dollars, but I remember the one boy stood there and looked at my identification. He said my name, and then asked me if I was German, if I was a Deutscher. I didn't say anything. And then he tossed my wallet back onto my chest, and they left me. I got up, and after making sure the lady wasn't hurt, I brushed myself off and went back to the front of the hotel. Anyway, a few minutes later the other man came down, and we went to breakfast. I really didn't think anything more of it, although I was glad to come home, and glad not to have to go back to New York anytime soon. I'm not sure what happened has anything to do with this, but it's the only thing I can think of."

"But...but these statements—they aren't true." Emma had heard about a Japanese family that lived in Lexington. They'd been taken away the previous spring, placed on a bus heading south to an unknown destination. They'd lost their home, and their business, a small grocery store. There were others as well: an Italian family she had seen a few times at Randall's, and a German couple who had arrived in town just two months ago, and had just as quickly been escorted away.

"Carl, I think we should burn this."

"Do you think we should move?"

"And go where?" Emma went to the cupboard, pulled out two glasses and a small bottle of brandy. Carl poured.

"I wish I smoked," she said. She looked through the papers again, the brandy calming her nerves, steadying her hands. Finally, she looked up at Carl. "I'll tell you what I think. I think this is the only record anyone has about us. Mr. Hannigan has gone out of his way to protect us. So, I think we just pretend this never happened. We hold our heads up high, smile, and greet everyone the way we always do. You go to work, take the dogs to the park, keep everything the same. I'll take the children to school, and keep volunteering at the hospital. Let's see what happens."

"Do you think we should write to Henry? Do you think he knows anything about this?" asked Carl.

Emma took another sip of her brandy. "No. Henry has his own life now, we should leave him out of this. I doubt he knows anything. He would have contacted us, let us know it was coming, don't you think?"

Carl nodded. Emma continued, "Let's just leave it—put the documents away if you don't want to burn them."

The next day, Carl went to work. He greeted his secretary as he always had, ate his usual lunch at the diner. He took the same route home, and greeted those he passed with an open smile and warm 'good evening' as was his usual custom. Nothing happened. Nothing changed. No one else knocked at their door, no police car pulled up as he walked home to take him away. Time passed, and the Smith family went on as they always had, breathing a little easier as the weeks went by, until finally, they put the threat behind them.

Henry did know about the document. He was stationed in Georgia, at an isolated facility on one of the little islands that swam in the Savannah River just before it plumed out into the ocean. The document was sitting on his desk one morning, a note taped to the front with the words 'Process Correctly' crisply written in large capital letters. Henry read through it, debated as to what to do. After all, this was the main reason he'd accepted this post, and spent his days interpreting documents and breaking German codes. He finally called the Boston branch of the OCD, just to see what the procedure would be, what he might say or do to protect his family. He was as shocked as he was relieved to find Joe Hannigan on the other end of the line, serving as the supervisor in charge of Middlesex County's local Alien Enemy Board. After a brief conversation, Henry sent the file by courier to Boston, where Joe received it, reviewed it, and then let it go. It wouldn't be the only record, but it was the only one that mattered.

Chapter 35

The next eighteen months flew by. George accepted the post of Selectman, and his business continued to thrive. His days were full and long. Claire maintained her own schedule, and although she didn't exactly abide by her husband's wishes, he rarely noticed anything was amiss. Philip Andrews paid out what he considered a paltry sum to maintain peace in his personal life.

Louise never saw Claire, but felt her presence in Winchester, saw her influence in the form of successful fundraising projects, and heard from Dot and Mrs. Humphrey that Claire was active, and doing some very good work in the community. Louise listened to these comments, but had difficulty believing Claire's motives were purely philanthropic. Still, time had passed, and Louise thought it was possible she was judging Claire too harshly.

It was Sunday, a few weeks before Christmas. Louise sat with George and Oliver at Randall's, and over their usual late breakfast of eggs and toast, discussed upcoming holiday plans. Louise mentioned Claire's activities to George, in the specific attempt to find something good to say about her sister-in-law.

"Mrs. Humphrey said Claire did a wonderful job with the Fortnightly's Christmas collection for the hospital."

George looked up from his plate.

"Hospital?" asked George, confused.

"Yes, apparently Claire managed the whole fundraiser. They'll be able to refurbish some of the equipment, and buy new linens. Mrs. Humphrey said you must be very proud."

Louise took a bite of her toast, and looked at her brother. The expression on his face was a blank, and she knew he was thinking.

"Well, George," she asked, "aren't you proud?"

George gave her a half grin, and said, "Of course. The hospital needs new linens, and I did hear that some of the equipment in the surgery needed to be repaired. Yes, of course I'm proud."

George was not upset with Claire. He was disappointed, maybe, but mostly with himself. He had once again he allowed his focus on work to blind him to Claire's activities.

That evening at dinner, he broached the subject.

"I heard today that you did an excellent job raising funds for the hospital."

Claire caught her breath, took a moment to respond. She was so careful. How did he find out? Then it struck her. George had met Louise for breakfast after church that morning.

"I may have made a few suggestions," she replied, cautiously.

"I heard you managed the whole fundraiser."

She looked at him. He wasn't angry. Maybe more curious. She took a sip of her Scotch.

"I was needed. I did what I could, and it worked out well."

"Explain to me how it worked. I remember telling you to limit your activities, to stay home with Oliver, and take care of the house. It's obvious you've at least skirted those directions."

Claire sat up straight, lifted her chin. "Ruth comes. She helps out. We're a team."

"I see," he replied. He put down his fork, and looked directly at her as he spoke. She met his eyes, unflinching.

"I'd have appreciated it if you had at least discussed your intentions with me; however, it seems you're useful, and benefitting others. I'm only going to give you this one caution, Claire, one I'm sure you appreciate. Be careful that what you do doesn't damage my business or interfere with my duties as Selectman."

Claire took a quiet breath. She knew he was referring to the affair. That had ended ages ago, why was he dredging it up? Besides, hadn't she always said that everything she did was for the benefit of the family? Weren't her current activities of benefit to his business and position in the community? George simply didn't understand her motives, and apparently never had. Claire decided, in that moment, he never would.

"Of course," she replied.

They finished their dinner in silence. But Claire's mind was busy. It was time, now, to follow through with the plan she had put into place almost two years before.

When Ruth showed up the following Tuesday, Claire sat her down again, this time over precious cocoa and ginger snaps.

In the course of what was an otherwise innocuous conversation, Claire let it slip that Louise was attempting to share production processes and information about Davenport's contracts with her brother, George.

"They're in the same line of work, you know," Claire began. "Of course, George has never accepted any of her information, but he's very upset that she's doing this, I suppose out of some sense of family loyalty. But if she can steal from her employer, what else is she capable of? My word, George was so upset last night, I thought he would bring the roof down. I'm so proud of him, though, for refusing to accept the information. He's always been very conscientious that way."

Three days later, a red-faced Mr. Davenport pulled Louise off the production line and into his office.

"Louise, you're fired. Here's your last day's pay. I expect you to get your belongings and leave, and don't come back."

Louise was stunned. "What? Why? Wait, I don't understand. You want me to leave?"

"Louise, you're a good worker, but I just found out that you are sharing, or at least attempting to share, information with your brother, information about our business here—contracts, machining processes, work activities, and such. I took you on knowing that you were George Duncan's sister, but I naturally assumed you wouldn't share inside information with him, especially in light of all the training from the government about keeping work secrets at work. He's my competitor, Louise, and I can't take the gamble. Frankly, I think you should be ashamed of yourself. You're the kind of person who looks good on the surface, but underneath is a—well, I don't want to say traitor—but I will say a significant risk, not only to my business, but to our country's security."

Louise was aghast. "Mr. Davenport, I can assure you—" she started, but he cut her off.

"Now, Louise. I can't have you in my employ."

She looked at him open-mouthed, ready to say something, but the words were no more than air.

"Now!" Davenport yelled.

Louise stumbled from the office, tears smarting. She made her way to her locker, where Mrs. Davenport stood waiting.

"I'm sorry it had to be this way, Louise. I'm sure you'll find something else."

Louise collected her coat and boots, and gathered her few belongings from the locker. She looked at Mrs. Davenport.

"He's wrong," Louise half-whispered, still reeling from the shock.

She turned and hurried through the factory to the side entry door, and pushed through. For the first time in nearly two years, she left Davenport Machining with the glaring midday sun in her eyes.

Chapter 36

Louise couldn't remember the trip from Woburn to Winchester, or how she managed to get from Winchester Center Station to her room at Dot's house. When she arrived there, though, she shut herself in, and sat on her bed, numb.

It wasn't until she heard a timid knocking that Louise woke up from her stupor.

Dot's voice came through from the other side of the door, a careful "Louise? Louise, it's me. What are you doing home so early? Are you all right? Can I come in?"

Louise stood up and crossed to the door, opened it. She sat back down on the bed as Dot followed her into the room.

"Are you sick? Should I get the doctor? You look awfully pale."

Louise sighed. "No, I don't need a doctor, thanks, though."

Suddenly, the hurt and injustice of the day rose up, and hot tears started to roll down Louise's cheeks.

Dot got a handkerchief out of the dresser drawer and handed it to Louise as she sat next to her on the bed.

"What happened? Please tell me."

The Lights of Pembroke Road

It took Louise a few minutes. Dot waited.

"I...I got fired today," finally came out. Then, in a tumble, Louise explained the whole sordid story, of how she was working one minute, then in Davenport's office the next, being accused of stealing information about Davenport's business and giving it to George; and worse, the insinuation that she was some sort of traitor, and could not be trusted.

"Oh, Dot, it was just awful! I don't know how I dare show my face again, all those nice ladies at the machine shop will think I'm a monster. I just want to hide in a hole and never come out." Tears ran afresh.

Dot hugged her friend. "Now, you know those accusations aren't true, and you're not a traitor. Why, Louise, you're the most steadfast, trustworthy person I know, with the exception of Mother." She sat back and looked at her friend. "There has to be a way to fix this. Your reputation has been sullied, and I won't have it. I'm going over to George's right now, and you're coming with me."

"Oh no, I couldn't go out!" exclaimed Louise, horrified.

"Have you done anything wrong?" asked Dot. Louise shook her head no.

"Of course not. So we need to fix this before it gets out of hand. Dry those eyes, put on your coat, and we'll go together. George needs to know, after all, it's an accusation against him as well."

A half-hour later Dot and Louise entered the office at Back Bay Machining. George, on the phone with a client, held up his hand, and then pointed to chairs.

"I'll just be a minute," he whispered.

The phone call ended, and George stood up. "Well, ladies, to what do I owe the pleasure of..." George stopped mid-sentence, seeing Louise's red-rimmed eyes. "Why, Louise, what's the matter?"

"Louise was fired today, George," said Dot.

"Fired? But you know their line, you've been there for more than a year—I thought you were doing very well over there. What in the world happened?"

"Louise was accused of stealing information from Davenport and giving it to you. There was an implication that if she was capable of that treachery, she might be capable of worse. We though you should know, since your name was mentioned."

Up until that moment, Louise had been silent and still. Now the tears started to flow again.

"It's just so unfair!" she blurted. "I haven't done anything wrong, you know I haven't. But they treated me like some sort of criminal! I didn't even get to defend myself or anything. Davenport yelled at me to get out. And now, now I'm sure everyone at that company thinks the worst of me, George. Soon it will be all over Winchester. How will I ever go out again? And what about you? He didn't say anything about you, besides that he thought I was giving you information. What does it mean for you?"

George's face was flushed with anger. "I'll get to the bottom of this. You girls go home, let me sort it out."

What happened that day between him and John Davenport, George would not say. Louise only knew that George went in person to Davenport Machining and obtained an immediate meeting with Mr. Davenport. At the end of it, not only was Louise absolved of any misconduct, but the two men parted ways on friendly terms. Back Bay Machining was not equipped to produce large metal parts; Davenport did not manufacture small pieces. When George left Davenport's office late that afternoon, the two businessmen shook hands heartily, each agreeing to notify the other whenever a contract came out that was not suited to their particular end of the business.

Louise didn't want to return to Davenport's, even though George explained that her name had been cleared. George didn't know from where the awful accusation had sprung, but he knew it was squashed. Still, Louise could not bring herself to go back. The incident had soured her on factory work, on any kind of work where she could be accused so easily of wrongdoing. It was time to do something different.

"So what will you do now?" asked Dot one evening over dinner. It was late February, and the snow was still piled high outside.

"I've been thinking about it. I have to say, I don't mind the last few weeks. I've caught up on my reading, and feel better about what happened, or at least, that it's been resolved. I haven't missed trudging through the snow every morning and every night, either!"

"You do seem to have recovered nicely," agreed Dot. "You know, with the money you have sitting in the bank, you don't really have to take a paying job.

You could be a full-time volunteer if you wanted."

"Hmmm—yes, I could, except Claire seems to have her hand in just about everywhere, and frankly, I don't want to have to deal with her, which I certainly would if I volunteered here in Winchester."

"So what are you thinking? I get the feeling you're mulling something over, but haven't spilled it."

Louise nodded. "Dot, you know me too well. I made a trip over to Town Hall last week, and spoke with Mr. Lowell again. He presented some options, one of which looked very appealing."

Dot waited expectantly. "Which is?" she prodded.

"There's a group called the Victory Farm Volunteers. I saw an article about the need for women in farm labor last summer, something in *McCall's*, I think. I didn't really pay attention, I was already working at Davenport's. But Mr. Lowell mentioned that there are several farms nearby that are looking for help starting in late March. I could serve for as little as two weeks, or as long as six or seven months, depending on the farm. I'd get some training, and room and board, and a stipend, too, although not what the factory was paying. Still, it would be out of Winchester, and something different."

Dot was stunned. "You must be joking!" she exclaimed. "Did you hit your head, or something? Because that sounds just awful. Months on end of back-breaking labor, herding cows or pigs or sheep, or digging in the dirt, then having to harvest everything. And what about your room? Would you be giving that up to go live with strangers? I'd never see you! And what about George and Oliver? When would you visit them?"

Louise took a breath to explain, but Dot continued. "Oh Louise, I think you must be out of your mind, and Mr. Lowell was off his rocker to suggest such an idea. There has to be something more civilized you can do here in town." Dot shook her head in disbelief as she speared a carrot.

"As I was about to say," chimed in Louise, "there is a nice farm in Lexington, Weatherby's Farm—remember we used to go there sometimes to pick strawberries? Remember Mrs. Weatherby? The nice lady who gave us taffy as a treat when we brought our buckets in to be weighed?"

Dot scowled. "Yes, I remember."

"Well, she needs help. All her sons are gone, and she was widowed last year. I would work at her farm, and have a room there at her house. Then, on the weekends, I can come back to Winchester. I'll keep my room here, and see you, and go to church, and see George and Oliver as well."

Dot was silent, eating another carrot, then a piece of potato. Finally, she spoke.

"Well, maybe it isn't the most horrifying thing you could do. I still think that you should stay in town, but I understand why you want to get away. As long as you promise to come home every weekend, I suppose it's almost tolerable. So, when does this training start? What do they teach you? Cow milking?"

"Actually, they teach me to drive a tractor, along with cow milking and chicken feeding."

Dot, appalled, looked as if she'd eaten a slice of sour lemon.

"Drive a tractor?! Good heavens, Louise! Are you sure you want to do this?" Dot looked at her friend with genuine concern.

"I'm sure," came the confident reply.

Chapter 37

Louise looked up over the fields. The bush beans were coming in in abundance; the tomatoes in the adjoining field were ripening on their vines by the hundreds. An acre of corn, located at the west end of the farm, promised a thousand ears just days away from perfect sweetness. A profusion of blueberry bushes would be ready for picking throughout August. Row after row of raspberries, their long vines trailing through wire hedges, would be ready soon as well. The strawberries, large and sweet and juicy, were already done, their season finished just a week before.

Louise shifted her position as she moved down the row, her broad-brimmed hat shielding most of her face. July was turning out to be warmer than expected, and she was already perspiring in the midmorning sun. Glancing over into the row of bush beans next to hers, she watched as Janet, a lithe, small-boned young woman, collected handful after handful of the beans, dropping them into the basket at her side with alacrity. Louise wiped her brow, and returned to her task, like Janet, of picking the tender green beans.

From the fields, Louise, Janet, and three other women hauled their baskets to a small barn, where the beans were weighed, packed, and collected by someone Louise only knew as 'Hank'—a worn old man who rolled up each afternoon in an equally worn old truck. The Weatherby Farm was one of over a dozen local farms on Hank's route, where he collected similar bundles of beans, or corn, or berries, and whisked them away to an unknown processing center.

When Louise first arrived at the farm in early April, she received a warm welcome from Mrs. Weatherby herself, a strong, good-humored woman in her mid-fifties. She gave Louise a tour of the farmhouse and the outbuildings, talking all the way.

"Here is the barn where the two cows are stalled." Mrs. Weatherby pointed into the barn, where Louise could make out the dim outline of two brown cows standing at the hay trough. "There's Phoebe and Charlotte. My daughter named them, Lord help us, but they're good old girls. They're usually out in the pasture, but they come in for milking twice a day, so you'll be doing that sometimes, and sometimes the stalls need mucking out or their water and hay needs to be refreshed. Each of you girls takes a turn tending the livestock, so it doesn't get to be too tiresome."

They walked quickly to the next building, of a similar size and shape as the barn, but set up for processing the produce from the farm. There was a large sorting table in the center, and scales, the largest Louise had ever seen in her life. Rough cotton bags sat piled on a bench beside the scales, and baskets of various sizes filled the shelves that lined one wall. Wooden crates were stacked high in neat rows against another wall.

"This is the sorting area. It's simple enough—the produce is brought in here, sorted, weighed, and bagged or boxed for pick up. You'll see, the girls will show you."

From there, they went on to a large, fenced-in portion of the yard where the chickens were kept.

"We have about thirty chickens here—they have to be fed, and their eggs picked up every day. Sometimes the coop needs cleaning—what a dirty job!—but it has to be done. Again, you girls rotate through this assignment, so no one gets stuck with it all the time. Come in, now, and I'll show you the house and your room."

They entered the kitchen, and passed through a tall, narrow door near the oven. They climbed down a flight of steep stairs, at the bottom of which was the root cellar, a large, immaculate, red-bricked room lined with shelf after shelf of preserves. Potatoes filled open-wire racks stacked six feet high against a far wall, and a few winter squash rested on a bench under the staircase. Louise was stunned. She knew the work it took to line even one long shelf; she couldn't imagine putting up enough preserves to stock a store.

"This is my root cellar. My husband put those shelves up when we first got married, and I have kept them fully stocked ever since," said Mrs. Weatherby, with considerable pride. "This farm has been in my husband's family for eighty years, and each generation has had a hand in improving it."

As they headed back up the stairs, Mrs. Weatherby continued. "Not only did my husband put up those shelves, he and my boys built the barn where we sort the produce, and he was able to acquire another five acres of land, so the farm now sits on a total of fifteen acres. Of course, we're not using all the land right now, we simply don't have the hands to do that, but we're still producing quite a bit."

Up in the kitchen again, Mrs. Weatherby gestured toward a very large pine table, surrounded by a dozen chairs, which sat in a large open room next to her kitchen.

"Plenty of space for everyone—not fancy, mind you, but I like to think that all you girls are part of my family, and I like to see everyone eat and enjoy themselves at mealtime. Now let's go upstairs, and I'll show you your room. Bring your case, we'll get you settled in."

Louise grabbed her small suitcase and followed the woman up the stairs. As they reached the landing, Mrs. Weatherby pointed to her left.

"You'll be pleased to know we have indoor plumbing. That was an improvement from my husband's father, hated going out in the cold to do his business, so when the sewer line came through, he hooked up to it. Got a big water heater, too, and a huge bathtub. I guess they had a devil of a time getting it into the house. Anyway, you'll see. The bathroom is at the end of the hall. You girls seem to work out your shifts in there pretty well, so I'll leave you to work out your schedule with the others. But your room is here." She opened the door to the right at the landing.

"You'll be sharing a room with Eve. She's a very nice lady from Cambridge, a hard worker, a little older than the rest of you girls," and then in a whisper, "I believe she's a widow. Her husband passed away last year, a stroke or something."

The bedroom was cheerful and spacious, with two large windows admitting the sun and fresh air. It was furnished with two single beds, each with a small table and lamp next to it. Two dressers and a cupboard filled in the remaining wall space.

"That's your bed there, on the right. That's your dresser, and you'll have to share the cupboard if you have anything that needs hanging up. I don't think Eve has that much," Mrs. Weatherby noted as she opened the cupboard. Two dresses hung to one side, and a pair of plain, black shoes sat at the bottom. A similarly plain black hat sat on the shelf above.

"Yes, plenty of room for you," she stated as she closed the cupboard doors. Turning to Louise, she asked, "Do you have any questions for me, dear? You've been awfully quiet."

Louise smiled. "No, thank you, Mrs. Weatherby, I don't have any questions. At least, not at the moment."

"Well, then, I'll let you get settled. Dinner is at 5:30, you'll hear the bell." As she passed through the door, she turned and added, "I hope you'll be happy here, Louise. Your help is very much needed and appreciated." She closed the door behind her, and Louise heard her footsteps as she retreated downstairs.

At dinner that evening, Mrs. Weatherby introduced Louise to her cohorts, and Louise was cheered by the lively conversation and laughter the women shared at the table. The food was plentiful and good, although Louise was somewhat taken aback at the portions the women ate. She thought she couldn't eat half as much, even if she tried. As one of the women heaped a second large spoonful of chicken casserole on her plate, she caught the look of wonder on Louise's face. She laughed and said, "Trust me, in a week, you'll be eating this way, too!"

After dinner, when Louise and Eve had settled in for the night, Eve shared Mrs. Weatherby's story.

"She's seen her share of hardship, I can tell you. Husband died just six months ago, and her three boys off and fighting. She had field hands in up until last October, and then one by one, they got called up. Her daughter came to help, but the girl lives in New Hampshire, and has her own family, so she was very limited in what she could really do. Mrs. Weatherby heard about the Victory Farm Program, and signed up right away to get help. So here we are. The work is hard labor, no two ways about it, but it's a necessary work, and Mrs. Weatherby feeds us very well, keeps the house tidy for us. She's used to feeding a lot of men, and I think you got an idea about that at dinner tonight."

Eve turned over in her bed, and turned out her light. "Well, five o'clock comes awfully fast. Hope you don't mind, I'm calling it a night. See you in the morning!"

During the first few days Louise worked at Weatherby Farm, she thought the physical labor might very well kill her. Whatever training she had received through the Victory Farm Program, it had not prepared her for the intensity and constancy of farm work. Each night she fell into bed utterly exhausted; in the mornings, it took her half an hour to ease the stiffness from her arms and legs sufficiently to allow her to dress and hobble downstairs.

By the second week, though, her muscles became accustomed to the work. Louise began to enjoy a sense of satisfaction at the end of each day, and a comfortable kinship with her fellow laborers as they shared laughter and gossip each evening when they gathered at Mrs. Weatherby's expansive kitchen table.

Some women only came for a few weeks or a month; others stayed longer. But the local office of the Victory Farm Volunteer program kept Mrs. Weatherby's farm fully staffed, so that there were always at least five hands readily available for work. Currently, six women worked the fields and managed the livestock.

The routine was the same every day, except a half-day on Saturday, and all day Sunday, when the women were permitted to take a well-earned rest. The daily schedule was quite simple. Mrs. Weatherby rang a bell in the kitchen at five each morning. As the women arrived downstairs for breakfast, she offered a hearty 'good morning, ladies' to her workers, and set out tea, eggs, biscuits and oleomargarine, pancakes and jam. After breakfast, each woman was given her assignment for the day, to pick, plant, or weed a section of the farm; to clean out the chicken coop; muck out the cow stalls; or to sort, weigh, and pack the day's harvest.

After dinner, some of the women would play checkers or cards. They sat in the front room, listening to the radio, or out on the porch, smoking if they had cigarettes. By eight every evening, though, they started to make their way upstairs.

Louise knew that not all farms were so well run, or as well equipped. She heard some stories about how the women were asked to do household chores, and some were physically or sexually abused by their hosts. Some were housed in deplorable conditions, unsafe and unsanitary. Not only was Mrs. Weatherby's home clean and safe, and the company enjoyable, it was perfectly located—close enough to visit Winchester on the weekends, but far enough away so that she felt she was in a different world during the week.

Louise grew strong. Her hands were calloused, more so than they'd been at Davenport's. Her skin was freckled, in spite of the large hat she wore faithfully every day; and she had muscles now, a definition in her legs and arms that she'd never seen before, that she caught sight of in the mirror sometimes when she stepped out of the tub. Her body was becoming lithe and powerful, changes which reached over and touched her mind and heart as well, stroking her independent inclinations, poking at her self-determination.

At the end of August, several of the women rotated out, returning to school, or home. Louise felt a sting of despondency as each woman left, as if a little piece of her was leaving with them. Louise wrote to some of them, and the return letters talked about classes, or how hard it was to get nylons or shoes. Some of women said they missed the farm, and would try to return next summer if the war was still on; others admitted they would find another, less taxing means of service. Louise pressed on, resolved to stay at the farm as long as she could.

Chapter 38

One particular Sunday, an overcast, blustery day in early October, George had stayed home with a cold, unable to attend Mass or meet Louise for their usual breakfast. Louise thus found herself with a spare hour, as the young woman with whom Louise would return to the farm was delayed in order to visit a friend in town. Louise decided to call on Mrs. Andrews to see if she'd heard from Mike.

Louise headed toward the Andrews' house. Orange, yellow and red leaves swirled in the air around her, sharp gusts of wind pushing them along to form a frenzied tarantella of color before they fell back gracefully to the ground, only to be blown up and around again, dancing with other leaves similarly displaced.

She wrapped her scarf closer around her neck as she hurried along. The last time she had heard from Mike was in January, just a brief note saying that he wouldn't be able to write for a while, but not to worry. Ray had written similar letters to his mother and Dot, intimating that they were shipping out, finally going to see some action. Since that time, neither Louise, nor Dot, nor Mrs. Simard had heard any word from either of the young men. Louise hoped that maybe Mrs. Andrews had some news.

Louise rapped at the Andrews' door. Margaret Andrews answered.

"Hello, Mrs. Andrews, I'm so sorry to bother you, but I was wondering if you'd heard from Mike? He hasn't written in such a long time…"

Suddenly, Mrs. Andrews disappeared, and Amy, Mike's older sister, took her place in the doorway. She came out onto the porch and closed the door behind her. She hugged a sweater around her as the chill breeze pushed her hair into a flurry around her head.

"Hi, Louise."

Amy moved a strand of hair away from across her forehead, shifted to stand so the wind would blow her hair away from her face, blinked as the cold air hit her eyes.

"Please excuse my mom, she's having a hard time. We haven't heard from Mike. The fact is, about a month ago we received word that he was missing— you know, missing in action. I've moved back in—Mom and Dad are just beside themselves, and…" Her voice trailed off.

Louise felt a cold, acid knot tighten in the pit of her stomach, and it took a moment for her to catch her breath.

"Oh, Amy, I'm so sorry. I can't believe it. Please tell your mom how sorry I am. Please tell her…" Louise couldn't say any more.

"I know Mike liked you, Louise, I know you and he had—have plans. I'm sorry too." She dropped her gaze. "We just want him home. Or at least, to hear something."

She looked up again, over Louise's head, scanning the empty street.

"Thanks for coming by, Louise. I wish I had better news to tell you." She turned and walked back into the house, closing the door gently.

Louise wanted to cry, but there were no tears. There was just the grip of anxiety around her heart, so tight she could barely breathe. She nodded and whispered a thank you to the closed door.

The next few days were a blur. There was no time, now, to sit and ponder what might be lost, to luxuriate in heart-wrenching sorrow, for the hot summer had passed, and the final harvest was at hand. The work at the farm nearly doubled, and as the days became incrementally shorter, the few remaining women at the farm carried lanterns with them as they walked out to the fields on those dark, frigid mornings, and then lit them again as the day closed, the lights bobbing like fireflies as they moved back toward the house.

When each day was done, the women gathered at Mrs. Weatherby's kitchen table for dinner, as they always had; but exhaustion now replaced the convivial atmosphere of the summer, and the women ate their supper in relative silence, broken only by occasional discussion about the next day's work, or a request for the salt or the wretched oleomargarine to be passed. For Louise, complete and utter weariness prevented the shedding of tears under any circumstances; and as she climbed into bed at night, merciful numbness crept over her mind as a comforting warm blanket over a compliant child, and she was blessed with sound and deep sleep. No dreams of Mike invaded; in fact, hardly any dreams at all.

As October waned the fieldwork was finished, and the vast stretches of open land lay fallow, spotted only with hedges of bare bramble, long devoid of fruit, a few tired leaves clinging to the vines until the next north wind tugged them away. Over the course of the summer, thirty-eight women had rotated through the farm and its workload, some staying for a week or two, some a bit longer. From the farm, they had returned home, or to school; a few of the women, who had no significant ties to bind them, went to work in factories. Two of the women joined the Women's Army Corps, and another made her way overseas with the Red Cross. A note from her indicated she was 'having a wonderful time,' and really felt of use as she 'rode around in a jalopy truck and served coffee and donuts to the men near the front line.'

By the end of the month, most of the work was confined to the farmhouse. Only Eve and Louise remained, and they spent their days canning pears, drying apples, and selling the last of the squash to a local grocer. Their service was fast coming to a close, with less than a week remaining before a new young woman arrived to take their place, just one person to manage the cows and the chickens during the winter months. Louise would leave upon her arrival, to go back to live full-time at her rented room at the Humphrey house.

Louise's thoughts turned to her future as she cleared the dinner dishes one evening, knowing that there was so much she could do, so much to be done, and not knowing how best to serve, not knowing when, or if, Mike would ever fit into her future. She sighed deeply as she thought that, once again, she was at an impasse.

Mrs. Weatherby, swaddled in a large blanket on the divan, looked up from her crossword puzzle and cleared her throat.

"You'll be going home soon. Do you have any plans for yourself?"

"I've been thinking about it. I keep hoping to hear from Mike, or some word about him. I'm sure I'll continue to work somewhere, but it would be so much easier to choose a direction if I knew what was going on with him."

Mrs. Weatherby shook her head. "I've watched you over the summer, Louise. You're smart and pretty, and a hard worker. You have everything a young woman needs to do something really great with her life, especially now that so many new opportunities have opened up for women. I'd hate for you to have regrets, regrets for things not done, for a life not fully lived. I hope you take some time to think about it, to think about what you could do that would make you truly happy."

"I don't know," Louise replied. "I just thought I'd marry Mike when he came back, and I'd be a wife and mother. It is true, I've learned a lot, and things are very different for me now. I know I can take care of myself, and I like working and making my own money. Still, I've always planned to wait for Mike."

"Of course you have, and I truly hope that he comes home to you safe and sound. But think about it, Louise. You have a lot to offer, and I believe it'd be worth your while to explore your options." With that, Mrs. Weatherby picked up her crossword and focused her attention there once again.

Louise couldn't help but smile as she mulled over Mrs. Weatherby's advice. It was true, she was a grown young woman making her own way in the world. Over the last few years she had found that she could care for herself through her own diligence and hard work; that she could milk a cow, drive a tractor, or machine metal; that she was likeable; that she was strong.

The next morning Louise placed the last jar of late pears in the basement, where it stood neatly lined up with hundreds of other jars filled with tomatoes and relishes, jams and preserves and applesauce. The open wire racks were once again filled with potatoes, and a new harvest of winter squashes sat carefully placed on the low benches in the space under the stairs.

With this final task completed, Louise's service at the farm came to a close. As bitter cold days and freezing nights enveloped New England during

November, she found herself with time to think as she once again arranged her few belongings in her rented room at Dot's house. There was still no word from or about Mike, or Ray. Her recent visit to the Andrews' had only deepened her concern that something was dreadfully wrong.

As for herself, she was in between—unwilling to return to factory work, and no longer needed at the farm. She had enough money, and was grateful to George for his honesty and fairness. At least that was one thing she didn't have to worry about.

Chapter 39

"It's good to have you home," said Dot.

She and Louise sat in the Humphrey's living room on the great white couch, swaddled in flannel pajamas and soft, warm blankets, sipping hot coffee and eating biscuits left over from dinner the night before.

"This is wonderful, Dot. I feel like I'm in the lap of luxury. Here it is, seven in the morning, and I'm still in my pajamas, all bundled up, eating these delicious biscuits, and sipping this wonderful cup of hot coffee. Where did your mother get it? I thought it was like finding a needle in a haystack to come across even a half-pound of the stuff."

"She made a little dress for a woman in Boston; well, for her two-year-old daughter, really. Mother got a quarter-pound of coffee as part of the payment. We'll re-use the grinds tomorrow, of course, but this is the first brew."

"Just heavenly," Louise sighed, relishing the aroma of the coffee. She looked at Dot and gave her a warm smile. "I must admit the last few days have been so nice—sleeping in a bit, having my things around me, and best of all, having you to chat with. I don't think I realized how much I missed you until I moved back in."

"I missed you, too. It's one thing to be busy at work, and then catch up on the weekends. But it's not the same as seeing each other every day. I think the holidays would be very hard for me this year if you weren't here."

"Yes, we'll have a good holiday together. Although I suppose I'll have to stop in at Town Hall to see what Mr. Lowell can find for me to do. After all, I can't spend the rest of my life comfortably ensconced on your couch, although a part of me would very much like to." Louise glanced out the window. It was going to be a bitter cold day, an insistent wind beginning to blow dark, icy clouds inland over Winchester.

Dot shook her head. "Why don't you wait until after the holidays to see Mr. Lowell? If you really want to do something right away, you can help me in the classroom. We still have a few weeks before school lets out for Christmas, and I could really use your help. The children are putting on a play this year, a simplified version of *A Christmas Carol*, and I'm having a devil of a time getting Tiny Tim to limp properly; and the Ghost of Christmas Future insists on saying lines like, 'ooohhhhh, Ebenezer, you are going to die a horrible death, your eyes will be eaten by worms' and other similarly revolting things. I love them, you know, but I have to admit that sometimes I'm very glad to send them home at the end of the day."

"You're not making the offer very tempting, you know," Louise chuckled.

"Oh, well, then, you could read stories, and we'll be making ornaments, too. You might enjoy the sequins and beads."

Louise put down her empty coffee cup. "For you, my dear, I will come help you in your classroom with whatever you need, as long as it's not past the beginning of the year."

"Will you consider staying in Winchester this time?"

"I don't know. Claire is so very busy, and I don't particularly want to work with her. I would like to stay close, though, just in case there's some word from Mike. And of course, so that I can visit you, dear Dottie." Louise shifted in her seat, and adjusted her blanket. "Did you see Mrs. Simard yesterday? Has she heard from Ray?"

"I stopped at her house on the way home from school. They haven't heard anything. It's odd, really. Some families are getting v-mail every week or two, and others are going for months, even more than a year, with no contact at all."

Dot paused for a long moment, then asked, "Nothing from Mike, either?"

Louise shook her head.

"Well, then we wait," said Dot, "and keep good and busy in the meantime."

Dot glanced out the window at the darkening sky. The wind was picking up.

"Unfortunately, that includes today. I promised Mother I'd get supplies in for Thanksgiving, and I want to get it done before the weather gets much worse. Come on, let's get dressed, I want you to keep me company as I sacrifice my ration stamps for our little Thanksgiving feast. Bring yours too, I'll need them!"

Chapter 40

Ray and Mike spent the better part of three days sitting next to each other on the landing craft. They had loaded up on June 2nd for the scheduled June 5th strike, but bad weather delayed their attack by a day, with no time to return to Devonshire. Their craft, along with other ships and transports, circled the Isle of Wight, as the rain drove down in sheets, and waves chopped at the boats; and leaden misery permeated the spirits of the men as deeply as seasickness did their physical bodies.

Then the call came. Desperately relieved to move forward, Ray and Mike, along with two hundred other troops from the 4th Infantry, loaded up on the transport that would carry them from the landing craft to within wading distance of the shore. It was just after three o'clock on the morning of June 6th, and from their position off the French coast, they could see the flak that signaled the landing of the 82nd and 101st Airborne Divisions. The Germans had finally detected the Allied fleet off the Cotentin Coast, and began their attack on the naval armada. The battleships returned fire, the deafening explosions spiking the already heightened tension among the men.

The transport moved slowly toward the beach, and just after six in the morning, Ray and Mike jumped off into the frigid sea. The transport had managed to pull close enough to the shore so that they were only waist-high in the water, but the weight of their pack, plus the weight of the water, made it tough going, and it took nearly ten minutes for them, along with the rest of the troops, to clamber up on to the shoreline.

They had landed almost a mile south of where they were supposed to be. Still, this part of the beach wasn't well guarded. They heard some machine-gun fire overhead, but it wasn't the heavy attack they had expected. The men made their way as fast as they could up the shore, taking cover against a broken sea wall. Brigadier General Theodore Roosevelt, Jr., was on the beach with them, encouraging the men to keep moving, to get ready to complete their first mission, which was to take control of the local exits and causeways leading inland from the sea. Mike and Ray moved with the rest of their unit toward their original target, code-named Utah Beach.

For the next three weeks, the 4th Infantry, along with the 9th and 79th Infantry Divisions, fought through hedgerow country until they claimed the harbor town of Cherbourg. Ray and Mike looked out for each other as best they could. One afternoon, when things were quiet, the two men were resting in a field, leaning back against a stone wall, sharing a cigarette. Ray looked to his left and saw a group of about twenty Germans, bent and worn, walking inland, retreating. Ray turned his head to the right. It was already wearing on him, wearing on Mike. They believed in their mission, wanted to defend their home and country, but they weren't killers, weren't inclined to shoot anyone whose face they could see.

From Cherbourg, the 4th Infantry traveled south over the Cotentin Peninsula, through to Periers. From there, they pushed on in an unrelenting eastward offense. In late August, they were the first troops, along with the French 2nd Armored Division, to enter Paris, and effectively liberate the city from German occupancy.

They would not rest there long. The 4th Infantry was to give chase to the retreating German forces, and eventually cross the German border. With orders to reconvene the following morning, ready to leave Paris, the American troops dispersed to enjoy a brief liberty among the celebrating Parisians.

Ray and Mike wandered down a small side street off the Champs-Élysées, hoping for an hour's respite from the frenzied revelry nearby. They passed a small pâtisserie, where an elderly couple stood in the window, waving to them. They waved back, thinking nothing of it. But then the old couple scrambled into the street, stopped them with exuberant embraces, kissed each of the young men on the cheek. The couple spoke in broken English, invited the men into their shop, where they made them sit at a little table. Soon, hot coffee appeared, and a little bit of cream, and a plate of bread.

The couple pulled up a table next to them, and told the two men their story of covert resistance, of relatives dead or missing, of constant fear, not for themselves, but for their neighbors, their beautiful city, their country. They took them upstairs to their apartment, asked the young men to stay, offered them a bath. The old woman would make them dinner, and they could sleep in real beds. And so they stayed, relishing a dinner of cassoulet and warm bread and cheese; and red wine, a couple of bottles the old man had hidden under a floorboard near the oven in the shop below. The old woman gave them pajamas. They belonged to her son, she said, it was good someone could use them while he was away. The old man sighed, and smiled at his wife, and agreed it was good. That night Mike and Ray slept in clean, soft beds, with eyelet-trimmed sheets and down pillows.

Ray rolled over in the early morning, forgetting for a few glorious moments where he was, savoring the unusual comfort. He heard something that made him open his eyes, the sound of someone weeping. It was Mike, sitting up in his bed, head in his hands.

"Mike, what is it?"

Mike shook his head, brushed away the tears. "I'm tired, Ray, so very tired. All I want is to go home. I almost wish we hadn't stayed here last night. It made me realize how much I miss my family, my friends…simple things, like a hot bath and cotton pajamas, and easy conversation around the dinner table."

He got up out of bed and went to the window, looked out onto the street below.

"I gotta tell you, Ray, the only reason I've lasted as long as I have is because of you. You've been my touchstone, my link to home, and I want you to know I'm grateful for it. And I hope we get to stay together throughout this whole damn war, because I have a feeling we haven't seen the worst of it."

Ray rolled over onto his back. "What do you want to do when you go home, Mike?" It was a question they asked each other when things were quiet, when they needed a diversion from the anxious thoughts that crowded in too easily. The answers were always the same.

"I want to sit with my family around me. I want to have a house near my parents, I want my family and friends to come over for barbeques in the summer, and spend Christmas and Thanksgiving all together. I want Louise and lots of children. I want to go to college. I want to sit in the reading room at the library and read a book. I want to go into every shop in Winchester and know every shopkeeper. I want to go home and stay home forever." His eyes were dry now, focused on a group of children passing underneath him. One of them looked up, saw Mike. Mike waved, the boy waved back, smiling. Mike turned from the window, sat back on the bed. "What about you, Ray, what do you want?"

He looked at Ray, no longer the chubby kid from Pembroke Road, but now lean and muscled, with lines of strain etched on his forehead.

Ray was quiet for a moment, pensive. "I want to hold Dot."

Over the next two months, Mike and Ray were separated twice as their unit was divided, then reordered. In early November they found themselves together again at the northern limit of the Siegfried Line, just inside the German border near the Hürtgen Forest, a swath of pines and fir trees that towered over a thick undergrowth carpeting the forest floor. Steep ravines and high ridges threaded through the landscape, a series of natural barriers that provided essential protection for critical German holdings, the Duren and Cologne plains, the Roer dams, the Rhine. It was heavily defended. The Germans were entrenched, with machine-gun nests and rows of minefields strategically placed throughout the terrain.

In mid-November, the 4th Infantry began to push through. The American troops faced hard enemies, the first being the Germans; but equally oppressive were the elements, for snow, rain and sleet consistently hampered their efforts. An outbreak of trench foot added to the misery. The troops made slow headway in the frozen, treacherous landscape, every foot gained a foot hard-earned. The plan was simple. Each day was spent fighting to gain the next line of enemy bunkers, and then hold the new line overnight. Each morning started with movement to gain the next line of bunkers. It was a slow, grueling, and costly effort.

It was three weeks before Christmas Day. Mike and Ray, like the other men in their unit, had spent the night in a German bunker, which offered protection from the wind and snow, if not the frigid cold. The morning broke as an overcast, frozen icicle, a light snow trickling from the sky. It was early, and the world around them was silent. Ray stretched, half asleep, trying to warm any part of his numb body that he could. In a few minutes the order would come, and they would push forward with the others, hoping to gain the next line of bunkers before digging in for another night. He peered out of the opening to scan the surroundings, a stand of burnt and broken trees poking like jagged spikes thrust up out of the mud and snow, victims of vicious and ongoing artillery-laden combat.

Mike looked up in time to see Ray's expression change, and then see him fall over to his side, half out of the enclosure. Mike scrambled to Ray and dragged him back under cover, and then rolled him over onto his back, looking at his face, looking for the wound. Mike couldn't hear the cracking sound of gunfire going on around him now, he could only see that Ray was still. He found the wound, a hole in the right side of Ray's jacket, under his arm.

"Ray!" he shouted as he shook his friend. Mike took off his scarf and wedged it under Ray's head.

"C'mon, Ray, don't you dare do this to me!" Then, into the frigid air outside, he screamed, "Medic!"

Ray's eyes came back from somewhere far away, focused on Mike.

He tried to speak.

"Dot," he spat, trying to breathe, unable.

"Yeah, Dot, I know."

"Help me."

Ray began to mouth the words to the Our Father, whispering with the force that he had left. Mike joined him, saying the words with him and for him. A cough of blood and a spasm of pain wracked Ray's body. Ray was gasping now, the breath finding no purchase. Mike knew he was drowning in his own blood.

The prayer finished, Mike looked at his friend, knowing what he wanted, knowing it was the last thing he could do for him. He didn't know the whole form, but he knew the words, had learned them in Catechism. He wasn't a priest, it wouldn't count, but he did it anyway. He had no oil, so he took off his glove, and spit on his thumb. He touched the spit to Ray's forehead, and bowing his head in prayer, said, "Through this holy anointing, may the Lord in his love and mercy help you with the grace of the Holy Spirit. May the Lord who frees you from sin save you, and raise you up."

He lifted his head, and looked at his friend, took his hand. "I'll take care of everything, Ray, I promise."

The last light of recognition dimmed, and Ray fell away into unending sleep.

Mike placed Ray's hand down gently. He went through his pockets, and retrieved two letters, both from Dot; and a few pictures, one of the Simard family, formal and stiff, Mr. and Mrs. Simard obviously holding children still for the photograph; and one of Dot posing near a tree, Mystic Lake glistening in the background.

There was a third picture, taken when they were children. Mike couldn't remember who took the picture, but it was of everyone he'd grown up with, all the kids from the end of Pembroke Road—Walter, and his brothers, Patrick and Daniel; Ray, Henry and Mike; Beth; and even Louise, from before her father's death. They were so young in the picture, grouped together in Walter's back yard, squinting into the sunlight, unused to posing for a camera. Impossible, now, Mike thought, to come together like that ever again.

Mike turned to sit next to the body, stuffing the pictures and letters into his pocket. He was numb with cold and exhaustion. Tears flowed down his cheeks, freezing by the time they reached his chin. All Mike could feel now was the precipice of loneliness that seemed to surround him, a sheer drop into a hazy nothingness. He didn't move, sure he would fall into it if he did, sure it would envelop him if he breathed too deeply.

He didn't know how long he sat there. When he looked again at Ray, a light dusting of snow had covered his face and upper body, pushed in by a breeze stirring across the scarred land outside. Mike looked away. Sensation was slowly returning, and with it, he heard the artillery fire, the shouts of other men in his unit, and started to feel the one place on his body that was wet, and warm, no, burning. He looked at his left leg. A pool of blood had collected underneath it, dripping onto the bunker floor. He could see his left calf was shredded, the meat hanging where a bullet had caught him and torn through the flesh. He'd never even felt it. He reached over and gently pulled his scarf from under Ray's head, and then wrapped it around the wound, grunting as he tightened the makeshift field dressing.

He moved, just enough to yell outside the bunker.

"Medic!"

It took nearly an hour for the medic to arrive. The fighting finally moved away to the east, and the medics moved through. When one of them came near, Mike gathered his strength and pushed himself out of the bunker, and whispered 'hey' as loudly as he could. The medic reached him. Mike looked up at the man, a thin, gaunt teenager, and for a bad moment, Mike thought it was Death hovering over him.

"You're going to be okay," said Death, after a quick assessment. Suddenly, the wound screamed anew as the medic poured sulfa powder over it. He applied a new field dressing to the gaping hole, and whistled for two corpsmen to come move him out.

"My friend," Mike whispered.

The medic peered into the bunker, pulled Ray out and laid him on the open ground.

"Sorry, kid, I can't help your friend. But I promise we won't leave him here. Let's take care of you."

Then the medic moved out of view, and corpsmen appeared, and placed Mike gingerly on a litter. As they lifted him up, Mike turned his head one last time to see his friend. His last memory of that forest was of Ray, lying outside the gray stone bunker, snow falling gently on his body.

Chapter 41

Gus watched from his front room window as the officer rapped smartly at the front door across the street. He knew what it meant. He watched as Mrs. Simard opened the door, her husband beside her. The officer delivered his message, and Gus saw Mrs. Simard turn in to her husband's shoulder, saw Mr. Simard, pale and somber, put his arm around her. There was a brief discussion, Mr. Simard not looking at the officer in front of him as he they talked, only nodding acknowledgement as the officer handed Mr. Simard an envelope. Gus picked up the phone, and called the Rectory at St. Mary's Parish.

Ten minutes elapsed, and in that span of time, the officer departed, and Father Glenn took his place at the Simard's front door, black stole in hand. Gus went into his kitchen and began to cook, all the while talking to Helen, for although it wasn't summer in the garden, she had appeared to him, sitting at the kitchen table, as he pulled out an old recipe card from the box.

"Do you think this will do?" He felt her nod. "Yes, this was always a favorite for us, real comfort food. I wish you could make it, though, no one made this like you, mein liebstes. Ah, well, you can tell me if I'm doing something wrong, yah?"

Twenty minutes after Gus started making the casserole, Ann, Ray's older sister, bundled up in her warmest winter clothes, left the Simard house and headed toward St. Mary's.

The church was warm, almost stifling. Ann took off her cap and scarf and mittens, crossed herself with holy water before entering the nave. Through the doors leading into the church she could hear the choir, practicing "Silent Night" for the Christmas Eve performance. She stood for a moment at the back pew, looking to make sure Dot was at practice. Satisfied that she was present with the others near the altar, Ann sat down. She waited patiently, listening to the voices, the direction of the choir mistress, another song, "God Rest Ye Merry Gentlemen."

Choir practice finished. The members said their good-byes, and filtered out of the church. Dot stayed behind to talk to the choir mistress for a few minutes. Finally, Dot made her way to the back of the church, trying to button her coat as she walked. She caught sight of Ann sitting in the pew, and stopped short as she saw the look on Ann's face.

"No," Dot said quietly, almost under her breath, a sick terror creeping in an icy wave through her body.

Ann stood up and approached her, wrapped her arms around her, and whispered, "My sweet Dorothy, I am so sorry."

"No," Dot repeated, tears starting to spill onto Ann's sweater.

Ann pulled her gently to the pew. "Come sit down. We only found out an hour ago. It was in Germany, two weeks ago."

Dot was now sobbing hard and deep, so that she could barely catch her breath. Ann handed her a handkerchief.

It took nearly ten minutes before Dot caught her breath well enough to ask, "When will he come home?"

"I don't know. It seems it's very difficult. The officer who came to tell us said he will probably be buried over there."

"What? Oh, no!" Dot's sobbing began in earnest again. "They can't do that, he should be here, he needs to be here. How else can I visit him and talk to him?"

Dot stood up. She was suddenly furious, and wanted desperately to get out of the church. All her prayers, all the candles she'd lit, all the hoping, it was all for nothing. Where was God when Ray needed protection? And now it seemed she wouldn't even have a gravesite to visit. It was just too much.

Turning to Ann, she said, as softly as she could, "Thanks, Annie, for telling me in person. I have to go now." Dot rushed out of the church, desperate to get home.

Word spread about Ray. His loss was felt keenly, in part because he made people laugh, because he sang so beautifully, but mostly because people knew him as a friendly, caring, and generous young man. There were others from Winchester, of course, who made the ultimate sacrifice—one young man at Omaha, another in Japan, a woman working for the Red Cross, another young woman who had joined the WAC. As families mourned their losses, the community as a whole pushed on, supporting those who were suffering in their midst, supporting those still fighting overseas.

As for Dot, she was inconsolable, and confined herself to her bed. Her mother brought meals to her on a tray, only to take them away again, untouched. Visitors came and went, dropping their condolences and cards at the front door. Louise wanted to sit with her friend, but Mrs. Humphrey gently suggested that Louise give Dot some time to grieve.

After nearly a week, however, Mrs. Humphrey asked Louise to see if there was something she could do.

Louise tapped at Dot's bedroom door, and went in.

She sat at the foot of Dot's bed. Her friend looked haggard from her self-imposed fasting and mourning.

"Dot, what are you doing?" Louise asked.

Dot looked away. "I'm just thinking."

"Dot, I'm inviting you out to lunch today. You need to get dressed and get out of this house and get some fresh air. I have something I want to show you, and I can't show you here."

"No, thanks anyway, Louise. I'm so tired, I want to stay right here."

Louise would not be put off.

"What are you going to do, Dorothy May Humphrey? Lie here until you rot? Oh, I'm sure Ray would be so proud of you right now, refusing everything, letting everyone feel sorry for you, feeling sorry for yourself. I have to say, I'm disappointed by your selfishness. This isn't like you, and it's not right, and you know it."

The Lights of Pembroke Road

"Shut up, Louise. Just stop right now, you don't know anything," Dot warned.

Louise pressed. "You think you're the only one who's been hurt by Ray's death? His mother and father are beside themselves, and Ann doesn't even have time to grieve properly, poor thing. She's taking care of everything for her parents, making all the arrangements. Are you at least going to go to the service?"

Dot's brow furrowed. "Service?"

"See, you're so wrapped up in your selfish little world that you didn't know there's a service, day after tomorrow at St. Mary's. Will you be there?"

"I don't want to go back to church. I—I don't know."

"Oh, you're going to go. And you're going to get up out of that bed right now, Dot, and take a bath, because you stink. And while you do that, I'm going to pick out some clothes for you, and you're going out with me today, and you're going to the service on Saturday."

Louise pulled the covers off her friend.

"Awful, just awful. You really are ripe, Dottie, you know that? Ray would be appalled."

With that, Louise moved over to the window, and pulling back the curtains that had been drawn against the daylight, she cracked open the bedroom window, letting in a shimmer of the frigid, fresh air. Without another word, she headed out of the room and into the bathroom, started a bath, and pulled tooth powder and soap from the cabinet. Back in the bedroom, she saw Dot had made it to a sitting position. Her friend looked so pale and thin, her hair disheveled into a rats' nest.

"Come on, do you want help or can you do this yourself?" she asked.

"I am a little bit smelly. I can do it."

"Be sure to wash your hair, too. I'll help you comb it out after."

While Dot bathed, Louise changed the sheets on her bed, and tidied her room. She laid clothes out on the newly made bed, and got a fresh towel and comb ready for Dot's hair.

Two hours later, Dot was clean and dressed, her long brown hair arranged in a simple braid down her back. Mrs. Humphrey had stayed out of the way during this whole time, but smiled and nodded at Louise in thanks as the two girls went out the door.

They went to Randall's. Louise ordered soup and sandwiches for both of them, and when the food arrived, insisted that Dot eat at least half her soup and half her sandwich. "This is no time to waste food. I'm not your mother, so don't make me cajole you like a little baby into eating a few bites of anything."

Dot ate, and Louise could see some relief in her friend as she ate the first solid meal in almost a week.

When they had finished, Louise pushed an ad across the table.

"Look at this."

Dot looked. It was an advertisement for a one-year nursing course at Massachusetts General Hospital. Applications were being accepted, with tuition subsidized by the government, and participants would receive a stipend for living expenses.

"What about this? You can't think that I can go do this. The course starts in three weeks. There wouldn't be any openings left." Dot pushed the advertisement back across the table.

Louise pushed it back again. "I spoke with the Director. There are still spaces open. I signed up. And I signed you up, too."

Dot looked at her friend, disbelieving. "You did not!"

Louise continued. "Tomorrow I'm heading into Boston to meet with the landlady who will provide the housing for this program, maybe even get a room assignment. I want you to go with me."

"Louise, I can't believe you did this! You must be out of your mind." Dot sat for a few minutes, looking at the advertisement. "Well, I'll go with you tomorrow, just to keep you company. But I don't plan to join up for a year of classes. If Ray comes home, I want to be here."

It was after the Mass for Ray, during the reception at the Simard home, that Dot heard with certainty that Ray's body would not be shipped back to Winchester; but rather, that he would be interred at a cemetery in France, along with hundreds of other fallen soldiers.

She found Louise in the Simard's kitchen, washing dishes. Picking up a dish towel, she started to dry.

"Did you hear, Louise?" Dot had been in shock until now, but as the words flowed out, so did the tears. "Ray...Ray isn't coming home. They're burying him over there, in some foreign cemetery, with people he doesn't know. They can't even say yet which cemetery." She stopped drying, and hid her face in the dish towel. Sobbing now, the words came out stilted and distressed. "I…won't….get to see him…or talk to him….he…won't be here… with his family…or his friends."

She cried for several minutes more, her head buried on the shoulder of her best friend. A few people walked into the kitchen, only to turn around and walk out. Mrs. Simard stood in the doorway for a moment, her own fresh tears evident. Louise shrugged her shoulders, and Mrs. Simard disappeared again.

Finally, Dot quieted. She looked up, blew her nose into the dish towel. Her face was red and blotchy, her nose and eyes swollen.

"Come on, I'm taking you home," said Louise. "Now you can go to bed."

A few days later, Dot sat across from Louise at the breakfast table, pale but steady. She told Louise she would go with her to Boston. She would take the nurse's training.

"Are you sure? What changed your mind?" asked Louise as she spread a thin layer of jam on her toast.

"I don't really have any reason to stay anymore. What will I do with myself? I can't bring myself to go back to school. All those little children, just reminders of what I was dreaming about ever since Ray left. So the nursing program would be very different, and I guess, well, I guess it's something constructive to do. Besides, Mother and Daddy both said it would be good for me to get out of Winchester a bit, start living my life. I don't have to do it forever, but for the time being, I can be useful, even if it's not what I had envisioned. And…Ray would have wanted me to move forward, I think, and he would have been right. So we'll go together, and make the best of it."

Louise stood up and went over to her friend, and hugged her. "Yes, we will."

Chapter 42

Mike's leg was still very sore. The bullet had gone clean through the fleshy part of his left calf. Since the day that he'd been wounded, the day that Ray died, he'd only heard bits and pieces of information, something about the 4th Infantry saving Luxembourg, and about some of the men lost. He didn't care. He only really knew what had happened to him, and to Ray.

Mike spent Christmas and New Year's Day in an Army hospital in a cast, another four weeks recuperating in a big country house in Surrey, surrounded by other men, some British, some American, all in various stages of recuperation. Some would be sent back to fight. He was on his way home.

In early February, Mike was transferred north into Scotland, to the cold, evergreen fishing town of Gourock. He was surprised to see the *Queen Mary* at dock, covered, still, in the gray paint which had adorned her since the beginning, when she'd first been pressed into service. She was a fast ship, successfully eluding Axis attacks from the sea and air as she transported troops and cargo from Britain to New York and back again, nearly a hundred voyages since 1940.

Mike boarded the ship. There were rules to follow, Standing Orders and Daily Orders; berth assignments, mess assignments, and work assignments for those who were fit; but after instructions were given, Mike was left to fend for himself for the six-day journey to New York. He caught a couple of movies that were showing in the ship's theater, got his hair trimmed at the barber. The skies were fair, and Mike spent much of the trip on deck, smoking, reading, and gambling a bit, even though it was against the rules.

The ship pulled up to the Cunard's New York Pier. Looking over the rail, Mike saw hundreds of people below, a carnival of waving ribbons and handkerchiefs and flowers. A band was playing "She's a Grand Old Flag," a welcoming fanfare for the troops now starting to make their way down the gangplank. He could smell something over the swampy sea air and diesel fuel, something savory and rich—hot dogs.

Mike scanned the people on the dock, hoping against hope that someone would be there to meet him, unsure if his telegram reached home. Suddenly, he caught sight of his mother in her fox fur hat, then saw his father beside her. He waved at them, waved like a madman, but the sun was in their eyes, and there were so many people and so much noise.

Mike started to choke up, but only for a moment. He picked up his gear and made his way slowly to the gangplank, keeping to the side as he limped along, keeping his eyes on his parents now that he'd found them. It seemed to take forever to get down that gangplank, as other soldiers jostled, as respectfully as possible, to get off the ship. He saw his parents still searching the flank of the boat, and then his father's eyes caught him as he stepped onto the dock. Mike could see his dad pointing and shouting, tugging at his mother.

"Look, look, there's Mike," he heard above the roaring din. Mike made his way through the throngs of expectant parents, wives, and sweethearts, and those already reunited, forming clusters of people hugging, kissing, and crying; until finally he dropped his bag and clasped his father's hand, followed by a hearty hug from him, and then his mother, and they were like the other clusters of people on the dock, standing, hugging, crying.

"Thank God you're home, son, thank God you're home," his mother said as she hugged him tightly.

"I missed you, Mom."

Finally, she let go, and Philip Andrews clapped his son on the back. "Let's get out of here and go home. Your mother wants to feed you and tuck you in."

Two days after arriving home, Mike crossed the street to the Simard house, and knocked at the door. Mrs. Simard smiled when she saw who it was, and invited him in.

"Why, Mike, I can't believe you're home. Thank God! But what happened? You've been hurt!"

"Oh, I got shot," he said, indifferently, "but it's much better now, it really is."

"Well, come in and sit down, Mike. Let me get you something hot to drink. We don't have coffee, will you have tea?"

"Yes, ma'am, that would be very nice," he said as he followed her into the kitchen.

He sat at the kitchen table as she put the kettle on.

"Your mother didn't say anything about you coming home, Mike, when did you get here?"

"Day before yesterday. Came in on the *Queen Mary*, beautiful ship, very fast."

The conversation remained carefully light as Mrs. Simard went through the motions of making a pot of tea, pulling cups from the cupboard, and a plate, which she piled with crackers.

"Where are all the girls?" Mike asked. "I half expected to walk into, well, a house full of girls."

"Oh, well, the younger girls are at school. Annie and Janie are done with school now, and they are so busy, working at the Red Cross, or at the hospital, or with the En-Ka Society, I hardly ever see them myself."

Mrs. Simard placed the plate of crackers in the center of the kitchen table, and carefully poured the tea. Mike could see she was shaking a bit and was relieved when she finally sat down across from him.

"I'm sorry I don't have any sugar for the tea, Mike. Oh, but I do have some milk, let me get it."

She jumped up and retrieved a milk bottle from the Frigidaire, and sat again.

Mike pulled the pictures from his pocket and slid them across the table.

Mrs. Simard stopped short at the sight of the pictures. She reached out to touch them, moved them so that they were spread out in front of her.

"You were with him?" she asked, her voice low and steady.

"Yes, ma'am. He had these with him. I thought you might want them."

She picked up the picture of Dot. "She would have made a lovely daughter-in-law. I got so used to her being here, she fit in so well with all of us." She handed the picture back to Mike. "Give this to her, will you, Mike? With my love."

"Of course, Mrs. Simard. It would be a privilege," Mike answered.

She picked up the photograph of the group of children. "Look at all of you together. Do you know who took this picture, Mike?"

Mike shook his head.

"I did," Mrs. Simard said, a little smile popping up. "I'll never forget the day. It was a Saturday, Labor Day weekend. We were having a barbeque at the Hannigan's. Everyone was bringing something, a pot luck, really. I brought a potato salad. Mr. Simard had bought a new camera, and I wanted to play with it, try my hand at photography, you know, just to see if I had any talent. Anyway, I wanted to get a picture with all of you, since it seemed all the neighborhood children were gathered in that one back yard that day. I couldn't get my girls to cooperate, but the rest of you managed to hold still for a few moments. That trellis behind you was brand new, and I thought it would make an interesting backdrop. Look at Beth, her hair was so short then. And all of you squinting in the sunlight. Heavens, it was a hot day, I remember that too."

She put the picture on the table and slid it back toward Mike. "You hold on to this, Mike. The children in this picture are your friends, I want you to have it."

"Thank you, Mrs. Simard. That's very kind of you."

Mike picked up the picture and looked at it again, remembering the day he'd found it in Ray's pocket. He thought he would always think of that moment whenever he looked at the picture. He wasn't sure that's what he wanted.

Mrs. Simard smiled as she picked up the third photograph. "And I'll keep this picture. I remember when this was taken, too. Oh, what an awful time we had, all the children were so squirmy, the clothes were itching at them, they just hated it! I think Ray pulled off everything but his underwear within about a minute after the picture was taken, and I couldn't be angry with him for doing it. Even my clothes were so full of starch I couldn't wait to get home to change."

The following weekend, Mike's parents invited neighbors, relatives, and friends to a party to welcome their son home. Mike's sisters were there, of course, and Amanda and Beth Crowley came an hour early to help Margaret set up. The house was a like a bustling beehive, and Mike and his father hid in the den and read the newspaper, out of the way until Margaret Andrews sent for them. Once in a while, Mike got up and peeked into the living room to observe the almost dizzying scurry of activity.

"Who is that?" he asked his father.

Philip Andrews got up from his seat and stood next to his son at the door, saw the young woman in question.

"Oh, why, that's Beth—you remember her, you two used to walk to school together." Philip nudged his son. "Sure turned out a looker, didn't she? You'd never have known it five years ago, but, well, there she is now." He returned to his chair and his newspaper, grinning.

Mike watched her as she placed plates of sandwiches on the dining room table. The last time he'd seen Beth was at the dinner Rose Hannigan held just after he and Ray joined the Army. The Beth he knew, had always known, was a gangly, freckle-faced girl that he'd been forced to walk to school with, who had been accepted as a member of their pack only because she could pitch and catch. No, this was someone different. This young lady had her dark blonde hair pulled back into a soft ponytail, and she was wearing a simple pink dress with white pumps. She wore a soft pink lipstick that framed her wide smile. But there were the dimples, the part of her that she hadn't outgrown, the only confirmation that this young lady really was the odious Beth.

During the party, Mike looked for Louise. He finally asked his mother if she was coming, if she'd been invited.

Margaret Andrews' answer was evasive. "Oh, she's gone off to work at one of the local farms. Last I saw her she was in one of those awful uniforms. Really, it's a shame how she's let herself go."

Mike persisted. "Did she know I was coming home?"

"Of course she did, everyone knew," his mother replied, reassembling a cookie platter on the punch table. "Now you mustn't think about it too much. I'm sure she'll stop by to say hello soon." And then Harriet whisked her away to see about more napkins and sandwiches.

"You didn't invite her, did you?" asked Harriet in a hushed tone.

"Certainly not," Margaret Andrews whispered back. As the two women made their way into the kitchen, Margaret looked behind her, and, sure that no one was within earshot, continued her train of thought.

"Louise is safely tucked away in Boston, and I have no intention of contacting her at all. The last thing I want is to have any member of that vile Duncan family wheedling her way into my family. Could you imagine if they got married? I'd have to see that hideous wife of George's at every holiday, maybe even speak to her. Oh, no," Margaret shook her head emphatically, "that would be entirely unacceptable." Her husband's affair with Claire ended more than three years ago, but it left a bitterness in her soul that she simply couldn't shake, and a prick of her pride that would not allow any member of the Duncan family to cross her threshold, let alone marry her son.

Harriet nodded her head in agreement. "You're absolutely right, of course. I certainly won't say a word. Here, let me help you put together some more sandwiches, and then I'll get another pot of coffee ready. I'm so glad you were able to get the real thing, everyone out there appreciates it so much; and everything is absolutely delicious!"

"Thank you, Harriet," said Margaret. "You have been a godsend the last several years, I don't know what I would do without you!"

Mike wandered through the party, accepted hugs, made small talk, enjoyed his first decent cigarette in months. His heart skipped a beat when he saw Walter standing alone on the back porch, looking out over the grounds, a patchwork of melting snow and brown earth dappling the formal gardens. He put on his jacket and headed outside.

"Hey, Walter!" Mike clapped his best friend on the shoulder, shook his hand happily.

"Well, there you are!" Walter chimed, glad to see his friend home, alive, standing there in front of him like they were kids again.

"Jesus, Mike, you're looking pretty good for a guy who's been through the mill."

They talked for a while, pulled chairs outside from the kitchen table, smoked. Mike didn't talk about the war, Walter didn't ask. They talked about what people were doing in town, and Walter's work at the *Star*. Finally, Mike asked if Walter knew what happened to Louise.

"Didn't your mom tell you? She's in Boston, with Dot. After, well, after we heard about Ray, Dot just fell to pieces for a while there. She lit candles for him at St. Mary's nearly every day, you know, and then, there was no reason to light candles anymore. Then we heard Drew Pearson's announcement about the 4th Infantry being wiped out. After that, with no word, we all thought the worst. Even after they got the story straight, we didn't know anything, and by then Louise and Dot had left. Louise was the one who saw the program openings, convinced Dot to go with her to join a nursing program at Mass General, and now they're both in it. I think it was good for both of them, you know? Louise really wanted to move away from Winchester, and Dot needed something to focus on, something meaningful, after all she'd been thorugh."

Mike's brow furrowed. "Does Louise know I'm back?"

Walter took a last drag and stubbed out his cigarette.

"Geez, Mike, I doubt it. I only found out on Wednesday, and I'm at the newspaper! I think your folks really wanted to keep you to themselves until today, you know, just to make sure you were real and they could fuss over you a bit before everyone else smothered you."

He lit another cigarette. He was conscious that this was two in a row, but this was a special occasion, so he indulged.

"Hey, Walter...she hasn't, ummm, found someone new?" He couldn't say any more, suddenly choking up. Walter laughed a little, reassuring Mike.

"No, Mike, she hasn't. She's, well, I don't know, become stronger, more self-reliant over the last few years, like most of the women I know. I think the last she heard about you was that you were missing, and then we heard about Ray—oh, I can tell you, it was an awful time here, Mike. I can't imagine what you went through, but I can assure you that the whole town was really in pain, and it was like you came back from the dead when you were all of a sudden here. She's been waiting for you, Mike. I mean, she's been keeping herself busy, doing a great job supporting the war effort here at home and everything, but she hasn't found someone new."

He took a deep drag off his cigarette, blew it out slowly. "I don't want to assume anything, Mike. After all, you've been gone a while, seen some things, maybe had a change of heart. But if you want her address in Boston, stop by the *Star* tomorrow morning, I'll give it to you. Up to you to follow through."

It never occurred to Mike that he could have a change of heart. If any-thing, everything he'd experienced sharpened to a fine point his needs, his wants, his goals. He wanted a home of his own, here in Winchester, with Louise by his side, children at his feet, dogs in the yard, flowers in the garden. He would go to college, go to work, and settle in Winchester for the rest of his life. There was no question in his mind. He could see it, grasp it, it was his, now that he was back on American soil, at home in Winchester, with his family and friends around him. All that was missing was Louise.

Chapter 43

The next morning bloomed cool, clear, and bright. Mike stopped by the *Winchester Star* office when it opened, picked up Louise's address from Walter, and took the train into Boston. The boarding house where Louise and Dot were living wasn't far from the train station, but Mike took a wrong street, turning left when he should have turned right, and it took him a while to recover. When he did, he found himself at the end of Blossom Court, a long cul-de-sac lined with three-story brownstone houses, with only a painted number over the door, or the odd barren planter on the step, to differentiate one from the other. He stood, finally, in front of one of the brownstones. The number 26 was painted in neat black script at the top of the doorframe, and Mike looked again at Walter's notes to be sure. He climbed the steps, and knocked on the door.

Mrs. Lasby, a fiftyish woman of not inconsequential girth, peered over her spectacles at the uniformed young man that stood on her stoop. He was asking about Louise. Her gaze went over him again, taking in the uniform, the medals, the smile, the earnestness.

"Well," she started, "I don't give out personal information about my young ladies. I have very strict rules, you know. But I can say that she's not in, she's working today, and sometimes I've seen her over at that little park by the Charles River at lunchtime." The woman pointed a round finger toward the far end of the street, where Mike could make out some trees, and beyond that, rising over the treetops, Massachusetts General Hospital.

He tipped his cap, thanked her, and headed off toward the park.

He arrived at a shady bench as the clock tower struck eleven. He sat for a moment, thinking he would just wait, but then he saw a flower shop across the street, and a delicatessen on the corner. What an idiot he was! Of course, flowers, and sandwiches for a nice lunch at the park. He retrieved a small bouquet, and two sandwiches, along with two root beers, and returned to the bench. The clock struck the half-hour, and Mike watched as people went in and out of the hospital, walking from one place to another, many of them turning their heads at the sight of the uniformed man sitting at the park bench with flowers and a sack of food. They smiled at him, nodded their heads; he smiled, nodded back.

The day was warming up. The clock tower struck noon, and groups of young women poured out of a hospital side door. The minutes ticked by. The flow of hospital uniforms slowed to a trickle. His hopes flagged. Maybe she wasn't coming to the park today.

"Michael Andrews?" A familiar voice said his name from somewhere over his right shoulder. He turned, and saw Dot Humphrey standing a few yards away, staring, incredulous. He was up and by her side in an instant, at first, he thought, to greet an old friend, but suddenly he was holding her up as her knees gave way. He helped her over to the bench, where he sat next to her, and opened a root beer.

Handing it to her, he said, "Here, Dot, drink this, the sugar will help." She took a sip, then another.

Dot looked up at Mike, pale from the shock, eyes starting to tear. He handed her his handkerchief.

"Oh, Mike," was all she could say. She sipped the root beer, pressed a few tears away into the handkerchief; he kept an eye on the hospital side door as he waited until she was ready. Finally, he looked at her.

"Want a sandwich? It's ham, the real thing," he offered, and she laughed. "Where did you come from?"

"I came back on a boat, about ten days ago. It's been a kind of whirlwind. My mother is fussing, my dad keeps saying 'it's good to have you home, son,' my sister just keeps busy helping around the house, asking every two minutes if I need anything. But I missed Louise, so here I am. I heard the two of you are in a nursing program—I think the uniform looks very smart on you, Dot."

Dot patted her cap, self-conscious, making sure it was straight.

"Thank you, Mike." Then, "I, that is, we, heard that you were missing, and I think we feared the worst, especially when we heard about Ray." She pulled in a deep breath, and went on. "We, that is, Louise and I, both needed a fresh start, in a fresh place, for different reasons maybe, but still. It was very hard at first, but we were determined to press on. Louise has been my angel every step of the way. And now we're here, working at the hospital, training to be nurses, and it's been good for both of us." She took another sip of the soda. The bubbles gave her something to focus on.

Mike sat back on the bench. He looked over at some children playing in a sand pile, industrious toddlers building castles and roads, their mothers sitting on nearby benches, smoking, engaged in lively conversation. From his coat pocket he pulled out a small bundle, which contained the photograph Mrs. Simard had asked Mike to return to Dot; and Dot's letters, the ones he'd retrieved from Ray's jacket the day Ray was killed. It was time to let these go. He handed the bundle to Dot.

With just enough breath for her to hear as he said the words, Mike spoke, trying not to waver, trying to keep his voice even. "I may never have another chance, Dot, I may never be able to say it again, so I'm going to tell you this now. It was fast, he didn't suffer. And I was there. I talked to him at the end, held his hand as he passed. He was with a friend when it happened. I just thought you should know."

Dot fingered the letters for a moment, saw the photograph. She held her head up and took another deep breath, followed by another drink of the soda. "Thank you, Mike. Thank you for telling me. I'm grateful you were there."

They sat quietly for a few moments. Dot put the bundle in the pocket of her uniform. She went on, cheerfully, changing the subject. "I bet you'd like to see Louise now, wouldn't you?" He nodded, smiling sheepishly. "Well, I know she'll be over the moon to see you, Mike. Can you wait here for just a few more minutes? She's in the dungeon today training men to be medics in the field, so she won't come up for air unless it's important. And this is important." She got up. He rose to his feet.

"Dungeon?"

"The hospital basement. A dreary place, really, you have to pass the hospital morgue to get to it. You'll be a welcome excuse to get out for a while. Just wait here." She started toward the hospital, called back as she walked, "I'm so glad you're home, Mike." She disappeared beyond the hospital entrance.

Ten minutes passed, then fifteen. And then Louise popped out of the hospital side door, scanning the park, looking for him.

"Louise!" he called, waving, walking toward her. She ran across the street, reached the park, reached him, enveloped him in her arms, she in his. They kissed, not caring who saw. They hugged again, and he breathed in the work scent of her, starch mixed with sweat, and something medicinal. They stood at the edge of the park, holding each other. Louise pressed her cheek against his chest, heard his heart beating, felt the familiar strength of his arms as he held her.

"Oh, Mike, I can't believe it, you're really here, home again." She pulled away to look at his face. "It's true, isn't it? You're home to stay?"

"Yes, forever and ever, yes!" He laughed, and they made their way over to the bench and sat down.

"I thought you might be hungry, I got you a sandwich. Oh, and these are for you, too." He handed her the flowers. She took them, wiped a tear from her eyes.

"No crying," he said, "Dot walked away with my one handkerchief!"

Louise laughed, and Mike looked at her, drinking her in. She was different, somehow. Her hair was shorter, maybe, although it was hard to tell with it caught up under her nurse's cap. Her face had matured a bit, and he thought she was more beautiful, if that was possible.

"Thank you for the flowers, Mike. And yes, I will have a sandwich, I've been buried in the basement all day with twenty-two young men teaching them how to apply field dressings. You'll have one too?" as she held out a sandwich to him.

They ate, and talked about who was doing what in Winchester. When the sandwiches were done, they took a turn around the park, and talked some more. The clock tower chimed two.

"Mike, I have to go back inside. I have a class to teach in fifteen minutes, I don't dare be late."

He turned to her, smiling. "But, I'm home now, you don't have to teach. I want you to come home with me, I want us to be married and have a family."

In Mike's mind, there was nothing as simple as what he wanted.

Louise looked at him, trying to be careful not to show too much. She reached up and cradled the side of his face. "I have an idea. Meet me for dinner tonight. My class will be over at four, I'll just dash home and tidy up, and I'll meet you at five. Do you remember that sweet little restaurant, La Vie Heureuse, over on Mapleton? Let's eat there, and we can talk about our plans."

Mike thought about it, and although it wasn't how he'd envisioned things, he agreed. "I'll just see what's going on at Faneuil Hall, maybe read a newspaper, get caught up a bit. I'll see you at five," he smiled at her, thinking that she would be back in Winchester soon enough, and everything would move ahead as he had planned.

She hugged him again. And then he watched as she hurried back to the hospital, waving before she went through the doors to return to the dungeon.

He stood outside the restaurant, staring at the young woman headed his way. This woman was Louise, he was sure of it, but she was so different from the woman he'd greeted that afternoon, now with her hair down, and a touch of mascara and lipstick enhancing her already beautiful features. Over her shoulders she wore the old black pea coat, still warm and serviceable after all these years. Her dress was simple, well-fitted, a deep burgundy which set off her fair skin and mahogany hair. She kissed him on the cheek in greeting, and he noticed the stale odors of her workday were gone, replaced by a hint of perfume, something new for her, light and floral. And underneath, still, the scent of sweetness, cookies baking in his mother's kitchen. This, he thought, was worth waiting for.

They stepped into the restaurant, and took a table in the back. Over dinner, Louise shared what had happened with George and Claire, and Mike shared the few funny stories he could tell from his time overseas. When dessert appeared before them, Mike turned the conversation to the future.

"I need you to come home with me. If not now, then soon. I want us to build our life together, to pick up where we left off, and move forward."

"No, Mike," came the soft reply.

"What? Why not? I thought…well, I thought we were waiting for each other. I'm here now. We don't have to wait any longer."

"Winchester isn't my home anymore, Mike. I don't want to go back. I love Boston, I love what I'm doing. The war is still on, and I'm useful here. I think we should wait just a little while. Let's wait until I finish the training program. When I complete the program, I'll be a registered nurse. Then we can talk about what to do next." She paused, placing a cool hand on Mike's arm. "It doesn't mean I don't love you, Mike, that I haven't waited for you. It just means I want to be here, doing this work. And I don't want to live in Winchester."

"Oh, come on, Louise, they can get someone else to do your work." He said it flippantly, without thinking, without understanding the depth of her commitment, her strength of purpose.

"Michael Andrews, I cannot believe you just said that."

He pushed away his dessert plate. All he knew was that all of his plans were changing form before his eyes, from something concrete and structured to an amorphous muddy cloud where nothing was tangible, nothing defined. He was silent for a long while. Louise waited.

Finally, he said, "I need my family, Louise. I need my home, and my friends, and a future with someone who wants the same things I do. I won't leave Winchester. I suppose at one time, before, I would have thought nothing of it. But while I was away, I kept seeing the life I wanted to come back to, the life I wanted to build. It all came into focus. Everything I've planned, everything, is founded on living there, with the people I care about, the people I missed so much while I was gone, the life I have always known and loved."

Louise sighed. "It seems to me that as determined as you've become to stay in Winchester, I've become just as determined to live somewhere else. Over the last few years I tried different things, looking for a place for myself, for a place where I could become someone I respect, someone free of the obligations that others wanted to impose on me without my say-so. I landed here. Now I have a life here, and a wonderful career if I want it," Louise paused, took a breath, "and I do. I like working, especially at something where I can really help other people. And I'm sorry, Mike, I simply can't live in Winchester."

"Are you sure? Do you want to wait and see if you'll have a change of heart, maybe at the end of your training? I can wait until then."

This was the turning point. Louise was tempted to say yes, to say she would think about it. But in her heart she had already decided her own future, one that she could live with if Mike hadn't come home, one that was of her own making. She couldn't sidestep the truth any longer.

"Mike, I've signed up to work at the hospital at the end of my training. They asked me, especially, if I would consider staying on, working while I learned surgical nursing and physical therapy. I want to do that. I'll be here for at least another two, perhaps three years."

Louise attempted to bridge the growing gap between them with a suggestion of her own.

"You know, Boston isn't really that far from Winchester. Are you sure you don't want to move here, just to give it a try, to see if you like it?"

Mike took Louise's hands in his, looked at her beautiful face, the tendrils of her soft hair framing her temple and jaw. He looked in her eyes, the depth of their emerald-green still amazing to him. He closed his eyes, breathed in her scent one last time. And then he said the words, resigned, in saying them, to letting go of this beautiful woman whom he loved.

"No, my dear Louise, I don't."

"Oh," she replied softly, and she gently pulled her hands from his.

He sighed. He wasn't sure if he was truly disappointed, or just exhausted. "Let me walk you home?"

"No, Mike, it's getting late. The last train will be leaving soon, you should be on it. I'll be fine."

They held each other for a brief moment outside the restaurant. "God bless you, Mike."

"And you, too, Louise." Then as cheerfully as he could muster, "Oh, and hey, don't forget, you owe me a dance!"

She nodded. "Yes, I do."

They let go, moving away from each other into the cool spring evening, each sorrowful, each relieved. Neither one looked back.

Times were still very difficult. The passing of President Roosevelt in mid-April stunned the country. Activity in Winchester came to a halt as the community absorbed the news, tried to determine how to press forward. In the end, the community went on as they had up until then, working for a common cause, doing without, praying for a victorious end to the war, praying for the return of their sons and daughters.

By V-E Day Mike was well recovered from his wound. He celebrated the news of the Allied victory with his family and friends, and joined the festival held at the Town Common, even giving a short speech commemorating the sacrifices of those who had fallen in the line of duty, choking up for a moment when he mentioned Ray, the solidarity they had shared, the support they'd given each other through the darkest days.

Mike worked to build a new life for himself with a fury. He applied to Harvard Law School, where his high school grades, his service to his country, and his family ties were welcomed. It would be another three months before the term started, time that he spent reading and working at his uncle's law firm; and when the weather was warm enough, he helped his father patch the roof on the house, helped his mother with the garden. When the new semester started, it would be an easy commute to Cambridge, and Mike saw himself spending his days in classrooms, strolling the Cambridge Common Park, playing devil's advocate with professors and other students alike; and returning every evening to hearth and home, to his family.

As for Mike's heart, it had been wounded, but not irretrievably; for as quickly as the wave of disappointment and loss washed over him, it just as quickly receded. Mike and Louise reached out to each other, first in brief, careful conversations on the phone, then meeting sometimes over sandwiches or a soda. They talked about what they were doing, what they hoped to do. They encouraged each other to follow their dreams, to follow their hearts; and while the young love they first shared fell away, a new affection took its place, and with it, a comfortable and easy friendship.

Chapter 44

It was the Fourth of July, and Mike found himself in downtown Winchester with Walter. The streets around the Town Hall were blocked off for the day, and the celebration was in full swing when they arrived in the early afternoon. There was a carnival atmosphere, V-E Day still in recent memory, and hopes for a quick end to the war with Japan swirling within grasp. Flags and balloons lined the streets. The Red Cross occupied the largest booth, centrally located to ensure it wouldn't be missed. The En-Ka Society hosted several smaller booths, each dedicated to a particular fundraiser: the British War Relief; the Greater Boston United War Fund; the National War Fund; the Winchester Hospital. War Bonds were available at every turn. There were baked goods for sale, punch and lemonade, too.

Gus manned the one barbeque. He had procured a supply of ground beef, enough to make a hundred very thin hamburgers, to be sold as a fundraiser for the Red Cross. Part of the Common area was roped off, and a riser and microphone placed for speeches. Mike watched as a parade of elementary school children, followed by the Winchester High School Band, passed by. He was proud of his town, more grateful than ever to be home. These people, his friends and neighbors, the shopkeepers and volunteers, the citizens of Winchester, were his life's blood. He could never do enough for them, and his determination to stay, to support and enrich his hometown, enveloped him.

Walter looked at Mike, saw tears streaming down his face, tears he obviously didn't know were flowing. "Mike?"

"You're my best friend, Walter. I hope you always stay close."

"I'm not going anywhere." And then, "Hey, Mike, let's go on over to the Red Cross booth. Beth said she'd have some numbers for me for the paper."

Beth stood up as Mike and Walter approached the booth. "Walt, it's good to see you! I have those numbers for you, hold on just a minute." Beth pulled out a notebook from a box under the table, and flipped it open.

"Auntie Beth? Look what we have!"

Three young children, two boys and a girl, appeared at the front of the booth, each holding a hamburger. Amelia Crowley stood behind them, eating a hamburger of her own.

"Well, look at you three! Aren't you the lucky ones! Are those hamburgers good? They look good!"

The three children nodded. The youngest, a girl no more than five years old, held her burger out to Beth.

Beth leaned over and took a tiny bite of the burger.

"My, that is good!"

The older boy stuffed the last of his burger into his mouth.

"Can we get ice cream?" he asked, his words muffled by hamburger. The younger boy smiled, nodding, all the while devouring his burger as fast as he could.

"Don't they feed you at home? Slow down, chew your food, or we'll be up all night with tummy aches. But yes, of course you can have some ice cream." She reached into her purse, and handed a coin to each child.

Amelia Crowley stepped up as the children headed off to the ice cream stand. She put her hand out to Beth's arm. "You'll make a wonderful mother someday."

Mrs. Crowley turned to Walter and Mike. "Boys, it's so good to see you here. Are you having a good time?"

"Yes, Mrs. Crowley, we're having a very good time," Walter answered. Mike looked at the three of them, confused.

"I'm sorry, I don't understand. When did you become an aunt, Beth?"

"Oh, well, let's see…it will be two years ago this August." She smiled. "I just love them, you know, they're really wonderful children, and they've been through so much. But of course, it's not forever." She watched as the children approached the ice cream stand. Mr. Withers, who was doling out the sacred portions of ice cream, caught her eye, and she nodded back to him. He doubled their portions.

Beth transcribed information from the record book onto a piece of paper, which she handed to Walter. "Here are the numbers, Walt. Let me know if you need anything else."

"Thanks, Beth, this is great." Walter glanced at the paper, folded it, and put it in his pocket. There was a line forming in front of Beth's table. "We'll let you get back to it, and catch up later, right?"

She nodded, and turned her smiling attentions to the patrons at her table.

Mike and Walter walked from booth to booth. They spoke with the volunteers, the patrons and donors, and two of the town Selectmen. They listened to speeches, Walter scribbling notes on a pad of paper all the while. By the time they headed back to the *Star* office, Mike's arm was sore from shaking so many hands; and it was gratifying to him, and he said as much as he and Walter climbed the stairs to the second floor.

They sat for a while, and Mike asked again, "When did Beth become an aunt? She doesn't have any brothers or sisters that I know of. And it was odd, but I could swear the boy had a British accent."

Walter laughed.

"Mike, I can't believe you don't know. Everyone knows. How did you miss it? You've been home, what, five months now, and you really don't know?"

Mike threw his hands up in the air. "Know what?! Please, Walter, just tell me!"

Walter shook his head. "Beth signed up to house war orphans. Those children were sent here from England. Their parents live in London, and now that the war is over in Europe, they'll go back, probably pretty soon. But in the meantime, she takes care of them, sends them to school, cooks for them, buys their clothes…everything. It's really a great thing, you know. Not everyone has the wherewithal to care for other people's children. Of course, Beth's mother and grandmother help out. You know, they all live in that big house together, always have. But it was Beth's idea, and she is there for those children every single day. It's her true contribution to the war effort, giving those children a safe and loving home."

The next day, Mike walked over to Beth's house. In his youth he'd walked down Pembroke Road a thousand times, but always to Walter's house, never to visit the hideous little girl across the street. He could only remember the odious task of waiting for her in the mornings before school, walking with her trailing behind him as he escorted her to St. Mary's every day before he could head off to his school.

Amelia Crowley welcomed him, asked him to come in. He hesitated.

"Actually, I came to see Beth."

"Beth took the children to the library. There's a story time from ten to eleven. You're certainly welcome to wait, but you may want to go over there if you really need to speak with her."

Mike thanked Mrs. Crowley and headed toward the library. Maybe he could speak to Beth while the children were at story time. He hoped she wouldn't be too difficult to find.

He entered the library, and headed toward the Children's Reading Room. He could start his search there, maybe even ask the librarian if she'd seen Beth.

As he approached the room, he heard Beth's voice. "When Georgie saw the puppy's tail go wiggle, wiggle, wiggle, he laughed. 'I'll call you Wiggle-tail,' he said."

Mike stopped outside the door, listening to the children laugh, to Beth reading. After 'Wiggletail,' she read Mother Goose rhymes, and invited the children to say the rhymes with her. As the story time hour came to a close, mothers started to arrive, and waited outside with Mike. They talked with him in hushed tones, asked after his mother, told him how glad they were that he was safely home. Finally, story time ended, and Beth gave each child a hug as they passed out of the room.

"Where are my three favorites?" she asked, giving her three charges each a hug. Mike knocked at the open door.

"Hello, Beth."

"Oh, hello, Mike," she said as she picked up her purse.

"May I walk you home, or—or wherever you're going next?"

She looked at him, her eyebrows raised, a shadow of doubt cast across her face. "I suppose so," she said.

They left the library, the three children skipping ahead toward Beth's house. At the turn to Pembroke Road, Beth asked Mike, not unkindly, "Mike, what did you really want to talk to me about? I don't think it was the weather, or my mother's recipe for cobbler."

Mike was caught off guard. He had intended to take his time to ask his questions, skirting around them for a while with general conversation before actually discussing her temporary adoption of the English trio.

"No, you're right. There was something else. I wanted to know more about those children. I think it's a wonderful thing to do, but why? It's such a heavy obligation for you to accept."

He realized he'd said too much as soon as he said it. It had come out all backwards, and his tone could be construed as derogatory rather than one of inquisitive concern.

"Why, Mike, I'm really surprised at you." Beth stopped walking and faced him. Her jaw was set, her eyes flinty. "Did anyone ask you why you took on the responsibility of going overseas, of fighting for our country, of comforting one of our dear friends when he was mortally wounded? Did you ever ask yourself? I'll answer for you—no, you didn't, the thought never crossed your mind that you shouldn't accept that responsibility, to do everything you could to defend our home and do the right thing. It wouldn't have mattered to you if you were alone fighting the enemy, or had a thousand others flanking around you—you would do your best. Do you think it was any different for those of us left behind, that we wouldn't do everything in our power, whether as individuals or as part of a community, to defend our home and do the right thing?"

She was starting to warm up now. Mike could tell she was insulted, that she thought he was degrading her work effort, questioning her ability to contribute in a meaningful way.

"Beth, I didn't mean..." but it was too late. She was irked, and there was nothing for it but to let it run its course.

"Well, let me tell you something, Mr. Michael Andrews, or corporal or sergeant, or whatever the hell you are. We, all of us, all of Winchester, gave everything we could. Each one of us did as much as was humanly possible, whether it was knitting a hundred scarves, or rolling a thousand bandages, or fundraising, or selling war bonds, or collecting metal in huge scrap piles. We did without sugar and coffee and gasoline and meat, and gladly so, for the sake of those who were fighting overseas, for Ray, for you." Beth jabbed her index finger into the center of Mike's chest.

"We worked hard in our gardens and community plots, not for the pleasure of a few sweet tomatoes, but as a sincere effort to free up farmland produce for the war effort. And some of us were graced with the opportunity to care for British children who no longer had a safe place to live, whose parents sent their children into the hands of American strangers hoping that they would see them safely home again in better times. Can you imagine the desperation those parents felt? The anguish?"

Beth stopped.

"Beth, please, it came out all wrong."

"Yes, I'm sure it did. I just want you to know that I'm proud of the choices I've made, of the work that I've done, and will continue to do. You know, Mike, not to put too fine a point on it, but you were never kind to me while we were growing up. I knew I was the most loathsome creature on the Earth to you, and that you resented my presence, even when all I did was follow after you on the walk to school. But we're older now, and I don't have to follow you anywhere. And you don't have to be in my presence to feel any resentment. Now if you don't mind, the children are waiting for me, and I have work to do."

Beth walked away toward her house, stiff-backed, head held high.

Mike stood on the street, immobile. Beth had said the first harsh words anyone had said to him since he came back.

"Heard that," said Gus, stepping up from his porch chair. "You have quite a way with the young ladies, no?"

"I didn't mean it…" Mike started, but Gus cut him off.

"Doesn't matter, does it? She took it a certain way, and rightly so. She's right, you know, you weren't very nice to her growing up. I know, I watched you walk as fast as you could through snowdrifts and rain and everything else, while she had to run to keep up with you. Probably one of the reasons she could outrun you now if she had a mind to. You were meant to give her some company, help her a bit if she needed it, but you never did. You just went along, a scowl on your face all the way."

Mike hung his head.

"Oh, now, don't be like that. You're all grown up now, the both of you, and both of you have seen your share of hard times. Why don't you act like the grown-up you are and go after her and make it right? She's a nice young lady, and you turned out all right, probably. Seems to me you should at least be on nodding terms, yes?"

Gus lit his pipe, puffed a bit, coughed. "This stuff is terrible, I can't wait for this damned war to be over so we can get some regular tobacco back on the shelves." He looked up at the horizon over the trees. "Looks like it might rain." Nodding to Mike, he turned, and went back into his house.

Mike stood at the corner or another minute or so; then, making a decision, he hurried down Pembroke Road to Beth's house.

Chapter 45

The trains bustling up and down the Eastern Seaboard were full of men and gear, and it had taken Henry a few days to secure a seat for his trip home. It was a late train, leaving Savannah at ten o'clock at night, and wouldn't arrive in Boston until midmorning the next day. He tried to sleep, but it was impossible to do more than doze for a few minutes at a time, the crowded compartment buzzing with the excitement of young men returning home, the train itself lurching into and away from each station, complaining noisily at each shift of speed under the weight of the cargo it carried.

From Boston, Henry caught the Boston & Maine line into Winchester Center Station. As he stepped off the train onto the street, he drank in the town around him. It all seemed so much the same, but it was different. There were flags everywhere, and a grocer's now occupied the space where a hardware store once stood. It was busy, too. There were cars on the street, and people, most of them vaguely familiar, walking along the sidewalk, or chatting with one another under an awning, for it was a warm, almost hot, mid-September day. Henry took a deep breath, and with this act, the adrenaline that had carried him from Georgia melted away. He was home.

He walked from the station to his house on Pembroke Road, nodding hello to the people he passed, some of them recognizing him, stopping him to welcome him back. He received the attention politely, but didn't linger too long. He was so very tired, and eager to get home, to see his family, to take a hot bath if he could, maybe take a nap.

He called out as he walked through the front door of his house, "Halloo! Anyone home?"

Silence. The house was empty. He called out again. It was all quiet, except for the sound of a bird chirping in the back yard, carried in on a warm breeze through the open kitchen window. He had a bad moment when he wondered whether he had walked into the wrong house, or perhaps his parents had moved. But no, there was their couch, and their table, and the same curtains across the dining room windows.

He wasn't sure what he'd expected. But it made sense; he hadn't told anyone when he was arriving, he'd only sent a letter saying he would be returning sometime in September. His father would be at work, his brother and sisters would be at school, and his mother obviously had stepped out, maybe to shop. That was all right. Henry was more than content to settle in and greet people as they arrived home.

He made his way upstairs to his room, dropped his bag on the floor. It was as he'd left it, although he could see the room was freshly dusted, and there were new sheets on the bed in anticipation of his arrival.

He pulled open a dresser drawer. His clothes were there, freshly laundered. Mom was a good egg, he thought. He pulled out a shirt. He was thinner now through the waist, broader across the shoulders, a result of rigorous daily PT, required whether he sat at a desk all day or not. He tried on the shirt, then another—they were tight across his back, he would have to get some new clothes. In his closet he found a few pair of trousers, freshly pressed, and his dress shirts. He found a pair of pants that fit well enough, a little loose, perhaps, but they would do. Back at the dresser, he pulled out another drawer and found T-shirts and pajamas. It was warm enough, as long as he wasn't going out, a T-shirt would be fine.

He took a bath. Soaking in the soapy hot water, he cleared away his own tired odor, along with the lingering odor of too many men in a cramped boxcar; and the smell of the soaps the Army had provided for the last three years. He rinsed off, and it seemed that all his time away from home disappeared down the drain with the water; and for a few minutes, he felt a lightness of heart and spirit, as if it had all been a long, uncomfortable dream.

The relief was short-lived. His thoughts turned, involuntarily, to the phone call he'd received from Major Branson just before leaving his post in Georgia.

"So, you'll be shipping off home soon, I suppose," Branson had said.

"Yes, sir, I'll be on a train within the next few days," Henry replied. He liked Branson well enough, having dealt intermittently with him during the war regarding one matter or another. Still, Henry sensed the Major wanted something from him. He hoped not. He hoped this was just a courtesy call.

"Will you be at home for a while, do you think?"

"Yes, sir. I'm not quite sure what I'll do next, but I want to visit with family, of course, and then decide what the next step will be."

"Ah," Branson said, "then you may be very interested in why I called. I want you to know I've followed your service rather closely, and I'm pleased to say you've done excellent work, Henry, better than we expected. Your country is grateful for the service you've provided. Hopefully the few little trinkets we've pinned to your uniform have shown that in a more tangible way than just my words today."

"It's been an honor, sir. I'm glad to know that my service was useful."

Henry waited, knowing more was coming, unsure if he really wanted to hear what it was.

"We'd like to offer you a commission, Henry. You'd start off as a Second Lieutenant, of course, but I imagine you'd move up quickly. Maybe you'd like to go to West Point? We could arrange that."

Henry knew he was supposed to say something here, but could only sputter a "Well, sir, that's very generous, I don't know…"

Branson waited to see if Henry would say more, but, after a heartbeat, continued.

"Think about it, Henry. You haven't had a decent break since the beginning. Go home, take a little time, visit your friends and family. We'll touch base again in a month or so, how's that sound?"

"Yes, sir, that sounds fine. Thank you, sir."

Henry had pushed that conversation back in his mind as he packed his bag, and still further back as he boarded the train that would carry him home. By the time he'd stepped off in Winchester, he'd almost forgotten it entirely. But as he put on his own clothes for the first time in three years, the conversation, its possibilities and implications, rolled forward, insistent and consuming. With effort, Henry pushed it back again. He wasn't ready to think about it. He sat on his bed, found his pillows, and then laid back for just a moment, just to rest his eyes.

When he awoke, it was to the sound of children calling to each other, a game of tag, maybe. It was nearly dark outside. Henry could smell food cooking, garlic bread toasting. His mother was making spaghetti, he thought, and then he heard her voice, no, her laughter, at something his father said just a moment before.

Henry was up. He took a moment to make sure he was presentable, and then ran downstairs, calling out, "Halloo, everyone! I'm home! I'm home!"

It was almost as if he'd never left. After a shriek of joy from his mother, followed by hugs and kisses and exclamations of surprise, the Smith family sat at the kitchen table as they always had, spaghetti and garlic toast piled on the plates. The conversation was easy, although Henry's brother and sisters sat through much of dinner quietly observing the familiar-looking young man sitting at the table, slightly unsure of who he really was. Finally, upon repeated assurances from their mother that this was Henry, their older brother, who used to push them on the swing outside, and who took them to Ford's for ice cream, the children agreed that he was probably all right; but suggested he would have to take them to the ice cream shop before they could be sure. Henry laughed, and promised that by the weekend he would take them to Ford's, and they would be happy to have their old brother back.

After the children went to bed, Henry sat with his parents for a few minutes. While the nap had refreshed him, he could feel the wear of his travels creeping back over him, and he thought he would sleep well that night.

"We'll have to call Eric and Rachel. They'll be thrilled that you're home, Henry. Maybe we could have a little barbeque this weekend? You're going to be here for at least a while, yes?"

"A barbeque sounds wonderful, Mom, and no, I don't have any immediate plans, so if it's okay with you if I stay…"

"Of course!" his mother exclaimed. "You're home now, Henry."

The Lights of Pembroke Road

Emma looked at Carl, wondering if they should broach the subject. Carl shook his head 'no' ever so slightly, but Henry caught the exchange.

"What?" Henry asked. "You might as well tell me, or I'll be up all night."

Carl started. "I don't imagine you've had a chance to really talk to anyone in the few hours you've been home. I don't think you've heard the news, and I guess it's better you find out now, from us."

The serious tone of his father's words settled as an anchor in Henry's chest.

"You know Mike and Ray went overseas. They were there at D-Day, on Utah Beach. They fought through with their Division until they ended up just across the German border. Mike and Ray were both shot there, last December. Mike came home. He's recovered well, just started a term at Harvard. But Ray...well, Ray didn't make it. They buried him in France. He never came home."

Henry sat back in his chair, silent, absorbing the news. His mother leaned forward, searching her son's face for his reaction, and finding a somber mouth and furrowed brow, reached out and put her hand on his arm, the way she had always done when he was growing up and knew he was distressed.

"I'm so sorry, Henry. Ray was a good friend, and a kind and caring young man." She started to cry, now, not for Ray, but for Henry, because there was something in his face, something in the set of his jaw and the distance in his eyes that frightened her a little, something that marked a bridge inside her son that she could not cross, a piece of him she could not reach, could not protect.

Henry recovered enough to go sit next to his mother, to put his arm over her shoulder.

"It's all right, Mom, don't cry. I'm glad you told me now, I didn't know. It's better I should know."

Carl agreed, "Well, of course, Henry. And although maybe it could have waited until tomorrow, we didn't want you to hear it from someone else, have it come as a shock outside of this house."

Carl stood up. "It's been a big day. Emma, schatz, come on up to bed. Tomorrow we'll start fresh, and I'll call Eric and tell him the good news. Henry, you'll have to be sure to stop by the *Star* tomorrow, let Walter know you're back. He'll put a piece in the paper for you, maybe a headline or something. He's pretty good about that stuff," and then, "Are you coming up, too?"

"Yes, I'll be up in a minute," said Henry.

He kissed his mother good night, and whispered in her ear, "It's all right, Mama, don't cry anymore. I'm home now." He pulled away from her as she stepped toward Carl, toward the stairs.

That night Henry lay awake for a long while. Memories rushed at him, some sharp, some faded, of the Hill Boys, the four fast friends who played and joked and worked together for more than ten years before war separated them forever, one way or another, from the children they had been, and the childhood they'd shared.

He spent a while thinking about his interview with Major Branson, sitting in that office in the basement of Winchester Town Hall, remembering how he thought he might be able to help his friends, only to discover once he reached his assigned base that he couldn't. Henry had entered a different type of Army, and once he was within the perimeter of his training camp, he was not permitted to leave, except on duty as a courier. His letters home were reviewed and blacked out wherever the text was considered sensitive; his calls home were made within earshot of a captain who would cut him off if the conversation veered in an unacceptable direction. It was true, he'd managed to help his parents, but Henry decided that had been a coincidence, a freak of happenstance that Mr. Hannigan would be in a position to protect his parents from the accusations raised against them. In any event, he'd stayed stateside, working in comfortable surroundings, eating three squares a day, while his friends had gone over and fought in the trenches.

Mike had been wounded, and Ray—Ray was dead. Henry could remember, just, the last time he'd seen his friend, the morning they had all left Winchester to report for duty at their assigned posts. Ray had spent the whole morning talking about Dot, the plans they had made for when he returned, how they were going to buy a house and have lots of children, and Ray would own a hardware store in town. Ray talked about how their children would all play together, and then their grandchildren, and they would be the Hill Boys forever. And then it was time for Henry to board his train, and he was half out the window at his seat as the train left the station, waving to Ray and Mike as they stood on the platform, wishing them luck, promising to see them again when they all came home.

Henry let the tears fall as he lay in the dark, in his warm, safe bed, in his warm, safe home, with his parents two rooms away, his brother and sisters down the hall. Ray, the round-faced, eager young man, who had been desperate to go so that he could all the more quickly return, would never see his family again. He would never marry Dot, or have children or grandchildren, or own a hardware store; and he would never again set foot in Winchester, not even as a resident of Wildwood Cemetery.

Chapter 46

Men were returning home in droves. The women who had served in factories and farms were quickly and easily fired. Most of these women willingly returned to the business of managing hearth and home without fuss, knowing that they had played a role, understudies filling in for an absent star; but now the men were coming back, and center stage belonged to them.

Still, some women were not so easily removed. Self-sufficiency in the form of a paycheck had become a habit, one they liked, and refused to give up. As it happened, there was room for them. Not every man returned home, and many of those who did were unable to shift gears so quickly from the war front to the home front. Some of them couldn't shift gears at all.

Henry began to regain his footing in Winchester. He took a part-time job at the library, a temporary situation until he could decide about college. He rebuilt his friendships with Walter and Mike. It was easier with Walter, picking up where they'd left off, catching up over a dinner at Randall's. But Henry felt an uneasy guilt over what happened to Mike and Ray, and Mike had a devil of a time assuring Henry that all was right between them, that each of them played the role they were assigned, that Ray's death was not something Henry could have changed. Henry understood all these things, but it took months before the weight on his conscience began to ease away.

When Major Branson called in late October, Henry had long decided he would not accept the commission. He told the Major that while he appreciated the offer very, very much, he was unable to accept. Major Branson didn't press, and wished Henry well, thanking him again for his service, and reminding him that the offer would remain open for a while if he changed his mind.

"What will you do?" Eric inquired of Henry over Thanksgiving dinner.

"I don't know," Henry replied, "There are so many jobs open, it would be easy to find something. College might be a better option for the long haul, but I can't decide what field."

Eric nodded. "College would probably be your best bet. You're an intelligent young man, you would do well."

Then he added, "I'm going to visit an old friend this weekend in Nashua. Would you like to come with me? We'll drive up, you'll get a day out. I'll treat you to lunch at a nice restaurant."

On Saturday morning they drove into New Hampshire. Eric pulled up to a large house settled on the outskirts of Nashua, situated on an expansive, well-manicured property. At first, Henry thought it was a private mansion, and Eric's friend was very, very wealthy. But as they pulled up in the drive, Henry noticed the placard at the front door. The building was a hospital—a hospital for the mentally ill. Henry looked at Eric.

"Why are we here?"

"I told you, I'm visiting an old friend. Come on, it'll be okay."

As they entered the building, Henry detected a strong odor, some kind of cleaning fluid, he thought. He looked around. The receiving hall was nicely decorated, with a plush carpet underfoot, and a chandelier over the staircase. A few highly polished tables of walnut and rosewood, some with exquisite marquetry, sat against the wall spaces, and pictures of pleasant country landscapes hung carefully centered above them. In front of the staircase was a desk, and Eric was talking to the nurse sitting there. There were rooms to the left and right of the entrance, their great walnut doors closed against prying eyes. This made the entryway really rather dark, save for the light from the chandelier, even though a sparkling late-November morning blazed brightly outside.

The nurse led them down the hall behind the staircase, and ushered them into a patio. The patio was enclosed, but windows spanned the breadth of the room, admitting sunlight, and a view of the back garden, which currently sat brown and barren.

A number of men, perhaps a dozen, occupied the room. Some of them were in wheelchairs, some in cushioned chairs, two of them sat on the floor. They were either dozing, or staring at nothing, or rocking gently back and forth. All of them were quiet. A nurse sat at a small table near one of the windows. She was reading a book, a romance novel, Henry thought. She looked up as they entered.

"Where is Mr. Dunning?" the nurse from the front desk inquired of her.

"There, in the corner, blue chair, green blanket." She nodded in the direction of the man in question, and returned to her reading.

"Would you please put down your book, Nurse Lundt, and escort these gentlemen to Mr. Dunning?" The front desk nurse was obviously irritated, but maintained a cool, civil tone.

"Of course, Nurse Bingham," replied Nurse Lundt, just as irritated, just as coolly civil. She placed her book on the table, and offering a grimacing smile to Eric and Henry, said, "Right this way, gentlemen."

Nurse Bingham, satisfied that her request was being fulfilled, turned to leave the patio, when she heard Nurse Lundt mutter 'bitch' in a low breath.

"I heard that," Nurse Bingham called, sing-song, as she walked away.

Nurse Lundt walked Eric and Henry to the corner of the patio where Eric's friend sat. With a point of her finger and a curt 'there he is,' she turned and walked back to her table, picked up her book, and resumed reading.

Eric pulled up a couple of chairs, and he and Henry sat on either side of the man. Henry thought he couldn't be more than twenty-five years old, although a streak of white-gray lined his temples, a sharp contrast to his otherwise jet-black hair. His forehead was lined with deep furrows, and his brown eyes were sunken, red-rimmed, and hollow. He was too thin, Henry thought, but would have been a decent-looking man with another twenty or thirty pounds on him.

Eric did most of the talking, Henry chiming in now and again, trying to be kind, trying to help Eric talk to his friend, who sat mute, staring at his hands for the first half-hour of the visit. Henry was surprised, and almost frightened when the man looked up from his hands and looked straight at Henry, with tears starting to flow.

"I—I can't," he whispered.

"Jim," Eric said, "this is Henry, my nephew. Jim, do you remember me? I'm Eric, I saw you last week."

Jim turned to see who was talking, and found Eric's face.

"Oh, yes, I remember you. My hands don't work. Is Mother coming? She can fix them. I—I can't make them work." And here the tears flowed more freely, and Jim Dunning started to sob a little, his hands still motionless in his lap. Eric took out a few tissues from his pocket, and wiped Jim's eyes, wiped his nose, encouraged him to blow.

"There, now, that's better. I'm sure your hands will get better, Jim. I'll see if I can get Mother to come."

Then, in a low whisper, he said, "And I've brought you something, Jim, something I know you like." Eric deftly pulled a piece of candy, butterscotch, it looked like, from his coat pocket. He unwrapped it carefully, quietly, and held it out in front of his friend so he could see what it was. Jim's eyes lit up, and he nodded vigorously.

"All right then, just be careful," and Eric placed the candy into Jim's waiting open mouth. "Soon enough you'll be able to eat these without my help."

Eric and Henry waited as Jim sucked at the candy, a glow of sublime happiness crossing his face. After a while he bit into it, and then it was finished, and Jim licked his lips, and closed his eyes. With that, Jim Dunning's mind went to another place, beyond the confines of the chair, the patio, the hospital, and beyond, once again, the reach of his friend.

Eric and Henry left, and drove to a little café along Spring Street, a place known for its chicken pot pie.

"Who was he? What happened to him?" Henry asked.

"Jim used to work for me. Nice kid, hard worker. We used to have lunch together sometimes, he would tell me about his family. He had a nice girlfriend, they were going to get married. Then the war started, and he was one of the first to get called up. While he was away, his mother died, and his girlfriend moved to California to live with an aunt, and work with one of the big military contractors, Boeing, I think. She did it without telling him, without leaving a forwarding address. In the meantime, Jim was in the trenches, fighting, watching his friends die next to him, and forced to kill other young men, some of them in hand-to-hand combat. He finally got shot, a belly wound that sent him home. It wasn't until he arrived at his house that he found his mother had passed, and his fiancée was gone. It seems his whole mind was a house of cards already, finding out about his mother and his fiancée was the flick of a finger that brought it all down. Now he's at that hospital, supposedly getting some sort of treatments, although he doesn't seem to be getting better."

"What about the candy?" Henry asked. "He liked the candy, he recognized that."

"Oh, well, those were his favorite. He used to keep a dish of them at his desk at work. I'd come by a few times when I first heard he was in the hospital, and he never recognized me, never even lifted his head. I happened to open a candy wrapper one time, and was just about to eat it myself, when he raised his head to see what it was. It was a butterscotch, the kind he always liked. He opened his mouth, and I popped it in. It was the first time I saw some recognition, maybe pleasure, even. So now I always bring one just for him. It opens the door, even if it's just for a minute or two."

"And all those men at that hospital, are they all like Mr. Dunning?"

"To one degree or another, I imagine they are. And that's just one hospital, and a nice one, at that. Some hospitals are like prisons, but all the patients are inmates, no matter how nice or horrible the living conditions."

Eric finished his lunch, and sat back in his seat. "That was good. I won't be able to eat dinner, now. Rachel will be furious, I think she planned on lasagna tonight. How's your food, good?"

Henry nodded, the last bite of chicken pot pie filling his mouth. It was good, but that wasn't what he was thinking about. Eric continued with his former line of thought, answering Henry's unspoken questions, raising still others.

"War is a terrible thing, Henry, no matter how right the cause. It's an unnatural and unrelenting process, and sometimes a man will lose his life, or an arm or a leg or a hand, in the doing of it. Sometimes what they lose is the rational, functional part of their mind. You would think that it would be the one thing they could recover, since it sits there, somewhere, between their ears, and you can't see the damage. It's not something you can cut out, or stitch up. It's like a sore, I think…maybe it heals, maybe it doesn't. Either way, it's a tenuous recovery, at best. It's an awful way for a human being to live, Henry, even for a short time; for most of them, it's for the rest of their lives."

Chapter 47

Louise flew into Logan Airport. She rented a car, and drove across the Charles River into Cambridge, where she picked up her nephew, Oliver. They chatted lightly about the recent remodel of his house, and his six grandchildren. They headed south, picking up Highway 1 at Dorchester, and then Highway 6 just over the Cape Cod Canal. From there it was east and south, along the 132, and then the 28, through Hyannis. Finally, they exited at Seaview, and cut down toward Yarmouth, toward South Shore Drive. They arrived, finally, at the Keystone Inn, a small, quaintly decorated hotel that overlooked Sea Gull Beach, a stretch of tan-white sand that cradled bundled strands of dark kelp washed up with the tide, and sprouted tender green grasses among the low dunes behind the tideline.

Despite her busy schedule, Louise always made time for these reunions. It was an excuse to see Oliver, who often accompanied her; and it was a way to reconnect with her old friends, and give herself a break from work. Henry and Mike didn't attend these events, but Dot came to every single one. Walter, as Class President, had the honor of organizing them, and hosted them alongside his wife, Susan.

For all of Louise's early determination to leave Winchester, her thoughts often ran to the people she grew up with, her classmates and friends; and seeing them, sharing news and life events, gave her a sense of connection to her past that she could not find anywhere else. There would be those that passed away since the last reunion just five years ago, forever absent now, except perhaps as a ghost next to the memorial presentation at the entrance to the event room, their pictures framed and surrounded by flowers, words of sorrow and loss whispered by those who stopped to look, to remember. But this time, Louise wasn't here for Dot or Walter, or those who had passed. Walter's phone call, a special request that she attend this reunion, had shifted her focus. She was here for Mike.

The years following their break had been kind to Louise, if not romantically, at least in productivity and wealth. She married once, an internist she met in 1947 at a conference. Their marriage lasted a grueling six years, long enough for Louise to refine her understanding of men's strengths and weaknesses, long enough to understand she preferred the company of dogs. While married, she continued in her chosen profession as a nurse, but once divorced, she moved to California, where she bought a small bungalow off State Street in Santa Barbara, and started a business providing home health care for the ill and injured.

In time, Louise built an empire for herself, eventually overseeing a staff of more than a hundred. She returned to Winchester twice after she married: once, to attend the wedding of her nephew, Oliver; and again at the death of her dear brother, George, who passed from a stroke on the eve of his 58th birthday. George's will left Claire the house on Dix Street, and the proceeds from a hefty insurance policy. To Oliver, he left the Winchester rifle, an heirloom passed down to him from a grandfather he never knew, and George's business, which Oliver promptly sold. Oliver was looking forward to retirement, and the sale of Back Bay Machining allowed him to pursue that course several years ahead of schedule.

One crisp autumn day, several weeks after the funeral, Louise received a box in the mail, sent from a solicitor in Boston. Enclosed were two items, and a brief letter informing Louise that the contents were items which her brother George directed should be given to her upon his death.

One item was a check in the amount of $167,635, the final distribution of principal and interest on her 1942 investment in Back Bay Machining. If Claire knew of, or was livid over, the money, Louise didn't know, and didn't care. Louise donated the windfall to St. Jude's Hospital in Los Angeles.

In addition to the check, the box contained her father's Waltham pocket watch, a token of remembrance of a family long divided by death. Louise held the old timepiece in her hands for a few minutes, traced the swirling design on the silver case with her finger; noted that the glass was clear of scratches, and that the mechanism still worked, still kept time. After that, she'd placed the watch back in the box and sent it to Oliver. She had no use for it. Her memories were held in the picture of her parents on their wedding day, the one she'd retrieved from the old house on Pembroke Road, and which now sat in a simple silver frame on a table in the den; and in her mother's brooch, which Louise still wore on special occasions.

Louise last saw Claire as she stood in widow's garb at the side of George's open grave at Wildwood Cemetery, where George himself had spent two hard summers as a teenager, digging graves for others. They stood on opposite sides of the trench, still unable to bear more proximal closeness than absolutely necessary. Louise never again heard from Claire, although Oliver mentioned once that she had remarried a sharpish, wealthy older man, and remained in the house on Dix Street, fussing over her great-grandchildren and volunteering, still, at the local Red Cross.

Louise and Oliver arrived at the inn by midafternoon, and settled into their rooms. There would be a Welcome Dinner that evening, and a chance to sign up for a trip to Martha's Vineyard the following day. The highlight of the event would be the big Reunion Dinner the next evening. It would be a dressy affair, with a live band and a multitude of what Louise hoped would be relatively short speeches.

That first evening, Louise and Oliver had a chance to talk to Walter and Susan. They sat at a table in the hotel's smaller ballroom, where a buffet dinner was arranged, and the decorations were simple and pleasant.

"People are still coming in," said Walter. "Looks like about half of the folks we expected are already here. Hey, there's Dot!"

Hugs and kisses ensued, and Dot introduced her daughter, Samantha.

"I'm living in Florida, now, you know. Since Ed died last year, that big house in New Hampshire became too much for me. Samantha was such a help getting me into my new place, and now she and the grandkids are just a block away. I'm having a wonderful time. Besides," Dot added, "I think my joints are a lot happier in the warmer climate!"

"I was so sorry to hear about Ed," said Susan. "I met him at the last reunion, and he was such a gentleman."

Dot nodded. "Yes, he was, and he had a good sense of humor, too. You know, I met him at Winchester Hospital. I had finished the nurse's training—you remember, Louise, that program that you and I went through? And then Mother became very ill, so I went back to Winchester and took a job at the hospital there. And there he was, a goofy intern, and I thought he was incredibly irksome at first. I can tell you it took a long time for me to agree to have a soda with him," Dot smiled. "But it ended up all right."

Walter nodded. "And Louise, I know you're still working. How is California treating you?"

"California is just beautiful. I walk down to the ocean whenever I get the chance, and the mountains are just an hour away. And as for work, well, work is as busy as ever, but I love it."

"You've always been a hard worker, Louise," Walter remarked. "I remember seeing you one night coming home from that factory in Woburn. It was bitter cold in the middle of winter, and there you were, slogging your way through the snow to Dot's house. It was during the war, remember?"

"I do! I was always so grateful that you didn't shoot me as a German spy!"

Walter laughed. "No, no guns, I was just making sure the blackout was enforced. But you were really growing up, then. I remember Claire was very unkind to you, but you did what you needed to do, moving out on your own, working in a factory. I never could understand why she was so mean."

Louise was thoughtful for a moment, then said, "It's true, Claire was motivated by a different set of rules, and she adhered to them like glue. But she gave me the wherewithal to get off my rear, to come out of my shell, and build a future for myself. So in a way, I'm actually very grateful to her."

"But what did George see in her?" asked Dot. "I never understood how they meshed."

Louise sighed. "I think, when they were first going out, she was a different person. She laughed a lot, and made George laugh too. But after they were married, things changed. Claire was concerned with appearances, I think, and George was probably a little too focused on work. But in the end, they managed, and I think they were happy enough, eventually. All I know is that I hated living in that house, and I was so glad when I finally moved out!"

Louise turned to her old friend. "And thank God for you, Dot. You helped me get through it, and I've never forgotten how good a friend you've been to me."

Dot reached over and grasped Louise's hand. "We've helped each other. All our lives, we've been there for one another. We've been very lucky."

The foursome talked for a few more minutes, until Louise finally asked the question.

"When do we expect Mike?"

Walter answered, "Beth says they'll be here tomorrow for the Reunion Dinner. Henry will be here too."

"Will Jennifer be with him?" asked Dot. "I really like her, she's got quite a sparkle to her personality. Henry certainly couldn't have chosen a better woman."

"Yes, she'll be here," replied Walter. "You know, when Henry first came back from his war service, I wasn't sure what he was going to do. I don't think he knew either. I know they offered him a commission, but he didn't accept. Then he went to Boston University, and that's where he met Jennifer, in a psychology class. He was smitten, and the rest is history."

The next evening, Louise and Oliver made their way downstairs for the formal Reunion Dinner. The event was held in the larger ballroom, already decorated in anticipation of the upcoming holiday season. White lights laced the columns that stood at the corners of the dance floor, and oversized ornaments, sparkling and beribboned, hung from the ceiling. The tables were set with white linens, and centerpieces of red and white roses sat atop mirrored rounds. A five-piece band was playing a slow, easy jazz piece. Walter, with his best host face on, greeted Louise and Oliver as they entered the ballroom.

"Hello, there! Oh, Louise, you look lovely! And you look quite dapper, Oliver! You'll excuse me for a few minutes while I tend to some of our guests, but I think you'll find the bar is open, and you two are sitting at a reserved table with me and a few others, over by the far wall—table number three, I think it is. See you in a bit!" he exclaimed, and went to greet two other couples that had just walked into the room.

Louise and Oliver retrieved drinks from the bar, and, wine in hand, crossed the room to their table. The table was actually two rounds pulled together, set so that ten people could sit comfortably. Louise and Oliver found their names and sat down for a few minutes to take in the atmosphere.

Dot and Samantha soon joined them, and as other tables began to fill, the excitement in the room grew high. Walter and Susan, relieved of their hosting duties for a few moments, made their way over to the table, bringing along Henry and Jennifer. Louise thought Henry had aged very well, looking very much like the handsome man he was at eighteen, still well-muscled, now with a head of salt-and-pepper hair, and a few laugh lines around his eyes.

Henry introduced Jennifer. She was Henry's counterpart, a naturally attractive woman who reminded Louise vaguely of Lauren Bacall, with intense, intelligent blue-green eyes above a warm, engaging smile. She was as witty and charming as Dot had said, and Louise liked her immediately. Henry, Louise thought, had done very well for himself.

The evening progressed. Dinner service was over, the speeches were made, and desserts and coffee sat on the tables, half consumed, as the guests danced to the live band, or chatted enthusiastically in groups.

Dot asked the question that everyone was thinking. Where was Mike?

"Oh, he'll be along shortly. Beth sent a message that they were a bit delayed, but they should be here any minute."

Chapter 48

Louise saw Mike and Beth first as they stood at the entrance. They started into the room, Mike leaning slightly on Beth's arm, his cadence slow, but steady. Louise stood up, and Walter, seeing her movement, stood up as well. The two of them made their way to the door, and Beth greeted Walter with a quiet, "Hiya, Walt!" And he responded, smiling, "Hiya, Beth!"

Louise gently clasped the large hands that had once held her so close. She looked up at Mike, knowing what to expect. He was gaunt, no longer a strapping young soldier, but hollowed out, his suit much too big, covering over the worst evidence of just how severely the cancer had ravaged his body. But she could see also the broad, kind smile, and a bit of sparkle that pushed through the pain that showed in his eyes. He stooped to receive a welcoming kiss on his cheek, received from the woman he had loved first, and whom he considered a lifelong friend, even if most years had passed with only the exchange of a Christmas card.

"Hi, Mike, it's been a long time; hello Beth, I'm so glad you both could come," Louise said.

"Louise, it's so very good to see you." Mike thought she was still beautiful, her emerald-green eyes still happy, her smile still sweet. He looked at her, with just the tiniest tinge of regret striking a chord in his heart, not for the lost love, but for the distance in time from where they started. And then Henry was nearby, and Dot as well, all gathered to greet the couple and escort them to their seats at the table.

Louise knew that Beth had been good to Mike, and good for him, and still was. She knew that Mike had spent an earnest year convincing Beth that he wasn't the foul troll she thought he was. It hadn't been easy. Mike was attending Harvard Law School on the new GI Bill, commuting to Cambridge every day from home; and in between classes and studying, Mike worked tirelessly to win Beth over with his sincere friendship, his support of her efforts, and his dedication to service in Winchester. She had eventually agreed that perhaps he wasn't entirely objectionable, and yes, she would have dinner with him sometime.

Mike proposed to Beth one balmy June afternoon as they sat along the shore of Mystic Lake, the swans paddling through the lily pads as the sun shimmered off the ripples in the water. He gave her his grandmother's ring, a white gold band set with opals and diamonds. A year later they married, and while Louise did not attend the wedding, she sent a beautiful Waterford vase, and a card wishing them both every happiness.

Then the boys came, one after the other, and Mike and Beth juggled work, school, and children until he passed the bar. Mike joined the family law firm, Andrews & James, welcomed this time as a junior partner. Mike and Beth bought a house on Church Street, a large, two-story Tudor, with an expansive front lawn, and a back yard suited to the barbeques the couple hosted every summer. Mike's law practice thrived, and the years passed from Farm League to Little League to Varsity and Homecomings. Every now and then Mike thought he should call Louise, just to see how she was, hear the sound of her voice. But the busyness of the life Mike built for himself left no room for action on these thoughts. Every fall the leaves had to be raked and the gutters cleaned, every summer the broad lawn at the front of the house needed mowing, and every holiday brought party plans and family visits. In addition to his work and family life, Mike served several terms on the Winchester Board of Selectmen, and, in turns, served on the Building Commission, the School

Committee, and the Finance Committee. His mind and heart were irretrievably dedicated to his family, and to serving the community that he loved.

Beth was just forty-nine when she was diagnosed with breast cancer, and Mike had his hands full, running the firm during the day, and taking the night shift with Beth after the day nurse left, holding Beth's hair while she vomited after chemo, tending the sutures from surgery, gently spooning into her mouth the warm broth that a neighbor made for her.

When Beth was given a clean bill of health, she asked Mike if they could go away for a few weeks, somewhere where she could feel the sun and the sand and the sea. He took her to the Bahamas for a month. Every day, she rose and walked to the beach and sat out on a blanket. She soaked up the warm rays, watched the surf, read and slept, and breathed the sea air as deeply as she could. She walked along the shore, sometimes with Mike, sometimes alone. When they returned home she felt renewed, and ready to move forward.

Three months later, their eldest son announced at a Labor Day barbeque that he and his wife were expecting a baby. As the cheers went through the gathering, Mike reached for Beth, smiling at her, so proud, so excited; and she smiled back at him, just as proud, just as excited. And at that moment, Mike let go of Louise completely, as if a thin, frayed thread that had tugged at his heart for decades finally snapped. For the first time since high school, Mike felt he could take a full breath. His purpose, for the remainder of his life, was crystal-clear to him, and he could see Beth with fresh eyes as the woman he loved, and who loved him, who had given him so much. And when his granddaughter was placed in his arms for the very first time, he wept and laughed, and looked at his wife, and said simply, thank you.

Beth was the one who reached out to Walter before the reunion. Mike's health was declining rapidly, and he spoke persistently about his friends and classmates from high school. Coming to this reunion, asking Walter to be sure the right people attended, was something Beth could do for her husband. Walter understood. He knew Mike was sick. He and Mike had remained close friends all their lives, even after Walter gave up his work at the *Star* and moved to Boston to work for the *Globe*, and then later, when he went on to start his own business with *The Weekly Boston Reporter*.

Now they were here, finally, surrounded by friends of a lifetime. They spent a happy half-hour at the table, catching up, laughing over things that happened when they were kids, decades ago. They spoke for a few minutes about Ray, and drank a toast to their long-absent friend. And then Louise excused herself, disappearing for a moment in the direction of the dance floor. As the band struck the first chords of "Moonlight Serenade," her hand was on Mike's shoulder.

"I believe I owe you a dance."

He turned to her. "Yes, you do."

He turned to Beth. "I'll be right back." Beth smiled and nodded.

Mike and Louise made their way to the dance floor with a half-dozen other couples. The music was slow and easy, and as they danced, Mike allowed the music to carry him back to the gym at Winchester High School. In his mind and heart he was there again, at the prom, with the world all new, every oyster open to him, every well-laid plan awash in a sea of blissful ignorance. This was the dance he was supposed to have had, and he wondered, for a split second, if it would have made any difference.

Louise held him as tightly as she dared. She knew in her heart it would be the last dance, the last time she would ever see this man. But it was no time for tears, they would simply have to wait until later. She bit her lip. It took all her resources, everything she had, not to weep in his arms, not to weep for the lost years, the lost love, and now the lost life.

The music faded out, and as the other couples pulled apart and clapped politely, Mike and Louise remained in tender embrace, his chin on her head, her cheek against his shoulder; until finally, Louise hugged him a bit tighter, and then pulled away, and held his hand as they returned to the table. She sat down, but he remained standing, looking down at her. "Thank you for the dance, Louise."

She looked up at him, still working hard to control her expression, to stuff back the tears that threatened to burst through her resolve. "Yes, it was a lovely dance," she managed.

Then he turned to Beth.

"Care to take a whirl around the floor?"

Beth looked up at him, surprised.

"Well, I don't mind if I do." She took his hand, and he escorted her out to the dance floor. The band was playing Dorcas Cochran's "Again," and Mike crooned the lyrics softly to Beth as they danced... 'Mine to hold, as I'm holding you now, and yet never so near, mine to have when the now and the here disappear. What matters, dear, for when this doesn't happen again, we'll have this moment forever, but never, never again...'

Louise watched them dancing, watched the words at Mike's mouth, saw Beth lean against him as they made their way slowly around the dance floor. A surge of deep regret washed over her; and then it was gone, and she only saw her good friend dancing with his wife, a woman who had once been a childhood neighbor, someone who had cared for Mike and supported him in a way Louise knew she never could.

Mike and Beth returned to the table. The band picked up with a quick-paced waltz, and the dance floor filled with those whose legs remembered the steps and whose hearts could bear the strain. Louise caught the look on Mike's face as they stood by the table.

"Is it time?" she asked.

"Yes, I think so," Beth replied. "We're going to head back to the room, and I think we may go home first thing tomorrow." Louise stood up, hugged Beth and wished her a safe journey home. Then she turned to Mike.

"Good-night, Mike. It was so very good to see you." It was all she could say.

"Thank you for the dance, Louise. About time you paid up." And then, "God bless you, see you on the other side." She nodded and turned away as the others came up to the couple to say good night.

Louise never saw Mike again. He and Beth left the next morning, Mike complaining of pain that couldn't be managed by the medications on hand. He died six weeks later, Beth and his sons at his side, ready to let go.

Walter called Louise with the news. She'd known it was coming, but that didn't stop the hard ache from rising in her chest. It hurt more than she'd ever imagined.

A few days later, she received a letter from Walter, which included an obituary cut from a page in Walter's newspaper, an article he had written himself.

'Today the Town of Winchester, Massachusetts, lost one of its vital treasures, Michael Charles Andrews, age 69. Mike grew up in Winchester, son of Buick Vice President Philip Andrews, and his wife, Margaret. He graduated from Winchester High School and immediately joined the United States Army, serving with the 4th Infantry. He served bravely with his cohorts until he was shot at the Hürtgen Forest, just a few months before the end of World War II. He returned to Winchester to make it his lifelong home. He attended Harvard Law School, and joined the firm of Andrews & James, where he became Senior Vice President and CFO. As a citizen of Winchester, he served three terms as Selectman, and served on the Boards of the School Committee, the Finance Committee, and the Building Commission. He leaves behind his wife of 45 years, Elizabeth; two sons, Raymond and Walter; and four grandchildren. Mike also leaves behind countless friends, whose lives were made richer for having known him; and a community that he loved, and actively supported every day of his life.

For those who were privileged to know Mike, the statistics don't mean much. We've lost a lifelong friend, a brother, and a kind and caring human being the likes of which we shall not know again in this lifetime. For myself, a part of my heart has been cut away, and I won't find it until I see Mike again.'

Louise was comforted to see the picture that accompanied the article. It was a picture of Mike, taken sometime during his late thirties, she thought, from a time she never knew him, a time between gawky teenager and very sick, older man; a time when he had been the man she knew he would become, handsome, devoted to his family and friends and hometown, a man sure of his purpose, sure of himself.

She didn't attend the funeral.

Book Discussion Questions

1. The Hill Boys share a friendship that spans their early years, and binds them, even at a distance, as they grow older. Can you think of friends from your childhood with whom you still share a bond? Why are such bonds important?

2. What does the hill at the end of Pembroke Road symbolize for the boys? How does Walter's view of the hill change after Christine's death?

3. When the United States becomes actively engaged in the war, Joe Hannigan goes out of his way to protect the Smith family. Why? How does he do this?

4. From early childhood George Duncan feels responsible for the welfare of his family. What factors play into this feeling? How does the weight of responsibility affect his relationship with Louise? With his wife, Claire?

5. With the onset of World War II, people of German, Italian, and Japanese heritage often found their loyalty as Americans in question. Gus Osprey is obviously of German descent, but his loyalty is never challenged. Why do you think this is?

6. Claire's portrayal in the book shifts between apparent devotion to her family and community, and blatant self-absorption. Which one is the real Claire? Why?

7. Louise is deeply hurt when she is fired from Davenport's, unjustly accused of sharing production secrets. Can you remember a time in your life when you were unjustly accused of wrongdoing? How did it make you feel? How did you resolve those feelings?

8. Death is a roaming character throughout the book. Discuss how different characters deal with death. Why do you think some of the responses to death are so different from each other?

9. We don't find out much about Joe Hannigan until the start of the war. What kind of father do you think he is? What kind of husband? Why? What are Joe's redeeming qualities?

10. How does Louise mature during the war years? How does this affect her reunion with Mike?

11. When George returns Louise's inheritance to her, she has enough money to live comfortably without working for a long time. Instead, she continues to work, often under physically challenging circumstances, first at Davenport's, then the farm, and finally the hospital. Why do you think she does this?

12. How does Helen's appearance to Gus affect you? What does her appearance mean to Gus?

13. Claire's mother, Mrs. Radcliffe, seems heartless and cold. Is she? Why do you think she works so hard to distance herself from her daughter and her new family?

14. George seems painfully unaware of his wife's needs or activities. Why does he seem to avoid meaningful interaction with her until something goes very wrong? They didn't start out that way – what changed?

15. Henry believes he might be in a position to help his family and friends by accepting Major Branson's offer. Does this hope pan out?

16. Who are the lights of Pembroke Road, really? Do some shine more brightly than others?

17. At the end of the book, the remaining characters come together one last time. Louise and Mike both seem to experience a fleeting moment of regret. Is it genuine sadness over what might have been, or is it something else? Did they ever really love each other? Do they still love each other?

18. Hard work is a fact of life for most of the characters. Is it oppressive, or is it liberating?

19. Mike's relationship with Beth changes dramatically during the course of the story. What factors influence this change? Is it just Mike who changes, or does Beth change too? How?

20. How do Louise and Claire represent the roles and expectations of women at that time? Does George have different expectations for Louise and Claire? What are the differences? Why does he have them, if he does?

21. Claire's mother wanted her daughter to marry into an upper middle class scenario. Claire married George, who was from a working class family, but she did not adjust to the lower class into which she married. How was this evident?

22. The Duncan's would have initially been considered a working class family. How did George and Louise rise to the upper middle class? The middle class in America grew tremendously after WWII ended. What factors drove that growth?

23. At the outset of the story, do you think Winchester would be identified as a middle class town, or a mixture of classes? Why? How did class distinctions change through the Depression? How had they changed by the end of WWII?

CPSIA information can be obtained
at www.ICGtesting.com
Printed in the USA
FSHW021136260119
55186FS